THE STARS COULD SAVE US

BOOK TWO

VALERIE RIVERS
& STEPHANIE COMBS

Midnight Tide
PUBLISHING

Published by Midnight Tide Publishing
www.midnighttidepublishing.com

Cover illustrations and design by Valerie Rivers
Character art by Valerie Rivers
Map by Gustavo L. Schmitt

Interior formatting by Stephanie Combs

Developmental/Copy/Line Editor - Rachel Bunner
Email: rachels.top.edits@gmail.com
Instagram: @rachels.top.edits

1st edition 2025

Paperback ISBN: 978-1-964655-29-1
Hardcover ISBN: 978-1-964655-30-7

Content Note

This story contains content that could be sensitive for some readers. There are scenes/mentions of violence, blood, torture, death, and loss of loved ones. There is also mild sexual content.

If you have specific questions about any of these, or any you do not see listed here, please reach out to us at silverflamebooksllc@gmail.com

Characters

Aella - AY-luh
Arianwen - Ah-ree-AHN-wen
Estrella - Eh-STREH-luh
Faber Ludi - FAY-ber LOO-dee
Helio - HEE-lee-o
Himmel - HIM-el
Jara - JAR-uh
Kairi - KYE-ree
Kaleidos - Kal-EYE-dos
Katye - COT-yay
Lewenne - LOO-wen
Lucris - LOO-kriss
Nephos - NEFF-os
Ona - OH-nuh
Solanos - So-LAH-nos
Valerik - Vuh-LAIR-ick
Verus - VAIR-us
Viera - Vee-AIR-ah
Wynn - WIN

Elemental Fae Races

Adamas - Uh-DOM-us - air elementals/opalescent, ivory skin/white hair
Aereus - AIR-ee-us - earth elementals/bronze skin/red hair
Argenti - Ar-JEN-tee - water elementals/silver skin/black hair
Aurum - OR-um - fire elementals/gold skin/blonde hair

Early Praise for
The Stars Would Curse Us

"The Stars Would Curse Us is a heart grippingly romantic story filled with fairytale like trials, beautiful friendships and so many kick your feet and giggle moments. With just the right amount of swoon, banter, page turning adventure and a cliffhanger that is not for the faint of heart, Stephanie and Valerie have crafted an outstanding debut." - M.A. Brown, author of The Songs That Beckon

"Faex! What a journey. I didn't want either story to end...and the last page... Torture!" - Elle Beaumont, author of Immortal Realms Trilogy

"Combs & Rivers perfectly blend together a high fantasy adventure and an ACOTAR meets Hunger Games style plot that had me on the edge of my seat the whole time." - Lou Wilham, author of Witches of Moondale

"The Stars Would Curse Us is a mesmerizing world, weaving a tapestry of slow-burning tension, perilous gambits, and a twist that leaves readers spellbound till the very end." - DeAnna Hill, author of The Heat of Seas

"This intriguing series starter just isn't what it seems. Beautiful, dangerous, and a commentary of all things too real, The Stars Would Curse Us embraces femininity, the woes of naivety, and the exploration of a realm under the hand of oppression." - Shar Khan, author of Maiden of the Hollow Path

Places

Concordia - Con-KOR-dee-uh
Easthen Forest - EAS-then Forest
Esterra - Eh-STAIR-uh
Ilithania - IL-ih-THEY-nee-uh
Iveria - Eye-VEER-ee-uh
Lakehaven - LAKE-haven
Prisma - PRIZ-muh
Zephyria - Zeh-FEAR-ee-uh

Dedication

ℛℰℂᴀᴘ

The Stars Would Curse Us

Aella and her best friend, Viera, were chosen to compete in the prestigious Matri-Ludus, a contest to marry the Iris prince, Kaleidos. Taken by ship to Prisma, Aella was quickly overwhelmed by the Palatium Crystalis' opulent surroundings and the Iris' glamorous lifestyles. Her simple upbringing left her feeling like an outsider.

Although winning was seen as great fortune, Aella was too preoccupied with her farewell to family and home to actually desire it. But when a forbidden, late-night swim in the garden brought her face-to-face with the Iris prince, she couldn't deny the connection between them. Their encounter sparked conflicting emotions as they bantered and offended each other in the same breath.

The Matri-Ludus commenced with dazzling revelries and perilous challenges in which the elementals were horrified to discover the true nature of the competition. Aella was hunted by shadow fangs in a glass maze, forced to dance until her feet bled, and spelled to see her fellow contestants as enemies, resulting in many violent deaths and a growing hatred toward their Iris rulers.

All that mattered to Aella was surviving the trials with her best friend, yet she found herself falling for the prince in spite of herself. After an over-consumption of fructus amare led her to become a little too friendly with the prince, she called him out for his role in the competition. But her growing passion and lowered inhibitions weren't enough to sway him, and his inaction thwarted their connection.

When Viera was taken by the king's tithe, Aella broke the rules to go find her. While wandering the halls in search, she was assaulted by the Iris courtier, Gaelor, who'd been pretending to help her. Upon finding them, Kaleidos' jealous cousin, Estrella, played savior while scheming and tricking her to sleep in another male's bed, accusing Aella of scandalous conduct. Kaleidos' trust in his cousin waned further as he saw right through her manipulation, but the situation gave him reason to suspect Aella had secrets of her own.

Once Viera returned, the best friends confided in each other. Viera revealed she was a spy for the rebellion, that she believed Aella had a star-blessed destiny, and she speculated some of her fellow contestants were falling victim to the nameless key—an enchanted artifact that stole identities. Together, they plotted for the rebellion while Viera tried to help Aella hone her hidden air powers.

As the competition neared its climax, Kaleidos opened up to Aella about his tortured past and the loss of his mother, a nameless Argenti contestant. Aella had won his heart, but with uncertainty around the deadly trial, she begged the prince to give his last favor to protect Viera. Aella's growing feelings for the prince made her question if he was capable of good and if the Iris might reform their ways under his rule.

When the final event ended in Viera's death, Aella, fueled by grief, unleashed her powers on the arena and the king. Her strike killed many Iris but ultimately backfired, knocking her out. Aella awoke locked in a cell to find her assassination attempt had failed while her cruel handler, Himmel, stripped and searched her for the condemning star mark that identified the chosen one spoken of in prophecy. The birthmark on the back of Aella's neck exposed her as an enemy to the Iris.

Arianwen, having slipped through the first marriage draft of the season, was preparing herself for an arranged marriage to Verus, a male she had never met. But it appeared fate had another path in store as she stumbled upon Wynn, a handsome, wounded stranger, who had impossibly fallen from the sky. She risked all to heal his fatal injuries and journey with him to a hidden kingdom among the clouds.

After they traveled together to Zephyria, Wynn's true identity as the prince of the lost Court of Air was revealed. Their friendship blossomed, but an intense attraction sparked between them as well, and Arianwen began finding more reasons to stay than return home. Arianwen's worldview changed as she witnessed firsthand the atrocities of the ruling Iris while healing injured refugees and uncovering shocking truths about the Iris' origins and sinister intentions. A secret prophecy that spoke of one marked by the stars who would be the Iris' downfall was also revealed.

No longer willing to sit back and do nothing while knowing the truth of the Iris, Arianwen accompanied Wynn and his cabala on a rescue mission to Ilithania, where she nearly fell into the clutches of the Iris guards when her glamour unexpectedly fell. Their perilous but successful journey brought Wynn and Arianwen closer together, leading them to finally give in to their growing feelings and attraction.

Despite finding freedom, purpose, and friendship in Zephyria—as well as a fledgling love—Arianwen continued to waver between listening to her heart and staying, or returning home to her family and duty. However, her new life crumbled when she discovered a devastating truth: Wynn was already betrothed. Refusing to stay as his mistress, she gathered her strength and fled into the night, leaving everything behind.

Arianwen returned to Iveria, and despite the scandal of her disappearance, her original betrothal to Verus remained intact. She wed the stranger, who had as little desire to be married as she did. Verus had lost his mate in the marriage draft and, after swearing off love, thought marrying a female who was already expecting a child was the best solution.

Not wanting to draw attention from the Iris or give anyone cause to question her child's parentage, Arianwen and Verus tried to make everyone believe they were a love match. Their forced proximity and attraction brought conflicting emotions as they struggled to mend their broken hearts. Aella's birth drew them closer, and they found healing and love together over time.

Twenty-five years later, using the connection she forged with the Iverian rebel leader, Lucris, Arianwen returned to Zephyria to beg for Wynn's help to save their daughter, Aella, the prophesied one.

ESTERRA
ZEPHYRIA
COURT OF AIR
COURT OF FIRE
EASTHEN FOREST
EASTHEN OCEAN
LAKEHAVEN
COURT OF WATER
IVERIAN SEA
IVERIA
PRISMA
WESTHEN OCEAN
RUINS OF CONCORDIA
COURT OF EARTH
ILITHANIA

A PROPHECY

Stars forgotten, the rebel roars
Through grave destruction, she restores
A thousand tears, the tempest sings
None can halt what storm it brings

What unlocks cannot be taken
Like honored virtue once forsaken
At the event, one shall remain
A dark horizon power drain

Hold not what isn't earned
In the stars, truths may be learned
Suffer the land until price is paid
Yours or hers, the choice is made

PROLOGUE

The sun beat down on us, its reflection almost blinding as it danced off the water below. Armor glistened, sparkling in an oddly beautiful way. Ugly sneers flashed across unfamiliar faces, all while blood seeped through the white tunic, quickly turning it a crimson shade. There was no sound, everything was bright, blinding light and blood pooling, dripping . . .

Ringing, something was ringing, or was it screaming? Something was breaking. Shattering.

As if suddenly returning to my body, every sense crashed back into me—the metallic scent of blood most overpowering of all. My throat was on fire, and I realized the scream was coming out of me.

No. Not like this. Not like this.

All my hopes had been dashed on the rocky cliffs below. I cursed the stars. I thought they would save us.

Unending rage as powerful as the sea itself flooded my body. I'd make them pay.

Throwing my hands out, I screamed louder as I called on my element, tunneling as deep into my source as I dared. They were fools to meet here with my element so close and quick to command.

The roar of a tidal wave rose up, gathering behind me. It would destroy anything in its path, but I no longer cared. Let them drown in the sea of my despair.

PART I
THE LUX VERAX

UNKNOWN SOURCE

"For while there is always more than one side to a story, there is also truth."

In the beginning, Esterra was a continent divided. The four races of elemental fae belonged each to their own respective corners, content in their ways and in their ignorance of each other. Water knew only water, fire knew only fire, and so forth. It was not until the Lux Verax made their descent upon the land that they learned more was outside of their small worlds.

The Lux came—beautiful, shining, and full of magic—leaving the elementals entranced. They were quickly referred to as "the Iris" for their many colors and magical abilities vastly beyond simple elemental controls. First appearing to the air elemental fae, a folk who lived among the clouds with a penchant for controlling the wind and sky, the Lux observed that the faes' powers were drawn from Esterra's source and the stars. Adamas, the Lux called them, for their crystalline hair and opalescent skin, which they likened to diamonds.

"We come with hearts open and vulnerable in our hour of greatest need," the leader said in a meeting with the Adamas king and his advisors, straightforward with their intentions. "Our people are aging, and we have no more younglings. The last birth was five hundred years ago, and before that, longer *still. We fear a societal collapse in our near future should we be unable to find a cure. Millennia of truth and knowledge will be lost if we do not find a way to save our people."*

An offer was made.

"Give us thirty of your brightest sons and daughters to take home with us so they might learn and pass on our truths and ways, and in return, we shall give you thirty portions of aether."

"You think our lives are worth so little?" the Adamas king said, offended by their offer.

"It is more than a fair trade," the Lux argued. "Each receiver of aether will live many lifetimes longer. Not only that, but it will give you access to draw on more source, strengthening your air powers. You will be like stars amongst fae."

After much discussion, the Adamas king refused. He feared the cost was too high and the reward too dangerous. Concerned the Lux might make this offer to his people and he'd have no way to deter them, he called up arms against the Lux to pressure them to leave.

"We cannot help you, and you are not welcome to stay. Vanish from this world, or we will make you regret it," the Adamas king declared.

The Lux Verax fled Esterra through their door between worlds, disappointed by their failure, that after so many years, they'd finally found a match only to be rejected. But in their haste to leave, they did not notice that one Lux remained.

CHAPTER 1
STAR–CURSED DREAMS

ARIANWEN

"Aella!" I lurched up in bed, my body drenched in sweat.

Verus bolted upright next to me. "What's wrong? Did you hear something?"

I shook my head while taking deep breaths, trying to calm my racing heart. Verus rubbed my back in calming circles.

"Another dream?" he asked softly.

"They're getting worse," I replied. "Are the stars trying to tell me something?"

My shoulders curled inward. They felt so real. Dreams of shadows and fangs, dreams of an arena bathed in blood with Aella at the center of it all. The latest had her floating above the ground with lightning in her veins, and I worried about what it meant. Was it a warning?

"Tell me about it?" Verus asked.

I buried my face in my hands, allowing myself the small comfort of his touch.

"It's just more of the same." My voice came out muffled.

"We've talked about this. It's probably just your subconscious dealing with the fear of the unknown," Verus said, pulling me onto his lap.

Looking up into his warm, teal eyes, I couldn't help but notice the dark circles marring the skin underneath. Neither of us had been sleeping well since Aella had sailed off to Prisma two months earlier.

"I wish I could believe that, but I don't think that's it. There has to be something I can do to protect her." I jumped out of bed and lit one of the lamps. Heading over to the wardrobe, I started digging around for my pack.

"For the stars' sakes, Ari. What in the dark depths are you thinking? Please come back to bed."

I frantically shoved random clothing items into my pack, the panic I'd tried to push down rising to the surface. "I need to do something, Verus. She's not safe there."

"What does that mean? You're going to go there and try to bring her home?" he scoffed. "The minute you set foot in Prisma, we will never see you again. Our children need you. I need you." His voice softened. "I am just as broken over Aella being chosen, but we have to believe she is strong enough to take whatever they can throw at her."

I dropped the shirt I was holding and collapsed to my knees, sobs wracking my body. "I should have sent her away. We have no idea what they might do to her if they discover . . . you know." I flinched as my hand burned at the thought of her secret—my secret.

Verus knelt beside me, wrapping me tightly in his arms, pressing kisses to my head. "This is not your fault, wife. If you had sent her away with the rebellion, the Iris would have come after the rest of us. You remember what they did to the Iona family after their son disappeared before the drawing last year . . ."

"We don't know that for sure! There may have been more to it than that." I shook my head. "Maybe we could've made up a story about her getting lost on her matri-ritus or something."

Verus huffed a dry laugh. "Like mother like daughter, huh?"

I couldn't help laughing, even through the tears. Taking a deep, cleansing breath, I considered what I *could* communicate through the oath's barriers without going too far. To break the oath meant death, and all my research looking for a loophole over the previous twenty-five years hadn't returned any ulterior options. Because of how it pained me, physically and emotionally, Verus had always tried to avoid the subject of my time away and anything regarding Aella's powers.

"I have some contacts who might be able to help," I finally answered. "There's no guarantee they can do anything, but they're more connected to the other courts than Lucris is here. I doubt he would lift a finger to help rescue Aella anyway. Did you see how callous he was toward Heather when Viera was chosen?"

Verus bristled, his body tensing up next to me. "You know how I feel about Lucris. I don't trust that seasnake any more than I do the Iris. What if he turns you in this time?"

I gripped his hands in my own, looking deep into his eyes, willing him to understand me. "I hear what you're saying, but this is different from the dangerous missions he's sent me on in the past. I think Aella might have a bigger role to play, and the stars won't let me rest until I do something about it."

Verus sighed in a long-suffering way but leaned forward to kiss my forehead. "I will support you in whatever it is you have to do. Just know I am worried for your safety . . . What if we all came with you?"

I shook my head. "I need you to stay behind with the children. If our entire family disappears overnight, the Iris might come after us."

Verus' shoulders tensed. "You're right. I want to make sure you have the best chance of getting where you need to go. Promise you'll come back to me?"

I dropped his hands, throwing my arms around his neck. "I promise I will do everything in my power to return and bring Aella back with me. I'll send word as soon as I can, but, Verus, if you catch even a whiff of trouble, please take the children and run."

I saw pain flash through his eyes, not liking what I was implying, but he nodded. "I promise."

My lips found his, and our kiss was full of longing, pain, and desire. Everything I'd ever wanted to say to him but could never fully express. He laid me onto the floor and made love to me gently, tenderly. For a moment, I was able to forget my worries and bask in how he adored and took care of me. My fingers mapped his skin, trying to memorize all the dips and hard edges. He pressed kisses all over my body, making it sing for him, a symphony of unspoken promises.

All too soon, it was time for me to leave to meet Lucris.

"Be safe, wife," Verus said.

I tried to put on a brave face and gave him a slight nod.

The waters were dark and cold as I swam toward the surface. I'd left while the children were asleep so they couldn't ask too many difficult questions, but I'd kissed their sleeping faces, memorizing them just in case I failed. Verus was the best father. They would always be safe and loved with him, no matter what happened to me.

CHAPTER 2

INTO THE WOODS

Arianwen

My scream pierced the night sky as I grappled for purchase on the side of the mountain. Suddenly, I was falling. Images of everyone I loved flashed before my eyes. Was this it? Was this my end?

"Oof!" The air was knocked out of me as I hit the ground with a thud. I lay there, stunned, unmoving, staring up at the stars. My chest spasmed as I tried and failed to fill my lungs. Distant, twinkling lights swam in the corners of my eyes. I couldn't breathe.

Panic took over.

I was alone.

I'd never make it like this.

Hopelessness overwhelmed me.

The moment the spasms stopped, I sucked down wheezing breaths. Every muscle in my body ached, and I tried to take inventory. When I was able to wiggle my toes, relief coursed through me that I hadn't injured anything too severely in my fall. A bloom of warmth pooled near my stomach, and I gasped as I looked down at the ice pick impaling me.

Stars, could this get any worse? Faex. Better not tempt fate by even thinking that.

My eyes fluttered shut as I used my power to search my body for internal injuries. I was stars-damned lucky the pick hadn't pierced any vital organs.

I let out a guttural groan as I pushed myself up to a seated position, leaning against the cruel mountain.

I wasn't going to make it. I'd come so far . . . Perhaps this had been entirely a fool's errand.

2 weeks earlier

"Ready to go?" Fide asked.

"Absolutely," I replied.

The leaves crunched underfoot, and I breathed in the crisp, fresh autumn breeze. The path reminded me of the one I had traveled with Wynn twenty-five years earlier. Retracing my steps brought back so many memories, some of them fond after all these years. I looked back at my younger self and saw how much I'd grown and changed since then—no longer the girl on her matri-ritus, inwardly fighting against the system and the arranged marriage in store for me. Thank the stars for that.

Lucris had sent word to Zephyria requesting an escort, so I'd made the trek to Lakehaven to wait for my contact, and we were finally off. My guide was a peculiar fellow. He told me his name was Seadial Fidelis, but I could call him Fide because no one but his ma had ever called him Seadial, and that was only if he'd been in trouble.

Lakehaven wasn't the same village I'd visited twenty-five years ago. Rather than the cozy lakeside town springing with life, it was quiet, almost abandoned. With boarded-up windows and doors, less than half of the homes still had smoke rising from their chimneys. I'd been relieved to find Siris still there, having taken over the shop after her mother's untimely passing. The shop was now a skeleton of its former self with only the bare necessities available for purchase. She'd told me that after a particularly devastating Iris invasion, many had left Lakehaven. Her daughter, Lewenne, had gone to Iveria to put her name into the draft and hadn't returned. I tried to remember the names of the other chosen females, but could only recall my all-consuming heartbreak and dread after Aella's name had been called. For Siris' sake, I prayed Lewenne had decided to stay in Iveria. Seeing my own daughter drafted off to Prisma had turned out to be the most painful experience of my existence. One I feared I might never forgive myself for.

"How did you get tangled up in the rebellion?" I asked Fide as we made our way up the mountain path. I glanced over at my guide, the morning sun reflecting off his silver skin—he looked to be in his mid-twenties.

"Now that's a stars-damned good story . . . Pardon my foul mouth." The tips of his pointed ears turned pink.

"Well, we have plenty of time." I smiled. "I'd love to hear it."

"I'm not even gonna get into how it all started—those no-good, slippery, rotten Iris goin' 'round takin' our land, tryna round us up like some kind of animals or somethin'. Don't they know? We lake dwellers don't answer to the Capitol." He grumbled some more unintelligible curses under his breath. "That's beside the point."

He whacked a branch out of the way of our untraveled path through the forest.

"Are you from Lakehaven?"

"No, haven't you been listenin'? I'm not from the big cities. I betcha you've never heard of where I come from. A lake so far north, it's practically in the Court of Air, yes, ma'am, it is." He grinned proudly. "Growin' up, we told tales of the Adamas. Never thought I'd see one with my own eyes. And now look at me. Workin' with them myself. I tell you, my ma woulda been proud." He teared up slightly, and when he realized I was looking at him, he turned away, clearing his throat. He pulled a rolled-up map from his pocket and studied it carefully before tucking it back. "Never steered me wrong."

"So, how is it you came upon them? Or was it them who caught you?" I asked, careful how I spoke. The slight burn in my hand alerted me to be cautious. Even though Fide knew of the Adamas, I was still unable to speak of what I'd experienced. I silently cursed the oath that had made my life so incredibly challenging for the past twenty-five years. There was no way around it unless Wynn released me.

"Ahhh, like I said"—he chuckled—"that's a stars-damned good story."

"You're going to make me pry it out of you, aren't you?" I teased.

"Always in such a hurry, you city folk." He shook his head. "Now, have you ever tried spit-roasted brook trout? I betcha you never tasted anything like it in the Iverian seas."

"I'm not much of a cook, but I do consider myself a food lover." My stomach grumbled at the thought of Verus' impressive skills in the kitchen.

"Oh, you'd love it. Nothin' like it in the great seas."

"You sure are skirting around the subject of your involvement with the rebellion. Is there something you're trying to hide from me? Should I be concerned?"

Fide blushed again.

"Well, it's not that . . . It's just that . . . such a respectable lady as yerself . . . erm . . ."

I raised my brows at him as he stopped in his tracks.

"All right, fine. I'll tell you. But you better not laugh."

"Promise."

"Okay . . . I was checkin' my traps in the woods. My family was tryna stock up on food for the winter months—we need to be real careful not to ruin the delicate ecosystem of the lake by overfishin', you see—and I . . . set off my own trap."

"Oh no!" I exclaimed, biting back a grin.

"There I was, hangin' from the tree upside down like a fool. I kept tryna reach up and cut myself down, but then my britches split right down the middle." His face turned bright red. "I was strugglin' and hollerin' for hours, hopin' someone—anyone—would come and find me, but I'd set my traps too far."

"That's terrible!" I really did feel bad for the poor male. I would have been mortified if something like that had happened to me.

"Imagine my surprise when a group of Adamas came flyin' to the rescue!" he said excitedly. "They had arrows aimed right at my heart, but never fear, I managed to convince 'em to trust me with my good manners and charm, and they cut me right down."

"You must be star-blessed," I said with a smile.

"You bet yer sweet arse I am." He grinned, reaching out to help me over a cluster of overgrown tree roots like the well-mannered boy his ma had raised him to be. "It's okay. You can laugh if you want. It really is funny. Only I'd meet a buncha Adamas with my arse on display."

A laugh bubbled out of me at that, and he joined me. His guffaw was so infectious, I had to stop and found myself doubled over with tears.

"Okay, okay. Enough pokin' fun at me now." He grinned.

"Thank you, Fide. I really needed that."

"When you got tears leakin' outta you that way, you most definitely did," he agreed. "You looked so sad when we first met. I was wonderin' what could have broken yer heart so much to make this journey . . ."

A long, shuddering breath helped center me as I considered how to reply. The last thing I wanted was for him to ask a question I couldn't answer and offend him in some way. "Oh, I just miss home, that's all," I said, trying to remain vague.

Thankfully, he was chatty, and my lack of response didn't hinder him from continuing on with his tales.

"I really do get tired of them Iris treatin' us all like playthings. Makin' us abide by their laws like we hadn't been fine mindin' our own," he grumbled. "At least with the rebellion, I feel like I'm doin' somethin' about it. Takin' back control. Y'know? Never saw myself as much of a fighter, but I'll fight for what's right. And the Iris ain't right. No, ma'am."

I can relate.

"Well, thank you for escorting me," I said.

"No problem at all. They asked me if I could be a guide since I know these woods so well. Chances are I'd be wanderin' them anyway."

"Have you ever been to Iveria?"

He shook his head. "I've never had much desire to go to the big city. I like the simple life we lead in Silverveil Springs. If only the Iris didn't have to come and ruin everything." He spat on the ground in disgust. "They used to leave the smaller villages like us alone. Not sure what's different in the waters these last years, but they seem to be comin' 'round more and more, pokin' their noses where they don't belong. For star-sent saviors, they sure don't leave anythin' good in their wake. Things like that make you question things, y'know? And I tell you, I'm not the only one questionin' things. There's a brewin' resentment in these lands. Us peaceful Argenti might just surprise 'em."

The young male radiated anger. His clenched fists and tight shoulders made me want to reach out and soothe him.

"I'm so sorry. I truly hope we can somehow make a better world for our children. That's why I'm here."

"Is that right?" He looked back at me and quirked a brow. "I have to admit, I'm curious. I haven't led anyone on this path in well over a year now."

"Argenti sure love to stay close to the water, don't they?" I said with a smile.

He laughed. "You ain't wrong."

"To be completely honest, I'm on this journey because my daughter was drafted by the Iris. I'm hoping our friends might help me save her."

His steps faltered for a moment before he continued trudging up the mountain path. "Stars, I'm sorry to hear that. That's either the bravest or the most foolish idea I've ever heard."

"They're all I have."

It's the Adamas or no one.

"Hey, don't feel too bad, ma'am. You're in good company. I'll help you get where you need to go, and if the stars are good, I'm sure they'll honor yer request."

I nodded, unable to form an adequate response with all the thoughts and regrets storming around in my head.

The forest was dense with trees so tall and vibrant, they blotted out the bright morning sun. I was lucky to have a guide, because there'd be no stars to lead us in these woods.

Fide stopped again to eye his map.

"So where do we go from here?" I asked.

"The Adamas won't come this close to Court of Water territory any-more, so we need to go as far as we can on foot."

Testing the bounds of my oath, I asked, "What do you mean?" Relieved that it was vague enough not to singe my hand in warning, I waited for his response.

"Apparently, an Iris patrol caught one of 'em."

Faex. Had it been anyone I knew? My thoughts jumped immediately to Wynn and his cabala—Helio, Rik, Glint, Kairi, and Eden.

"After that, they started sayin' it was too risky," he continued. "It's almost as if they think the Iris are out here waitin' to catch someone else."

This new information was unsettling. Hearing of Wynn's faction of the rebellion essentially withdrawing from the water court was not a good sign considering what I was planning to ask of them.

"Do *we* need to worry about Iris?" I glanced around. "It's not as if I could use my rite as an excuse for being out here." A nervous chuckle left me.

"We *should* be fine."

I frowned. That didn't make me feel better at all.

We continued our trek in companionable silence, stopping only briefly to refill our water pouches. As we passed some wild winterberry vines wrapped around the trees by the stream, I made sure to collect the berries in a loose bit of fabric. They might have stained my hands and cloak, but their refreshing tartness took me right back to my matri-ritus.

I'd been trying not to think of what Wynn would say when he saw me again, but how could I not when so much hung in the balance? Would he even be willing to help, or would he be furious at this revelation? What if he turned me away? A pit formed in my stomach. The fear of the unknown would eat me alive. I had to tell myself he would help. Though he'd hurt me once, I knew he was good. I knew he would do what was right.

When we finally made camp for the evening, we slept back to back, huddling together for warmth in the frigid mountain air.

Standing in an arena, bathed in blood, I tried to let out a scream as a blonde Aurum female rushed toward me, blazing swords in hand. The malice in her eyes terrified me, and I turned to run. My feet slipped in the sand, and it was as if I couldn't move forward, as if I were running in place. Glancing over my shoulder, the Aurum female had almost caught up to me, the fire from her blades radiating heat.

Wake up, Ari! Wake up. This isn't real. Why did it feel so real?

I jolted up, gasping for breath. Despite the chill in the air, my clothes were drenched with sweat. The dreams were getting worse.

"So if it ain't askin' too much, why now?"

"Huh?" I shivered with the cold.

"Well, considerin' you know someone who can help you in the Court of Air. I guess I'm just wonderin' why you didn't ask them for help before yer daughter had to line up for the draft."

"Don't you think I've already asked myself that a thousand times?"

"I didn't mean it like that. I'm sorry."

I shrugged, abashed by my outburst. "No, you're right. The truth is, I should have sent her away . . . but I was selfish and scared."

"I guess that was rather stupid of me to ask, considerin' I know just how hard it is to leave the water you love. No matter how many times the Iris come 'round, I won't abandon Silverveil Springs. That's my home. And if she's anything like the rest of us Argenti, how do you even know she would have agreed to go?"

"I . . . I guess I don't," I admitted. "Maybe I'm just looking for reasons to blame myself."

He nodded. "Fair enough, but as my ma always said, no use worryin' about somethin' you can't go back in time to fix."

The further north we went, the more the temperatures dropped. I'd tried to prepare myself, but even with all the layers, nothing could shield me from the bitter cold. It wasn't as if Argenti had fur-lined travel clothes for barter in the markets. I was reminded of the vastness of Esterra as we spent weeks hiking toward Zephyria, tucked high in the northen alps. Without an aquila taking us most of the way, the journey was long and arduous. Tiny doubts crept into my mind with each step.

How could I have left Verus and the children back in Iveria? What if I didn't make it and never saw them again? What if I made it and Wynn turned me away? What if he refused to help Aella? What if Aella was already—

No. Stop it, Ari. Don't lose hope. Keep the faith. You won't let her down.

"Any chance we can risk a fire tonight?" I asked, rubbing my arms.

Before he could answer, a howl rent the night air.

Faex.

"I'll take that as a no." I grimaced.

The answering howls in the distance sent chills racing down my spine.

"Yeah, I don't think that would be a good idea." Fide frowned. "Sounds like the warg are out huntin' tonight."

"Great. Just great."

I'd never forgotten the terror of facing one of them, let alone an entire pack.

"I think there might be some caves we can shelter in up ahead," he said. "You're doin' great though. We're makin' good time. By my reckonin', we'll reach the meeting spot in the next few days."

"How can you tell?"

He pointed in the distance. "You see where those two mountain peaks meet? There's a lake hidden up there. It's a bit of a climb and will require some teamwork, but we can make it."

"The end is in sight," I said with a weak smile.

"Now let's get out of the open before we become a warg's dinner," he joked, motioning for me to hurry up and follow him.

"This is where it gets tricky," Fide explained as he pulled climbing gear out of his pack. "Here, loop this around yer waist."

He handed me some rope, and I used my fishing knot skills to tie it off. I looked up at the cliffside, and my jaw dropped. "You expect us to climb this?"

"It's easier than it looks. The rope is just a precaution."

"If you say so."

Suddenly, I started second-guessing everything. My entire body was exhausted from travel, and this final hurdle seemed insurmountable. I was weak from lack of proper nutrition—food had been sparse, and our rations were low.

What I wouldn't give for an Adamas to show up and fly me the rest of the way.

"So where are you off to after this?" I asked, trying to distract myself from the task ahead while also worried about Fide making it back on his own.

"Oh, I hadn't really thought that far ahead. Like to take things one day at a time."

"Well, what would you be doing if they hadn't assigned you to this task?"

"Ah, I'd be fishin' along one of them streams that comes down from the mountains. Best brook trout in all the lakelands come from these peaks. I got a nice stash of fishin' equipment not too far from here. So you see, while you're up there bargainin' with the rebels, I'll be sittin' pretty by the stream, roastin' fish with a smile on my face."

"What I wouldn't give to be near a fire right now."

"When all is said and done, you can come by and I'll show you how we supper in the northen lakes."

"That sounds nice," I said through chattering teeth.

"I can tell you're used to eatin' so well, you haven't built up any stores like me." He patted his belly. "Hang in there. We'll meet 'em soon enough."

Fide tied the other end of the rope around his middle, and we started our climb. Using an ice pick where needed, our progress was slow, and Fide had even removed his gloves, giving them to me to borrow. He said he had better grip without them, which I doubted, but I couldn't refuse his generosity when my fingers were practically turning blue with cold.

I screamed as my foot slipped on a rock covered in black ice, but Fide was right there, grasping my hand and keeping me steady. "Thanks. That was close."

"No worries, ma'am. That's what I'm here for."

"I told you to stop calling me ma'am," I teased. "Ari is fine."

He blushed slightly. "Okay, fine, Miss Ari."

When we finally made it to a ledge that led into a deep cave, we crawled in to take a short break, sliding off our packs. A musty scent filled my nose as the packs disturbed piles of old, damp leaves that must have blown in.

The cave was barely tall enough to sit up in, and we huddled together. The wind had been so biting cold that I'd worried my nose might fall off, so the brief reprieve in the cave felt almost warm in comparison.

Fide rubbed his hands together furiously.

"Are you all right?"

His teeth chattered, and he nodded.

"I can try to help? I'm a healer," I offered.

"I reckon you can try if you want."

I took his hands in mine, pouring some healing energy into him, and they began to warm slightly.

"Ow, ow, ow," he cried out. "It burns!"

"I'm so sorry. I know." I winced. The pain radiating off of him hurt my soul. "Just a little longer. Hang in there, Fide."

His icy hands finally turned a normal shade of silver, and he sighed in relief. "Thank you, Miss Ari."

"Now put your gloves back on. Keep those fingers warm!" I handed them back to him.

He grinned as he reached over to his pack and started fumbling through it.

A loud hiss echoed through the cave, and Fide froze.

"Miss Ari, um, we might wanna slowly make our way out of this cave right about now," he whispered.

"What is it?" I tried to peek around him when I heard another hiss followed by the sound of something sliding along the cave floor.

"We really oughta be movin' now, Miss Ari," Fide said as he started pushing me toward the cave entrance.

"What about all our supplies?" I asked.

"Don't you worry 'bout a thing. I'll grab 'em."

I crawled backward out of the cave, and my eyes widened in horror as the largest serpent I'd ever seen came into view. Its head bobbed and weaved slowly, and it watched as Fide grabbed our packs and started to shuffle away on hands and knees.

A scream bubbled up in my throat, but I bit down on my tongue to keep it in. The last thing we needed was for me to startle it.

"It's okay there, Mister Snake," Fide said softly. "We didn't mean to disturb yer slumber. We're gonna leave now, okay?"

The loud, ear-splitting screech of a hawk sounded, and suddenly, the serpent lunged for Fide, its razor-sharp fangs dripping with venom.

"Fide!" I screamed.

The snake's fangs pierced Fide's jugular, and he clawed at the beast, trying to detach it.

Snapping myself out of my fear, I looked around frantically, spying one of our ice picks near the mouth of the cave. I reached for it and swung at the serpent, praying to the stars my aim was true.

The pick met flesh, and I pulled back, ready to strike again. Hot blood sprayed from the serpent's neck, and it reared back, hissing its displeasure at me, then launched itself toward me. I swung again, screaming, and opened my eyes to find the snake's head impaled on the sharp end of the ice pick. I dropped the snake and crawled over to Fide.

Fide weakly held a hand against his bleeding neck.

Faex. There was too much blood. Too much venom.

"Don't you die on me, Fide," I commanded as I knelt over him, trying to draw the poison from the wound without taking too much blood with it, but the poison had acted quickly and had already mixed well through his bloodstream and into the surrounding tissues. Dark green streaks spread out from the punctures in both directions.

"I'm so cold, Miss Ari. So cold," he said weakly.

"Stay with me, Fide. You're going to be all right."

I pushed more healing energy into him, soothing his pain as best I could. Fide seemed to relax a little, his eyes fluttering, but the streaks of green continued to spread.

"Tell me about Silverveil Springs again, Fide." I tried to sound reassuring, even as his silver skin paled, mottled with the green streaks that were now visible in the whites of his eyes, and it became clear there was little I could do but keep him comfortable in his last moments.

"Don't forget . . . After you rescue yer daughter, you're gonna come 'round Silverveil Springs, all right? Bring yer whole family for some brook trout. I'll make it the way my ma taught me." A dopey smile etched itself onto his face as the venom continued to work through his system.

I nodded, too choked to answer, tears streaming down my face.

"Miss Ari?"

"Yes?"

"I'm sorry I can't get you the rest of the way."

"No need to be sorry, Fide."

"I am. My ma taught me never to abandon a lady."

"You're not."

"It's just a little bit further . . . Just up that rock."

"You've been an excellent guide. Your ma would be so proud."

"She'll be real proud . . . won't she?" He smiled, closing his eyes briefly. "And Miss Ari?

"Yes?"

"I think . . . I think I see her."

"Go be with your ma, Fide. It's okay."

He took one final, shuddering breath, and he was gone.

Present

I awoke with a gasp, immediately wincing at the pain radiating through my body.

How long have I been unconscious?

My hand went to the ice pick wound I'd barely patched up before passing out. It would likely leave a nasty scar. Everything ached from my fall, and I knew getting back up would be even harder the longer I sat. Leaning my head back against the rock, I stared up into the night sky—praying to and cursing the stars in the same breath. I desperately needed to get to that lake, if not only to meet the contact, but to replenish my source so I could heal. How long would my escort wait for me to show up? If I returned home and waited for Lucris to arrange another guide, would it be too late? Could I even make it back home if I tried?

I glared at the side of the mountain. There was no turning back.

You will not defeat me. My love is stronger than my fear, stronger than my doubt.

The ice pick that had nearly taken me out stuck into the mountain, and I pulled myself up. Inch by inch, foot by foot, I climbed.

Remember what you have to lose. Remember what you have to gain. This is for Aella.

My fingers were numb from the cold, even with Fide's gloves, and I slipped again and again. I screamed in frustration. Why was this so stars-damned impossible?

This is for Aella. Mila. Arden. Silber. Liili. Dean. Verus. This is for a better world. This is for hope.

I reached up, holding back a cry as the wound stretched and burned. The trill of an aquila whispered to me on the wind. Faex. Was I too late? Had I missed them? No! Not when I was so close.

"Don't leave!" I yelled. "I'm right here!"

The call of the aquila sounded farther away, and I tried to hold back a sob.

Aella needs me.

I've come too far to give up now.

Reaching up again, my hand found a secure hold, and I pulled. Every muscle screamed as I reached and pushed with my feet. It was too hard. It was impossible. But my love was stronger than the voices telling me I would fail.

Suddenly, a hand stretched out from above, and I took hold of it. With a mighty heave, I was over the ledge and looking into a surprised but familiar face.

"Henri?" I rasped.

"Should I know you?" His eyebrows knit together.

I let out a choked, half sob, half laugh—the frozen tears cracking on my cheeks. "I'm just so glad to see you. We met years ago in Zephyria."

He awkwardly patted my shoulder until a flash of recognition lit up his face. "Miss Arianwen, was it?"

I nodded weakly.

"Where's your guide?" He looked over the edge as if expecting someone to be right behind me.

"He didn't make it . . ."

"I'm so sorry."

"Me too," I said softly.

"You look like you're freezing," he said, pulling off his leather coat. "Here, you can wear this."

"Are you sure?" I asked, even as I wrapped myself in the warm, fur-lined leather.

"The cold doesn't bother me." He smiled.

"Thank you."

"Let's get you to Zephyria."

CHAPTER 3
HOLD NOT WHAT ISN'T EARNED

KALEIDOS

My eyes darted between the two females whose lives I'd promised to protect. It was pure torture repressing the dread that lanced through me, let alone watching yet another event unfold in which I might be proven a failure. I stoned my expression to nothingness, concealing my true thoughts and fears. I was bound to the chair by my obligation to watch and by the weight of expectation, yet something was wrong, impossibly wrong, and those ever loose, invisible tethers were slackening.

Without the tonic, Aella would not stand a chance at winning the final event, but she could live—all she needed to do was survive. She would. She always did. As favored, her best friend, Viera, had gotten the tonic instead. It should have made the earth agree with her, it should have protected her, yet she struggled in the back, at a crawling pace, almost as if she hadn't taken it, or worse.

"This bores me." Estrella picked at her nails. "The Aereus are so far ahead of everyone, it's no contest. I had expected a little more blood," she complained to the Faber Ludi. "No one wants to watch an easy win. This is the final event of the Matri-Ludus. Don't you think we deserve a grand finale?"

"Do you doubt my ability to deliver one?" he asked with a sneer.

"Surely after the last event, everyone doubts your abilities," she scoffed.

"So impatient, your generation," he said. "Some prefer to save the excitement for the end."

"The Aereus are nearly at the top of the mountain. Even the dullest could foretell how this one will turn out. You think the audience is amused? I can practically hear crickets, it's gone so quiet in the stands."

And then, as Ramalia reached the top of the mountain, about to claim her ring, she paused. A mix of anger and grief crossed her face, and she turned away from the cairn. Her resolve was clear. Instead of taking the ring, Ramalia threw a boulder at it in a tremendous show of defiance. But it was repelled with a crack, knocking her back with a force that sent her right off the narrow edge of the mountaintop. There was a scream. Her fellow Aereus contestant, Ona, cried out in horror, barely diving out of the way of the massive pieces of stone that ricocheted down the rocky slope. The crowd cheered and laughed at Ona's several failed attempts at shifting the earth to stop Ramalia's fall. More rocks and boulders were dislodged and rolled down the hill toward the others. I leapt from my seat when it became clear who was trapped in Ramalia's path.

"You can't interfere." Estrella tugged at my shirt, urging me to sit back down as she taunted me.

"Faex off, cousin." I shrugged her clawed hand away from me.

Estrella's eyes heated the back of my neck as I left the viewing box. I couldn't risk her following, so I took my time, making it appear as though my actions were nothing more than to attend to my personal needs. As soon as I was out of sight, I bolted to the holding rooms below. I forced my way through the throng of drunken attendees, but before I could make it out into the arena, the guards stopped me. Four blocked my path, not one of them Iris—their commanders would have been delighting in the sordid festivities up above. I did not wish to fight them, but I had no other choice. I readied my stance for their resistance, but the guards' eyes widened, armor rattling as they quivered in their boots.

Then, out of nowhere, my surroundings shook, and screams echoed throughout the ancient, blood-stained halls.

"Get out of here while you still can," I ordered, to which they nodded in fearstruck appreciation and fled the premises.

One lingered, bowing low to the floor. "How may I serve you, Your Highness?"

"Send word for a healer. Meet me in the crypt below."

He paused, puzzled by the order. He'd likely expected a command to escort me out of the chaos, not bring more in.

"Go!" I roared, then kicked the doors open, running out into the arena. I'd lost my ability to care if Estrella or any of the other courtiers saw me.

But to my surprise, no one shouted my name in accusation. The air was thick with dust, and what I could see of the arena was in disarray. Ominous screams pierced the air, panicked crowds fled to the exits, rocks and boulders were strewn about the stands, and there were crushed bodies everywhere.

And then the cloud of dust parted, and she appeared. Like a goddess of ruin, Aella hovered in the air, a bolt of lightning in her hand, ripples of electricity pulsing over her skin. My heart leapt at the sight. She was glorious in all her power. But I had to stay on task. No time to marvel.

Carefully, I scooped Viera into my arms, her skin still warm, her pulse thready and breathing shallow. I had half a thought to grab Ramalia too, but it was too late—her head was cracked open, the source of the pool of blood they were both lying in.

Just as we made it into the holding room, a blast displaced the air, almost knocking us to the floor.

"Hang in there, Viera," I said as I carried her down a spiral set of stairs to the crypts. "I made Aella a promise, and I intend to keep it. So for both our sakes—" I nearly choked. I'd forgotten the putrid odor of the narrow halls below. I kicked in doors until I found a chamber less atrocious than the others and set Viera onto a table in the center of the room. "Help is on the way," I uttered. Though as I said the words, taking in the state of her, I could scarcely believe them.

Unsure how to help or if my attempts would make her situation worse, I paced the room anxiously as I waited for what felt like an eternity for the healer to arrive. Every second seemed to stretch, yet my heart pounded in my chest in an unnatural rhythm. Too many breaths raced in and out, overcrowding each other, trying to keep up. This was taking too long. Far too long, and I didn't have enough time. *She* didn't have enough time.

This never should have happened.

This is all wrong.

I gave my word I'd protect her.

My actions had defied law and reason—I was forbidden from interfering in the games—I did not care. I'd done everything in my power to get to Viera in time, to save her. I prayed to the stars that I was not too late, that she still had a chance.

The Argenti healer burst into the room, her mouth falling open briefly before she ran to the table, getting to work on the wreck that was Viera's body. Blood, dirt, and swelling had left her nearly unrecognizable if not for her silver skin and hair. The healer was overwhelmed trying to repair the damage. It was like trying to fix a sinking ship—as soon as she patched one leak, another revealed itself, and the healer rapidly grew more fatigued from the energy spent keeping Viera alive.

"You must not give up," I said to both Viera and the healer. My hands clenched into fists, completely useless in this battle. If only the arena had more healers I could have called on. As it was, they were probably already searching for this one at this very moment to save the wounded Iris in the stands. There would be no healers to spare.

"You must not give up. You must not give up," I pleaded, my voice a low snarl.

"I am trying," the healer gritted out, like it took great effort to even speak. Her hands trembled, and sweat beaded her brow.

Viera's eyelids fluttered, a strangled breath escaping her lips. No, not a breath, words. I leaned in to listen.

"The choice . . . will be hers . . ." She faded out.

"Viera, stay with me," I growled.

The healer trembled with such force that I feared she might faint. I rushed over to support her. Tears poured from her eyes.

"I'm so sorry, my prince. I'm so, so very sorry. I cannot save her." She wiped her brow. "It's not enough . . . Her injuries . . . They are too severe." She panted, her breaths breaking up her words as she tried to explain. "I . . . I can't . . . I'm so sorry . . ." She collapsed into my arms.

"No! This isn't right." I set her down carefully and placed my hands on Viera in her place. I had no idea what to do, but I would do anything, try anything.

When our skin made contact, it was clear . . . she was gone. And nothing I could do would bring her back.

A swell of anger built up inside. At the stars, at myself. I'd failed. I was weak. I was powerless. Just as my father had convinced me, just as I'd always known. Powerless to protect my mother, powerless to protect the one I adored. I couldn't even save Viera. Part of me wondered why I'd even tried. After all this time, why now, why her? I stared at Viera's still form, the pale freckles on her cheeks, the aqua tint of her silver skin, the wavy ends of her tied-back hair. She almost reminded me of my mother, if my memories could be trusted.

Mother hadn't been given any honors. No funeral rights had been made for her. Carted off with the rest of the dead, she had been disposed of like an animal while my father laughed and drank. Like she'd meant *nothing* to him. When I sometimes caught him staring at me with cool resentment in his eyes, I wondered what he saw. Did he regret what he'd done? Was there even a shred of remorse? Or did he resent it all, including me?

Aella had been right. This *all* needed to end. It's what my mother would have wanted. As impossible as it seemed, I had to find a way. But I couldn't stop this on my own. No. With Aella's help, perhaps together, we could find a way. But she'd never forgive this failure.

"I'm so sorry," I whispered. And then a thought occurred to me. It was a foolish, wishful notion.

I was no healer. The Iris weren't bred to heal the world but to take from it. Yet, somehow, I could not remove my hands—give up, walk away. In spite of everything telling me it was too late, I could not stand by and let her slip away without giving it my all. Even if it meant attempting the impossible.

I focused on Viera, pushing my magic into her until I felt myself shaking. It fought against me, refusing to leave my body, refusing to enter the void resting before me. Viera, who meant so much to Aella, whom I'd promised to favor, to protect in this final event, lay on the table, still, motionless as the dead. No more agonal exchanges of breath, no more erratic pulse of life, no hum of source. She was gone.

I will not accept this outcome.

She needed more time, she needed *more* magic. She needed something else altogether. Without another thought, I funneled aether into her, and with it, source raced across like it had finally been granted a pathway in. As far as I knew, it had never been done before.

Our aether was not meant for elemental fae, who drew upon source power from the stars and the elements of Esterra. Our aether was from another world. It was what set us apart, made us stronger, more powerful, superior to them in every way.

Stars knew if her frail, elemental body could even take the aether or if she'd explode from the sheer force of it. But I was out of options, and she'd be dead anyway.

My hands were glued to her, aether and source rushing through her body seeking out injury, when Viera jolted as though struck by lightning. And all at once, blinding rays of light shot out from the creases of her eyes and lips.

I stumbled back, shielding my face against the harsh luminance.

Through squinted eyes, I saw Viera glowing, an aura of colors radiating off her skin. She floated upward from the table, and I backed away further, my powers drained. Fear like liquid ice in my veins.

What have I done?

Will I ever get them back?

Viera came slowly to stand before me. In place of her bright, teal-colored eyes was only white, blazing light, like staring straight into the stars. I lost my balance, feebly catching myself against the wall behind me. She opened her mouth to speak, though it was not her voice but a chorus of souls that exited her lips.

Stars forgotten, the rebel roars
Through grave destruction, she restores
A thousand tears, the tempest sings
None can halt what storm it brings

What unlocks cannot be taken
Like honored virtue once forsaken
At the event, one shall remain
A dark horizon power drain

Hold not what isn't earned
In the stars, truths may be learned
Suffer the land until price is paid
Yours or hers, the choice is made

Viera walked forward, placing her glowing, silver hand directly over my heart. Energy surged into me, all that had just been flowing through her returning to me in a mournful relief. Then she collapsed into my arms, unconscious again. I slid down the wall, head hung heavy with her limp body in my arms.

The healer awoke, scrambling to return to her feet. "I need water . . . I need . . ." She looked around the room, searching, tapping at her temples frantically.

"It's too late," I said.

She looked at the empty, bloodstained table and then down at me where I slouched against the wall, Viera's body in my lap. She darted toward us, knelt down, and took Viera's hand in hers.

"My prince . . ." Bewildered, she poked and prodded some more, a tearful laugh escaping her.

"What in heaven's name—"

"You've done it, stars above, you've really done it! She was gone . . . I *felt* her die on the table." She shook her head in disbelief.

"I was there," I growled, unable to comprehend her attitude in such a moment.

She shook her head, still laughing and crying all at once, her display of emotion making me increasingly uncomfortable.

"You misunderstand me." Before I could deny her, she took my hand and placed it over Viera's chest. I flinched, unprepared. "Do you feel it?"

I saved her.

I stared at the wall, the room practically spinning around me as the healer confirmed Viera was alive, all her wounds somehow healed.

After pulling myself together and giving the healer instructions on what to do with Viera, I stepped out into the narrow, underground halls where only one guard stood watch. What remained of the passageway was an obstacle course of fallen stone.

"No one in or out of this room except with the healer, understood?"

"As you command, sire."

I needed to get back to the palatium unnoticed. There was a slight chance they thought I was dead. I'd take advantage of the chaos to make proper arrangements for Viera. But first, I needed to find Aella. As I navigated through the dusty rubble and chunks of fallen stone, my mind replayed the powerful image of her in the arena and the devastation of her attack. It had all been her, hadn't it? I shook my head to clear the memories as I emerged from the debris that nearly blocked my exit.

"He's alive! The prince is alive," guards shouted as they swarmed around me and escorted me to a palanquin. *So much for sneaking back into the palatium unnoticed.* Making use of my resources, I requested a quill and parchment and began scribbling down Viera's utterance before I could forget a word of it, combining it with what I remembered of the ancient prophecy.

If the prophecy was correct, Aella was it, the tempest, the one who had come to destroy my world and everything in it. Whatever I'd just heard from Viera's lips held even more truths to unravel . . . truths or omens I wasn't sure I was ready for. But this much was clear—Aella was an enemy to my people, a threat to me.

The tempest had been unleashed.

CHAPTER 4
A COLD HEART

WYNN

The book closed with a thump, and I ran my fingers through my hair. I needed to get up and stretch my legs. It had been another long day, full of comforting my weeping mother and making sure I was on top of all the important things I needed to know and do to run the Court of Air. My father's passing had been sudden, and we'd been ill-prepared. The healers had said there'd been a problem with his heart and that he'd likely felt no pain, but my mother was a wreck, and I was left to pick up the pieces and grieve in my own way. My father and I had never been close. Once I'd decided to go on rescue missions and put my life at risk, he'd sworn I'd be the death of him and our small kingdom.

I'd never ceased to be a disappointment to my father. I had wanted to be the son he'd needed me to be, but my traitorous heart had made other plans. If only my father could have, just once, let me know he'd been proud of me . . . perhaps I wouldn't have rebelled so hard against him.

As I walked the halls of the palatium, I thought I heard voices followed by the echoing thud of the front door slamming shut.

Who in the stars would be visiting at this hour?

I ran down the stairs and nearly missed Emil as he slunk off toward his chambers.

"Emil!" I called out.

"Yes, Majesty?" he said as he turned around.

"Who was at the door?"

Emil frowned. "You needn't worry. I sent her away. I'm sure she will return tomorrow at an appropriate hour."

"Who was at the door, Emil?" I growled, irritated at his attempted diversion.

Emil sighed loudly as he rolled his eyes. "I think her name was Arianwen or something. I told her the royal family is in mourning and to come back tomorrow."

I felt the blood drain from my face. No. He had to be mistaken. There was no possible way she had come here. My feet were frozen to the floor.

Misreading my expression, Emil frowned. "If you do not wish to see her, I'll keep her away."

"What? No. Start preparing her old room."

Emil bowed stiffly. "As you wish, sire."

A million thoughts raced through my mind as I rushed to the door. Why had she come? How had she managed to find her way back? Did that mean she—

I flung the door open and watched the only female I had ever truly loved walk away from the palatium.

"Arianwen," I called out. She paused before turning around to face me.

"Wynn . . ." she whispered before weakly dropping into a curtsy. "Your Majesty."

My eyes roved over her face, taking in every detail. She looked just as I remembered her, the years had barely touched her face, but there was sadness and worry in her eyes. Her windswept tresses framed her face where they had come out of her braid, and I felt the strongest urge to brush them behind her ear. Her silver eyes shone in the starlight as if they were stars in their own right. My heart that had become so hardened over the years started to thaw, and unwelcome emotion overwhelmed me.

"What are you doing here, Arianwen?" My words came out forced.

"Your Maj—"

"Stop. I'll always be Wynn to you." The formality of my title coming from her lips felt wrong.

"Wynn, I came here to beg for your help. I can't lose her. Please. You must help her escape."

My entire being was drawn to her, and I moved in closer.

What in the stars was she talking about?

"Help who?"

The tension in her body was palpable, but I tilted my head and watched as she rolled her shoulders back and looked me in the eye with defiance. "Our daughter."

I reared back.

No. She could not possibly have just said what I think she said.

Anger. Disbelief. Hurt. My emotions started to consume me and must have shown on my face, as she flinched away from me.

"I don't have a daughter. Surely, if I did, you would have had the courtesy to tell me before now," I replied, unable to keep the raw distress from my voice. Her eyes glistened with tears, making me immediately regret my outburst.

"I'm so sorry I never told you, but you chose *her*, and I wasn't going to be your mistress. I had no idea when I left—"

"You could have found a way to tell me! I had the right to know I was a father!" I flung my hands into the air in frustration. How could she have kept this from me?

All this time . . . Stars.

"She has a wonderful father. Verus has always treated her like his own blood," she challenged, her own anger bleeding through in her tone.

How dare she show up here and remind me of the male she chose to run home to.

Part of me wanted to send her away out of spite.

"So why are you here asking for my help?" My voice dripped with disdain. She'd said the girl already had a father, why did she need me? "Let Verus help her."

"Don't you think he would if he could? The Iris have her! She was drafted, but I know in my heart that she is not safe. She carries your element but has never learned how to wield it, and if they discover her secret . . . I think it's her. She's the one the prophecy spoke of. She is marked by the stars."

For the second time that night, I felt the blood rush out of my face. A sudden fear for a child I didn't even know overcame me. "No . . ."

"If they harm or kill her . . . I couldn't live with myself if I didn't at least try to save her somehow, but I can't do it without you. Please . . . help me."

"No one has ever attempted a rescue out of Prisma, it is far too dangerous." Once again, a large part of me just wanted to tell her to leave, but she looked so broken and defeated. My heart ached when I remembered the last time I had seen that look on her face.

"I should have tried to send her away, but I never thought they'd choose her . . . Faex, what have I done?"

The pain in her eyes chipped away at the ice that encased my heart. I raked my fingers through my hair, wondering if there was anything I could do to help but fearing I would only give her false hope. "I cannot promise you anything, but I will gather my cabala and try to reach out to contacts I have near Prisma. Perhaps we can mount a rescue, but there is no guarantee."

Arianwen's eyes lightened just a little as she gave me a tremulous smile. "Thank you, Wynn. You have no idea how much this means to me." She wrapped her arms around herself protectively, and it took everything in my power to not run over and take her into my own.

"Arianwen, you look exhausted. Please come and rest while I make arrangements." I waved a hand toward the entrance, then squeezed my eyes shut for just a moment, trying to come up with the right words and not lose my temper again. "We are not done talking. I am *so* angry with you for keeping this from me! After everything—"

"I tried to do what was best for her," she interrupted, her chin held high. She lifted her hand, showing me the mark from our stars-damned oath. "You guaranteed that I could never tell her about you or where she came from."

Faex.

She had me there. If she hadn't left in the middle of the night, maybe I could have defied my father and released her. I prepared to respond, but nothing I could possibly say would even matter. The past could not be undone.

I offered her my arm to walk her into the palatium, but when she stepped toward me, she lost her footing. She must have been traveling for weeks or more, stars knew how long. The closer I got to her, the more I could see the utter exhaustion and weariness. Now was not the time for arguments. Knowing she would likely reject my help if I offered, I swept her up into my arms before she could stop me.

"There is much I regret about those days but never you. I just wish you would have gotten word to me. Everything would be different," I whispered into her hair.

I couldn't help but imagine a life where she had never left and we had raised our child together. Surprisingly, she didn't fight me and stayed quiet. I felt her relax into my arms, the feel of her so familiar that it made my heart ache, and I fought the unwelcome tears. *How dare she still have this effect on me?* When we arrived at the door of her old chambers, I gently set her on her feet.

"What is she like?" I couldn't help but ask.

"She's beautiful, stubborn, and strong. Her eyes are a darker shade of blue than yours, but I can still see you looking at me when she smiles."

"What's her name?"

"Aella."

I blinked, trying to mentally create an image of the daughter Arianwen had painted for me. No matter how hard I tried, I couldn't picture her, and something broke inside me.

"I'll let you get some rest," I finally replied, and I quickly turned on my heel and left. If I stayed any longer, I wasn't sure what I would say to her. I was vacillating between anger and grief, hope and despair. Like a whirlwind, Arianwen had swept back into my life, and I feared I would not recover this time . . . or perhaps I never had.

The wind whistled through snowcapped mountain passes, their knife-sharp ridges sparkling in the early morning light. Despite our powers, it was always winter here, and my heart grew ever colder.

I paced the balcony that jutted out from my chambers while Valerik lounged comfortably on one of the fur-lined chaises. His eyes closed as he soaked in the morning sun, light bouncing off his opalescent skin.

"A daughter. Can you faexing believe it?" I blew out a frustrated breath. "Why in the cursed stars did she have to show up and turn my world upside down all over again? She didn't just leave me twenty-five years ago, she left with my firstborn child. My heir." The words shot out of me, and it was as if I'd been punched in the gut. I was *so* angry with her.

"Wynn, I—"

"She never even gave me the chance to explain," I interrupted Rik as I ran my hands through my hair. "Faex!" The curse echoed through the mountains.

Arianwen had been the light in my darkness—my star. Then she'd left, taking my heart with her, plunging me into despair.

"What are you going to do?" Rik asked, leaning forward, propping his chin on his fists.

I shrugged. "I don't know what I *can* do. She's lucky my father is dead. He would have sent her away immediately."

Rik scoffed. "You say that as if you wouldn't have found a way to tear the stars from the sky in order to help her."

I glared at him. "I just wish she could have done something, anything, to let me know I've had a daughter all this time. Maybe if I'd known—"

"But she couldn't have told you because of the oath," Rik said.

I groaned. I'd thought I was doing the right thing for my people, for my court. I couldn't have been more wrong. "You're right. I know. It doesn't hurt any less though. I just can't believe I have a *daughter* who is trapped in Prisma—in the Palatium Crystalis, no less."

"Faex," Rik murmured.

"Exactly."

I stopped pacing and leaned against the railing, looking out at the alpine city below. Rik was right. I would do everything in my power to help Arianwen, but I didn't know how I was going to do so. We'd never attempted a rescue out of Prisma in all my years with the rebellion. The risk was far too great.

I took a deep breath, letting the cold air sink into my lungs and wake me up.

"There has to be some solution I'm not thinking of," I said, the metal railing groaning underneath the fierce grip of my fingers.

"Well, that's what you have us for," Rik said as he joined me, placing a calming hand on my shoulder. "You're not alone, Wynn. I know you've tried to keep us out, but you don't have to shoulder this by yourself."

I straightened my posture and took another cleansing breath. I was the king—I needed to show strength even when my world was crumbling all around me.

"We should go. The others will be waiting. We'll figure this out," Rik said.

Giving him a nod, we headed inside.

The only solution that kept coming to mind was a terrible one and would most likely end in death. I just wasn't sure whose.

CHAPTER 5

TEMPEST

KALEIDOS

"Bring her to me," the king demanded.

"It is not advised at this time to—"

"Don't make me ask twice!" he snapped at the Faber Ludi.

"My king, it hasn't even been a day since the attack. Might I suggest we take care of the problem first before we bring her forth?" Himmel asked sweetly.

"No, I want her alive. I want to see the light fade from her eyes. Use whatever means you must to restrain her, but I will see her before nightfall," he warned, drumming his fingers impatiently, the bulging vein in his forehead betraying his otherwise perfect complexion. "Now, where is my son?"

Although it was true, calling me his son felt like a humorless farce. I could no more think of him as a father than he could look at me without disdain in his eyes. I took a sip of wine and pushed off the pillar I'd been leaning against in the council chamber, knowing my lack of urgency in submitting to his request was one small act of defiance I could still afford. Unhurriedly, I positioned myself before him and the rest of his council, giving only the slightest bow of my head.

King Solanos sat at the flat end of the triangular table with his advisors and high-ranking officials facing him on the other two sides. To brave the king directly, one stood at the sharpened point, a feared position, but I'd been in worse.

"Did you know?" he accused, his voice deep and rumbling.

Did I know? My shoulders shook as I became half hysterical with laughter. I covered my face, attempting to conceal the madness that overtook it. *Did I know that my Aella, my little Sea Nymph, had been plotting to destroy us?* I'd known she'd had secrets, but that . . . ? All I could do was laugh.

"DID—YOU—KNOW?" he thundered. Enough of a warning that I finally managed to rein myself in with a modicum of control.

"What is it that I should have known, Father?" I began to stroll leisurely along the side of the table where Himmel and the other handlers sat. "That the marriage draft was so poorly executed this year, not one of the contestants managed to win? Not one was capable of proving themselves worthy of marrying the crown?" The handlers stiffened at my words, and I signaled to the serving staff to pour me more wine.

Solanos let out a dark, humorless laugh. "Worthy!" he spat in my direction. "This is actually fitting for you. Sadly, it's no surprise you failed to incite true strength in any of your contestants. Remember, they were a reflection of you. Surely your weakness and incompetence rubbed off on them, as it has on every task I've assigned you. If you couldn't inspire them, that is on you."

"Before you point fingers, you may want to have a look in the mirror. Haven't you always told me that everything I do is a representation of you, Father?" I tossed back the goblet of wine sloppily, rivulets of burgundy running down the sides of my cheeks, likely leaving blood-like stains.

Solanos maintained eye contact as he slammed his fist onto the table so hard that it splintered into several dozen slivers before collapsing into a heap on the floor. Startled curses flew from the gathering council members while some jumped out of their seats. I rolled my eyes, unphased by his outburst, then chose an abandoned chair that looked reasonably comfortable and dragged it screeching across the floor to an appropriate place near the king's seat.

The Faber Ludi used the pause to worm his way back into the discussion. "All things considered, we have some contestants who survived the attack. What would you have us do with them?"

"I'd hardly call it an attack." Solanos scoffed. "She threw a few stones. Little more than child's play. How many casualties were there?"

"It's still early for the exact numbers, but we've calculated nearly seven thousand deaths, Your Majesty. And up to twenty thousand are reported injured or missing."

Solanos' nostrils flared, betraying his cool. "Like I said, child's play."

"We *could* use this to our advantage." The Faber Ludi steepled his long, spindly fingers, tapping them lightly. "A sign from the stars that the offerings have not been plentiful enough."

"Now that is an idea I could get behind. Demand more tributes," my Uncle Ventius said. "We could host more games, whether we need them or not. Estrella is in need of a new husband. I wouldn't mind a new toy to play with either."

Solanos smirked.

The wine soured in my stomach, threatening to crawl back up my throat. Unsure if from the obscene amount I'd consumed since returning from the arena a few short hours earlier or from the discourse I was presently hearing.

The handlers didn't appear thrilled with the idea either and whispered furiously amongst themselves. Though a brief twitch of a smile curled at the edge of Himmel's lips.

"Fascinating idea," Nephos remarked, stroking his glittered beard. "But with the limited number of skilled elemental fae we have working on the arena, I'm afraid it will be months before it's ready to host another Matri-Ludus."

"I find myself in agreement with Ventius—we should demand more tributes," Himmel chimed in, a calculating look in her eyes. "With the declining birth rates and the loss of a considerable number of Iris citizens, it would not hurt to replenish. However, a royal wedding must still take place. Now, more than ever, we *must* project an image of strength. Show the elementals we have not lost control."

"Not without an apparent winner." The Faber Ludi scoffed and folded his arms.

"Who says we don't have a winner?" Nephos asked, sounding thoughtful. "Stories are written to be changed. *We* tell them what happened, and that is what they will believe. As it has always been."

"Who should it be?" Himmel asked innocently, although it was clear she was scheming.

"Might I suggest Jara?" the Aurums' handler prodded. "Her beauty rivals our own, and her victory in the second event showed us the ruthlessness in her blood. A fine choice she would make."

"We all know Ona is the apparent victor . . . She made it farthest in the final event!" the Aereus' handler cut in. Himmel sighed heavily.

"You speak as though the boy isn't here to choose for himself," my uncle said. Knowing him, he'd expect me to repay the favor in kind.

"Have you considered your options? Or would you like us to take the trouble from your shoulders and make the choice for you?" Himmel asked in her sweetest tone.

"I'll take the tempest," I said before I could think twice. "Give me the girl with lightning in her veins." She might have been lying and scheming behind my back, but I didn't want her dead.

Himmel gasped. "You couldn't possibly consider making that wretch your bride!"

"Hasn't she proven herself strongest? Or is the competition all just for show? She is the *only* logical choice."

"The people will think you've lost your mind. There will be an uproar the likes of which we have never seen!" Himmel exclaimed.

"You forget your place," I growled. Himmel shrunk back as though slapped, hiding her face in the crook of Nephos' feathered shoulder.

The other two handlers grumbled amongst themselves.

"Have I not stared the prophecy in the face and defeated it?" Solanos declared. "All these years . . . all this time . . . and the prophesied one came right to me. Presented herself on a silver platter." He chuckled. "I hate to admit it, but the boy is right. *This* is what we *must* do. To show the world I cannot be defeated. That I am not afraid of some witless prophecy."

The Faber Ludi nodded eagerly. "All shall look upon thee and be humbled in your presence."

Always the suck-up.

Nephos bellowed, "Behold, King Solanos Stellaris, Son of Parthalos, King of Esterra and all surrounding seas, the Unyielding, and Defier of Prophecy. He who has etched his legacy as the greatest of all in our recorded history."

Pride shone upon Solanos' face.

Cocky bastard.

"Poison her, shackle her in iron, take her name for all I care. She struck me with all her power and failed. The prophecy doesn't scare me, nor should an elemental fae girl," the king boasted.

The golden stem of my goblet warped in my hand. I was powerless to stop him, even more so if I objected to him now.

Nephos added, "All the world will know how powerful you are when they hear even prophecies bend to your will. Watch them cower before your might."

"Just bring her to me whole so I can witness the look of defeat before all her delicious pain is erased."

The Faber Ludi muttered to himself excitedly, "Iron, yes, yes." He scribbled maniacally on a roll of parchment stretched out on the floor beside the ruined table, panting as he worked. I glanced over, attempting to focus on his sketch, but the lines crossed as my vision doubled.

I may have had a few too many drinks since . . . well, everything. Or maybe it's from all the energy I expended saving Viera. My mind wandered back to the note Kasha had found on her. The note that changed everything.

When Aella had asked me for books on the Adamas, I'd suspected she'd had ulterior motives, but I'd let my suspicions slide. After seeing her wield the power of air in the arena and then reading this note found on her best friend, whom she'd wanted me to protect, all the pieces started coming together. She'd been using me to further her cause the entire time, which apparently included ending the Stellaris line.

As much as it displeased me to know she had been planning to kill me, I couldn't escape the inexplicable draw to her, even if it would lead to my demise. I supposed it didn't matter what I felt—the king would get what he wanted in the end. And perhaps that was part of the reason I was so compelled to help her, if only to seek vengeance against him.

If the prophecy was true, was it even possible the king could change the course of destiny simply by making the marked one nameless? Did he think he was so much greater than the stars that he'd dare defy what had been foretold?

These were dizzying thoughts, and I wasn't nearly as drunk as I needed to be to cope with them. I threw back another goblet of wine in an attempt to rectify my state, then slumped down in my chair, allowing my eyes to drift shut.

"What is this foul mess?" the king's voice cut through my drunken slumber. "Couldn't you have at least hosed the wretched thing down before prancing it in here?"

"And risk strengthening her?" Himmel hissed. "This is for your benefit, I assure you."

I had half a heart to tell them to shut up because they were disturbing my respite, but that would require using my voice, and I couldn't find it in me to care enough to make the effort.

Heavy chains scraped against the marble floor, then a small grunt and a thud startled me like a kick to the chest. I suppressed a gasp, as it felt like the air had been knocked out of me. I peeked an eye open to see that which I was not yet ready to see.

Midnight blue eyes connected with mine through a curtain of thick, black hair. Void of hope, stars no longer glittered in them. It pained me to look at her. So much, it shocked me sober. So frail, so . . . broken. Though she'd captured a piece of my heart, I questioned if any of it had been real, or if she had just been playing the long game. Had she really thought she could use me, that I could be the one to arm her just to stand by as she took everything?

She closed her eyes, severing the connection between us. She may have been secretly plotting against me, but I welcomed the challenge.

CHAPTER 6
A Place No One Would Dare Look

AELLA

Phantom screams rang in my ears. Fearful echoes of suffering, uncharted and unnamed. Had it been hours? Days? I wasn't sure. I'd let darkness swallow me whole and had welcomed the void until *they* had returned.

Now, every waking moment was consumed by the cold iron that bit at my skin and sent searing pain down to the bone. Tormenting enough to distract me from the memory of what I'd lost. Rough, heavy chains hung from the collar around my neck. My throat burned from the inside out. Too many screams, too much iron. The last I'd tried, nothing more had come out.

I'd thought I'd been done, thought I'd had no more fight, but it turned out even giving up took strength I didn't have. It shamed me to know I'd given in to Himmel so easily just to avoid torture. I just wanted them to return me to that dark, endless abyss—or better, let me die.

I could hardly open my eyes, too swollen from crying, and my limbs were heavy as I was dragged forward, the guards jerking me along. A boot in my back to keep me stumbling forward. With each fall, the cool marble was like ice to my flesh. My skin so raw, so weak, unable to heal. But when

I didn't get up quickly enough, they tugged the chain, yanked me by the throat, choking me. I had to keep moving.

One step at a time.

Ignore the sounds, ignore the pain.

Ignore the hissing and the taunting.

The Iris courtiers cursed me and spat on me, like I could get any lower than I already was. Their curses, full of formality, sounded petty coming from their crisp, accented tongues. I marched naked, blanketed only by the caked-on mud, blood, and knotted cape of my hair. This was a march I feared might never cease, though whatever awaited me at the end of it couldn't be much better.

Upon our arrival to the triangular hall, the heavy boot collided with my back once more. I fell forward, collapsing into a heap. A loud voice boomed over me. Solanos. But there was something more, a rhythm in the air, a scent familiar. Opening my eyes, they connected with the owner, the breath of whom I knew better than I should have.

Kaleidos stared at me with a consuming hatred, clear in the furrow of his brow. A look of pain or disappointment flickered across his eyes, replaced by disgust. What we'd had, what he could have been, all of it had been nothing more than lovesick rationalizations. Deep down, I'd known this but had been too lovesick to admit it to myself. As much as I wanted him to, he would never stand up for me. His feigned interest in me had been nothing more than another contest for him. Another form of entertainment.

His nostrils flared, and he stood abruptly, as if to leave.

"Is this some kind of vile jest?" he clipped. "She is to be my bride, but you dare to make me suffer the memory of seeing her like this?"

His what? Was it not over yet? Did they intend to put me back into the arena? Into yet another event? I began to sweat, dizzy, saliva pooling beneath my tongue.

"Perhaps it will open your eyes to what she truly is, what they *all* are. Without us, they'd be nothing more than animals," King Solanos said with a dark chuckle. "Though I do have to admit, this is probably one of the more strategic choices you've made in your life. Those powers should do quite well mixed into our line . . . And I agree, we shouldn't have to endure the sight of her as she is at this moment. Ladies!" He waved his hand toward Himmel and the other handlers. They scurried forward, surrounding me. Then, prismatic light shot from their fingertips, connecting to form a circular dome around me. It bubbled out slightly before shrinking in on me, and I held my breath as I was encapsulated in a glittering light that undid all of the filth. Though I could still feel the itch and the pinch of the dried blood underneath, my skin appeared sparkly clean with a pearlescent hue. An illusion was all it was.

Without all the visible layers of filth, I should have felt more bare standing before the king, but that was insignificant in comparison to all I'd just been through. Losing Viera. My failed assassination. The cell. Himmel's search.

Let them stare at the broken shell of the person I used to be. I glared at Kaleidos, daring him to show some remorse.

"Much better," the king declared, his sophisticated accent giving off an air of superiority. "There she is, the girl who thought she could kill me." He barked a laugh, his sycophants joining in a chorus of amusement with him. "The 'Star-Blessed.' The prophesied one. Tell me, silverfish, what do you have to say for yourself?"

I wanted to scream, but no sound would come out. I'd torn my voice to shreds and now suffered the consequences. Beyond that, I'd never been more weak, all source power drained out of me by the presence of iron around my neck. If I wanted to summon a drop of water, even that would be too much.

"What's wrong with it? Doesn't it speak?" Ventius asked.

"She most certainly hollers," one of the guards chuckled behind me.

"Kaleidos, if you want to choose another bride, I wouldn't blame you," Ventius added. "But I am curious to see if her abilities pass on to your descendants. It's not as though you can't pick another female once this one fulfills her purpose."

I swayed. This couldn't be happening.

The prince marched to stand before me, his towering form blocking me from the king. Kaleidos only glanced at me with a cold disinterest, as though unphased by the sight of me.

"Perhaps she might continue to surprise us all," Kaleidos muttered under his breath.

"Fetch the key," Solanos said.

I squeezed my eyes shut. The key, the nameless key, it *was* real. Viera had been right. The Iris truly did wield a key that would render its victim as a blank slate to be molded as they pleased. Perhaps this was for the best. I couldn't live like this anyway. Stars knew what more torture and punishment they would plan if I kept my identity. If I could be made nameless, there was still a chance my family would be spared. Nothing would matter anymore because I'd be gone, joining the stars with Viera and the rest. Or would my soul remain trapped here somehow in a nameless form until my death?

The Faber Ludi stepped forward with two open palms. In one hand lay a dagger clear as glass, and in the other, a set of iron forceps, the handheld portion enveloped in some type of shiny material to protect the bearer. My eyes widened as they summoned Zaita over, who had been lingering listlessly near the back of the room. I recalled Viera's words about Zaita being used for the king's pleasure, my former fellow contestant turned nameless. Zaita obeyed without hesitation, kneeling before the Faber Ludi.

Without warning, he stabbed her through the gut with a sick squish. A soft gasp parted her lips, and her eyes connected with mine as he dug greedily through her with the forceps. I screamed a silent scream. I wanted to look away, but to leave her alone when she was so clearly in trouble felt like abandoning her. All I could offer was my presence in her final moments. When the Faber Ludi withdrew his hand, her head lolled back, and she collapsed to the ground. Kaleidos just stood there, squeezing and opening his fist, staring at the ground, at the puddle that slowly grew around Zaita.

"I rather liked that one. Couldn't you have used a more surgical approach?" The king harrumphed.

The Faber Ludi appeared drunk on violence. "I'm sorry, my king. I lost control of myself. I will do better next time."

In the forceps, he held a key—so plain for such a magical artifact. But clearly so powerful, they sought to hide it in a place no one would dare look. Were they going to put it inside of me? My breathing quickened, and my heart hammered in my chest. I dared the storms to come, to wipe out this city and every last member of this kingdom. I begged the stars, but as I prayed, the iron seemed only to cut deeper into my skin, like it knew I needed magic so it leeched harder at my source, sucking me dry. Unfathomable fear penetrated me, and my body began to tremor.

Kaleidos turned to face me finally, and all I could see was his stony, cold expression. So shockingly beautiful yet so heartless, so full of evil. I had been a fool to ever put my faith in him. He was no better than the rest of them.

Where were you? my eyes threatened to say. His only response, a tensing of his sharp jaw.

He stepped toward me, and I flinched back, which seemed to spark more anger in him. Grabbing me by the hair at the back of my head in a show of dominance, his hand seemed to almost tremble. Or was it my imagination? Tears bled from the corners of my eyes at the sting of betrayal.

"That's right, nephew. Show her who's master," Ventius said.

Kaleidos' eyes were filled with so much hate, so much disgust, I could practically feel the heat radiating off of him. And in a voice lower than ought to have been possible, he growled, baring his teeth. "If you want to survive, follow me."

I swallowed the aching lump in my throat, the humiliation of having once wanted this male, having once trusted him, and tried to process what he could possibly mean. His grip loosened ever so slightly on my hair before he pressed my head down and I followed suit in a bow.

The Faber Ludi extended the key toward me.

"All you need to do is touch it," Himmel crooned, "and all your sorrows will be gone, washed away like the sea. And you shall begin a new life, a blessed life with no attachments. You will be free."

I squeezed my eyes shut again as I felt the pull to touch the key. A thousand images played of my family, my home, my best friend. Knowing I wouldn't be able to take them with me where I was going. My last exchanges with my mother and father. My heart ached, and I hated how horrified they would feel if they knew what had really happened to me. I was exhausted with the shame of failing to end the Matri-Ludus, failing to protect my siblings from this ongoing evil.

I'm sorry, I sent with my heart. *I love you,* I proclaimed one last time to my family.

Perhaps my mother had believed I was star-blessed, but she couldn't have been more wrong. If anything, I was cursed with misfortune. Tears streamed from my eyes as I braced myself for what was to come. My final choice, my final move.

I reached a shaking hand forward, eager now. I didn't know if I'd still hurt once this was over, but what could hurt worse than this? Desperation tempted me to grab for the key, like I'd never wanted anything more. Was I a coward to want it, or was it self-mercy?

I looked to the prince one last time. How much I had changed since our first glance all those months ago, since our first encounter in the garden, since our first kiss, and since he'd made me his first promise. A promise he hadn't kept. He'd made me fall for him, he'd given me a taste of what could have been. But his acknowledgement that he was on the wrong side paired with his continuous failure to do anything about it . . . That had been uglier than the Iris being cruel.

"You are the worst of them all." I mouthed my final words to the prince before closing my hand around the nameless key.

CHAPTER 7
Marked by the Stars

Arianwen

I squinted against the bright sunshine pouring into my room. It had been so long, and I'd forgotten what it was like to awaken to the light bouncing off the snowcapped peaks. Sunlight never woke me in my underwater home in Iveria. It felt completely surreal to be back in my old rooms in the Zephyrian palatium, filled with my belongings from another time. Stars knew I had never wanted to come back here—to the memories that haunted these halls.

Since leaving, I had found my purpose—a beautiful family and doting husband waited for me back in Iveria along with my fulfilling work as a well-respected healer. All I needed now was my Aella, our whirlwind and light. Fear tried to strangle the air out of my lungs at the thought of what she might be enduring in Prisma. It left me wondering if I'd taken too long to get here, if I would be too late.

I replayed the look on Wynn's face as I told him about our daughter for the first time. The shock, anger, and despair—the knowledge he might never look upon her face now that she was in Prisma, competing for their wicked prince.

The wound in my abdomen throbbed, and I pressed my hand against it, trying to send in some healing energy. Healing never worked quite as well on oneself. I was rummaging through my pack, looking for my numbing salve, when a knock at the door startled me. Grabbing my old robe off a chair, I hurried over to answer it. Perhaps it was Wynn with news.

I flung the door open, surprised to see Mari there with a tray of breakfast items.

"Miss Arianwen!" she exclaimed with a smile. "I never thought I'd see you here again."

Unable to stop myself, I threw my arms around her in an awkward hug, trying not to disrupt the tray. "Mari, it's so wonderful to see you doing well."

She brushed a blonde strand of hair behind her ear with her free hand, then rubbed her swollen belly. "I don't know if *well* is the correct term, but my life is full and quite exhausting."

I couldn't help but laugh. "I have five still running around at home. I fully understand your pain."

"Stars! Five? Your husband must never let you out of his sight."

I smiled. "Something like that."

"Forgive me for asking, but what are you doing back here in Zephyria? When I was informed who I was to prepare a bath for and bring food to this morning, it was quite the shock."

Uncertain how much I should reveal and what Wynn wanted people to know, I hesitated. "I . . . uh, I came to ask Wynn—the king—for his help. My eldest daughter was taken to Prisma, and she's in great danger."

Mari looked at me with pity. "Oh . . . I am so sorry for your loss."

I squeezed my eyes shut, trying to hold back tears. No, I would not believe that. She was alive. She was not lost. I would hold her in my arms again.

As if uncomfortable with my sudden show of emotion, Mari turned away and set the tray of food onto the table. "I didn't mean to upset you . . . You think the king might be able to help?"

"It's about time someone stood up to the Iris, Mari," I said, trying to keep the frustration out of my voice. "It's been twenty-five years since I found out about the rebellion, and what do we have to show for it?"

Mari turned to look at me, brows raised at my sudden brazenness. "The king has saved so many. You should know. You helped him."

I covered my face, taking a deep breath. "Yes, I know. I just think it's time we do more. No more mothers and fathers should have to say goodbye to their children and never see them again."

Seeming slightly put off by the conversation, Mari nodded curtly, then headed off to the bathing chamber. "I will prepare your bath now and come back with some fresh coffee if that is all right with you."

"Yes, thank you, Mari."

Perhaps I had spoken out of turn, or perhaps she was angry with me for how I'd left. If I was completely honest with myself, perhaps I had been holding a slight grudge that she'd never warned me about Katye. Wynn was her king—of course she would stand behind him. Regardless, Mari had always been so sweet. I owed her an apology.

My anxiety was at an all-time high, taking away from the comforting nostalgia of the warm bath and coffee I'd dreamt of. I wrung my hands while I paced back and forth in front of the fireplace. Wynn had not called for me, and I was somewhat nervous about roaming the halls of the palatium, not knowing who I'd run into. The thought of bumping into Queen Katye brought me back to my insecure, twenty-five-year-old self. I'd never forget Katye's tinkling laugh and the smug look on her face at that dinner. What would she do when she found out about Aella? I shuddered. Surely nothing good.

What is wrong with you, Ari? You're not some naive, infatuated girl anymore. You're better than this.

Still, I had no desire to run into Queen Astrid *or* Queen Katye without warning—those females who had constantly looked down their noses at me.

I sat back down in the chair, pouring another large cup of coffee. Oh, how I'd missed it. I would seriously need to figure out a way to smuggle some home so I could finally introduce Verus to it. Admittedly, I was slightly bitter at Lucris for flaunting his coveted coffee stores in front of me and never deigning to share. Loathsome male.

Another knock startled me, causing my coffee to splash out and burn my hand. Cursing under my breath, I set the cup down and hurried to answer the door. The smile fell off my face—Emil stood outside.

"Miss Arianwen, if you'd follow me, I'm here to take you to the king."

"Of course," I replied, smoothing my hair while following him down the hall. I tried to bite back my irritation that Wynn hadn't come for me himself, but things had changed. I'd have to get used to that.

Emil led me to a part of the palatium I hadn't frequented. Far too many stairs and hallways later, we reached a large set of double doors that were open to a meeting room with floor-to-ceiling windows overlooking the surrounding alps. It reminded me of the dining room but must have been on the opposite side of the mountain.

As I walked into the room, I shrank as all eyes turned toward the entrance. Faces I recognized greeted me, their expressions hard to decipher. I'd left without a word, so they'd have every right to be angry.

To my surprise, Helio jumped out of his chair and crossed the room in quick strides, throwing his arms around me. I held in a wince as he jostled my injury.

"Ari! Look at you! It's as if no time has passed. You look wonderful as always." The copper-haired Aereus fae grinned.

My cheeks flushed with warmth. "You don't look so bad yourself."

Aging dramatically slowed for elemental fae once we reached the age of twenty-five. We were not quite as long-lived as we'd been before our oppressors had come, but we still lived decently long, unlike the Iris, who seemed almost immortal.

Valerik walked over and gave me a brief embrace. "It's good to see you, Ari."

"You too, Rik."

"Wynn called us all here today but hasn't told us what's going on," Helio said. "How in the ancient tree roots did you make it all the way back here?"

"I was wondering that myself," Wynn chimed in as he entered the room from behind me. A gust of air closed the doors, and he gestured for me to take a seat. His icy blue gaze was filled with storm clouds, a reminder he was still quite upset with me.

I took a seat at the table. Glint and Kairi nodded in greeting, then turned to whisper to each other. Despite Helio's warm welcome, I felt like an outsider in this group that had once treated me as one of their own. Eden—the other Aereus in Wynn's cabala—was missing, but perhaps she was on a mission.

"Will the queen be joining us?" I asked hesitantly, wanting to prepare myself for all possibilities.

Wynn frowned. "She has never been a part of my cabala and is currently in mourning. The absolute last thing she needs is to be concerned with this matter."

I looked down at my hands, full of nerves. Was he going to tell them, or would he ask me to do it?

Wynn cleared his throat, and I looked up as he settled back into his seat. Being king suited him. He commanded the room in a way he had always been meant to, the wildness of his youth a memory.

"As eager as I am to hear how you made it here, we have more pressing matters to attend to. Would you like to tell them, or shall I?" Wynn asked.

I clasped my hands in front of me on the table, gathering up my nerve as I faced the questioning looks and judgment of the cabala. A strained laugh came out of me, and I looked to Helio's kind eyes for strength, noticing him nodding encouragingly. I took a deep breath.

"I am here because my daughter was drafted into the current Matri-Ludus, the one for Prince Kaleidos."

Helio tilted his head and reached across the table, giving my hand a squeeze. "That's terrible, Ari, and I hate to ask, but what does that have to do with us?"

I dared a glance at Wynn, his eyes shuttered and jaw tight.

"Well, you see . . . when I left Zephyria, apparently I did not leave alone."

"I'm sorry, what?" Glint exclaimed. "Are you saying what I think you're saying?"

Helio looked at Rik, shrugging, not fully grasping what Glint had deduced.

Not wanting to drag it out any further, I took another breath and said, "I wasn't aware when I left, but the stars blessed Wynn and me with a child, and that child is currently in Prisma."

The cabala froze as my words sunk in, then all at once, the room was in an uproar as they started talking over each other, throwing questions my way.

"The heir to the throne is in Prisma?"

"What do you mean a 'child?'"

"Wynn, what in the faexing skies did you do?"

"Ari, why didn't you let us know sooner?"

All I wanted to do was climb under the table and hide from the hurt and angry faces.

"Enough!" Wynn commanded with a roar. "I know you all have questions, and I doubt they are even close to all the questions *I* have, but that's not what's important." The room quieted as everyone turned to look at Wynn expectantly. "*My* daughter, *my heir,* is in the hands of the Iris, and we must find a way to get her back if she is still alive."

His heir? Because she's his firstborn? But she's not even fully Adamas. Why would he say that?

"That has never been done before," Kairi added. "What do you think we can do? There are bound to be even more guards and patrols in Prisma with it being the prince's Matri-Ludus."

"Yes, I'm aware," Wynn growled. "That is why we are here—to see if we can come up with a plan. I would like to send someone to see if any of my contacts outside Prisma are still around, and if they're not, I'll need one of my trusted spies to go and glean any information they can. Unfortunately, it is incredibly risky, and we won't hear back for weeks. Either way, we need to act as soon as possible."

"Forgive me if this seems callous," Glint said softly, "but there can be other heirs. What makes this one worth risking everything for?"

I couldn't help my own growl at her comment. Every life was valuable and Wynn's other children could take the throne, but it angered me for anyone to speak as if my daughter were an acceptable loss.

"The prophecy!" Rik uncharacteristically blurted out. "Do you think it's her? '*Born of courts united . . .*'"

I stood and paced the room, all my anxiety threatening to overwhelm me. "When I came upon the prophecy here twenty-five years ago, I thought nothing of it. Then the rebels in Iveria got their hands on it, and I heard them speculating about who it could be referring to, and I started to wonder."

"What makes you think it is about your daughter?" Glint asked, full of skepticism. "She is not the only child born of two courts. In fact, there have been a few here in Zephyria."

"Are any of them marked?" I asked.

"That's a good question," Glint replied, tossing her golden hair back.

"My Aella was born with a star-shaped mark on the back of her neck, she was born under the stars . . . Of course I cannot be fully certain, but everything within me says it's her. When I read the prophecy again weeks ago, something clicked. Call it intuition, call it the stars trying to speak to me, but I just *know* in my heart she's the one we have been waiting for who will finally bring down the Iris." I stopped pacing and turned back to the table, meeting each gaze one by one before landing on Wynn's. "The time to act is now. Stop hiding up here in the alps! We need to take them down before they destroy her or find out her secret!"

"Hiding up here in the alps?" Helio said, hurt coloring his voice. "We've been risking our lives for years helping refugees."

I swung my gaze back to his. "I know you have, but what happens when Zephyria is overrun with refugees and you have nowhere else to put them? How much longer will those of us still living in our courts be forced to send our sons and daughters to be slaughtered and enslaved? When is enough going to be enough?"

Wynn stood, staring out the windows, his brow furrowed in thought. "I hear what you're saying, Arianwen. Perhaps if we can rescue . . . Aella . . ." He seemed to struggle saying her name out loud. "If we can convince the rebel leaders of the other courts she is the prophecy come to life . . . maybe we can finally rally them to work together."

"That sounds completely doable," Kairi groaned with sarcasm. "Let's just break into the Palatium Crystalis, steal a contestant out from under their noses, and then somehow gather all the courts together to take down the Iris."

"There is far too much fear among the rebellion, but if we have a figurehead, it just might work," Rik said thoughtfully.

"Ooh, yes. This could definitely work." Helio grinned.

A glimmer of hope rose within me. At least they hadn't completely given up yet. We just needed to find a way in.

"Any brilliant ideas?" Glint asked.

"Time is of the essence here," I stated.

"You think we don't know that?" Wynn bit out.

"Stars, Ari, I haven't seen Wynn this out of sorts in years," Helio said, leaning back in his chair and putting his feet on the table in a completely irreverent manner. "Maybe you two should find a room and 'talk it out' or something."

"That is completely inappropriate, Helio. We're both married!" I gasped. "To other people!"

"Unless Wynn has been hiding another major secret, that is news to us," Helio quipped.

I turned to look at Wynn, eyebrows furrowed, my heart sinking all the way to my stomach. "What does he mean? Didn't you marry Lady Katye?"

After an awkward pause, Glint and Helio started whispering back and forth, but I couldn't make out what they were saying. All my attention was focused on Wynn and what his response would be.

Wynn rolled his shoulders back, his eyes hard and unyielding. "Whether or not I am married is of no consequence to you. You have your life in Iveria—you don't need to concern yourself with mine."

An overwhelming feeling of hurt swept through me. I murmured a quick, "I need a minute," before escaping to the hall.

Wynn had never spoken so harshly to me, yet I understood his pain. Having truth withheld was hurtful, and I had kept one of the greatest secrets possible. Despite the anguish he had caused me at the end of our whirlwind romance, I had forgiven him. But now I couldn't help but wonder if he had ever forgiven *me* for leaving.

A throat cleared behind me, and I turned around to see Wynn.

"I'm sorry. That was harsh of me," he said, his tone softer.

I nodded before taking a deep breath. I was going to be honest with him, even if it hurt. "Wynn . . . I am sorry for how I left. I hope you can believe me. I just couldn't bear the thought of living a life as your mistress while you were duty-bound to marry Katye. I knew if I told you I was leaving, you'd somehow convince me to stay . . . I had to choose myself."

A loud gasp came from the open meeting room doors followed by the sound of a chair crashing to the floor. "You did *what?*" I heard Helio exclaim.

Had we been that loud?

"Stars-damned nosy elementals," Wynn muttered, pinching the bridge of his nose.

"Faex, Wynn—"

He held up a hand to stop me as he turned and marched into the meeting room.

"One would think you all would have enough sense not to eavesdrop on your king," he admonished. "Kairi . . ."

I sheepishly followed Wynn back into the meeting room, noting the shocked looks on everyone's faces except Rik's.

"With all the secrets you've been keeping, can you blame us?" Kairi retorted, a blast of air kicking up around her, ruffling her white, bobbed hair. "So what if I let your words drift on in."

"I obviously knew Ari left, but you never explained what happened!" Helio blurted out before he turned to me, his brows pinched together. "Faex, Ari. It hurt when you didn't even say goodbye—I thought we were friends—but now I understand. I just wish you would have told us so we could have kicked Wynn's arse and knocked some sense into him."

"I think Ari and I have some things to discuss," Wynn said. "In private."

Helio groaned. "Just when we were finally getting some answers."

Rik motioned for the cabala to get up and follow him. "We'll give you two some space."

Helio squeezed my shoulder on his way out. "For what it's worth, I will do everything in my power to help you and Wynn rescue Aella. Despite everything that has happened, you're family."

My eyes welled with tears as all the emotions crashed over me. "Thanks, Helio."

As the doors closed behind them, I turned back to Wynn. "Can we just start at the beginning? I'm so confused right now."

"What is it you would like to know?"

"Are you married?" I asked.

"No."

"Why not?"

"Does it even matter now?" He frowned.

"Yes. It does."

Wynn ran his hand over his face and through his hair, sighing loudly. "Okay. No, I did not marry Katye. Faex. After you left, I just couldn't bear to go through with it . . ."

I couldn't hold back the half laugh, half sob that came out of me. "But what about your duty?"

Wynn's shoulders tensed as he trained his eyes on the floor. "I was wrong, all right? All those things I said to you that night were completely foolish and idiotic. Yes, my parents had been talking about a betrothal to Katye for years, but she'd been away, and I guess I'd hoped it would just disappear. When we showed up at dinner, I was completely blindsided by her presence and the sudden talk of making the betrothal . . . the marriage official. I felt trapped." His pain-filled gaze finally met mine. "I am my family's only heir, I've had responsibilities and duty ingrained in me since I was a small child. I was desperately trying to cling to the idea that I could please my parents—please my people—and still have you. If only I'd realized sooner that, without you, none of that mattered. *You* were all I wanted. You had completely stolen my heart . . . and I can't say it has ever fully recovered."

A wave of pity swept over me. I'd assumed he'd gone on to fulfill his duty and was married with children of his own by now. I couldn't have been more wrong. I had found my joy . . . my peace. I had found a deep love with Verus, and here Wynn was, alone. No wonder he was so angry with me.

But I had never asked him to be lonely and miserable.

I reached over and put a hand on his arm. "Wynn . . ."

His glacier eyes bored into mine. "You never even gave me a chance, Ari. Why couldn't you have stayed and worked things out? Didn't you realize—"

"I didn't think there was anything to work out. I thought you had made your choice," I interrupted. "Not that it even matters now because—"

"I came looking for you."

"What?" A fleeting memory swept through me.

"I tried to let you go, but I had to make sure you were all right. I came looking for you in Iveria."

"When?" I asked, my eyes wide.

He shrugged. "I don't know, maybe a month or so after you left. I was utterly miserable, and Helio convinced me to go after you. They didn't know what'd happened, only that you'd left suddenly. I know I'd promised to let you go, but I had to make sure you were all right."

"The market . . ." I said under my breath. "I thought I scented you."

He focused on the floor again, unable to look me in the eye. "You were with a male, covered in his scent, and you looked happy. What was I going to do? You had obviously moved on."

I closed my eyes, and just for a moment, I imagined how different things could have been if he had approached me in the market. If he had told me he'd chosen me, would I have gone with him? Would I have raised children with him in Zephyria, Aella safe from harm? Verus and I had been married, but our marriage could have been annulled. Verus would have let me go . . . I shook my head. No. Dwelling on what ifs and what could have beens would only cause heartache. I refused to mourn a life I hadn't lived. Wynn needed to let me go as I had let him go years earlier. Telling him that things might have been different would do him no good. I cared too much to allow him to continue hoping for something that could never be.

"Wynn, once again, I am so sorry for the way I left and for never telling you about Aella, but the past needs to stay there. Verus has my heart, and I have built a life with him. It's time for you to build a life of your own."

His eyes shuttered. "Understood. And if we rescue her—if we rescue our daughter, would you continue to keep her from me?"

"That choice would be hers. She is no longer a child. She deserves the truth after all these years, and I only hope, if we can save her, she'll forgive me."

A calm acceptance came upon Wynn's face along with what looked like resolve. "I don't know how, but I want you to know I will do everything in my power to free her. I would love to get to know her, but I will respect her choice. We should gather the others and come up with a plan."

He started walking toward the door, but I stopped him with a hand on his shoulder. He stiffened beneath my touch. "One last thing . . ."

He slowly turned toward me, the tension in his body screaming the weight of his burdens. I didn't want to add to them, but I had to ask.

"Can you release me from the oath? I'll release you too."

"Yes, of course. Under the stars tonight."

CHAPTER 8

SEVERED OATHS

WYNN

My heart was heavy as I knocked on Ari's door. I had promised to dissolve the oath, and I was a male of my word, even though it was all we had left.

The door opened, and those molten, silver eyes looked up at me with a pained smile. Everything about her took me back to those days. I'd never thought it would be so difficult to see her again.

"Is everything all right?" I asked.

"Just worried," she said, biting her lip.

Those lips . . . Stars help me, I still want her.

If it hadn't been for the scent of *him* entwined with her, I would have been tempted to try to pick up where we had left off, but no. She was no longer mine, despite how my very being screamed against that fact.

She took a step back, as if she could read my thoughts, and let me into the room.

"We should probably get this over with, Wynn," she said softly as she walked toward the large balcony that jutted out of the mountain.

I nodded, unable to speak for fear of what might come out of my mouth. I was a fool for holding on to the vicious hope that someday we'd make our way back to each other. The fickle stars mocked our connection, and still . . . they had blessed us with a daughter, one I had never laid eyes on and perhaps never would. Aella—whirlwind. What a name her mother had chosen. Perhaps that had been her way of honoring me, or I was grasping at straws, hoping she had not completely forgotten what we'd had.

We stepped out under the stars, and I quickly created a dome of protection around us to keep out the bitter chill of the wind sweeping through the mountains.

"Thanks," she mumbled.

"Of course," I replied, glancing down to glare at the mark on my hand. This damned oath had tied us together long enough and had kept her from getting word to me, from even telling our daughter where she'd come from. Anger writhed under my skin once again that she had withheld something so vital, but I tried to temper it. Maybe once the oath was severed, I could let go. Perhaps I was wrong and it was the oath that made me feel the incessant pull toward her. "Are you ready?"

She nodded, her eyes luminous under the stars as she held her palm up to me.

Damn it, Wynn. Control yourself.

I unsheathed my dagger and quickly sliced into the mark on her hand before doing the same to mine.

"I release you, Arianwen, from the oath you swore to never reveal anything of the Adamas people or the places you have seen. May the stars bear witness."

"I release you, Wynn, from the oath you swore to not harm me or my family, and to allow me to leave whenever I chose. May the stars bear witness."

We clasped our bloodied palms together, and a flare of heat went through mine as the oath was dissolved.

From the glassy fringe of trickling icicles overhead, Ari summoned an orb of water to clean off our hands, and when I looked down, the star-shaped scar was gone. There was merely a slightly reddened mark where the wound had sealed.

Ari sighed as she turned to look out over the alps, her shoulders loosening as tension melted off her. "I don't know about you, but I feel as if I am lighter. I didn't even realize the weight I'd been carrying all these years. It no longer burns when I think about telling Aella or Verus about where she came from."

It took all of my willpower not to pull her into my arms right then and there. How I had missed her. But I had lost that privilege with my foolish choices and misplaced duty. I had hoped releasing her from the oath would have released me from her, but I had been mistaken.

I cleared my throat. "Now that that's taken care of, I'll let you get some rest. Tomorrow, we will need to make some decisions."

She turned to me, starlight shimmering off her skin. "Thank you, Wynn. I know this means you need to trust me."

"I do . . . trust you." Out of habit, I reached forward and tucked the stubborn tendril of hair behind her ear. She took a step back, distancing herself from me.

"Wynn, stop. You can't . . ."

I raised my hands in submission. "I'm sorry. That won't happen again."

She looked shaken, but she nodded. "It's all right. I realize this is all very strange for you . . . for us."

"I should go," I said while backing away, every fiber of my being wishing she would ask me to stay but knowing she wouldn't.

"Good night, Wynn."

I turned on my heel and fled to my wing. The way she still managed to get under my skin after all these years . . . We needed to finish this mission, and then I needed to keep my distance. Being around her was more than I could bear.

CHAPTER 9
A Good Little Pet

Vines and a clamor of other plants hung from the ceilings above me. They crept along the walls, decorating the space in a wild but beautiful show of life. Light filtered in through lofty, vaulted windows, and by its cast on my surroundings and by the color of the sky, I guessed it must have been late in the afternoon. Books filled the empty spaces along the walls in neat but uneven stacks. The room was furnished in dark woods and deep, rich fabrics, both sophisticated and extraordinary and not at all like anything I'd seen in the Palatium Crystalis except . . .

Muffled voices filtered in from the adjacent room, growing louder as they neared. Not servants—I could tell by their demanding and un-hushed tones.

A door swung open, and without turning to look, all of my muscles tensed. I knew he was there, I was certain of it. I could feel his presence as surely as I might have felt the presence of any divine creature. I swallowed, mouth dry, heart racing. The last I'd seen him was in the king's councilroom . . . Zaita had been stabbed . . . I'd touched the key . . . I should have been nameless. Yet I'd woken up here. *How?* What would they do if they found it hadn't worked?

Kaleidos will take one look at me and know.

All of my hatred for him would be written across my face. How could I hide it from him? How could I possibly fool him into believing the girl he'd come to know was gone? Revealing that the key hadn't worked to the prince . . . it wasn't a gamble I could risk taking.

Breathe, Aella. Breathe.

He wasn't alone. I'd have to fool them all if I wanted to stand a chance of surviving . . .

I focused on the thick, iron cuff around my neck, how it burned. As long as I didn't move around too much, I could potentially grow accustomed to the pain. If I could get used to it, or at least focus on it, I could block everything else out. This was just another challenge, and I'd made it this far, hadn't I? I squeezed my eyes shut, unable to shake the feeling that perhaps the key hadn't worked for a reason. Perhaps I still had a role to play in this star-cursed world.

I sat up in bed, turning to face the intruders with a blank stare. The prince stood at a distance, arms folded as the Faber Ludi, Nephos, and Himmel entered the room, followed by at least a dozen royal guards and two servants carrying a heavy, plated trunk.

I didn't allow myself to look at Kaleidos' face, as much as I wanted to see his reaction to this procession. Himmel taunted me with a perverse grin, and I bowed my head, dropping my eyes to the floor, trying my hardest not to let them trigger me into any emotion that would reveal myself.

"Any signs of . . . recovery or violence? I can give her an iron-infused tonic to—"

"No." Kaleidos raised a hand to halt the Faber Ludi.

"Better not," Himmel added. "Could prevent her from carrying an heir. Chances are she is with child already based on Kaleidos' eagerness last night."

My stomach twisted at the implication, and I stiffened all over at the idea Kaleidos could do anything of the sort. Not reacting was so much harder when he was watching me.

Don't think about what they said last night, about marriage to the prince, about everything that's gone so terribly wrong. Not about what's in that box, or the malicious looks on their faces. Just think of the iron, become one with the pain, the emptiness. It can't possibly get worse than it already is.

The servants set the trunk down at the foot of the bed with a heavy clunk that made me flinch. Whatever was inside couldn't be good.

"I had this designed for her presentation," the Faber Ludi gushed as he opened the trunk, revealing the iron monstrosity inside. I found myself physically repelled, shrinking away from the polished, metallic contraption.

Himmel burst with a haughty laugh and gave Kaleidos a salacious grin. "You're going to love it."

Himmel had the servants erect a semitransparent room divider to give me the illusion of privacy, and I practically sighed with relief when the males left to have tea in the adjacent room while I dressed. The less people watching me, the better until I perfected this new act.

"Did you see what they brought you?" Himmel asked, waving a hand toward the trunk.

I couldn't bring myself to look at it, instinctively backing up a step, but before I could back away further, Himmel grabbed me from behind, pushing me toward the chest. I stumbled, catching myself weakly on the open edge of it.

"Get up and stand still," Himmel said.

When the two maids donned gloves before touching it, that was all the confirmation I needed that it was, in fact, wrought iron. A hiss of pain escaped my lips when they fastened the brassiere to my chest and the cold metal dug into my shoulders and ribs. Next, they secured an iron-chained belt that rested low on my hips, two long, white panels of silk fabric hanging down the center in the front and in the back. The look was complete with a set of layered, iron thigh chains and wrist cuffs that coiled up my forearms like snakes.

Himmel stood me in front of the mirror so I could see my reflection. "Do you like it, my dear?"

I forced a smile. "It hurts," I rasped.

"Oh, you'll get used to it, I'm sure. It's for the safety of the crown . . . and for yourself. You are a very dangerous girl and not to be unchained, do you understand?" she asked in a patronizing tone. I nodded.

"You killed so very many people. You wouldn't want to hurt anyone else now, would you?" She gently stroked the side of my face. "Don't worry. In time, you might be trusted again, but presently, this is your fate. Now, put on a smile. You don't want the males to see you sad . . . And don't forget to express your gratitude for the impeccable design of your garments. They will be drooling over you, I'm sure." She waved a hand dramatically and spun on her heel to leave without further notice.

As the maids combed and styled my hair, I compulsively reached my hand back to cover my neck. Even though the iron collar covered it and my mark had already been discovered, the habit was hard to break.

"What's the matter, miss?"

"I . . . I'm sorry. I had an itch," I lied.

After giving me a dramatic makeup look that appeared to double the size of my eyes and a midnight blue pout, they dusted the exposed areas of my skin with a prismatic glitter. I was then draped in a fine, transparent veil that hung down to my toes with a wrought iron circlet, a mockery of a crown, to hold the cloth in place.

"A moment alone please." Kaleidos' aristocratic voice cut through the silence, making me flinch.

I hadn't heard a door open, and all the nerves had me extra jumpy. The maids hurried off, and soon, we were alone together. I wasn't ready to face him yet, terrified I'd lose control of my emotions. I wondered if he would treat me differently, thinking of me as nameless. If he'd drop the charm he'd used on me in the past and show his true colors. I'd been bitterly reminded who he was in the king's hall. Iris. Yet I feared I was still defenseless against him, with or without the collar.

I stood from the vanity. Ready or not, there was no avoiding this confrontation. I tensed at the sensation of him standing behind me.

"Aella," he said, barely above a whisper.

Stars, I can't do this. I spun around, dropping to my knees before him, my head bowed to hide my face. "Do I please you, Your Highness?" My voice was hoarse.

Kaleidos cleared his throat, then took long strides across the room. I let out a breath, daring a peek only to see him rubbing his face, a dark, humorless laugh escaping him. He made to leave, then paused at the door.

"Stand up," he ordered. "I won't have my *bride* groveling or behaving like a slave." The last word came out with a sneer. "You are going to be paraded through the Palatium Crystalis this evening. Made to show your submission to the crown. My father wants the court to see he has defeated you and that you and the prophecy do not threaten him in the least. He is going to use you to manipulate the people. Do you understand?"

Unable to find words, I stared blankly forward. Kaleidos pinched his nose, then took another long look at me. My skin tingled as he raked his eyes over me, the sheer veil doing little to hide so much exposed skin. I kept my eyes trained on an imaginary point beyond the wall, allowing my vision to blur. Despite doing my best not to notice him, his observation was tangible, as though his eyes left behind a trail of heat.

What I really wanted was to yell at him, to hit him, to tell him to stop staring at me. And then sink into his arms and cry. But I couldn't help thinking of how he'd handled me, how rough he'd been when he'd brought me to the key. How he'd made me think he cared about me. How he'd let Viera die and then let them do *this* to me.

Kaleidos cleared his throat again, then called for the others to return.

"Do you think you used enough iron?" he asked as though slinging an insult. "How in the bloody deep am I to touch her when she's covered from head to toe in the cursed metal?"

"I fully understand your frustration, Your Highness, but this is what you chose for yourself. It is not too late. You could choose another less risky option. The Aurum fae, perhaps?" the Faber Ludi offered.

Kaleidos didn't respond but practically shook in a silent rage.

"We could remove the collar so her neck might be bare?" Himmel suggested.

Kaleidos nodded his assent.

The Faber Ludi crept near, his spindly fingers grasping the veil, lifting it up and over my head, and my cheeks burned with shame. Though they had seen me through the veil, I now felt that much more exposed. I'd been stripped completely naked and paraded through the palatium to the king's council room, but this was different. Then, I'd still been covered in the proof of my suffering—sorrow, blood, and tears. My dirty, tangled locks, a cape of protection. I couldn't have cared less about what they'd seen. But as I stood in a room full of mostly males, scantily clad in a provocative display of iron-wrought underthings, their eyes stole something from me.

I squeezed my own shut, feeling the rush of gooseflesh cover my skin with the cool air dancing across it. I was supposed to thank them for this. I was supposed to smile. Stars, this was impossible. I opened my mouth to speak.

"Hand it to me," Kaleidos demanded.

"But you need to wear the protective—"

With a small click and then a chink, the collar fell apart, crashing to the floor. My tense shoulders dropped a little, some of the weight lifting.

Nephos strolled over. "You have indeed won yourself a rare prize, young prince. Don't worry, I'll have my designers come up with a solution that works for both of you."

Himmel interjected, "Well now, we still don't know how much force is necessary with her, so it will be a slow weaning process, but in time, once she's proven herself a good little pet, she may walk freely as most nameless do."

As she said the word *pet*, the Faber Ludi brought over yet another chain. I couldn't help the trembling fear that overcame me as he approached, but I obeyed when he asked me to step into it. The chain cinched tightly around the most narrow part of my waist and became tighter still when he handed the leather-handled leash to the head guard, who tested it with a little tug that had me crying out, nearly falling as I stumbled forward. The Iris guards chuckled. In a moment of weakness, I let my eyes meet Kaleidos' in the reflection of the mirror, let him see a split-second glimpse of me.

One of the many vining plants that decorated the room grew furiously toward the guard. A thick, thorned vine circled the guard's throat, constricting as it snaked around and around. The guard dropped the leash, his body going taut. But he didn't fall, he just hung there, face turning purple, blood dripping down his neck. It was so gruesome, I had to look away.

"Let me make myself *very* clear. She is *mine* to taunt. *Mine* to torment. Anyone who touches her without my express permission will find themselves in his position," Kaleidos threatened.

Himmel gave me a sharp, accusatory look, shaking her head at me. It was my fault. My reaction had caused this.

"I'm sorry," I quickly corrected myself. "I shouldn't complain when you have all been so gracious with me." I straightened myself and put on a fake smile as I addressed the Iris. "I am humbled and honored by your attention. I do not deserve it." I bowed my head in deference.

"All right, we're running short on time now. File out," Himmel declared. "And get someone to clean up this mess."

"Your Highness," the Faber Ludi prodded as he attempted to pull Kaleidos away. My shoulders relaxed an imperceptible amount, and I counted my breaths as the group filed out of the room. But in the reflection of the mirror, I cast one last look at the prince, and he stalled on his exit, a puzzled expression apparent on his brow. Had I given myself away already? I could only pray I had not.

Chapter 10
My Nameless Bride

Kaleidos

Aella was gone.

I found it nearly impossible to peel my eyes away from my bride as guards escorted her to a small, crystal palanquin to be carried throughout the endless halls of the palatium for all to see. Practically naked, she was shielded by little more than the iron that bound her and a flimsy, translucent veil. Though I had claimed her, it was made clear by the king's bold presentation of her that she wasn't truly mine.

"Make way, make way," Nephos exclaimed. "He is all powerful. He is impenetrable. He is Solanos Stellaris, Son of Parthalos, Defier of Prophecy, King of Esterra and all surrounding seas!"

With his grand palanquin before hers, the king was so proud to show himself off unharmed. Though I hadn't witnessed her attempted assassination, his surviving of her attack in the arena had probably been attributed to more than just his might. More than likely, it had been the quick response of his guards. Naturally, he'd claimed all the glory, and my bride had become little more than a prop for him to parade his triumph.

"Fix your eyes upon the champion of the games! The king, in his great and benevolent mercy, has not only forgiven her but has granted her the honor of marriage to his own beloved son. She will strengthen the royal bloodline with her powers, but do not be afraid. She has been molded into a prize worthy of our prince by giving us her name."

Riding behind her in a palanquin of my own, a bitter resentment churned within my chest at them using her this way. There wasn't enough wine in all of Esterra to dull the feeling of seeing her garbed in iron. I scanned the crowd for their response to this public display that could do just as much damage to my reputation as it lifted the king's. She was unmistakably gorgeous, and the courtiers couldn't take their eyes off her, no matter how much they wanted to hate her. Somehow, she managed to make iron appear the most luxurious metal in all of Prisma.

It gave me no satisfaction to see them ogling my bride, even knowing it wasn't really her anymore. She was mine, and I did not like sharing.

Aella is gone, I reminded myself.

I tried to detach myself from the harsh reality of what I was seeing. Tried to rationalize all my choices up until this moment, tried to strategize my next steps, but it was like spiraling between who I was and who I wanted to be.

Aella had betrayed me in the cleverest of ways—Viera's secret note was proof of that. Still, the memories of her last moments would haunt me . . .

Her skin was soft beneath my fingertips, her hair thick and heavy in the palm of my hand. I yanked her head back, knowing full well there was a chance she wouldn't trust me after this. Though I didn't have much reason to trust her either, knowing she'd been seducing me whilst planning my demise from the very first day she'd set foot in the Palatium Crystalis. I had every intention of finding out why and by whatever means necessary. None of that would be possible, however, if my plan didn't work.

Though I'd never personally had a taste for violence when it came to pleasure, I'd long been surrounded by it, accustomed to the prying eyes and near palpable lust for cruelty that surrounded me wherever I went. The council appeared pleased by my show of dominance, and amidst the noise of their chatter, I whispered her a message. She needed to play along if I wanted even a chance at saving her. I couldn't be sure if it'd actually work, but it was worth the attempt.

If I hadn't given a good show to the king, he surely would have taken things into his own hands.

A strange, unfamiliar sensation pulled at my gut. Perhaps guilt. Was it selfish, forcing her to stay? The way she looked at the key and then at me, I feared maybe I was wrong to try to take that away from her. But I couldn't let go. I couldn't lose her. Not with so many questions left unanswered between us.

It all happened so quickly. One moment, she was there with me, eyes boring into mine, telling me how much she hated me, her lips curling into an anguished sneer—the kind that, in a twisted way, motivated me even more to make this work. The next moment, she collapsed into my arms.

I'd managed to stop her circulation just enough to knock her unconscious, but I wasn't certain if the forcefield I'd placed around her had shielded her from the magic of the key. I wouldn't know until she awoke.

Her body was limp and so delicate. Without the look of defiance and hate in her eyes, she was defenseless, and it took every ounce of willpower not to cover her naked form, not to brush the hair out of her face, not to press one last kiss to her sumptuous lips. Despite all her secrets and lies, I couldn't help the protectiveness that possessed me upon seeing her like this.

"So eager to take your prize. Let us get her properly cleaned up first, and we will send her to your bedchambers," Himmel said.

The Faber Ludi buzzed over. "My prince, I may have alternative means to restrain her, if you are interested."

"Let him have his fun," Uncle Ventius said with a wink. "It will probably be a while before she wakes up anyway. Don't shame the prince for how he likes it."

Before anyone else could cut in and tell me how or what I should do, I turned on my heel and made a beeline for the exit. Let them think me demented, let them gossip, I didn't care. I needed to get her out of here. I cradled her in my arms and headed out toward my rooms.

Once back in my bedchamber, I set her on my bed, searching her expres-

sionless face, dreading the moment of truth. Would there be an empty, confused look in her eyes when I said her name, or would I be hit by her immense hatred and disgust? Perhaps she'd even try seducing me again. I huffed a dark laugh, then got up to leave the room. Whether it had worked or not, I wasn't sure it was wise for me to be the first person she saw when she awoke.

A knock on the crystal encasement startled me back to the present moment, and I refocused my gaze. The door was held open for me to exit. I was back at the entrance to my wing. It was over. It was *all* over. It hit me in the gut. The presentation. The Matri-Ludus. The future we'd been meant to share.

Aella was gone.

But what of the look I had seen in her eyes in my bedchamber? Had I imagined it, or had she been pleading with me. Me, specifically, because she'd known me? Was my Aella still in there? Or had I just seen a face I knew and projected her onto it?

As I walked through my wing, pondering, I nearly went straight into my bedchamber until I remembered I'd given it to her. *Should I check on her? Should I leave her be?* My hand rested on the door handle as I stood there for a long moment, debating my next move. The clicking of heels and that damned overpowering lily scent alerted me I had a visitor. I shook my head, clearing the intruding thoughts before I risked acting on them, and I turned to greet my cousin.

Chapter 11

As If I'd Never Left

Arianwen

Memories of a coppery redhead filled my mind as I rushed out of the palatium the next morning. As much as I was dreading the possible rejection and anger from her, I had to see my old friend. I needed to see Liisa. Before the day's meetings were to start, I made the old, familiar trek to the hospitium.

The narrow streets were far busier than I remembered, the shops bustling with energy. Market carts that had always been overflowing with produce were now scant and picked over. I gaped as I took in all the new structures—every gap was filled in. In the light of day, I fully comprehended the growth Zephyria had experienced in the years I'd been gone.

"Oh, excuse me!" a stranger said after bumping into me.

"Don't worry about it," I said with a smile, grateful my sturdy boots had kept me from slipping off the side of the mountain. As soon as they passed, I winced, my hand going to my ice-pick wound. With any luck, Liisa would have something that could speed up the healing.

I dodged a child as he ran past me and gave the mother an understanding look as she hurried after him. Stars, I missed my children.

Perhaps I should have confirmed Liisa's whereabouts with Wynn, but he'd been acting so strangely around me. It was apparent he still had some unresolved feelings for me, but I would never call him out on it. The way he'd looked at me the night before and how I could picture us falling easily into those old, familiar habits . . . being around him brought a wealth of confusing feelings. Perhaps we needed to keep our distance.

My heart belongs to Verus. I came here to ask for Wynn's help, nothing more.

A glimmer caught my eye, and my gaze swept down the mountainside, searching for what had grabbed my attention. I inhaled a quick breath. A beautiful, shimmering lake that hadn't been there before bordered the outskirts of the city.

What in the stars?

I shook my head in disbelief. I would have loved having a lake so close when I'd been here last. I pulled myself away from the sight, refocusing on my task as I reached one of my favorite places in Zephyria.

As I opened the door to the hospitium, I was immediately transported to the past, all thoughts of the new lake pushed to the back of my mind for later. The smell, the soothing presence of the water trickling through, the humidity of the healing pools . . . How I had missed this place and the work I'd done. The hospitium in Iveria was nothing in comparison.

"May I help you?" an Aereus healer asked as she walked toward me. She was young, and I did not recognize her.

"Hello! Stars, it's strange being here again after all these years. I'm looking for a healer by the name of Liisa. Does she still work here?"

A huge smile broke out on her face. "Yes! I'm her apprentice. How do you know Liisa?"

"We used to work together many years ago. Is she available? Do you think she would have time to see me?"

"Oh, goodness, I'm sorry, yes. Let me go see if I can find her! Do you want to come along? Take a brief tour of the place?"

"Thank you," I said kindly. "I wonder how much has changed in the past twenty-five years."

The female led the way down the familiar hall. "So you're a healer too?" she asked. "What took you away?"

"Yes, I am." I left her second question unanswered, not wanting to explain my complicated past.

"It's very unusual for you to have been here and left."

"Yes, quite," I said, hoping she'd leave it at that.

"It must be so nice to have the advantage you Argenti have with your healing gifts," she said a bit mournfully. "But Liisa is such a good teacher, and I have already learned so much." She peeked into a few rooms as we walked back toward the apothecary.

"Believe it or not, I still use a lot of the Aereus techniques I learned while working with Liisa. They are just as valuable, even though they differ from the abilities I was born with."

"Fascinating. Good to know."

After checking the apothecary with no luck, the healer led me down another corridor.

"I probably should have checked here first, but you know how it is." She chuckled awkwardly.

"It's fine, really," I assured her.

We arrived at a door, and she knocked before popping her head in. "Liisa, someone is here to see you!" She whispered something I couldn't make out. "I'm sorry, what did you say your name was again?" She winced as she turned to look at me.

"Arianwen."

The door swung all the way open, and Liisa's mouth dropped at the sight of me before she got up and stepped around her desk. "Ari?"

Feeling shy, I gave a brief wave. "Liisa, it's so wonderful to see you."

The young healer turned toward me in shock. "You're *the* Ari I have heard so many of the healers talk about?"

"I had no idea I had such a reputation here." I shrugged sheepishly.

"That's putting it lightly," Liisa scoffed before closing the distance between us and wrapping me in a warm embrace. All the tension I'd been carrying seemed to melt right out of me.

"Liisa . . . I'm so sorry I didn't tell you . . ." My eyes welled up.

She squeezed me tightly. "I'm sure you had your reasons, and I won't say it didn't hurt, but I'm so very glad to see you are all right. Come in and sit. There is so much to catch up on." She pulled back, brushing a tear off her cheek, her smile still stretched wide. "I can't believe I'm looking at you."

Her contagious grin had me smiling right back. "It feels like a dream. I've thought about you so many times. I can only stay for a short while, as I am expected back at the palatium, but I had to see you, Liisa. You have always been my dearest friend, even after all these years. One of the hardest parts of leaving Zephyria was losing my friendship with you."

"You never lost it," she said, squeezing my hand before shooing the young healer away and closing the door. "Is everything all right?"

"I wish I could say I was here just to catch up, but I came here to beg for Wynn's—the king's—assistance."

"That sounds serious!"

"My daughter was drafted by the Iris this mating season, and it's very complicated, but we need to rescue her. She's in grave danger."

Liisa grasped my hand. "Oh, Ari, I am so sorry."

Everything spilled out of me, from the devastation of learning about Katye, to returning home and discovering I was carrying Wynn's child, and marrying a male who had lost his mate and had wanted nothing to do with me. My guilt over not finding a way to protect Aella weighed heavier than everything else.

"It's funny how one choice completely altered the course of my life, and yet I still ended up in Iveria. It's as if the stars were mocking me." I laughed. "I thought I was choosing my own path, but it led me straight back to the very same fate I'd been trying to escape."

"But you found happiness? Despite everything you lost?" she asked.

"Verus turned out to be a wonderful husband and is my closest friend back home." I smiled. "You were right after all. He has supported me and my dreams and accepted me, broken parts and all."

"What happened when he found out about your child?" Liisa asked.

"He loved and claimed Aella as his own from the start." I couldn't help the tears from reappearing. "We've made a beautiful life together."

"He sounds like a catch," she said.

I nodded. He was. While I knew I could never replace the mate Verus had lost, our love was true. He saw me and knew me, as much as he could within the binds of the oath.

"I admit, I am surprised," Liisa mused. "I always thought what you had with Wynn was a once-in-a-lifetime thing." She shrugged.

"Coming back here has brought out so many confusing emotions," I admitted. "Our love burned bright and hot, and the oath between us also created that bond I'd never felt with anyone else . . . Losing that hollowed out a part of me . . ." I shook my head. "But he released me. This confusion will pass."

Liisa pulled me into a hug. "While I can't pretend to have all the answers, maybe everything happened for a reason that we still don't fully understand."

"I truly hope so," I replied. "Before I go, do you have anything I can use on an ice pick wound?"

Chapter 12
As You Command

AELLA

Earning Himmel's trust meant soaking up her every hateful word as though they were drops of rain in a drought. Nodding and smiling politely, following all her contradictory and confusing instructions.

"Smile." Himmel slowed her gait as some courtiers passed by. "Show them your deference." I willed myself to smile, and she snapped, her voice lashing like a whip. "Don't smile too much. They want to see a little pain." She pressed against my gown of fine iron chains with her wooden pointer, making me wince as it dug into my skin. "They want to know you're paying for what you did. You deserve to be in pain. You deserve to suffer for what you've done."

My face heated, and tears threatened to escape. Not only for the pain and humiliation but at the knowledge of what I'd done. Whether the guilt was my own or what she'd pinned on me, I wasn't sure. I hadn't meant to kill so many people. Had it been justice or had it been rage when I'd allowed my powers to consume me, when I'd struck out at all those who'd attended the games? Was it forgivable in the face of all they'd done to us?

Or had it made me no better than the Iris, who saw our lives as worth little more than entertainment?

"No tears, child. You don't want to show you're feeling badly for yourself," Himmel tutted. She resumed walking along the hall filled with historical portraits and scenes carved into the massive stone walls. "Stars forbid you tarnish your makeup or rust the polished iron with those salty tears of yours."

I willed myself not to think of anything. I had no movement-limiting shackles on, but the iron gown and chain around my waist were just as potent at sapping the magic from my veins, leaving me helpless and disconnected from my source.

She laughed then. "I'm surprised you can produce any tears at all. How long has it been? Two days? I suppose I might reward you if you behave."

"Thank you. That would be most benevolent of you." I bowed my head.

"Chin up so they can see your face." She lifted my chin with her wooden pointer.

I allowed her to guide my face up, trying to follow her instructions perfectly. My mouth seemed to become even drier at the idea of a reward.

"Not too high or you'll look proud!" She ripped the pointer away.

I took deep breaths to keep from screaming. It was impossible to win with her. Knowing water was on the line raised the stakes to a new level. I needed her approval if I was going to get any.

We continued down the long hall, Himmel smacking her pointer against the histories as we passed. Teaching me, she focused on the most frivolous details—like what they were wearing in their portraits, how many colors reflected off their marbled skin, their hair color, or their gemstone preferences—rather than their significant accomplishments. I tried memorizing their names in case she quizzed me on them later, though there was a better chance she'd make up new details simply as a way to toy with me.

By the time we made it to the end of the hall, I began to sway, dizzy and lightheaded from the long walk. Himmel tsked, then, to my surprise, gave in.

"It's been a while since I was tasked to instruct a nameless creature such as yourself, and I forget you're just like a child." She picked at her nails, then snapped her fingers to the guard behind me. "A glass of water before she faints again."

Himmel played coy with the other guard while we waited, running her fingers along his biceps and batting her eyes.

"Eyes down," she reprimanded as she caught me looking. "Never make eye contact unless granted permission."

"I'm sorry. I'm so sorry." *How could I be so stupid?* I was so scared, and I was going to cry if she refused to give me the glass of water now.

When the guard returned, Himmel made a show of pouring almost all the contents onto the floor. I took a sharp inhale and steadied myself with a hand against the wall. She walked slowly toward me, her heels clicking against the marble. She handed me the glass and giggled with the guards as I chugged the small amount down, holding it up high, willing every last drop to fall onto my parched tongue.

"We're done for the day." Himmel waved. "Take her back to the prince's wing."

I stepped over the puddle as it lay there, unresponsive to me. I was terrified of what might happen if I tried calling to it. The iron blocked all access to source powers, so I doubted anything would happen anyway. I climbed into the crystal box at the entrance to the hall to be carried back to the prince's wing of the palatium, grateful for the small luxury that I wouldn't have to walk all the way back.

I hadn't seen Kaleidos since the king's presentation of me the day before. I shuddered to remember all those gawking eyes on me, what they might have done had I not been protected by the prince's claim on me. But while I was chained in iron at Himmel's mercy, he was likely busy reveling with his cousin, Estrella, and single-handedly ensuring the winemakers of Esterra never went out of business. It was probably best I hadn't had to face him again, because I wasn't sure I had it in me to fake pleasantness around him. He could go on filling his time with decadence and debauchery. I would never risk trusting him again.

Upon entering my bedchamber, the guard tethered me to the room with a long, iron chain that attached to the one encircling my waist. While it didn't restrict my movement throughout the room, it would prevent me from leaving or going any place I wasn't meant to on my own.

Different from the rest of the bright and airy palatium, my bedchamber was dark and hauntingly beautiful in a way that I wished it wasn't. The entire room reminded me of *him*, it even smelled like him, making it impossible to stop thinking about him no matter how badly I wanted to.

I was about to swap out my heeled shoes for softer slippers when I was caught off guard to find a visitor in my room. Kaleidos invited me to join him where he stood facing the large windows overlooking the gardens. The iron leash hummed as it dragged behind me across the black marble floor, fading as I took my place beside the prince. I made sure I was close enough to take in the view but maintained as much distance as I could without drawing suspicion. No distance was enough, as his aura seemed to radiate off of him, charging the very air with his presence. I hesitated, not knowing if I should speak first or do anything at all. I had to remind myself just to breathe.

Kaleidos tossed a side-glance toward me. "You don't have to be nervous around me. I'm not going to harm you."

I swallowed. When it was clear his words had done nothing to calm my nerves, he sighed audibly.

"Suit yourself. But we are going to have to spend significantly more time together in the near future, and I'm already dreading the idea of listening to that vindictive heart of yours beating away so quickly at every encounter."

Was he goading me? I squeezed my hand into a fist, focusing on the points of my nails digging into the palm of my hand. Still, I couldn't stop myself from mentally replying. *Thank you, Prince Kaleidos, for reminding me exactly how selfish and entitled you are. Am I really supposed to apologize for my well-earned fear after all your kind has inflicted upon me?* I bit my tongue, praying it was enough.

Kaleidos leaned in then, so suddenly, I flinched and assumed a subservient posture, chin tucked, making myself smaller. The crisp, clean, and earthy scent of him invaded my senses, laced with a hint of what I assumed was the amber liquid he swirled in the crystal goblet in his hand. I stood perfectly still as he studied me, keeping my head bowed as I attempted to appear meek but noticing with my peripherals how he stared.

"You see, I'm struggling to come to terms with the idea that the strong-willed, fearless girl is truly gone. But I do imagine there are things my Aella would never let me get away with saying." He grinned.

My racing heart pounded even faster at the sound of his voice when he said *my Aella*. After everything he'd allowed, he still thought to call me his? *Cocky Iris male.*

"I'm not sure what you mean by that," I murmured.

Kaleidos leaned in even closer, his lips skimming the veil that draped over the rim of my ear as he spoke. "Your fear is so palpable, I could hear your heart pounding from across the room," he said, his voice low and purring. "The only time it should be beating like that in my presence is if we were to continue what we started the last time we were alone in your chamber . . . with your legs wrapped around me."

"Uh, what had we started?" I asked, my voice breathless as I tried not to blow my cover. His nearness inflicted a sort of heady sensation, tempting me to give in. Allowing my desire for him to overrule all judgment, I remembered how much I'd wanted him that night.

"I thought—" Kaleidos turned away from me as he set his goblet onto the drink table. He rested his weight on it with two hands, broad shoulders curled inward. "I thought perhaps if my Aella were still in there, I might coax her out of you." He turned back to me with a deflated expression. "I fully expected you to at least *try* to slap me for that one . . . and it doesn't feel fair to torture you if you're not really Aella, or, well, you know what I mean . . . Perhaps not." He chuckled to himself. "I wonder . . . May I kiss you?"

I took in a small breath. *What would she do? What would this nameless girl do?* I couldn't say no without good reason. But if I kissed him back, would he be able to tell? A better question might have been, what did he think a kiss would do?

"A kiss to remember?" he suggested.

"I'm not sure what you want me to remember, my prince, but I shall do as you command."

Kaleidos lifted the veil, bringing it back over my head, and cradled my face and neck in his hand. I tilted my head back, eyes closed, waiting. He leaned in, and his lips came dangerously close, his nose brushing up against mine, his warm breath caressing my skin.

"Oh, Aella. I know you're in there somewhere," he murmured across my lips. "Whether you'd like to admit it or not, I'm going to draw it out of you, I swear. Even if it's just to earn your ire once more, I will. And you're going to yell at me. You're going to tell me how much you hate me. And I'm going to reward you for it beautifully." He stroked his thumb over my lower lip. And just as I parted my lips, welcoming him for the kiss . . . just as I expected him to slam into me, devouring me with the force of all his desire, kiss me like he had before, as though starved for affection . . . just as I wanted him to, no, desperately needed him to distract me, to numb the pain of my circumstance . . . he pulled away. A change of heart or merely his way of teasing the truth out of me. He left me to stand speechless and breathless, swaying from lightheadedness, tingles running up my arms replaced by the now cold and lonely hollowness of his absence.

Kaleidos stopped at the door, shaking his head to himself. "If Aella is not still in there, or even if she is but simply does not want me anymore, I did mean what I said. You need not fear me. Say the word, and I shall never lay a hand on you again."

He was toying with me, and I refused to let him win. I couldn't trust him. Besides, what was to stop him from turning his back on me as soon as he got what he wanted? That was how the Iris operated, wasn't it? They used us and then threw us away. And if I were to tell him I wasn't nameless and ask for his help, what good would that do? Even if he did side with me, it was hard to imagine he'd help me. He'd never been willing to step in or interfere with the Iris' tormenting of me in the past. Why would it be any different now?

If he really meant what he said and he obeyed, wouldn't that be a test of faith? He'd prove himself trustworthy by holding up his end of the bargain. It seemed like asking a lot, considering I was to be his bride. A bride he could never touch. A bride with no autonomy, no rights, no protection, no control. As much as my body wanted to revolt against the decision I was about to make, it seemed the only option.

"I do not know the female of whom you speak. But it makes me uncomfortable, and I wish you would not lay a hand on me again." My chest crushed in on itself as I uttered the words, understanding what fate of loneliness I might have just sealed, the possibility of love and passion I might have just denied myself. For all the things I had wanted so badly with him, knowing they could never lead to anything good, that I could never trust him, it was better this way. It had needed to be done. At least like this, I had some measure of control, and I could not pass up on my one chance at an upper hand when all other choices had been taken from me.

Hurt shone in his eyes, a muscle in his jaw feathering, but true to his word, he bowed and retreated.

"As you command."

CHAPTER 13
RAT BOY PRINCE

KALEIDOS

Foolish. Whimsome. Negligent.

I removed myself from her presence as promptly as I could. She didn't want me? Fine. At least I wouldn't have to suffer any more of her dangerous seductions whilst she plotted against me. Though it wasn't exactly fair of me to deduce that she was still in there, considering it had only been a smidge of a hunch that had led me to act on such an assumption.

"Ready my horse. I'm going to the arena," I ordered the guards.

"The arena is not yet secure."

"Good."

Better not to train amongst the prying eyes of the court at this time.

"Will you require an escort?"

"No, but send for Master Gladius to meet me there."

When I had first seen Aella yesterday, I'd believed without a doubt that I had failed, that she was nameless, and that it was finished. But as I'd replayed every moment over and over in my mind, I'd reconsidered. Was it possible this was another one of her ruses? Had I been imagining things, or had I seen the flash of a storm in her eyes? If she were a spy sent to kill me and put an end to the Stellaris line, wouldn't playing the part of a nameless be just as effortless for her to pull off?

If she was in fact nameless, it didn't matter. But if there was a possibility she was pretending, my impulsive actions might have ruined my chances of finding out. I shook my head.

There were no proven means of ascertaining if my shield had worked on her or not. To my knowledge, it had never been tested with the nameless key before, so it was up to her to reveal it. I hated not knowing.

I made my way down to the stables through the servants' passages. The last thing I needed was to run into my comrades, though perhaps a distraction would be necessary later.

I should just let it go. Block it all out. All of it from the moment we met until now.

She had asked me to leave her be. I would honor that request, whether nameless or not.

My onyx stallion's withers stood tall and strong, a testament to his breeding. I ran a hand along his sleek coat, then mounted and took off down the bridge toward the wreckage that was the arena. There, I could let my powers run wild, I could let out the contemptible emotions that threatened to consume me.

⤸

"Are you going to leave any part of the arena intact, or is the plan to level what is left of the entire stadium?" Master Gladius asked, leaping effortlessly over a fallen pillar as he made his way toward me.

"Just warming up," I said. The arena had seen better days, but why spare what was already ruined? This place brought only bad memories, and wrecking it further did seem to help.

"I see that," he snarked.

Elemental squires scampered through the rubble with hefty packs of training weapons. I ran my fingers over the hilt of an iron-tipped sword. It was in the usual Iris fashion of melded metals—gold, silver, and bronze— but it leaned heavier on its use of the silver alloy. I skipped over it, testing out the other weapons on display, but kept catching myself eyeing that damned silver one.

Fine.

Tossing the last weapon aside, I grasped the sword, and to my chagrin, it was perfect. From the weight of it to the feel in my hand, not to mention, it complimented my own skin quite well. It was the most beautiful of swords—I couldn't resist the allure of it. Even the damn sword reminded me of her. I rubbed at my temples, trying to rid her from my mind.

That little tempest and her friend were planning to destroy me.

I chose not to report or exact revenge on Viera. I was a male of my word, and I'd promised her safety, even if she was nothing more than a lying, scheming little rebel. Though, after what we'd put the contestants through in the arena, I could hardly blame them for their acts of treason. They'd done their fair share of penance.

Gladius and I trained late into the night, and by the end of our sparring session, the arena's outer structures were all but collapsed. It was like standing in a pit of rubble.

"What's gotten into you?" he asked as we made our way to the horses. "I haven't seen you bring that much ferocity to the ring since you were a child." *Since my mother was killed.* "Is it your upcoming nuptials?"

"Perhaps I'm tired of living in *his* shadow. Same time tomorrow?" I asked as I climbed into my horse's saddle.

"Of course," he said.

Just as he was climbing in, his horse reared back, snorting and whinnying in a panic, throwing Gladius to the ground.

"A faexing rat!" he screamed, using his Aereus powers to throw a chunk of fallen masonry at it.

It was a tiny, silver creature, more of a mouse than a rat. Though my faithful steed nearly threw me off his back too, I managed to shield the rodent. White stone shattered, pulverizing until it left Gladius covered in a fine mineral powder.

"What the . . ."

I hopped down to assess the little thing that had caused such great commotion. As I reached out to the trembling creature, Gladius marched over, prepared to take on the task himself.

"Diseased vermin, unfit for royal hands," he muttered.

"I think you've done quite enough." I waved the weapons master off.

What he'd said was true, perhaps, but I looked past my privilege for a moment. Hadn't I been surprised by the very elemental fae whom I'd been taught to undervalue, overlook, and give no compassion? With a wry smile, I gently scooped the rat into my hand, and she poked her tiny pink nose up toward me, sniffing curiously.

"So small, and you brought Gladius down on his arse? Not even the highest ranking king's guard can manage that." I laughed, then set my hand onto the ground to let the rat crawl off. The cursed little thing scurried up my arm, coming a bit too close for comfort as it tucked itself into the collar at my neck. "Easy, there!"

I pried her off, holding her to my face again.

"You cannot come with me."

⌇

"Was it truly that unreasonable of me to think she could've been pretending?" I asked, trying my best to keep my voice down and not slur my words, though I was only on my third or fifth bottle, who could've known.

Rat twitched her whiskers.

"Oh, fine. You don't have to rub it in my face." I stumbled back over toward the liquor cart to pour myself another glass. "She may have falsified her intentions, but her physical attraction . . . She could not hide that even if she wanted to." I swayed slightly after turning back to face my tiny little friend, who sat nestled on the settee. "It should have worked."

Rat gave a curious tilt of her head.

I shuffled back over to the settee and came lumbering down as I missed the step into the recessed area. Faex whoever designed these multi-level bloody lounge areas in my wing. *Lucky no one's ever snapped their neck.*

Rat squeaked.

"Don't all come running at once," I said as I picked myself up off the floor. "I'm all right. Thank you for your concern. Most fortunately, I have managed to save my drink!" I held it up proudly, but Rat wasn't impressed.

"Look, even if I could wipe the female from my mind, my draw to her goes against every one of my better judgements." I sat down beside Rat, leaning back on the settee, and I whispered, "I've really begun questioning everything I believed about the elemental fae. I'm still not sure exactly when it happened. She should mean nothing to me—a lowly water fae—yet my desire for her is so powerful, I think I might be willing to wage war on my father, on all of my people, if that means protecting her. But I suppose I may need to wait for her consent on the matter."

Rat gave another soft squeak.

"Thank you. You're an excellent listener, by the way."

Rat nestled into my hand and boggled in a sign of contentment, and it occurred to me that I was conversing with a rodent, of all creatures.

I suppose I talk to rats now. I sighed.

"Snuggle in close, Rat. It's a long tale. Dare I tell you, *she* was plotting to kill *me* . . ."

CHAPTER 14

RISKY BUSINESS

WYNN

As we sat around the table, ready to discuss a plan, I couldn't help but find my eyes drawn toward her. She was still so beautiful. Her spirit and hope lit up the room. Despite everything, I would do anything for her. It didn't matter that she hadn't chosen me, it didn't matter that there was not a chance in the stars of her ever choosing me again, I just couldn't keep myself from wanting to help her and the daughter I had yet to meet. Even though involving myself with Prisma and the Iris was quite possibly the worst idea ever.

The cabala was arguing among themselves about the safest paths in and out of Prisma and if there was any possibility of sneaking into the Palatium Crystalis.

"Enough." I pounded my fist on the table. "There is no possible way we can get in and out of Prisma undetected. There has to be another option."

"Can we get an ally to glamour some of us?" Helio asked, twirling a dagger on the table. "That's mostly worked well in the other courts."

It had until it hadn't.

"This is Prisma we're talking about," Glint said. "There are already tons of elementals walking around. I agree with Helio—we just need someone to glamour Wynn, Rik, and Kairi."

"We don't have enough information to simply waltz into Prisma." I ran a hand through my hair. "We have no more allies there. They either dropped off the map or disappeared before we could get any useful information."

"Then what business do we have trying to go in there?" Kairi tapped her fingers on her cheek. "If this is a suicide mission, there won't be any way to save her."

"There is one option I am considering, but you're not going to like it," I said to the group.

"What's that supposed to mean?" Arianwen asked.

"Perhaps we could propose a trade with the Iris. My life for hers."

The entire room went completely silent before exploding into chaos.

"Have you lost your stars-damned mind, Wynn?" Helio jumped to his feet. "You can't trade yourself!"

Arianwen's face went ashen. "I didn't come here to ask you to sacrifice yourself, Wynn."

"But what if that's the only path to get her out? Don't tell me you wouldn't choose her over me, Ari," I retorted.

As I'd suspected, she couldn't reply. And perhaps it had been wrong of me to even ask the question. I didn't know what it was like to be a parent.

"That's not fair, Wynn," Rik said, always the calm and collected one of the group.

"I'd trade myself in a heartbeat," Arianwen swore, her eyes glistening with tears, "but they have no use for me. Please, Wynn, there has to be another way."

I shrugged, even as frustration brimmed inside me. My daughter was at the mercy of the wicked Iris, and our discussions were going in circles. "There is no other solution I can think of that would get us quick results. You said time is of the essence, right?"

"We need another plan, Wynn," Helio pleaded as he sat back down.

"The Court of Air needs you—you're all we have. How do you even know they'd consider the trade?"

Every eye was trained on me, the tension in the room palpable enough to cut with a knife. My friends might not like it, but my idea was the only one so far with a chance of success. After Valerik's capture a few years back, the Iris had made it clear they'd been looking for me and there was a price on my head. Before he'd gotten away, Rik had overheard the Iris guards assuming they had caught *me*. The guards had been under strict orders to bring me back to Prisma in secret but alive. That had only reconfirmed my decision to stay in Zephyria. There was no telling what my parents would've given up to get their only heir back, and there had been no way I was going to risk the people in my court for my insignificant life.

Breaking the uncomfortable silence, I said, "Solanos has been after me for years. And besides, what else am I supposed to do? Just sit back and do nothing?" I pushed away from the table and stood. "Because that is the only other option I see right now."

"Wynn, you can't," Kairi pleaded.

"If we want to unite the courts to take down the Iris, the first step is to get them to meet." Arianwen spoke up. "If we can gather the rebellion leaders, perhaps one of them might have a means of getting in and out of Prisma?"

Valerik leaned forward, resting his chin on his hand. "It's never been done before, but perhaps now is as good an opportunity as any?"

"I don't know if there's time." I started to pace. "If there's any chance the Iris have discovered her heritage or suspect she has anything to do with the prophecy . . . the sooner we get to her, the better."

"Who knows if she will even survive those games?" Glint examined her nails. "Do you think the other courts would even be willing to meet without a guarantee that she is the prophesied one?"

I bristled at the notion and couldn't help but glance over at Ari and see the anger flashing in her eyes. The Aurum sure weren't known for their sensitivity.

"Those are all valid points," Helio chimed in, his hand draped over the empty chair next to him. "But if there's a way to avoid Wynn handing himself over to the Iris to save his daughter, we should take it, right?"

I rolled my eyes. I loved the members of my cabala like family, but it was clear they'd gotten a little too comfortable with my relaxed governing over the years. It was time I reminded them who made the final call.

Returning to the table, I leaned forward. "We will send messengers and find out if a summit is even possible. If they do not agree to come, my plan is the only feasible option, and I will carry it out with or without your support."

Helio frowned. "I'd do anything to keep you from defaulting to that plan, but what do you think will make the rebellion leaders even consider meeting with the risk involved?"

"Perhaps we can tempt them with information about the prophecy," I replied.

"If they say yes, where do you propose we meet?" Kairi pulled the map of Esterra toward her. "Zephyria is completely out of the question. As much as we might trust our allies, we don't trust them that much."

"Kairi makes a good point," Rik agreed, furrowing his brow. "What if we met in Concordia?"

"There's nothing there," Glint scoffed. "What, you think we should meet amid the rubble?"

"I was just trying to think of a place central to everyone and close enough to move on Prisma if the time comes," Rik said.

"That makes sense," I agreed, gripping the high back of my chair. "I'll send scouts ahead to check on the safety of the area and for Iris patrols."

"Why would they have patrols?" Rik leaned back in his seat. "It's been abandoned since they decimated it. I think it would be the perfect location to meet. We can have the Aerial Guard watch from the skies to keep us apprised of any Iris on the move and roll in cloud cover to keep the aquilas out of sight."

"I'll arrange a team of Aereus to go ahead of us. They can strengthen and secure the old ruins for us to gather and take shelter in," Helio offered.

"I'm still not sure it's the best idea," Glint complained, biting on one of her nails. "It's so close to Prisma."

Helio rubbed his hands together excitedly. "With enough overgrowth, we can cover any new structures we form so no one will even realize they haven't been there for centuries. As long as it appears abandoned from a distance, no one will be the wiser. And I agree with Rik, I highly doubt they have any reason to investigate the old ruins or be suspicious. It's not like they know we're coming for them. All of our rescue missions have been contained to the courts."

In spite of my hesitation, I couldn't help but wonder if the dream I'd had of courts working together might actually come to fruition. The petty squabbles we'd had with the other rebellion leaders had prevented us from uniting, but perhaps with the hope of the stars being with us . . . perhaps we could finally set aside our fears and our differences and join together for something bigger than ourselves—the dream of freedom after millennia of oppression and lies.

"Send word immediately to the other courts. We'll meet in Concordia in a fortnight. Helio, organize a team of Aereus to leave in advance to set up shelter. Make sure they are made aware of the risks. This is volunteer only."

"You got it, Wynn," Helio replied, his face split in a grin. "Ari, thanks for making things exciting around here!"

A small smile tugged at her lips, and I couldn't help but stare. Her smile widened the crack in the armor around my heart, and I ached.

"Helio!" Kairi admonished, looking up at him from beneath her thick lashes. "This is serious business, and it's not as if she came here for a holiday. Try to be a little more sensitive."

Helio looked contrite. "I'm sorry if that came across the wrong way, Ari."

"It's okay, Helio. It's been so nice seeing you again after all these years."

Helio walked over and planted a kiss on top of her head. "You really need to come meet my wife."

"You're married?" She gasped. "I'm so happy for you! If we can make it happen, I'd love to."

Helio left the room after promising to schedule something with Ari, and Glint and Kairi followed shortly after to go make arrangements for messengers to leave with meeting notices.

"How did you end up getting involved with the rebels once you left?" Rik asked Arianwen, drawing her attention back.

My ears perked up, as I'd been curious about that as well, and I returned to my seat.

"I was attending Lucris' daughter as a healer maybe a year or so after I left, and some things just started adding up."

"Such as?" Rik tilted his head.

"Hmm . . . The scent of coffee for one. Strange, secretive meetings . . . and then their daughter became sick with an illness not seen in Iveria. I suspected they had been exposed to elementals from other courts."

Rik laughed. "Figures you'd end up finding the rebellion without even trying."

"To be fair, I had wanted to find them. After my time with you all, I couldn't sit back and do nothing."

An unwelcome warmth bloomed in my chest. Arianwen's desire to create a better world had not dimmed, and I couldn't help but admire her for it.

"Lucris confronted me when he discovered my journal filled with notes from Zephyria. He thought he could hold it over me, but I had enough damning information on him that I was able to use that to my advantage to keep things on my terms," she continued, sitting up taller.

"He threatened you?" I pushed away from the table. The temptation to harm Lucris for endangering her even years ago was immense.

Ari's eyebrows rose as she looked at me strangely. "He did, but—"

"Did he hurt you?" I clenched my fists to keep from slamming them onto the table.

"Why would you even ask that?" Ari frowned. I gritted my teeth, but before I could respond, she said, "You lost the right to concern yourself with my safety when you chose Katye over me."

"Your safety will *always* concern me."

"I can take care of myself. Working with the rebels was a risk, but like you, I had to do something. After what I'd learned, my desire to fight for a better world only deepened. Imagine my surprise and disappointment when I discovered the Iverian rebels never planned on stepping up and fighting back; the rebellion is a front for lining Lucris' pockets and cementing his power and control in Iveria. I keep hoping something might change eventually . . . and to be honest, I thought *you* would have raised armies by now, but no. Here you sit in your ivory tower in the mountains, barely even accepting refugees anymore."

Her words cut me to the quick, pierced through my armor like finely honed blades. How dare she question everything I had done after all I'd risked and sacrificed over the years?

"You want to fight? Let's fight," I said. All of my attention was directed at her, though I could sense Rik leaving the room to give us some privacy.

Her molten, silver eyes did not break from my gaze as she glared right back at me. "I just want to rescue my daughter. I didn't come here to ask you to sacrifice yourself for her."

I laughed mockingly. "Isn't that what a parent is supposed to do? Give up their lives for their children?"

Arianwen rolled her eyes. "Come on, Wynn. You might share her blood, but that doesn't make you a parent. As I've already said, she has two parents who love her. While I won't keep her from you if she decides to allow you into her life—if we somehow manage to get out of this unscathed—she doesn't *need* you."

My chest tightened painfully, and my entire body tensed as I leaned forward. "Unlike your dearest husband, I was never given a choice to be her parent."

"Well that would have been pretty difficult considering I couldn't even talk about you," she retorted.

An unwelcome heat prickled through me, and I clenched my jaw. Despite my anger, all I could think about was pulling her into my arms and showing her how much I missed that smart mouth. *She's not yours*, I reminded myself.

"If you scented me in the market all those years ago, why didn't you come talk to me? You could have told me then," I spat.

She gaped at me. "Why didn't *you* come talk to *me* in the market?" she finally sputtered.

"As I said before, you looked content with your life." I leaned in closer, our faces mere inches apart. "And his scent was *all over you*."

She bared her teeth. "Not that it makes a difference, but we weren't even truly together. He knew about Aella, but he was giving me the time and space to grieve *you*." Her eyes shot fire at me, so unlike her usual calm. "I grieved for months."

"I grieved for *years*."

We sat staring at each other, the air taut with tension.

"I feel for you, Wynn. Truly, I do." Ari finally broke the silence. "But you cannot put that on me. You made your choice clear."

I groaned, leaning back, running my hands through my hair. "No, you're right. That's on me and my damned heart."

Her eyes softened slightly. "I honestly thought I'd never see you again, Wynn. I had to let you go . . . and Verus is a good male. He has loved me and our daughter, and now we have a family. It pains me that you've been here all alone, but maybe it's time to open your heart to someone new."

"Easy for you to say, Arianwen," I scoffed. "You got your happy ending."

"You deserve one too, Wynn." She reached across the table as if to grab my hand, but I pulled it out of reach and pushed away from the table.

The silence was deafening, and I couldn't meet her gaze.

"I need to go make preparations for our journey," I said, deliberately ending the conversation. "Feel free to do whatever you'd like in the meantime. We will likely head out in a few days' time if the other courts get back to us swiftly."

If our meeting with the rebellion leaders failed and my only option was to turn myself over to the Iris, I needed to come up with a plan for someone to rule the Court of Air in my stead. My mother would not be able to handle the pressure on her own.

"Who is contacting Iveria?" She interrupted my thoughts. "I need to get word to Verus that I made it here safely but that he needs to take the risk and run. If Aella is found out and they come after my family . . ."

"Where would you have them go?" I couldn't help but ask, despite not wanting to hear more about her perfect little family.

She shrugged, looking down at the table. "The plan was to head to one of the smaller lake villages on the outskirts of the Court of Water, but my guide made it clear that nowhere is truly safe from the Iris."

"Have them come here."

Her gaze shot up to meet mine, and a myriad of emotions flashed over her features—hope and excitement that morphed into worry and dismay. "Thank you for the generous offer, but I'm afraid there is no way I could send my children on that journey—I barely made it here." Ari's hand drifted to her midsection, and I stiffened. What had she gone through on her way here?

I fought the urge to ask more questions.   "Go find Rik. He can help you with whatever message you want to send and arrange safe travel for your family. We take extra care when children are involved. You need not worry."

She took a deep breath and slowly let it out. "Thanks, Wynn. I truly appreciate it."

I gave her a stiff nod as I got up and headed toward the door. Pausing, I dared a brief look over my shoulder at Arianwen. Any optimism had faded, and she sat looking somewhat defeated and bereft. That was all my fault. I had made so many mistakes in the past, but I was determined to make up for them, no matter the cost.

CHAPTER 15

THE WISE ONE

ARIANWEN

My fight with Wynn had brought a multitude of feelings to the surface, but instead of examining them, I fixated on my annoyance. I almost couldn't believe he'd been able to get under my skin the way he had.

Getting up from the table, I rolled my eyes at the fact that Wynn had sent me to find Valerik but had not even given me a place to start, though I tried to remind myself to be grateful and relieved he would help get my family to safety. The palatium was so large, and despite my months here, I had not visited even half of it. The majority of my time had been spent between Wynn's wing, my room, and the library of course. Oh, how I'd missed the delightful library full of books. I could never imagine reading even a fraction of the vast collection in a lifetime. How Aarifa had managed to catalog each and every one remained a mystery.

A million thoughts filled my head as I made my way down the hall toward the entrance. I could only pray Emil would help me track down Valerik.

The weight of everything hung heavy in my chest, every conflicting feeling leaving me unmoored. While I desperately missed my family, there was a sense of rightness being in Zephyria I had not expected. I felt almost guilty for being glad to be back, as if it was a betrayal to the life I'd built. The constant flood of good memories didn't help.

My mind flashed back to the moment Verus realized he couldn't accompany me on my journey, but I appreciated his trust. The unspoken words, the oath that had prevented me from sharing my secrets, and knowing I could never be fully known had been a challenge for our whole relationship. There was a certain excitement about reuniting with him and finally being able to share the parts of me I'd been unable to. But stars knew how long it would be until that happened. We would be long gone before my family made it up here.

"Ari!" Rik smiled when I almost ran into him. "Wynn sent me to come find you."

My eyes widened in surprise while a small wave of happiness washed over me.

Wynn might be acting cold toward me, but he can still be thoughtful.

"Oh, thank you so much. Yes, I need to get word to Verus with the messenger you are sending, Wynn told me you could arrange safe passage for my family."

Rik's brow furrowed. "I can, but I'm not sure I'm comfortable putting your name or a personal message in the note. The last thing I want is information about your family falling into the wrong hands."

I sighed in exasperation. "It's a risk I need to take. My husband will be worried out of his mind. I had to leave him and not even tell him where I was going, and now I need to convince him it's safe to change our original plans. They need to get out of Iveria as soon as possible."

"Will he be with the rebel leaders?"

"Unlikely . . . but I'm sure Lucris can get word to him. He owes me enough favors."

Rik's shoulders were bunched with tension, his discomfort evident in his stance and the way he narrowed his eyes. "This isn't how we usually do things . . ."

I placed my hand on his arm, sending some calming power through him. My healing powers had strengthened and improved over the last twenty-five years, and that included the ability to put people at ease, which had come in handy more than I'd thought it would.

"They're already at risk. It's going to be all right. Verus needs to know I'm safe and that it's time for him to get out of there."

Rik eased a bit. "All right then. I will let Lucris know to contact Verus and arrange travel for . . . how many?"

"Five children and my husband," I replied. "Thank you, Rik. You truly have my gratitude."

Rik's eyes narrowed in suspicion. "Did you work your healing mojo on me to get me to do what you wanted?"

A bright, cheery laugh burst out of me. "Wouldn't you like to know."

Rik shook his head and offered his arm. "Can I escort you anywhere?"

"I am actually quite exhausted after my travels and the excitement of our meetings. My nerves have made it hard for me to sleep and eat these past weeks." I laid my head on his shoulder as we walked slowly toward the wing of guest rooms. "You know, I did miss you all terribly," I confessed. "You became like a second family to me. You were the older brother I never had."

Rik cleared his throat but remained silent for a moment. "I missed you too."

"How have you been? Do you have a family of your own as well?"

He chuckled slightly, his shoulder shaking underneath my head. "No, I'm afraid I have not been able to settle down like Helio."

I straightened. "I'm honestly more shocked Helio settled down than anything else."

"I suppose the right person just hasn't come around. Also, I don't mind being alone, and there are plenty who have warmed my bed over the years," he quipped with a sly smile.

"As long as you're happy, Rik," I said softly.

We paused in front of my door, and he tilted his head. "Are *you* happy, Ari?"

"Of course," I nearly choked out. "Why wouldn't I be? I have a loving husband, more children than I could possibly ever need. I just . . ."

"What?"

"I feel guilty that I didn't do more to protect and prepare Aella. She knows there is something different about her, but I was never able to explain. I believed we could remain in Iveria and live our lives, but . . ."

"Yes?"

"My selfish pride over how things ended with Wynn prevented me from coming to you all for help. This is all my fault, and I will never forgive myself if something happens to her."

Rik remained silent for another moment, always the quiet, thoughtful one. "Did you ever think maybe the stars allowed this to happen to trigger the prophecy? If she had stayed hidden, maybe our chance to overthrow the Iris would have never come."

As much as I hated to admit it, he brought up a good point. "I want to believe in the prophecy, believe she can help free us, but I'm just a mother who is terrified of losing her daughter." I leaned back against the door, trying not to let the worry and despair overtake me.

Rik pulled me into his arms, embracing me in a comforting hug. "It's going to be okay, Ari. Trust that the stars will save us, even if we don't understand how."

"I want to, but what have they done so far?" I whined, my voice muffled in his broad chest.

"Who are we to question their design? Sometimes it's not for us to know but for us to trust and take the next step we know how."

"When did you get so wise?" I laughed half-heartedly.

"I've always been the wise one, Ari, or did you forget?"

I pulled away from him, giving him a wan smile. "Thanks again. Despite everything, I do feel a little better."

"It was my pleasure, Ari."

Before I could enter my room, I paused and turned back. "Rik?"

He stopped in his tracks. "Hm?"

"I noticed a lake earlier . . . Where did that come from?"

"Ah, Wynn's passion project." Rik ran a hand through his short, white hair. "Not long after you left, he decided to build a lake here for any Argenti who needed to flee Iveria."

"Really? That's incredibly thoughtful," I replied, warmth flooding my chest.

"Yes. He realized how difficult it had been for you and wanted to provide a home for Argenti refugees that was closer to their element."

"I'll have to go for a swim." I smiled.

Rik's brows drew together and he took a step closer to me. "I realize things are"—he paused—"uncomfortable—for lack of a better word—between you two right now, but he does care for you."

My gaze dropped to my feet. "I know. I care about him too."

"Chin up, Ari. We're going to do our best to help."

CHAPTER 16

DEPRIVATION

AELLA

Servants delivered another lavish presentation of food—trays covered in succulent meats, aged cheeses, seeded breads with a soft inner crumb, butters and spreads, cakes and pastries in all shapes and sizes, a splendor of colorful vegetables roasted and seasoned to perfection. The only fruit was dried and lacked variety in contrast to the vast quantities of rich cuisine. One thing the food all had in common: each left the mouth parched, and not one beverage was provided. I forced myself to swallow salted vegetables, which I guessed had slightly more moisture than the other offerings. Water was only offered in small quantities at Himmel's discretion, and today was apparently not one of those days.

Lethargic from dehydration, I collapsed back into bed, where I could dream of water and the sea. For days, I'd spent most of my free time lying in the immense, evergreen bed, watching light and shadows dance across the walls, speaking to no one.

My state of numb detachment was interrupted by a jingle. It was time for my daily scrub. I wasn't allowed to bathe, either for fear of what I might do or as another vicious form of punishment. My maids, whom I'd heard referred to as Yulema and Kasha, entered the room and began scrubbing my tight skin from head to toe with damp rags soaked in scented oils. Kasha, who was also Argenti, paid me a sympathetic look and murmured apologies under her breath. She understood better than my Aurum maid the depths of torture this water deprivation caused.

Later that night, I awoke to find a full glass of water on my bedside table. I leaned over feebly for the glass and gulped it down, mistakenly allowing some to spill over my oiled, dehydrated skin. The glass slipped from my hand, and it shattered over the hard floor, the last few droplets darkening the stone. Empty, tearless cries ripped from my throat at the loss of those precious drops that I could not call back to me even if I'd wanted to. If their plan was to break me, it was working.

Forcing myself out of bed, I stepped over the broken glass and walked to the large window overlooking the garden with the vast city of Prisma in the distance. I pressed my hands against the cool glass for support. More than ever, temptation begged me to give in and ask Kaleidos for help. Himmel's treatment was unbearable, but she'd promised to start giving me more water soon. She couldn't keep starving me like this if I was to be Kaleidos' bride. I needed to hold out a little longer.

The shattered remains of the glass I'd dropped glared at me, evidence of the contraband water I'd just consumed.

Could it have been from Kaleidos? Or had it been from Kasha, who had emanated such pity? Either way, I couldn't leave the mess, not knowing who might rat me out to Himmel if it was found.

On my knees, I carefully picked up the pieces, dropping them one by one into the soil of a potted plant nearby.

"I'm sorry," I whispered. *Apparently I talk to plants now.*

"Lovely day for a swim, isn't it?" Himmel asked as we walked along windows overlooking the sea.

I quickly averted my gaze, but not fast enough. Himmel smacked me across the face with her pointer. My cheek stung.

"Were you thinking about the water again?" She tsked.

Himmel used her daily lessons not only to exert her control over me but to fill my mind with endless negativity and hate toward my people, toward my element, toward everything that made me who I was.

I shook my head, posture bowed. It was easier to just go along with Himmel's nonsense, to stop questioning all her contradictions, even when she reprimanded me for doing something she'd previously instructed.

She whacked me again, evening out the pain, and I cried a pitiful sound. "Look at me when I am speaking!"

I raised my head slowly, bringing my eyes to meet hers.

"I don't want you looking at the water or even thinking about water. Do you understand?"

I nodded.

"You are an insignificant, nameless servant. Nothing more." She began pacing around me. "Do not think your belonging to the prince affords you any true value or special treatment. You are here for one purpose only, and that is to serve King Solanos. Your very life was spared due to his mercy. You neither eat nor drink except what is allowed by his graciousness. You have no desires of your own, no longing for water nor wind." She pointed to the water and then challenged, "Did you want to go for a swim?"

"No, madam," I murmured.

Days turned into weeks of nothing but seclusion and lessons with Himmel so I could be shaped into whatever they wanted me to be. The amount of iron I was to be clad in had not been reduced as Himmel had earlier hinted. But at least she'd been slowly increasing my water intake. I aimed to please Himmel for those precious rewards and was becoming "quite a good little pet," as she called me. I didn't care so long as I got my rations. I'd be damned if I missed a single one of them.

At first, I'd been thankful for so much isolation. I hadn't known how to behave or how to carry myself, and I'd needed to train myself into stoicism. How would a nameless person perceive this existence if they didn't know any other?

I couldn't allow myself to think of Viera, to think of anything I loved. The fine threads holding me together were already worn so thin, and I could feel myself falling through the cracks, bit by bit, day by day. Like a ghost, no longer a true part of the world, merely drifting through it. I was isolated and alone, forlorn, longing to be held.

In spite of numerous attempts at scouring Kaleidos from my mind, it seemed I'd never be rid of him. My pillows still smelled of him, and the room that was every bit chaotic as it was beautiful suited him but also spoke volumes about the kind of person he was. If his bedchamber was now mine, where had he taken up residence? Was he nearby, or was he with someone else? What would it be like, lying next to him in his bed, curled into the frame of his body, protected and safe? It was easier to imagine him as the person I wanted him to be. If only he were.

How could I still long for him after how he'd treated me? He'd done nothing to earn my love or my loyalty. Day by day, I was becoming more certain that any goodness I'd seen in him was no more real than the nameless person I was pretending to be. I'd been reckless to ever think he could have been on my side, that he could have changed our world for the better. The only person he cared about was himself.

Unable to sleep one night, I climbed out of bed and walked around the room, dragging my chain behind me as I regarded the hoards of books. More and more books had begun appearing each day, cluttering the room in uneven stacks along the walls. I wasn't sure why—perhaps Kaleidos was reorganizing his library. It was strange though—so many of them were either about Iveria, set in Iveria, or involved the Argenti in one way or another. It was hard to even think of picking one up after Himmel's efforts to create an aversion to water and the place I came from. For all I knew, filling my room with these books was another form of torture.

It was illogical to feel the way I did, but after being conditioned every day for hours, it was hard not to internalize Himmel's words. I fretted I would begin losing myself even without the key's effects. Without my best friend anchoring me to truth, without anyone to speak freely, honestly with, I could feel pieces of myself slipping away, just as my magic felt farther and farther from me, as distant as the inaccessible sea.

But I clung to my memories. I would live in them, an escape from this torturous place. They were flickering, becoming more and more elusive—my mother's voice, my father's smile, my siblings' laughter—now they were just fragments of stories I told myself over and over again, willing myself not to forget. With so many of Himmel's lies running through my mind, I sometimes questioned which thoughts were actually mine or merely fed to me in her efforts to shape me. For this reason, it was infinitely vital that I read about home. I could not let her win.

After checking over my shoulder twice for good measure, I allowed myself to take a book, reaching a shaking hand toward the stacks.

I am Argenti. I am of the water, I spoke to myself, whispering inside my head. Afraid that if my thoughts were too loud, Himmel might somehow hear me. I held my breath and lifted the book ever so slowly. As soon as it was in my hands, I scampered back into bed, curling up on my side away from the door, away from prying eyes.

The book I'd chosen was titled, *Tales of the Sea: An Unabridged Collection of Iverian Bedtime Stories*. Perhaps the comforting prose of the familiar stories and memory of home could quiet my mind and help me fall into a dark, dreamless sleep. I flipped through the book a few times, running my thumb along the papers' smooth edges before attempting to read, but I couldn't get past the first few pages. The book's tale about the stars and their all-knowing kept tugging my mind back to the prophecy. They had to have been wrong. Surely there was another braver, wiser, and more capable person who could fulfill it instead. Surely it could never have been me, or Solanos would have been dead. Unless he truly was more powerful than the stars. In that case, we were all doomed and there was no reason to continue fighting or keep going at all.

Perhaps I should just lie here, staring, watching light and shadows creep across the wall as the days pass me by, willing my heart into silence. Willing myself into nothing. I sighed.

But like a storm captured in a tiny vial, fighting to break free, I couldn't shake the feeling that somehow, against all odds, I was still here. It had to mean something. *Could it be the stars' doing?*

Day by day, as I suffered, as I *survived*, I clung more and more to the prophecy as a promise from the stars that I still had purpose, even if my path was hidden from me.

My name is Aella Kalani. I was born under the cloak of night. My father builds ships, and my mother is a healer. I have five siblings—Mila, Arden, Silber, Liili, and Dean. My best friend was killed by the Iris, and I tried to kill the king. I reached my hand to touch the star mark on the back of my neck for reassurance. *I am the one who was prophesied. The Iris know me as nameless, but I was blessed by the stars, and I will see this kingdom crumbled.*

CHAPTER 17
A PINCH OF ROSEMARY

ARIANWEN

Sweat dripped down the back of my neck as I carefully measured ingredients in the hospitium's apothecary. The blazing fire needed to simmer the concoctions had significantly raised the temperature in the room.

"Does this smell right to you?" I craned my neck over my shoulder.

Liisa hurried over and crinkled her delicate nose as she sniffed the mixture. "Maybe a pinch of rosemary will help with the odor. This one works wonders for travel, but the smell isn't great."

I laughed even as I tried not to gag. "Not great, my arse. This smells like a week's worth of unwashed travel clothes."

Liisa cackled as she started sprinkling in more herbs to counteract the potent odor.

"Is this the last one?" she asked.

I nodded. "I think we will be good for our travel to Concordia."

The days had rushed by in a flurry of activity as preparations to leave were underway. It still seemed completely surreal to me that we would be headed to the location of the cautionary tale told to all elementals about the dangers of mixing our races. What a load of utter garbage. The Iris had used our beliefs against us and had had us eating out of the palms of their hands all these centuries. It was time someone finally stood up to them and held them accountable for the countless atrocities they'd performed—the utter destruction of Concordia only one of them.

Liisa frowned. "I'm sad you're leaving. It feels as if you only just arrived."

I poured the rank concoction into a few vials and sealed them. "I'll try to come by and see you, Char, and Ethan at least one more time before I go."

"We'd love that." She grinned.

Liisa had a son Aella's age with her dreamy Aurum partner, Char. Ethan's fiery, fun-loving personality made me wish I could have introduced him to Aella. If they had grown up together, I just knew they would have gotten into all kinds of trouble.

"Has there been any word from Iveria?" she asked.

My shoulders drooped even as I sent a silent prayer to the stars that Verus and the children were all right. It had been a risk sending a message through Lucris, but I knew Verus would have been worried sick until he knew I was safe. I couldn't have been more grateful that Wynn was sending people to pick them up. "No, but I didn't really expect to hear anything. By the time they begin their trek this way, we'll be long gone."

Liisa rubbed a reassuring hand on my back. "I'll look out for them and try to help them feel at home," she promised. "And I'll try my best to make sure Char doesn't scare your husband off with his well-meaning but often inappropriate humor."

I gave her a knowing look. "Yes, like that one time he roasted you in front of his entire family and you nearly strangled him before realizing it was a compliment."

"He called my brilliant herbal concoctions *fancy salads* and said I might as well be made of plaster the way I dedicated myself to my work."

We both laughed.

"I'm used to it by now," Liisa said, swatting at the air.

I turned and squeezed her in a hug. "You're the best, Liisa."

"How did you two meet?" I asked Helio as I sipped the best coffee I'd ever tasted.

I had finally taken him up on his invitation to meet his family. He was married to a beautiful Adamas named Rachell and had three adorable children.

Helio's eyes glimmered with mischief. "I met Chells at Kristel's tavern one night after a particularly dangerous rescue mission. Wynn, Rik, and I were trying to blow off some steam, when she got into an argument with her arrogant former lover."

He briefly rolled his eyes, and Rachell smacked his arm. "That's not the entire story, honey," she crooned.

Helio stared at her as if she was the center of his world, his eyes following her every movement, especially tracking her lips as she spoke. "I didn't say I was done with the story," he retorted before pulling her onto his lap, his arms wrapped around her possessively. "Anyway, she threw an entire tankard of glogg on him and was rearing back to throw a punch when I rescued her before she got into a fight she couldn't win."

"Who says I couldn't have won?" Rachell said in mock annoyance. "I absolutely could have had him flat on his back if you'd given me the chance."

"The last thing I want to think about is you getting anyone other than me on their back, Chells," Helio countered.

I watched them go back and forth, grinning in amusement. She was perfect for Helio. He absolutely needed a female with some spunk to her.

"I still wish you'd have let me leave a mark." Rachell rolled her eyes. "He deserved it. That prick."

"Well I, for one, am thrilled I was able to save you from bruising your beautiful hand," Helio said with a grin. "The moment I laid eyes on you, I knew you were supposed to be mine."

"I'm sure you've said that to many a pretty female," she replied.

"You're the only one I've ever really meant it with though," he said before planting a kiss on her lips.

I chuckled and looked away, feeling somewhat like an intruder with their show of affection.

"What about you, Ari? Tell us about your husband," Helio said.

Looking back at them, I smiled. "Well, when I left Zephyria and made it back home, my mother was quick to make sure my arranged marriage to Verus was still on."

"Did you know him before you got married?" Rachell asked.

"No, the first time I saw him was on our wedding day."

Helio's voice went deeper and more serious. "Did Verus know about the child when you married him?"

I looked down, feeling shame tinge my ears pink. "Yes. I actually found out shortly after I returned home. His family was informed of my situation, and he agreed to marry me anyway."

No one said anything for a moment as the words sunk in. Ready to change the subject to something lighter, I sipped my coffee and smiled. "Honestly, Helio, they need to have you come teach them how to make coffee at the pala—"

"Why didn't you come to me or Rik before you left?" Helio asked, hurt coloring his tone. "We would have helped."

"I felt trapped, and you are his friends. I figured you'd try to convince me to stay in Zephyria, but I couldn't, not with Wynn marrying Katye."

Helio groaned. "I still can't believe he did that to you—asked you to be his mistress while he married her."

A sad smile graced my face. "We were both quite young and foolish. I don't hold it against him anymore . . . Anyway, it worked out for the best. I found the healing I needed in Iveria, and my husband raised Aella as his own along with our five other children."

"Aww . . . he sounds wonderful," Rachell said softly, her eyes full of warmth.

Helio looked impressed. "I don't know if I would have been so accepting."

"Oh, hush, you," she shushed him. "You have the best heart of anyone I know. You would've done the same."

"I agree with her. Even now, you've been so forgiving and kind despite how I left."

Helio blushed slightly. "Aw, you need to stop before my head grows too large."

"Don't worry, honey, I'll remind you of your place soon enough," Rachell teased.

We all laughed together and continued sharing stories of our lives and families. Helio chased his children around his cozy home, making them giggle and scream, which immediately made me miss my own. Rachell and I traded horror stories of toddlers losing control of their powers at such a young age. After speaking with her, I was more than grateful none of my children had the ability to shake the earth. Our conversation also made me realize how helpful it would have been to know some of her tips for managing the storm-brewing tantrums Aella used to throw.

As I walked through the crowded streets back to the palatium, squeezing my arms around myself to ward off the chill, I couldn't help but wonder once again how different my life would have been had I stayed here in the Court of Air. I loved my little home under the sea, but because of all the secrets I held, I had never truly made as deep of connections with friends in Iveria. Here, I could be entirely myself, fully accepted. Back home, there was something always holding me back. I wondered if that would change now the oath was gone. And yet, it wasn't as if I could tell my friends about Zephyria without putting them at risk. I groaned inwardly. The Iris needed to be stripped of their power, and that was that. Perhaps then we could create a better world for our children to grow up in, and refugees could return to their homes if they wished.

It was evident to me that space was running out in Zephyria. No longer as open and airy as I remembered, it now reminded me of the crowded city of Iveria. My quarters in the palatium felt spacious in comparison to the modest townhome Helio and Rachell were squeezed into. Homes were built on top of each other into the side of the mountain, and Rachell had told me many families had chosen to share spaces to make room. Life in Zephyria would not be sustainable as they continued to grow.

As I headed up the quiet street that led to the palatium, a gust of air swept over me, followed by a distinct scent of pine and sage. He had once said he could find me anywhere. Footsteps crunched on the snow, and I knew he'd purposely made the noise to alert me to his presence. He could be utterly silent if he wanted to.

"Are you going to say hello, or just follow me like a stalker?" I threw over my shoulder.

Wynn cleared his throat before matching my stride with his own and coming up next to me. "You looked quite lost in thought—I didn't want to disturb you."

"That's never stopped you before," I retorted.

What is wrong with you, Ari? What is it about being around Wynn that is making you act like a child?

Wynn snorted. "You say that as if everything's the same as it was before you left."

I stopped walking, squeezing my eyes shut to collect myself before I said something I'd regret. "You're right. Everything has changed." I braved a glance up into his eyes, his gaze full of curiosity. The hardness had softened just a bit over the days I had been here. "It's just . . . being here has brought back so many memories. I feel as if I've been transported back to those days. So much has changed, but much remains the same."

We walked in silence for a few moments before he said, "Tell me something about you that I don't already know."

Surprised but pleased, I took the peace offering for what it was. A reminder of the past but also an opportunity for something new.

"I completed my healer training and have become one of the most sought-after healers in Iveria."

"I always knew you'd do great things," Wynn replied with awe. "That doesn't surprise me one bit."

"Thank you, Wynn," I suddenly felt shy.

"But none of that is something I don't know," he prompted, the hint of a smile tugging at his lips.

I blew out a breath. "Well, you know I got involved with the rebellion because of my healing skills, but I don't think I mentioned I have to attend to the Iris as well. Lucris takes full advantage of my ability to get in and out of their homes without catching notice."

Wynn's body instantly went tense, and he turned away from me, concealing his face. "I hate to think of you being at risk like that," he grumbled.

"Trust me, it isn't where I want to spend my time either . . . but still, I am grateful it allowed me the resources to come back here to get help for Aella."

Wynn turned back to me, his eyes filled with an emotion I couldn't quite place. "Why couldn't you have come sooner? Why wait until now? I would have taken you all in if you'd only asked."

"You say that now . . ." I shook my head in frustration. I had enough guilt eating me alive—I didn't need more. "You know what, I think I'd prefer to walk back on my own." I quickened my pace, not mindful of my surroundings.

"Ari, wait!" Wynn called out. "There's ice—"

His warning came a moment too late, and I found myself slipping toward the edge of the cliff. Before I could even scream, a warm hand gripped mine and pulled me up into a rock-solid chest. Overwhelming feelings of pain and ice-cold fear shot through me, and I gasped. It was excruciating. Without even thinking, my source flowed out of me, searching for a way to heal and soothe the pain.

"What just happened? What are you doing?" Wynn asked, dropping my hand and taking a step back.

Filled with confusion, I shook my head. "What? I don't know what you're talking about! What did *you* do to *me*?"

"I was only trying to keep you from sliding off the side of the mountain," Wynn said.

"Thanks for that," I muttered, still shaken and confused at what had happened with the flood of emotions and pain I'd felt.

"Please try to be a little more careful where you walk. I don't think . . ."

I sighed, and when he didn't continue, I asked, "You don't think what?"

"Never mind." He started walking back toward the palatium, and I followed behind, my eyes glued to the ground in search of more ice.

Wynn must have been carrying some heavy burdens to project so much pain into me. I felt desperately drawn to help, but I didn't think he'd let me.

Chapter 18
Open the Floodgates

Wynn

What in the stars had I been thinking? I couldn't be around her. It was far too difficult. When I'd pulled her away from the edge of the cliff, she had somehow engulfed me with her healing energy, releasing years of built up tension and pain. It had been too much. It had opened a floodgate of emotions and feelings I did not want to feel, breaking through the carefully constructed barrier holding everything back.

I needed to avoid her.

She is not for me. She is no longer mine.

It had become an unwelcome mantra I had to repeat every time she was around—every time I sensed her nearby. She had carved herself into my heart all those years ago, and I had been left cut open, bereft. None of the females I had brought to bed had satisfied my need for her.

I'd finally given in to Kristel's advances after far too many tankards of glogg, but it had been empty and unfulfilling. Every meaningless encounter had felt like a betrayal to Ari, so I'd stopped trying. It had been years. After acknowledging the emptiness that could never be filled, I'd finally given up. No one could ever match up to *her*.

If I had only discovered the truth before she'd left . . . perhaps things would have been different. Alas, dwelling on the past and roads not traveled never did anyone any good. I couldn't keep living in regret instead of embracing potential futures. Maybe this was my chance to realize the reality of her did not live up to the sugar-glossed memories of the past. I had survived with half a heart until now, and I would endure. If I were truly honest with myself, being near her and dealing with the pain was still better than not being near her at all.

Perhaps the stars had another fate in store and I wasn't meant to rule. If I could save my daughter, she could rule in my stead. Knowing Arianwen, she would have raised her right, *and* she was star-blessed. What more could the Court of Air desire?

Death was an almost definite possibility if I turned myself over to the Iris, but if there was a guarantee I could save her, I'd make that choice.

CHAPTER 19

GROVEL

AELLA

Time passed in a blur of iron fittings. Like a statue, I posed, bracing for the iciness of metal on skin. Each outfit, a beautiful new torture device designed just for me. Woven of fine iron chainmail, always in the Iris fashion of showing off more skin than parts covered. I'd been showcased in an assortment of barely there bikinis and gowns with plunging necklines so low and leg slits so high that I could hardly move without revealing myself. The chained jewelry often resembled that which one might use to confine a prisoner or a beast, with locks dangling from the chains around my ankles and wrists.

At the end of each day, my maids would apply salves to heal the damaged skin underneath the biting iron, but I was still left with a deeper bruise no one could see, a constant reminder with its perpetual ache. Balmed and bandaged, blushed in pearl dust, my skin shimmered like that of an Iris, bearing no evidence of my continued suffering.

"In you go," Himmel said as she waved a hand toward the crystal box.

I climbed inside before it was hoisted up by four elemental bearers. They carried me around the palatium like I was some prize on display. *If only my little sister could see me now.* Not at all how she'd likely imagined it—practically naked, perched on a bed of cushions in my tiny prison, a guarded spectacle for courtiers to ogle.

I stared straight ahead as I'd been instructed by Himmel, allowing my vision to blur so I could try to tune it all out. With the elaborate gowns and my status as the prince's future bride, the defeated prophecy, I was the center of juicy gossip—I'd become quite the attraction. It was good for morale, Himmel had said. How they loved to see me helpless and in chains, how it made them feel so mighty. I tried not to be affected by the insults or threats flung at me. They too had lost some of their sting.

What was most insulting was the way faux iron jewelry and clothing had suddenly become the height of fashion. The Iris relished showing off their fake iron tiaras, bejeweled collars, and body chains—a mockery of my suffering.

The palanquin bearers lowered my box for me to exit, and I was escorted by a set of guards into a revel full of debauchery.

My ears twitched, overstimulated by the constant music—so loud, it thumped off the walls. The iron chains vibrated and buzzed over my skin in a painful hum. The latest look Nephos had curated for me was a sultry, gossamer gown made of long sheets of midnight blue fabric, anchored by intricately crafted, scalloped, wrought iron shells at my collarbone. The shells were linked by a delicate chain that connected behind my neck. Running down from the seashells to cover my chest and then converging at my naval, the sheets intertwined through an ornate buckle adorned with looping chains that cascaded over my hips and thighs in various lengths. The skirt of the gown concealed my rear with more of the bunched, dark fabric stretching from hip to hip while still exposing a significant expanse of leg.

I scanned the crowds for the other contestants as I always did. For Ilaria, Lewenne, Ona, Enneli, Rae, and Jara. Were they here? Had they survived?

The prince, if he showed at all, was never around for long. Since our agreement, he'd kept his distance. In fact, I hadn't seen him for several weeks now, possibly going on a month or more if I'd counted my days correctly. Sometimes I'd catch whiffs of his scent and I'd whip my head around in search of the culprit only to find him nowhere near. Perhaps it had merely rubbed off on me from spending so much time in his corner of the palatium. I'd play it off as just another nervous twitch, one of several I'd developed over the course of my time in Prisma.

There it was again—that scent—only this time, I was certain he was near. I could feel the burn of his eyes on me even without looking. I turned slowly, purposefully, as inconspicuously as I could. And there he was in an adjacent alcove. An Iris female was draped over him from behind, giggling as she whispered into his ear.

I wasn't sure why it bothered me so much, but even as I tried to tell myself I had been mistaken for ever trusting him, that I didn't want him, that I needed him to stay away from me . . . I couldn't stomach the sight of another female's hands all over him. Envy wrapped around me, squeezing tighter than the iron chains. But who was I to be jealous? I'd asked him to leave me alone. I'd pretended not to know him. I had no claim on him.

Trying not to stare was the hardest part as the female stroked a hand up and down his chest, her fingers disappearing under the fabric of his loosely buttoned blouse. I should have averted my gaze, but I could not as I remembered the warmth of his skin beneath my own touch.

Kaleidos watched me as the female licked and nipped at his neck, tilting his head to the side to make more room for her. Heat pooled low and throbbed with the beat of the music as he stared at me, eyes dark, his tongue gliding over his lip absentmindedly. He sat there, legs wide as the female slowly worked herself around to the front of him, straddling his knee. The girl was beautiful in an obvious way, and her moves proved she knew what she was doing, the way she angled and curved her body like a snake.

While this wasn't out of place for these revels, seeing him there, partaking like this . . . I hated myself for everything I was feeling both emotionally and physically, but still, I couldn't bring myself to avert my gaze. Even as my eyes burned with envy, I couldn't look away as the female stroked his thigh. I imagined it was my hand and that I was her.

The guards tugged on my leash, the chain locking one click tighter around my waist. It was time to go. I stole one last glance at Kaleidos, the girl giving it her all now. But when she dared steal a kiss from him, he turned his face away, flicking his wrist for her to leave. I hated the tiny part of me that felt relief in that moment. Because it would have been easier to hate him if he had relished in her kiss, if he had proven himself a liar.

The guards escorted me to a great room near the revel. Fortunately for me, my appearances were always kept brief to keep the Iris interested—to keep me mysterious. It was usually a relief to be done, but now I wished I could have stayed longer, if only to see how much more Kaleidos would have done had I not been tugged away. It was still early in the evening, and I would be waiting in this great room until they were ready to show me for the next one. There was no schedule for my appearances—they didn't want the Iris to expect me—so I could be stuck here for minutes or hours, I never knew.

My heart still throbbed in my chest, my body hot and sweaty as though I'd been dancing. I tried to clear my mind of what I'd just seen. But the more I tried, the more I kept thinking about it—about him. Had he been trying to make me jealous? To get a reaction out of me? Or was he simply moving on? Would he do it again? Based on my physical response and the turbulence of my emotions, I feared he still had more of a hold over me than he ought.

Times like these had me questioning why I still resisted the idea of him. I didn't have to push him away—I could just play along with his games.

I am to be his wife. He did choose me after all.

Wife. I'd always hated the idea of it. Before the draft, I'd dreaded losing my autonomy, of belonging to another, as so often happened in arranged marriages. Most Argenti females were not lucky enough to end up with a male like my father, who treated marriage more like a partnership. My parents' relationship was something to covet, but I'd known that even if the stars had chosen to bless me with a good match who had treated me fairly, I'd have just as quickly become a slave to motherhood. How naive I'd been to fear such a life. Even losing my individuality to the expectations of matrimony would have given me more freedom and choice than my current situation—which was made abundantly clear by the iron and chains they so brazenly controlled me with.

Lightheaded, I walked toward the plush settee until the chain tightened around my waist another notch. I couldn't decide which was worse, the rigid collar around my neck or the cinching belt around my waist. It was always one or the other depending on the look they were going for.

"Here, here, pretty kitty," said the guard holding my twelve-foot leash. Despite Kaleidos' warning, the guards still taunted me any chance they could so long as the prince was out of sight, some worse than others. The Iris guard tugged me closer when I didn't obey.

The newer guard standing beside him chuckled nervously. "You sure she won't report back to him?"

"I think she likes it," the first replied.

Gone was the horrified girl I'd been. I had no sympathy left for the Iris. How badly I wanted them to get caught. I'd paint the walls with their blood if I could.

"Do you think he holds her by the leash while giving it to her from behind?" the nervous one said quietly to the other, then chuckled to himself.

"Never had a taste for seafood myself," the first guard replied, "but now I can't stop thinking about how delicious she must be to have earned so much of his favor." He licked his perverse lips before stiffening and jumping back into formation.

Icy goosebumps crawled up my neck, and my vision tunneled.

"There she is," Estrella drawled as she strolled into the room with another Iris. She gave me a long, purposeful glare before her eyes swept over me in an agonizingly slow manner that raised the hair on my arms and legs. She kept a wide berth at first before narrowing in, like a shark circling its prey.

I'd seen her among the crowds in the revels, always watching, glaring. But this was our first moment together since she'd set me up. I wasn't afraid of her anymore though—I knew exactly how she worked. What more could she possibly do to hurt me that hadn't already been done?

"Have you seen what Kaleidos did to Gaelor after your little accusation?" she hissed. "First you seduced him, then my husband . . . now the prince." Her eyes were red and glassy as she seethed with so much hatred toward me. She ripped off my iron circlet, sending it flying into and shattering a mirror on the far wall. With her other hand, she swiped my iridescent veil and scoffed.

Estrella trailed a sharpened nail over the tender flesh of my throat. "You're no better than that slutty little friend of yours who tried to entice the king. But at least she'd known her place." She pressed her lips to my ear, then whispered, "It's too bad she had to take the fall. You were supposed to get the tonic."

My heart clenched in my chest, threatening to stop beating altogether, trying desperately not to fall to pieces. I couldn't breathe, stunned by the revelation of what Estrella had just said. Had she poisoned Viera thinking it had been for me? The amount of willpower it took to keep myself from attacking her or even showing an emotional response was beyond the strength I'd previously possessed.

The truth about desperation, about living in a constant state of survival, is that it teaches you what you are truly capable of. And sometimes that means letting a piece of yourself die.

I couldn't afford to feel. If she were to find out I wasn't nameless, my life would be forfeit. I pressed it all inward, crushing it into nothingness. The part of me who grieved her friends and family, the part who felt sadness and loss, she had to go in order for me to survive.

A weight lifted off my chest as I regained control of my thoughts. Feet rooted in place, I focused on the memory of Estrella being strangled by

Aedrus. I'd been doing the right thing when I'd asked him to stop, and it had cost Viera her life. I should have let him finish the job.

Estrella circled her hand around my neck, pulling my back against her. "Look at what you have done!"

She turned us to face the other Iris she'd come in with, and from the shadows, Gaelor emerged, pale and sickly. I almost didn't recognize him. At the ends of his once muscular arms hung heavy, silver prosthetics.

"Come, Gaelor. Now's your chance to seek revenge."

He stalked forward, swinging a solid metal fist into my stomach so hard, I doubled over, unable to breathe. Estrella grabbed me by the hair, pulling me back up while I was still silently gasping for the air that had been knocked out of me.

"It's too bad she doesn't fight back anymore. It doesn't feel as satisfying to torment her this way." She shoved me onto the ground. "In our presence, you will only grovel. Now, crawl over there and fetch my cousin a glass of wine."

Estrella and Gaelor made themselves comfortable on opposite settees in the center of the room.

My diaphragm finally ceased spasming, and I gasped for breath. Pulling myself together as much as I could, I crawled across the marble floor to the drink table, then poured a glass with shaking hands. When I turned to bring it back, Estrella snapped her fingers.

"No, no. I said *grovel*." She pointed to the ground with a venomous smile.

I looked around for a rolling cart, confused. How was I supposed to do that?

Estrella raised a slender brow at me expectantly. "Do you need Gaelor to give you another reminder of what happens when you displease me?"

Gaelor raised a mocking brow, making me cringe. I did not want to play this game, but what choice did I have? I swallowed my pride and placed the foot of the tall glass between my teeth, proceeding to crawl back over to them as they laughed.

"Such an obedient nameless wench," Gaelor crooned.

A good portion of the wine splashed over me as I attempted to balance the delicate piece of glass with my tongue. The iron chain scraped across the polished stone floors as it dragged beneath me.

Estrella was positively delighted. "I changed my mind—her acquiescence is so much more fun." She clapped her hands. "Now, give Gaelor a sip."

My hands trembled as I held it to his unkind mouth. Being this close to him after what he'd tried to do to me disgusted me all over again. At least he couldn't touch me now. I had Kaleidos to thank for that. Gaelor laughed as I poured wine down his throat, so it splashed even more, splattering over the two of us.

"How fitting that the son of a nameless Argenti whore would want one as a bride," he spat out, wine-tainted spittle flying from his lips. "Such fine taste for our future king."

"I told you this would be fun," Estrella sang.

The doors at the end of the hall flew open with such force, they cracked against the walls to either side in a clatter almost as loud as his voice.

"What is the meaning of this?" Kaleidos thundered into the room.

Estrella flinched before quickly recovering. "We were just discussing how impeccable your taste in females is."

Kaleidos glared at me where I knelt between Gaelor's thighs, crystal goblet in hand. The room shook with his fury. I dropped the glass and fell back from Gaelor, steadying myself with my hands on the low stone table behind me as the marble floor cracked and splintered toward us.

Gaelor trembled, and his pants darkened with urine.

"Calm down, cousin. We're just having a bit of fun." Estrella laughed, then pointed toward me in accusation. "Look at your nameless bride. She couldn't keep her hands off Gaelor before, and even now, she's fawning over him."

I clenched my jaw. Estrella had once again made me a pawn in her scheme.

In a flash, Kaleidos slammed into Estrella, knocking her to the ground so hard, she coughed up blood. But she wasn't playing the victim this time as she smiled defiantly up at the prince.

"Don't be jealous, cousin. It's in her nature."

"Don't think my patience for you is infinite. She is my bride and will be treated with respect from here on out," Kaleidos growled.

He turned to face Gaelor, who had already begun slowly sneaking out of the room.

"Run," Kaleidos warned, and Gaelor took off in a full sprint. Finally, Kaleidos turned to me, hands clenched into fists at his sides. "What did I say about groveling?"

I sucked my bottom lip as I rose on shaking legs, locking my knees to keep them from giving out under me. I went to collect my veil, but Kaleidos held out a hand to stop me.

"Estrella will help make you presentable again. Won't you, cousin?"

She narrowed her eyes at him, then begrudgingly swiped the shimmering veil off the floor where she'd tossed it.

"There will be no more appearances this evening. Take her back to my wing," Kaleidos said to my guards.

I swallowed, eyeing the males who had spoken such vile words about me. I must not have hidden the hesitant look in my eyes, because Kaleidos stilled suddenly as though darkness had taken over.

"I can't trust anyone with you, can I?" Kaleidos said more to himself. He cracked his knuckles and began rolling his sleeves. "It appears I have more things to take care of."

He turned to Estrella. "Escort her back to my room. No games, cousin. I trust I need not remind you again."

I could hardly stand to be so close to her, knowing what she'd done to Viera. If only Kaleidos knew . . . would he still spare Estrella? The one comfort I had was seeing the fear she'd failed to adequately hide after Kaleidos' warning, that she would not be dumb enough to try anything else. I almost wished she would. I wished she'd give him a reason to crush her windpipe.

As I stared at her, I pictured his thorny vines creeping around her neck, tightening until her face turned blue. I pictured her begging for mercy that wouldn't come, just as none had been extended to Viera.

On the way back to Kaleidos' wing through the palatium's grand halls, I rode in Estrella's palanquin, much larger than my own, affixed with the luxury of privacy curtains my crystal box didn't have. She bent toward me to fix the smudge under my eye, smoothed her fingers over my hair, then replaced the veil somewhat neatly upon my head. She could be tender when she wanted to be, but she made sure I knew how much I'd ruined her evening with the searing pressure she used when replacing the iron circlet upon my head. She slumped back in her seat across from mine, staring absentmindedly out the small gap in the curtained window beside her.

"He's become so boring ever since you came here."

We sat in silence the rest of the way.

Estrella dropped me off in front of Kaleidos' wing, kicking the end of my chain out after me. Since my guards had remained behind with the prince, I was free to roam for the first time instead of being locked up in the bedchamber. I explored the many rooms I'd never had access to before, my only company the unmanned chain of my leash scraping the stone floors behind me.

Kaleidos' wing was like a palatium in itself.

For a moment, I second guessed where I was as I wandered into his "not library." The once neat bookshelves were disorganized with empty gaps everywhere, and piles of books were stacked haphazardly around his desk. For someone who had claimed to be skilled in organizing his books, I couldn't help but let out a small laugh—this chaos would be a disaster for him.

This was his work though, I could see, as I glanced at the books on his desk. What appeared to be a compendium of ancient artifacts lay open, and various historical annals were stacked to the side, tabbed with strips of ribbon. In the center was a notebook in which it appeared Kaleidos had been recording the dates and locations the nameless key had been mentioned and what, if anything noteworthy or useful, had been gleaned from it.

Was he looking for a cure? I backed away from the desk, unwilling to accept he would do that for me. I'd seen him at the revel earlier. He hadn't looked like a lovesick male working tirelessly to save his lost love. I gripped the back of my neck. Even if he was doing this for me, it didn't change anything.

Back at the bookshelves, I trailed my fingers along their spines once more, stopping on that well-worn book on Iveria I'd seen what felt like ages ago. The one with all the notes in the margins. I opened it, flipping through the pages.

"Who are you?" I whispered.

Gaelor had confirmed a suspicion I'd had—that Kaleidos' mother had been nameless. If this had been hers, that meant she'd been searching for answers. He'd called her a shell of a woman, but she'd designed the waterways in the gardens, and these notes proved there was another depth to her far beyond what they had expected from a nameless. Perhaps this meant there was hope for the other nameless. Would she have remembered eventually, or would she have spent the rest of her life wandering in darkness, grasping for damp clues that would never spark?

I sighed. She hadn't had enough time. Kaleidos had told me his mother had been taken from him at a young age. It was a wonder he had any kindness in him at all after such a thing had been done to him. The morals he'd been raised on were the same that had nourished the likes of Estrella and Gaelor. Could I really blame him for his faults? I didn't know what I'd been expecting from him. Born of a people so indoctrinated to see us as less than. To see us as unworthy of choice, of life. To see us as nothing but a means of breeding and entertainment for our subjugators.

But Kaleidos was different from the rest of them, wasn't he? Was it possible that seeds planted by a mother—however small—might have still grown into something with the power to change the world? That the prince might carry the heart and will needed to bring such change? That he might still make an ally to the rebel cause?

Perhaps that was why King Solanos had made an example of his mother. Not only for his son, but perhaps also to show the other nameless what awaited those who began searching. How I wished Solanos could get a taste of his own cruelty. My hands shook, my vision blurring from angry tears.

I was done standing around. I needed to do something. I used to have so many hesitations, but what more did I have to fear losing now? My worst nightmares and more had already happened to me.

I'd been drafted to Prisma, taken from my family and home.

Forced to compete in deadly trials.

Watched as those I'd been competing with died around me. My best friend had been killed.

Imprisoned, starved of my element, chained in iron.

Humiliated.

All of those things had happened *to* me. Like I'd somehow deserved them for being born elemental fae. I'd been as helpless as seagrass in a raging current.

Was I not meant to fight back? Not meant to rail against my suffering?

The stars commanded it. Or so the Iris said. They said a great many things, and they said them so prettily. But I'd seen through their schemes, I'd seen how they operated—through glamour and illusion, through subtle mistruths and distraction.

They were liars.

I was marked by the stars. I had the power of not one but two elements. The Iris had spoken of a prophecy and believed I was the one meant to end them—that I was the biggest threat to life as they knew it. And instead of killing me, they'd had me chained and put on display in mockery of the same stars they so proudly proclaimed to have been sent by.

I'd make them regret that mistake.

I brought the book back to my bedchamber, my gilded cage, tucking it swiftly under the pillow when Kaleidos burst through the door, breathing heavily.

CHAPTER 20
WHAT IS NECESSARY

AELLA

Kaleidos eyed my hands briefly, and I feared being caught red-handed. But whether or not he knew what I'd just hidden, he seemed to brush it aside as he called for Kasha and Yulema.

He stood at a distance, fidgeting with his collar, a mix of unreadable emotions stirring in his fierce, green eyes. There were splatters of blood on his sleeves, and I wasn't sure if I should run to him to see if he was hurt or cower away at what he had likely done.

"Are you all right?" I asked.

He let out a dark, incredulous laugh that half frightened me. "You're asking *me* that?"

When I didn't respond, he strode somewhat closer while still maintaining a respectable distance. His expression changed to that of concern. "You're shivering."

Kasha and Yulema entered the room, and Kaleidos instructed them to remove the iron.

With gloved hands, Kasha removed the circlet and veil from my head while Yulema gently unwound the iron bracelets that snaked up my arms. I tried to hide the winces of pain as Himmel had taught me. *"You mustn't let the prince feel bad for you."* Kaleidos made an angry sound, and I dared a glance back at him, only to see the murderous look in his eyes that, if I hadn't known better, appeared to be directed at me.

"Is it always this bad?" he asked, barely restraining a growl.

"I'm getting used to it. They'll apply the balms, and then—"

"I didn't know . . ." He was practically shaking. "I don't know how you can bear it." All the glass windows buzzed as though ready to burst at any moment. "I've handled iron before. It wasn't comfortable, but it didn't *sear* my flesh like this." His eyes roved over the reddened, blistered skin on my arms, then over my dress. "And you're faexing covered in it!"

Kaleidos stormed out of the room. The rumbling followed him, increasing in intensity until the outer glass doors erupted in the other room, the spray of glass visible through my bedroom's crystal window panes.

The girls washed me with damp, oil-soaked rags, wiping away the scents of spilled wine and perfumed smokes from the revel, tending my raw flesh with potent, healing salves. They worked around the chains in a series of synchronized maneuvers while changing me into a diaphanous, silver sleeping gown.

Kaleidos trailed the Faber Ludi and his guards into the room, his presence hanging over them, fierce like a storm cloud.

"Have you seen the damage your devices have done? She is nameless, for faex's sake!"

"These are the necessary precaut—"

Kaleidos picked him up by the collar of his robes so his feet dangled, and he squirmed helplessly in his grasp.

"UN. CHAIN. HER," he roared into the older male's frightened face, "Or I will do to *you* what I find *necessary*."

Kaleidos dropped the Faber Ludi, who then scurried over, carefully donning thick, leather gloves before drawing the iron key from the folds of his robes. "When you handled the alloy before, I would guess that the amount of royal aether in your blood protected you in some way so that it did not burn your skin as badly. But you only handled it for seconds—if you'd touched it for much longer, it would have attacked the source you'd inherited, burning the weakened flesh underneath." He spoke nervously. "As you can see, they do not leave any permanent marks. Her skin already looks good as new." And it was true. The Iris' healing balm was so effective, all signs of scarring had been wiped clean. Even the scarring on my forearm from the shadow fang had dissolved as though I'd never been a contestant in the Hunt. The Faber Ludi fumbled with the key nervously, unlocking the mechanism at the end of the leash that kept the chain from opening.

"If you bring one more object made of iron near my bride, it will be *your* neck in chains."

"I would have to run that by the—"

"Look at her! She is starved of her element," Kaleidos growled as he gestured toward me. He made a menacing spectacle of himself, looming over the Faber Ludi. "What are you so afraid of?"

"But the prophecy—"

"Didn't my father already defeat her? Didn't he prove she was no threat to him? She is my bride. I will take responsibility for her. Out of my sight . . . Get him out of my sight!" Kaleidos commanded the guards, and the maids hurried out after.

I stood there, unsure what to do. My eyes welled up with tears. With the choking chain removed, I could finally breathe. I'd spent every moment of these past weeks in some iron imprisonment or another, so the simple awareness of its absence made me feel almost like I was floating. But more than that, what Kaleidos had just done was monumental. Filled with gratitude, I was ready to drop to my knees and thank him. But before I had a chance, Kaleidos stepped over to the bed, pulling the book from under the pillow.

"This . . . was my mother's." He held it reverently in his hands and swallowed. "I don't think she ever quite remembered who she had been, but she tried. This shows me that." He flipped through, smoothing his finger over the annotation in the corner of a page before handing it delicately over to me. "Perhaps you will find some meaning in it." His brows bunched together as he lingered, his hand still touching the book.

For once, I hated myself for hiding, for not just coming out and telling him I wasn't nameless. This male was so much more complex than I had given him credit for, and perhaps I should have tried to work with him instead of blaming him for everything. But what was I supposed to do in this moment of vulnerability after lying to his face for weeks? *Surprise! It's me! I've been here the whole time!*

Still, if I did tell him the truth, what would he do? Would he fight to protect me? Would he help me seek revenge? Although this was a big one, I had to ask myself, was this one act of his enough to trust him? I'd suffered through Himmel's torture too long to just give up now. And chances were, even if he did have a fascination with me, he'd continue to sit on his hands while injustices occurred, so long as they didn't directly affect him. Like he had told me before, *"It is the way it has always been."*

"Good night, my prince," I said to dismiss him. It was still early in the night, but I was truly exhausted from Himmel's lessons and the increasingly frequent late-night showings at revels. I'd use any opportunity to catch up on sleep.

Kaleidos gave the book a gentle pat.

"Take care," he said and then left the room.

I sighed, releasing my shoulders from where they'd practically migrated to my ears. Pretending was always hardest around him, but I'd made myself a promise. If I had to live this life, I would no longer let it float around me, helpless as an animal. I would plan and I would scheme until every last Iris paid for what they had done.

So long as everyone believed I was nameless, I stood a small chance at earning the trust of my Iris captors. One day, I might be permitted to maneuver throughout the palatium—perhaps even the city of Prisma—without raising suspicion. I owed it to myself, to my family, to my people, to Viera, and to all those I'd lost to find a way to fulfill the prophecy.

If I could wake up the nameless or, at the very least, turn them against the Iris, perhaps I could raise a secret army from within the palatium's walls.

CHAPTER 21

WATER

AELLA

"Aella, I have something I've been wanting to show you," the prince said, rousing me from my slumber. I squinted my eyes open to see him practically aglow with excitement. *What is he smiling about?* I rubbed my eyes and climbed out of bed. So much for catching up on sleep.

Kal called the maids to prepare me for a morning bath. I could have cried—it sounded too good to be true. Confused by this sudden afforded luxury, I was too afraid to risk asking *why now* for fear that he might change his mind.

"I'd rather you not stink up my room any more than you already have," he said as though answering my thoughts. It seemed a shallow reason, but he was Iris afterall. Besides, I agreed a bath was sorely needed, and this was not the time to argue logic.

Golden, glittering steam poured out of the entrance to the bathing hall. I flew to the open door to the pool I'd never seen before, stopping at the threshold. My breath caught in my throat, and I was unable to move even an inch forward. I had started to think I'd spend the rest of my life slowly desiccating. All the same, Himmel had been feeding me with the fear of water every single day, and as much as I hated to admit it, all her poisonous words had burrowed under my skin. Caught in a limbo of baseless fear, I found myself fixed in place, feet like bricks mortared to the ground, unable to move forward.

Kal slid past me, pulling his shirt over his head in one swift motion. Bronzed skin shimmered by candlelight, cast shadows contouring his long, lean, muscled back.

"Come on in." He grinned back at me with a wink before loosening the tie of his trousers.

Who is this male?

I closed my mouth, which I'd found hanging open at the sight of him undressing before me. I fidgeted with my hands. I didn't know what to do. Kal sauntered back over, his pants halfway untied, hanging dangerously low on his hips, the deep V muscles of his stomach drawing my vision south.

He rested his forearm on the doorframe above my head, leaning in close enough to whisper, "I'm sorry I've been such an arse." He tapped the door frame before sliding past me again, back out into the bedchamber. "Don't go anywhere," he quipped.

I pulled slightly away, befuddlement creasing my brow, and Kal threw his head back in laughter.

"Okay, maybe that was the wrong thing to say. Just . . . hold tight, okay?" He raked his teeth over his bottom lip, and I turned back toward the water before he could catch me blushing.

Smoothing my hands repeatedly over the silky, near-transparent fabric of my nightgown, I tried to swallow past the butterflies fluttering in my chest. My eyes were glued to the stretch of water that took up so much of the room. So vast, the extent of it blurred from view by steam rising off its surface. It bubbled and spilled over the edges of the bathing pool, rolling over the detailed mosaic tile before disappearing again. Humidity clung to me, my nightgown becoming a second skin.

He'd figured me out. That was the only explanation for his sudden flirtatious behavior.

Unless this was another way for him to trick me into admitting the truth. Or some kind of heartless joke he was playing on me before turning me in.

Although, he had ordered the removal of my chains, and he'd even defended me in front of Estrella and Gaelor. Whatever he'd done to my guards last night was unclear, but after seeing what he'd done to my guard that first day I'd awoken nameless, I imagined it hadn't been pretty.

Perhaps these were all signs I could trust him, especially, if not only, for the gifted luxury of a bath. Even if I wasn't quite sure how I could work past my new fear of water.

Is this really the proof I need, or is it simply that my standards have become exceedingly low, given my circumstances?

I shook my head. I hated the idea of admitting to him that I'd been faking it all this time. Where would I even begin?

Kal came up from behind me, sliding his hands around my waist. I shivered, tantalized by the warmth of his skin on mine.

"There you are," he breathed, spinning me around to face him, his charming smile from ear to ear melting away all worries about his agreement not to lay a hand on me.

I nodded, shyly peeking up at him again. "May I?" I motioned toward the water. His curious and playful demeanor seemed to bolster my courage, softening me to the idea that the water wasn't going to harm me.

"If you delay any longer, I may find it necessary to throw you in," he teased.

It could have been the way his eyes sparkled or the pure comfort of his arms around me, but I suddenly realized I didn't much care for secrets or past agreements anymore.

"Did something happen?" I finally asked, my fear he'd think better of allowing the bath long forgotten.

"Yes, Aella. *You* happened." He cupped the side of my face in one hand, tugging me ever closer with his other on my lower back.

I looked away, acting a touch coy. "I don't know what you mean by that."

He raised a brow. "Is that so, little sea nymph? Would you like me to help you remember?"

A kiss to remember.

Unable to answer with words, I gave him a slight nod. Kal lifted my chin, and I closed my eyes in anticipation of what would happen next.

"Don't close your eyes," he whispered just as he placed his lips over mine. It was so incredibly intimate, our eyes locked together this close. My breath hitched, arms hanging heavy at my sides. Energy buzzed up the length of them, and my fingers thrummed with an acute desire to touch him.

Stars, I am at his mercy.

Kal kissed me over and over again, softly at first as he walked us toward the slick mosaic wall. I melted into him, no longer able to resist, mouth opening to his. Hungry with desire, I sucked his bottom lip between my own, and I nipped at its plushness with my teeth. He was sweet like honey, like poison, and I'd do anything to slake my thirst with another taste of him.

Kal roamed his hands over my arms, my back, my shoulders, my legs, squeezing and discovering all the places I wanted touched, *needed* touched. His hands promised to relieve an ache, his body promised an escape. He kissed me harder, and his fingers found their way up my thighs in answer to the tingling waves pulsing through me.

"You're a pretty good actress," he teased between kisses.

"What?" I gasped into his mouth. I'd all but forgotten my own name, I was so engulfed with desire.

"Almost had me fooled," he whispered against my jaw. Kal picked me up, one thigh at a time, until I was nestled between the heat of his hard body and the cool, damp wall. "Remember this?" He rocked into me.

How could I forget?

My nerves thrummed with pleasure and desire, and I wanted nothing more than to relive that moment we'd once shared. The position he held me in angled our bodies together in the most advantageous way, and with only a bit of fine fabric between us, there wasn't much holding back the growing pressure in his trousers.

Faex it.

"It clearly wasn't memorable enough—you might have to leave a bigger impression this time," I whispered against his ear as I dug my fingers into his raven-black, tousled locks.

"Ahh, finally," Kal purred. "There's nothing I'd like more than to do exactly that." He hoisted me up a little higher, grinning into my neck as he angled himself dangerously closer to where I wanted him most.

The muscles in my hips and thighs flexed with need, and I squeezed my legs around his waist, clinging to his neck as he carried me into the bath. He walked down the steps into the water, submerging us inch by inch, deeper and deeper, kissing me over and over and over again as though searching out every tender spot along my neck and chest. Kal pressed his lips to mine again, the heady taste of salt on them.

"I could kiss you forever," I thought, as he had once said to me. My longing for him clouded all my better judgment. It was the perfect distraction from the fear of water that had been injected into my mind.

Kal settled me onto one of the reclined seats that lay submerged at the edge of the bath and floated in the water over me. I held onto him, desperate for the unending depths of pleasure his every move offered mine, for the freedom I knew he could deliver. The water between us swirled and twisted, drawing us nearer still, our bodies gliding effortlessly against each other. His hands gripped the flesh of my rear, squeezing as he maneuvered himself over me. I reached down to his trousers, but he chuckled, slipping just out of reach.

"Slow down, sea nymph. I don't think you're ready for me yet."

But before I could protest, he disappeared under the water, tugging my hand to follow him.

I dove in after him, and my eyes widened as I took in the sight of the pool that extended deep into an enormous, cave-like spring. Deeper we went, hand in hand, exploring the depths of the cavern. The water cooled the farther we went, and I choked back a sob—it was the closest I'd felt to home since coming to Prisma. The prince observed me with a boyish grin. I crawled back into his arms—*my* prince—and together, we sank down into the depthless cave. I closed my eyes, taking a moment to appreciate the water with all my other senses.

My source was dull, distant, and I suddenly felt very heavy. I looked down at myself. I was cloaked in iron. Chains hung from every limb, threatening to pull me deeper and deeper until I'd never get out. And when I called upon it, the water was foreign to me. Like it didn't know me, like I didn't belong. When I attempted to inhale, the water burned and lodged in my throat.

Can I no longer survive in my element?

Panicking, I pushed the prince away and frantically ripped at my clothes. The chains were weighing me down, and the immense heaviness of the water crushed in all around me. Kal tried to pull me back into his arms, but I fought, thrashing in terror. He held on anyway, swimming us up toward the surface. I kicked and screamed, a never-ending stream of bubbles escaping my lips. I looked to the surface, which appeared to grow miles farther. My vision narrowed as if I were looking through a straw. I didn't think I would make it. I was suffocating. I was going to drown.

My element had turned against me.

When we finally breached the surface, I gasped for air, only to find myself awake in my bed—Kaleidos' bed—held securely in strong arms.

"Breathe with me, Aella. Breathe," he said, stroking the hair out of my face. I attempted to calm my hyperventilation but couldn't stop the deep, gasping breaths that tore through me. My terrified reflection was amplified in the large blacks of his eyes. I touched my hair, which was damp, not wet, and my skin was slick with sweat, *not salt water*. I still wore the silver nightgown, and I was in bed, unchained, as I'd gone to sleep that night.

Kaleidos exaggerated his breaths for me, urging me to mimic him.

Still trying to reconcile what was real and what had been a dream, I closed my eyes and focused on his breathing—in and out, like the ocean's waves—relaxing into his arms more and more with each breath. I laid my head against his chest, his strong and steady heartbeat a soothing rhythm beneath my ear. Kaleidos placed tender kisses one after another atop my head as he held me. His arms felt like home.

Once my breathing started to calm, he broke the silence. "I came to bring you a glass of water. But when I found you lying here, you were impossibly still. Too still. Your body was cold. You weren't breathing, Aella. I know I promised I wouldn't touch you, but you were dying . . . I thought I was losing you . . . again."

I looked up at him, and he paused for a breath, then continued more slowly, each word intentional. "I tried to wake you, I tried to give you air." He dropped his forehead to mine. "Storm clouds, Aella, what happened to you?" he asked, concern etched across his handsome features.

I touched one of the shimmering streaks that lined his face, my finger coming back damp, and my heart stuttered over the evidence of tears he had shed for me. Kal dropped his gaze to my other hand, which he stroked affectionately in his spare one, then to my wrist, as though he too remembered my scars—now wiped clean as though nothing I'd been through had left lasting marks, as though my life, my struggles had never been.

"I couldn't breathe. I . . . I couldn't—" I began, then jerked back from him, sliding out of his embrace. The last thing I needed was to take comfort in his arms when I hadn't even told him I wasn't nameless. I needed space so I could think.

Wrapping a dark sheet tightly around myself, I jumped out of the bed to put distance between us, the excess fabric puddling in a heap on the floor. I couldn't keep lying to him. I needed to tell him everything, but I couldn't find the right words. And how would he take it? Would he be angry, or would he be kind?

As much as I tried to tell myself this was what I needed to do, I just couldn't bring myself to do it. I was too much of a coward, and I'd rather push him away again than admit the truth. I held my hand out as a sign to stay back. Looking at his face, his gorgeous, iridescent face, I saw it all in his eyes—the pain, the rejection, the fear, the longing.

Kaleidos got up from the bed, taking the hint that he should leave. "I'm so sorry I broke my promise to you." He walked toward the door.

My outstretched hand shook in front of me, my knees buckling as it suddenly became too hard to stand straight. Again, I felt around my waist, searching for the chain I'd grown so accustomed to, then around my throat for the absence of the iron collar. I was so tired of pretending. I was even more tired of being alone. *Perhaps loneliness is stronger than pride.*

I squeezed my eyes shut. "I could hardly hold it against you, Kaleidos. After all, you're so good at breaking your promises." *Scratch that, my pride is stronger than a mother.* I braved looking at him again in search of his reaction.

Kaleidos stopped in his tracks. Turning slowly back toward me, his face showed no emotion, and he was eerily still, making my heart skip.

"Aella?" he whispered.

"Please don't make me explain everything to you." I paused, waiting for him to respond, to reject me, to threaten me, anything. He just stood there, eyes wide, as though seeing me for the very first time. "I have no idea how it happened. And I know you gave me a chance to say something before, but I was really mad at you! I have endured weeks of torture because it seemed preferable to confiding in you." The words spilled out of me. "I am still furious with you . . . but I can't keep doing this alone."

Kaleidos gave me an incredulous look, which softened as a smile slowly spread to the corners of his lips. And then he was sprinting toward me. He knelt down in front of me, wrapping his arms around my waist and burying his face against my middle.

"Keep lying to me or don't," he said. "I don't care. I'm just so happy you're still in there."

"You're not angry?"

Kaleidos stood, his eyes glistening with unshed tears as he spoke. "I'm more angry with myself for not seeing it sooner." He let out a soft laugh. "You gave a very convincing performance."

"That's not what you said in my dream."

"You've been dreaming about me?"

My gaze dropped to his trousers and then snapped back up to his face. "Um, what?"

"Oh, you have, haven't you?"

My face burned, and I forced myself to look elsewhere, anywhere but at the prince. "I . . . It was only a dream!"

"How about we make a deal—you tell me all about your dream, and I won't ask you a single question about your nameless charade."

I squinted at him. "Too late. You already told me I didn't have to tell you."

"Ah, it was a shot worth taking." He winked.

I wrapped the bedsheet tighter around myself, trying to keep the dream from my mind.

"I fully understand if you don't want to tell me everything, but if anyone hurt you . . ." He balled his hands into fists, and a muscle flickered in his jaw, as though even the idea of it was setting him off.

I could deal with what I'd been through. It wasn't like he could go back and change the past. Most of what I'd experienced had only served to make me stronger. Except . . .

"It's gone, Kal," I choked out. "My element is lost to me." He took my elbows in his hands. "For weeks, I've dreamt of the sea and I've called to the water with no reply," I whispered. "I am afraid it has forgotten me."

Kal gathered me into his arms, resting his cheek on top of my head, taking a deep inhale.

"No one could forget you, Aella."

CHAPTER 22

ILLEGAL SWIM

AELLA

"Where are you taking me?" I whisper-shouted as Kal carried me out onto the terrace.

Still wrapped up in his bedding, he tossed me over his shoulder to free up one of his hands.

"What are you doing?" I shrieked.

"Something I should have done long before now," he replied, his voice smooth, as if it took no effort for him to haul me around. "Now stop squirming, or I may drop you."

"You wouldn't dare!" I snapped back at him.

Kal only chuckled, and my eyes nearly bugged out of my head when I saw he was climbing us over the side of the balcony to the gardens below.

Once we reached the bottom, he gently set me on the soft, manicured grass.

"If they catch us . . ."

"The midnight revelries have only just begun. They'd hardly be found patrolling the gardens when the palatium's delights await," he said. "Though, if it does come to that, I can place a glamour on you. You're unchained—no one will know it is you." He offered his arm. "Come, be with your element. Float under the stars. I'll stand watch."

I wanted that. Oh, how I did. But the idea of it flooded my mind with anxious trepidation. "Kal, I . . . I can't do this."

He cupped my face in his hands. "Yes, my little sea nymph, you can."

"What if it rejects me? What if it pulls me under, drowning me, refusing my command? What if my magic is too far gone and I can no longer swim or breath in the water?"

"Then you are fortunate to have me with you to pull you out," he said. "I know you're afraid, and those are valid fears, but what if the water greets you? What if it welcomes your return? What if it recharges you and lifts your soul?" He raised his brows. "You'll never know unless you try. Come. You are not alone. I will let no harm come to you." He held out his hand.

I swallowed the lump in my throat, taking another deep breath, then reached for him. His fingers laced with mine as we walked to the river, stopping at the bank. I glanced at the water. Longing settled like an ache in my bones, but terror seized my joints, the fear of rejection so strong, I couldn't move an inch, my nightmare still too fresh in my mind. It had felt so real. Noticing my pause, Kal tugged on my hand gently, bringing my focus back to him. His emerald eyes glittered in the dark, and a mischievous smile tugged at his cheek.

"Why are you looking at me like that?" I asked.

"I'm reminded of our last meeting at the riverbank."

My cheeks burned as I remembered how I'd practically thrown myself at him after devouring a bushel of a certain not-to-be-trusted fruit. Kal stepped closer to me, narrowing the space between us.

"Ready?" he asked, his voice low.

"Not really," I murmured, glancing at the water again, shaking now. "I don't know what's wrong with me. I know what I must do, but I can't. This fear . . . it's paralyzing."

"Then let us sit and rest. Your choice remains your own, always."

I sighed in relief, nodding. "Yes, let's do that."

As we sat beside the river bank listening to the trickle of water, the chirps of small creatures, and the otherwise silence of the garden, I watched the fireflies glow in and out of view like flickering stars. Kal settled onto his back, hands behind his head, making himself comfortable. I tried to be patient with myself. I tried to still my mind and relax, to allow the stars and the peace of the garden to sink in. And he'd been right—I was already feeling slightly better just being outside under the stars, enjoying the slight breeze. He'd known exactly what I'd needed without me even having to ask.

I studied Kal's relaxed expression. He appeared to glide through life without a care. The wayward prince who had the world at his fingertips and a reputation for rakish exploits and hosting revels past dawn. He brought forth swift and violent judgments when he deemed them necessary, yet it was like he held me to another set of rules. He was patient and kind with me, thoughtful even. How could he be so wickedly Iris and so incredibly gentle and forgiving at the same time? It was almost infuriating how he could remain so serene and treat me with such care after countless had suffered and died in his name.

My eyes were drawn to the strong cut of his jaw and the curve of his plush lips I could hardly believe I'd once kissed. I wanted to run my fingers through the wavy locks of his jet-black hair, so dark, it seemed to swallow all light but somehow kept a prismatic quality to it, reflecting various colors, depending on the angle. The marbled lines that covered his body seemed to glow against his bronze skin, pulsing as though energized by the night sky. It was unsettling but beautiful, if not mesmerizing . . . and I hated that, in spite of everything he symbolized, I couldn't help but like him.

Kal peered at me through the lashes of one vibrant green eye, then closed it again, returning to his baseline look of smug indifference.

"If looks could kill, I'd be dead," he said.

"If only . . ." I mused.

He chuckled. "Which part?"

"A death-bringing glare, or your swift demise? Hmm . . . That's a tough one," I teased, tapping a finger on my lips. "I'd say both, but against all reason, I'm afraid I still value the meager scraps of life I have left."

"You pretend to disdain me, yet you remain here at my side, at my mercy," he said.

"It is a strange thing, that I could somehow feel safer with an Iris prince than with my own element." I folded my arms across my chest. "Could it be a side effect of your devastatingly handsome appearance, or is it an acquired response from being your prisoner? Maybe it's because you're the only person in this entire palatium who seems at least a tiny bit sympathetic and I've become so desperate that I've allowed myself to believe you have my best interests at heart . . ."

"You find me devastatingly handsome?" he purred.

"Of course that's the only thing you heard me say." I huffed a laugh.

Perhaps not every feeling needs to be masked with sarcasm.

"It wasn't disdain for you that prompted that face, to be clear. I wasn't thinking of murdering you in your sleep. I've been told I look quite mean when I'm deep in thought." I rubbed the back of my neck, suddenly feeling vulnerable for admitting such a small truth about myself. I realized I so often put up my guard around people, I hardly knew how to be myself anymore. It felt good to speak freely.

Kal's lips quirked into a smile that showed off a glint of his pearly white teeth, amused, delighted even at my confession. "So you're saying that expression isn't expressly reserved for me? What a shame."

I focused on the water again, irritation flowing out of me. It was my life source . . . I closed my eyes, trying to remember how lovely it felt, but my dream came flooding back, sucking me under, choking me, the chains pulling me down.

All at once, I was spinning and nauseated. I forced my eyes open and gasped for air, reaching up to pull the phantom iron collar away. I had been holding my breath again.

Kal placed a hand on my shoulder, grounding me. "You're giving them too much power over you," he said, kneeling before me. "Your past, your hurts, your fears . . . they can only control you so long as you allow them." He tilted my chin up. "You understand?"

"How are you so good at this? You're so patient. You're so calm. How do you know all the right things to say and do?"

"Tell that to my father," he scoffed. "Though I'm not sure such words could ever describe me." He shook his head.

"I think he's wrong about you, Kal. I think he underestimates you, and what he sees as weaknesses are perhaps your greatest strengths."

He furrowed his brows, studying me for a moment, then dipped his chin, taking a deep breath.

I was afraid I'd broken him when he didn't come back with some egotistical or flirtatious reply. Did he really agree with everything his father said about him? I couldn't believe I was doing this, but I figured he just needed proof he had goodness in him. I could give him that.

"I'm ready." I nodded a little too dramatically. Perhaps still trying to convince myself. I sprung to my feet. "Let's do this."

Kal and I stood across from each other. He removed his shoes, then smirked at me while unbuttoning his shirt. Though I was tempted to look away, I held his gaze for fear that I'd change my mind about what we were about to do. I did, however, consider throwing his own shoe at him for the devious looks he was shooting at me.

"Stop looking at me like this is something more than it is," I scolded him.

"Now if you would direct a little more of that disdain toward your fear, perhaps it wouldn't continue wreaking such terror," he said with a wink.

The prince dropped his shirt to the grass, then dove into the water effortlessly. He came up, flicking his hair back, inviting me to join him with that boyish grin of his that made my heart do funny things.

The earth rumbled and shifted beneath my feet, and I braced myself until I realized Kal was now standing in waist-deep water and he'd slowed the river's movement so it was as still as a lake.

"Did you just . . ." I gaped at him.

I sat down at the edge, then slowly lowered myself into the water, keeping my eyes on the prince the entire time. With every inch that I slipped inside, I could feel my tense muscles loosen a tiny bit more. First my toes. Then my ankles. My calves. My thighs.

I breathed in and out, focused. I could do this.

I slipped deeper. My hips. My waist. And finally . . . I was in, my feet on the ground. I took one last breath, then let go of the river's edge, letting the water surround me, feeling the gentle movement as it enveloped me completely.

And at last, I was *free*.

My water magic hummed in and around me, coming back to me, filling me with energy, lighting up my source. It raced inside me, zipping and tingling through my muscles and veins. It had been so long, I'd forgotten what it was like. It was a rush of sensations. I felt like laughing and crying at the same time.

I fell back into the water and released the biggest sigh as I allowed it to carry me. With the stars and sky above, a gentle breeze tickled my skin. The current beneath me complemented the wind as it nourished me. I could almost pretend I was back home. It had been too long since I'd been under the stars, outside at night. Too long since I'd felt their presence, their blessing. I, who was supposedly marked by the stars, blessed even, was given a second gift.

The water swirled around me in greeting, and at last, I let out a giggle, perhaps the first true joy I'd had since this all began. Remembering the prince was with me, I became self-conscious briefly before deciding it didn't matter. I laughed wholeheartedly at how absurd the whole situation was. How terrified I'd let myself become of my own element.

I swam over to Kal, unable to hold back the huge smile that took over my face as I stood before him. He folded his arms with a self-satisfied expression he had every right to wear, then feigned confusion.

"Have you seen my bride? She's a gorgeous little sea nymph, about this high, with a permanent glower."

I raised my hand to give him a teasing smack, but just before making contact, he snatched it in his, which he used to twirl me out and then back into his arms. Then he slid a hand behind my neck and lowered me into a dip. The water whirled around us in a frenzy, propelling our bodies together, and I grimaced at the idea that it was my magic behaving this way.

"There she is," he said as I glared up at him. "The tempest."

"Tempest? Why would you call me that?"

"Isn't that what you are? A whirlwind? A storm come to torment me and throw my world into chaos?"

I paused. It felt strange being accused of such a thing, and I suddenly feared he was leading me into a trap. Had I trusted him too early? Had it been a mistake revealing myself to him? Though destroying Kal's world wasn't what I'd originally come to Prisma to do, if I was to fulfill the prophecy, it probably was now. I wouldn't directly admit to it, yet there was also no sense in denying it. I had to be careful with my words.

"If that's truly what you believe, why help me?" I asked. "Shouldn't you be afraid?"

"That's a very good question . . . One I keep asking myself. One with an answer I can't quite explain . . . I shouldn't help you, but somehow, nothing in my world has felt right since you fell into it. Perhaps it is unwise. Perhaps I've a death wish . . ." He idly traced the contours of my face as he spoke, eliciting a pleasant chill.

"But to answer your question, Aella, if I may honestly tell you . . . at least one of my reasons is a noble one. I want to help you because you were right—my people aren't meant to rule over yours. I want to help you because it feels good being on your side. I want to help you because nothing is more threatening, more terrifying than you. So I will support you until the day you plunge a dagger into my hollow heart. Tell me, Tempest, what could be sweeter than loving the monster who's come to destroy you?"

"A monster?" I sputtered, leaning away from him. "Now, even if that were true, I'm sure my colossal failure washed away any suspicion."

"You're still here, aren't you?" he said, pulling me back into his arms. His lips brushed against the tip of my ear. "It's quite clear you have more than a few hidden concessions. Tell me, what other rebellions do you have planned?" He spun me out and away from him again.

I scoffed. "I don't know what you're talking about."

"Don't you though?" he asked with a half smile as he made a slow circle around me.

"And if I did, what makes you think I would tell you?" I followed him with my eyes.

"Perhaps we could work together, you and I . . . Perhaps we could come to an agreement." The prince was behind me now, his hands encircling my hips, guiding them to move with him in a primal sort of dance.

"Such as . . .?"

He said he wanted to help me, but although it sounded pretty, it would take more than just words to convince me he truly meant it. This was a dangerous rhythm we were in, and I couldn't allow him to think he was fully in control just because I'd revealed a few things to him.

"You help me improve my reputation while I do something useful for you. So long as it's within my power, I will agree to it." He twirled me again until I came face to face with him.

"Your reputation?" I asked, halting our dance. "How?"

"Let's just say my comrades have taken notice of my poor participation in the revels and lack of enthusiasm in recent days . . . They fear I've gone soft and that I no longer share their values."

"Ha! I saw you at the revel earlier this eve." I made my way to the edge of the river, climbing out to sit on the bank while dangling my feet over the side. "You appeared to be doing just fine in that department."

"It was a show, yes." His voice deepened. "But that wasn't for them."

I snorted. "For who then?"

He raised a brow in a way that told me I should have been able to figure that one out on my own.

"What? You thought you'd make me remember by making me jealous?"

"Were you . . . jealous?"

My eyes flashed as I realized what I'd just admitted.

"I was . . . entertained." I tried to act nonchalant in my recovery.

The smile on his face only grew wider, and I rolled my eyes at him.

Kal made his way over and sat next to me on the riverbank. He rested a hand next to mine, so close, our fingers nearly touched. Though they didn't even need to make contact to make tingles race all the way up my arm. I pulled my hand away, squeezing it in my lap, and focused my attention on the swish of water between my toes.

"Assisting me would help you in the long run," Kal went on to say, "but in the short term, I'd still owe you a favor."

I couldn't say no to a favor. I needed all the help I could get. But there were far too many things to ask for. What was most important? How could I decide? What lengths was he willing to go for his reputation? I wasn't sure if the big want was too much to ask, if it were even possible.

"Kill your father," I blurted before I could reconsider.

He laughed. "You would ask me to do that . . ." He sighed, scratching his head, staring up at the stars. Perhaps I'd sentenced him to death with that request. He could always say no.

"You do understand it may take years, perhaps even a century for me to build up the strength to challenge him, if ever at all."

"Even more reason to challenge him now. He'd never expect it, Kal."

"It's a funny thing. Before you, I hadn't actually considered it much. But more and more, I can't seem to rid the thought from my mind. If you knew how much time I've spent dreaming of it, how much I've wanted it . . ." He shook his head dismissively. "While I do vow to challenge him one day, I cannot give that to you just yet. Ask for something else. Anything."

"Anything?"

He nodded.

"I want the truth. Tell me where you were during the final event."

CHAPTER 23

FIERCE, PRIDEFUL, A LITTLE BIT RUDE

AELLA

"What's her name?"

"Rat, I suppose, though she's really more of a mouse." Kal cradled the tiny creature in his hands. I slowly reached toward her, and she sniffed a few times, poking her wet little nose in and out of his hands cautiously before gaining the confidence to scamper across and say hello.

"Oh, she's so warm," I hummed, and Kal beamed like a proud parent.

Rat had been roaming freely throughout the prince's wing when we'd happened upon her but was now content to come along with us. Once back in my bedchamber, which Kal had confirmed was actually his bedchamber, I set Rat on top of a stack of cushions placed on a cozy armchair, so she could be closer to eye level, and offered her a tiny buffet of soft cheeses, dried fruit, and nuts from the side table.

"Fit for a princess," Kal joked as we sat together on the divan across from Rat. "All right. I fear I've put it off long enough. Where do I begin?" he asked, looking almost as nervous as I felt.

I feared what his truth would mean—if I'd still trust him after, if any of it would make me feel better. I didn't want to think of the final event, it was so painful to remember, but I needed to know where he'd been. I needed to know why he'd broken his promise to me—why my friend had needed to die.

"From the beginning?" I suggested, willing strength into my tone.

"Yes, I suppose that would be best." He took a deep breath and paused for a long moment, as though searching for the right words. "Do you remember when Ramalia fell during the final event?"

"Of course. That was when Viera . . ." I couldn't say the words aloud.

"Was struck down," he finished for me. "She would have died if I hadn't gone to her."

I leaned forward, confused. "Wait . . . what do you mean, 'would have?'"

"I saw she was in Ramalia's path, so I risked breaking the most important rule of the Matri-Ludus and ran to the arena floor."

"You—" My breath caught. "You went to her?"

"I made you a promise, Aella. I gave my last favor to Viera because you asked me to. I couldn't sit there and allow her to die, knowing how much she meant to you. I'd have rather taken any punishment for intervening than let you down."

My eyes widened, and a storm brewed inside—shock, disbelief, anger, hope. "Tell me everything," I demanded.

Kal recounted every moment of Viera's rescue, sparing none of the details, and it was like the room was spinning, like the whole world began and ended in this little place where we sat. Then, like a dam breaking, my emotions poured out of me, and I wept, shoulders shaking with weeks of pent-up grief. Tears of joy that Viera hadn't died but also of sadness for the pain losing her had inflicted. Never could I have imagined hearing such news after so many days of darkness.

"She's really alive?" I whispered, voice trembling once my sobbing had subsided. The words sounded nonsensical coming from my lips. "All this time . . ."

"And she is safe." Kal nodded. "I made sure of it."

A laugh bubbled out of me, and then I stood abruptly from the divan and paced the room, rubbing the star-shaped mark on the back of my neck.

I turned to face the prince with a tearful smile. "I won't believe it until I see her. After everything . . . thinking she was gone . . ." My voice faltered. "She's alive."

"I'm sorry I did not reveal this to you sooner. I should have—"

Before he could finish, I threw my arms around him. "Thank you for giving me this news. I thought I'd lost everything." I pulled back and wiped my eyes. "Can you take me to her?"

"Nothing would please me more than to reunite you." His face fell, and with it, my spirits as I heard his reply. "I've given this much thought. Truly, I have." He shook his head. "There is simply no way for me to remove you from the palatium's grounds without raising unwanted suspicion and attention. And to make matters worse, if my father were to learn Viera is alive, he would surely destroy her. I know that isn't the answer you seek, but if it offers any comfort, I assure you she remains safe."

Even though that made sense, it was hard to accept and pretty much impossible not to worry about her. "Where is she?"

"She's serving as a lady's maid in a respectable household in Prisma."

"As long as she's in Prisma, she can't truly be safe, can she?"

"Were it within my power to find her safe passage, I would have done so without hesitation. Do you not think I'd have tried to free you as well?"

I rejoined him on the divan, hugging my knees. I wanted to believe Viera was truly all right, but after seeing her fall . . . I shook my head. Not until I saw her with my own eyes.

"Do you know what Estrella did?"

"My cousin has done many things." Kal frowned. "What are you referring to?"

"Poison . . . She assumed you'd give me your favor. It was meant for me."

Kal let out a floor-rumbling growl that caused shivers to go down my spine.

"There is no place on Esterra she can hide from my wrath. That she would dare to touch what is *mine* . . ." His eyes shone with malice when he turned to me. "I would shatter the world for you, if only you would ask. If you would like her head served to you on a silver platter, I will sever it myself."

In that moment, revenge sounded sweet to my ears, enticing. I could even envision myself taking part in it, but I held back. I wasn't like the Iris.

"Don't do anything hasty," I said, laying a hand on his arm. The muscles of his forearm clenched under my fingers. "I'm sure we can think of something a little less . . . violent." It was my job to help improve his reputation now, and I doubted killing his beloved cousin would do him any favors with his subjects. Though, I could never be too sure where they drew the line.

"My patience for her wears ever thinner by the day." He pulled his arm away. "However, regarding Viera, there is something else I must disclose." Kal recited the prophecy and told me about the treasonous note he'd found on Viera, claiming me as the prophesied one. "For all I knew, you'd been seducing me with the intent of killing me from the very first day we met."

"So this is why you call me Tempest," I said, bemused, though I failed to refute the claim. "And here I thought I was the one who was going mad . . ."

"Not quite mad enough. Speaking of which, did you want me to gather you some of the fruit? I've rather missed that side of you."

I shoved at him playfully, which he countered by capturing my wrist and pulling me onto his lap. My breath caught as I stared into his deep green eyes. They seemed to swallow me whole. His playful, wholehearted grin threatened to break down the rest of my walls.

A door snicked shut, and the fear of being caught like this—irrational but threatening all the same—made me shift. Kal rocked back, reacting to my sudden movement, and flipped the divan we were on, spilling us out onto the floor. But instead of getting up, the prince rolled onto his side to tend to me.

"What startled you so?" he asked. "It was only the maid coming to collect the water glass I left at your bedside table."

"So you've been the one leaving them for me." My eyes betrayed me, glancing briefly over at the unhappy potted plants I'd hidden a number of glasses in.

"I'm afraid they don't turn to sea glass when you bury them."

I rolled my eyes. "I was hiding them from Himmel!"

I laughed then at myself, at how ridiculous this all was. Conscious of how close our bodies were and how easy it would be to continue lying here next to him, I sat up. I expected the prince to jump up and dust himself off. To my surprise, he turned onto his back, resting his hands behind his head as though it were the most comfortable place he'd ever been.

"I think I quite like the view from down here."

I raised a brow at him.

"Come lie next to me and have a look."

Lowering myself back down, my eyes widened at the ceiling. Tiny windows in the shapes of stars glittered the rooftop, allowing the faint glow of moonlight in, but beyond the overall impression of scattered stars, whether it was by clusters or coincidence, I swore they formed the outline of an elongated, eight-pointed star. The same star that marked the nape of my neck. I blinked rapidly, thinking I must have just imagined it, but upon further inspection, it remained indisputably the same.

"I've never noticed this before."

"You can't really see it well from over there unless you know what to look for."

As we lay sprawled out on the floor, staring up at the starry, vaulted ceiling sparkling down on us as though it were the night sky, nothing was off-limits.

"I hated every moment of it, from the last our eyes met until you lay limp in my arms. I didn't know if it would work." He finally sat up, looking away from me as he spoke, as though too ashamed to see my response. "It was selfish of me to shield you when I saw the need in your eyes as you looked at that key."

"Why did you do it?" I asked.

He turned back to face me, eyebrows pinched. "I couldn't let them take you from me, not before getting answers. Not before I had a chance to ask you if anything between us had been real."

It had been real for me.

"And when I woke up nameless?" I asked.

"When I looked at you—empty and confused, all of your fearlessness gone, unable to talk back to me in that special way that only you do, in the way no one else has ever dared—I told myself you were gone." Sorrow shone in his eyes. "I wondered if perhaps it was for the best, that you'd gotten what you'd wanted and your suffering was over."

If only my suffering had ended there.

"You could have wiped your hands clean of me," I said, shaking my head. "Why leave water at my bedside? Why defend me against those guards?"

"Yes, your becoming nameless afforded me the ability to walk away from all the shame of failing you, of never protecting you the way you deserved. Trust me when I say that sense of relief was short-lived, quickly replaced by an aching hole in my chest I swore would never fill. I was willing to spend the rest of my life as empty inside as you were. You have done something to me, something I'm not sure I can ever quite change or repair."

I had to remind myself to breathe, to process all he was saying. I had felt his absence just as strongly, even when I hadn't wanted to. Even when I'd wanted to hate him, he'd been missing from me.

Kal held my hands in his, staring directly into my soul as he spoke. "It didn't matter if it was still you or not, I did it in honor of you." His eyes brightened as he continued, and a dark grin spread across his face. "You know, I pictured our lives together, how I'd crown you my queen. You'd make an excellent ruler—fierce, prideful, a little bit rude . . ." He winked at me, and I scoffed.

"You wouldn't have taken faex from anyone, Tempest. You were born for this. Together, we'd have transformed Prisma—all of Esterra. Alas, those were only fantasies. Besides, what kinds of rulers would we have been? One void of spirit, the other void of heart."

My soul ached hearing his truths. I wanted to tell him it wasn't too late, that I wanted those fantasies just as much as he did, but a part of me held back, knowing they were nothing more than wistful dreams. If I was the one who was prophesied, they could never come true. And perhaps even love wasn't enough—we would still be enemies in the end.

"Did you ever suspect I wasn't nameless?"

"Every now and then, there was some small mannerism, a tone in your voice, or a storm in your eyes that would give you away. As much as I tried to convince myself you were gone, it was impossible not to see you underneath it all. At times, you played the role so well, I second-guessed myself. Nonetheless, I kept hoping you were just pretending, and I would have pretended along with you for as long as we lived if that was what you'd wanted, but when I saw you with the book last night . . . You reminded me of someone, and that's when I feared I'd truly lost you."

I opened my mouth to speak, to give him some kind of explanation, but found myself speechless.

"I don't blame you for withholding your truth, Aella. I have not earned that from you, but perhaps I might yet."

CHAPTER 24
A Cold Journey

Nervous energy flooded the air as the day to leave for Concordia finally arrived. What would we find when we got there? Had the people we'd sent ahead arrived safely? Had they managed to create shelters and a meeting place for us? Would the other courts show up? So many questions flitted through my mind as I finished lacing up my boots and pulled on a warm, leather coat.

The messenger Wynn had sent to Prisma for information still hadn't returned. Wynn had assured me the scouts we'd sent ahead would be on the lookout for him.

I was desperate for any news on the Matri-Ludus and whether or not Aella was okay. The dreams hadn't stopped, and I was finding myself even more concerned. I just had to keep reminding myself she was strong and the stars were on her side. She had to be all right. I would accept no other outcome.

With my few belongings packed, I made my way to the aquila aeries. Knowing we would be flying for hours, I appreciated the chance to stretch my legs and move around, even though my calves burned not even halfway down the never-ending stairs that wound through Zephyria. My breaths came out in cloudy puffs of air in the crisp, cold weather. I had forgotten what it was like to be up at this altitude and away from my element—though visiting the new lake had worked wonders for my soul. The others had gone ahead to make preparations, so I enjoyed my remaining moments of solitude.

I couldn't help but worry and wonder how my family would fare once news reached them. Would they be scared or excited to travel somewhere unknown? Rik had reassured me they'd send extra help to pick up the children and they wouldn't need to take the treacherous path I'd taken. A pang went through me when Fide's face flashed through my mind. I truly prayed he was at peace. He'd been such a kind soul.

The emotional and physical toll from that journey would last. Once Henri and I had taken off for Zephyria, I'd passed out for the duration of the journey. We'd barely spoken upon our arrival, as I'd rushed off to the palatium. I wondered if I'd see him at the aeries so I could once again express my thanks for saving me.

"Ari!" Helio exclaimed when I finally reached the aeries and caught up to the group that would be traveling to Concordia.

I spied Wynn discussing plans with Glint and Rik while I walked toward Helio adjusting the saddle on his aquila. Wynn hadn't even bothered asking me to fly with him. If I was being honest with myself, it would have been far too intimate. I didn't need more memories of the past muddling my present or my future.

"Is anyone else joining us?" I asked out of curiosity.

"Kairi is staying here to keep an eye on things, and we already have people waiting for us. We don't want the group to be too large," Helio replied.

"Yes, that makes perfect sense." I hesitated before asking him the question I was dreading. "Would it be all right if I flew with you?"

"Of course. I'd be more than happy to have you," he replied with a grin. "If we weren't both married, I'd use this time to make some inappropriate jokes, but alas . . ."

I couldn't hold back my laugh but stifled it when the others looked our way, questions in their eyes.

Helio helped me mount his bird, telling me her name was Lunaya.

"She's lovely!" I stroked her sleek feathers, gray like the moon.

Glint got on a bird with Valerik while Wynn simply nodded at me before calling out final orders to the team.

With the exception of Glint being on this trip, I couldn't help but compare it to my first mission with the cabala. The biggest difference being how Wynn could barely look at me now. I reminded myself he had every right to be angry. We were leaving on an extremely dangerous mission to rescue the daughter he had only just learned about. That was a lot to process. Along with the fact that he seemed to struggle being around me.

Glint smiled at Wynn, her golden skin and cornsilk hair shining in the light. They would have made a pretty pair, and I wondered if there had ever been anything between them.

"You know, your thoughts are written all over your face," Helio said before climbing up in front of me.

"I have no idea what you're talking about." I laughed awkwardly.

He chuckled. "Glint and Wynn are just friends—there's never been anything more between them."

The odd relief I'd felt that he *hadn't* married Katye returned in full force, but this time, I was happy he hadn't been with one of his best friends. Did that make me a terrible person?

"Like I'd care if there had been! I was just thinking they'd look nice together."

"Sure, Ari." Helio poked my shoulder.

"I want him to be happy."

There was an ache in my heart when I remembered the pain I'd felt inside him, a sadness I couldn't quite release.

"That's what we all want. Sadly, he's been pretty closed off for years." Helio said quietly, sounding defeated, as if he'd been carrying his friend's burden for just as long.

"What do you mean?"

"Wynn changed after you left. He never told us what happened—we just knew his parents were pushing for a big wedding with Katye and he refused."

"I honestly thought he'd be married to her with a whole bunch of children by now."

"He's never been with anyone the way he was with you," Helio said softly before pulling a pair of goggles out of his pack.

"What are those for?" I asked, arching a brow. "A pair just like them showed up in my room the other day with a note to pack them for the trip."

Helio grinned. "You're gonna want to put them on."

I tilted my head. "I never needed to before."

"Buckle up, Ari. You're in for a wild and chilly ride. I can't shield the way Wynn can up here."

My eyes widened in awe at the ingenuity as I pulled them out of my pack and slipped them over my head, tightening them while Helio donned his own.

"Bet you're wishing you'd asked to fly with Rik or Wynn right about now," he teased.

"Nonsense. It'll be totally fine," I replied as memories of my solo journey came back to me. I'd kept my eyes shut tight for most of the flight. "You didn't wear them last time I was here."

"That's because we didn't have them back then. One of our Aurum refugees, who joined the patrol maybe twenty years ago, invented them to help with his comfort while flying. I don't always use them, but they're nice to have."

"Brilliant," I replied, glad I had worn my hair in a tight braid woven around my head.

Our birds jumped off the cliffside, wings spread wide to catch the drifts, and my stomach almost lurched out of my throat at the feeling. The wind whipped at my clothing, the air freezing my exposed skin. I was grateful for the warmth of Helio in front of me, but the biting wind was still fearsome.

Maybe I should have asked Rik after all.

Our trip down to Concordia took us through the middle of the continent. Once we'd gotten out of the alps, the land stretched beneath us in rolling hills and forests. A serpentine river flowed far below, leading us south. After passing the smaller mountains on the outskirts of the Court of Water, we moved further west so we'd approach Concordia from that direction instead of the easthen side that was closer to Prisma.

It was our last night before our arrival in Concordia, and as we sat around the fire eating roasted game, Wynn nonchalantly looked over at me and announced, "I received a message over the wind from one of our scouts, the one we sent to Prisma for information."

My ears perked up immediately, my eyes wide. "Did you learn anything about Aella?"

"He said he would meet us in Concordia and fill us in," he replied gruffly, averting his gaze.

My shoulders slumped in disappointment. I'd wanted more news than that, but at least we'd hear more tomorrow. "Okay. Thanks for letting me know."

Helio knocked his shoulder into mine. "Hey, at least he got out in one piece! Thank the stars for that."

"You're right," I said, smiling up at him. "Thank you for being such an optimist. I'm usually more positive, but it's been hard."

Wynn suddenly stood and stalked off into the woods.

"Did I do or say something wrong?" I asked, my eyebrows raised.

Glint let out a small laugh from across the fire. "While you might have moved on from Wynn years ago, I believe he never lost hope you'd return to him someday. Let's just say being around you is chafing a little."

I blew out a frustrated breath. "I wish I knew what to do to make things easier for him."

"Just give him space, Arianwen," Glint replied. "I'm starting to see some hints of the old Wynn, and that gives me faith."

"What in the stars do you mean by that?" I frowned. "Even Helio mentioned that Wynn changed."

Rik, Helio, and Glint exchanged glances, all seemingly unwilling to divulge more.

"What are you not saying?" I asked again.

Rik finally shrugged. Looking around to make sure Wynn was still gone, he flicked his hand out, creating what I assumed was a sound barrier. "It wasn't immediate, but he kind of stopped caring to the same degree he used to. He'd always been one of the most active members of our rescue parties, always risking everything to save as many elementals as possible and taking every loss personally. After we lost Eden, he just stopped."

"Eden?" I gasped, remembering the kind Aereus female in Wynn's cabala. "I was wondering where she was . . ."

Helio teared up. "That loss hit all of us hard."

I leaned into him, the lump in my throat preventing me from speaking.

"Our missions became fewer and farther between, and it's been years since Wynn joined us on one, for multiple reasons," Rik continued. "I am slightly concerned about how this meeting with the rebel leaders will go, considering how distant Wynn has been over the last ten to fifteen years."

As Rik spoke, my brows almost reached my hairline. Yes, Wynn had been cold toward me, but I'd chalked that up to his anger at my secret and for putting him in the position to risk lives to get Aella back. Despite knowing his behavior was not all my fault, I couldn't help but feel slightly guilty.

"That sounds so unlike him," I said softly. "I guess he really isn't the Wynn I used to know."

Glint let out a small laugh. "Never underestimate the power love has to change or destroy us."

"We'd only known each other a few months," I scoffed, but even as I spoke, I heard the lie for what it was. "I'd hardly say we were in love. Lust, absolutely. But Wynn never once told me he loved me."

Lying to yourself doesn't make it hurt any less, Ari.

Glint's eyes flickered in the firelight, seeming to blaze with the reflection of her element. "You were young fools, highly infatuated with one another. Anyone could see that. But don't write off love." She looked at me pointedly. Did she see the truth written on my face despite my words? "He may have never said it, but the connection between you two was far deeper than lust."

I looked down solemnly at my hands. "I know mistakes were made, and perhaps I should've given him more of a chance to explain or tried to work things out, but the reality is, he shattered my trust. If I had told him I was going to marry Verus and fly off and visit him on weekends, do you think he'd have been satisfied with that? I doubt he would've shared, so why should he have expected me to?"

Helio groaned, palming his face. "Yeah, he really mucked that one up."

"Anyway," Rik spoke up again, "you asked how he's changed? Ultimately, he's been focused on learning how to rule the Court of Air and coming up with creative ways to replace resources. Zephyria would've been closed to refugees by now if it weren't for him."

My eyes widened, and I sat up straighter.

"Even still, we're running out of space. I wouldn't be surprised if we stopped taking in refugees sooner than later," Helio lamented.

"I noticed it was more crowded and the markets seemed a little sparse, but closing Zephryia? Even more reason to fight against the Iris. We've waited far too long to take action, and they only grow stronger," I said, raising my voice. "If what they've done in small towns like Lakehaven is any indication, the rest of the continent could be suffering the same."

"That sounds like reports of what we've been hearing from the east as well," Glint confirmed. "I hope you're right, Ari. Perhaps this is the spark that lights a fire underneath Wynn and he returns to the leader I first decided to follow."

Helio and Rik nodded in agreement.

"I still can't believe Wynn has a kid," Helio said with a laugh. "He's so grumpy—he'd be a terrible father."

An icy gust of wind blew right past me, pushing Helio off the log we'd been sitting on, and he yelped in surprise.

"You were saying?" Wynn said, clearly unamused.

Helio brushed himself off as he stood. "You only prove my point." He laughed.

Wynn growled in annoyance.

I wondered when Rik had dropped the air barrier and how much Wynn had overheard. I missed the Wynn who joked around with his friends. This overly sensitive and grumpy male was new. The Wynn I had known would have made an incredible father. I only hoped he'd have the chance someday, and perhaps Aella would at least want to get to know him.

CHAPTER 25

GLAMOUR

AELLA

Colored smoke surrounded us in a shimmering haze of violet and blue, partially concealing the sweat-slicked, writhing bodies of revelers as they sated themselves with the many pleasures offered. Iris drenched the elemental dancers in a mist of sparkling wines, then drank the golden liquid off their bodies. Music thumped too loud to even speak, the tempo hypnotic. I couldn't help but feel it pull me in.

Though the beat was fast, my heart pounded faster with Kal's arm slung around my bare waist. My dress that evening consisted of a tiny, indigo-colored halter, fastened with a false-iron collar at my neck and a fluffy skirt made of hundreds of layers of sheer fabric that started at the narrowest part of my waist. To keep up appearances, I was adorned in an assortment of false-iron jewelry, from the circlet atop my head to the thick, chained bracelets and anklets that resembled the ones meant to keep my powers from me.

Kal had insisted on ordering my lessons and appearances to stop, but I'd been adamant about keeping some of the revels. I couldn't very well accomplish any of my plans of rebellion if I remained locked up in his wing at all times. He'd initially rejected the idea after hearing about all of the torments Estrella and Himmel had put me through, but ultimately, he'd relented and had taken it upon himself to be my escort.

"You ready to leave?" Kal's breath danced over the tip of my ear, and goosebumps raced up my arms and neck. We'd only just gotten to the revel, and I sensed he was aiming to be respectful toward me, but standing in the midst of such antics together without actively participating was terribly awkward. I honestly couldn't blame him for wanting to get out of there. His lips brushed over my ear again as though he might say something else. I shivered, and his forearm flexed around my waist.

We'd agreed that I would help him with his reputation, but it seemed, by the looks we were getting, his escorting me to the revel was possibly hurting more than helping. I got the feeling his Iris subjects weren't at all impressed by his restraint and that they considered Kal's behavior too protective for a worthless, nameless elemental fae. He needed to gain the admiration of his peers, which I didn't think would happen so long as we stood as stiff as the guards.

Taking a deep breath, I willed myself to relax. *I can do this.* I closed my eyes for a moment to try to let the beat carry me away, let it guide my movement. This didn't need to be hard. Unless I was missing something, all I needed to do was make him look like the immoral Iris prince that he was. Though how exactly that would be accomplished remained a mystery. I shuddered to think I'd unknowingly agreed to more than I'd realized. *Perhaps a little wine might help.*

Untangling from his arm, I made my way over to grab us drinks from the table in our private lounge. I held out a flute for him, but he laughed, stealing the bottle instead. He took a hefty swig, then lifted my chin slightly before tilting the bottle to my lips and pouring the fizzing liquid down my throat. The buzz hit immediately, and I pulled back, some of the golden wine spilling down my neck. Kal's eyes followed the trail, and I half expected him to lick it off as I'd seen so many around us do. But he turned away, finishing the bottle instead and then took me by the hand to go sit with him.

I sank into the cushioned seating area, so soft, it felt like it might swallow me whole, and the prince spread himself out, resting his head in my lap as though to take a nap. I stroked a hand through his silky, black curls, and he shivered slightly but continued to lie there with his eyes closed, relaxed with a slight smile. His legs were crossed at the ankles, but he tapped a foot to the beat. Ever the careless prince.

I shook my head and closed my eyes, allowing myself to enjoy the pleasant thrill and somewhat tranquilizing nature of his company.

The days bled together as we attended more revels and began staying out later. We made quite the spectacle walking through the halls together. Kal had ordered his designers to craft us the most beautiful and extravagant outfits, not quite matching but complementing each other perfectly. From glamorous suits and gowns with intricate beading, to striking and powerful ones in which precious metals and jewels mimicked armor, ornamenting our shoulders and brows. Some of my preferred looks were the more simple and sleek ones made of light, breathable fabrics that highlighted and hugged the contours of our bodies, showing off all of my curves and the sharp lines and edges of his body.

We paired well together, easily outshining all others. I'd noticed the jealous glares and sneers of females who'd deemed me so far beneath them. As contemptible as it was, I'd started enjoying the feeling of having what so many of them wanted, even if it was only on the outside. For once, I had something over them.

This new show of the two of us together had a sort of ripple effect in the way it influenced the courtiers and revelers. The strangest response was when they'd started bringing more elementals into the palatium. I wasn't sure how I felt about it, because on one hand, it helped even the playing field between Iris and elemental fae, giving me more opportunities to see and interact with elementals, but on the other hand, it could be a dangerous new trend for the Iris to follow. Soon, they'd all want to show off their elemental pets at the revels. I wondered if it would bring in one of my fellow contestants, but I had yet to see any of them.

After making our rounds, Kal had made a habit of sneaking me out to the gardens for a midnight swim under the stars. He'd sit with his back against a tree, reading a book, sometimes with Rat on his shoulder, while I floated, renewed by my elements. I wasn't sure how he could actually read with only the glow of fireflies, unless the Iris had some kind of superior night vision. I hadn't asked. Just noticed his occasional far-off stares or his smoldering, stolen glances.

Since our agreement, Kal had spent most of his energy and attention tightening his connections and garnering support throughout the pala-tium. In his spare time, he poured through books, researching ways to overthrow his father's rule. He'd been keeping full transparency with me, earning my trust more and more each day. Outside of our evening plans, there had been no more affections shared between us, limiting all flirtatious interactions to the revels. I wasn't sure if they had all been for show for him, but they surely hadn't been for me. I couldn't deny how he'd captivated me—emotionally, intellectually, and physically. I was drawn to him as it seemed he might also be drawn to me.

One night, as we walked to our usual spot, I took off my slippers and hung my luxurious, black velvet robe on a branch of the tree the prince always sat under. I meandered over to the water, about to slip in, then paused with a daring thought.

"Are you going to sit there and pretend to read all night, or will you join me for a swim?"

Kal set down his book, raising a thick brow. "It's probably best if I stay here and keep watch."

"You can watch me from there . . . or you can watch me from here," I said, then pulled the silk gown over my head. Kal's jaw slackened, and I jumped into the water with a laugh I couldn't suppress any longer. Blush-ing furiously, I waited beneath, counting the seconds until a large splash disturbed the crystal clear water.

Kal swam to me with a devilish grin. He hadn't even bothered to take off his shoes, he'd come running so quickly. When he thought he had me, I bolted, making him chase after me. I'd been getting stronger, and while he could probably still outswim me any other day, the drag of his clothes slowed him down. It was a thrill, swimming nude, taunting him. For a brief moment, I could almost forget I was a prisoner, pretending I was wild and free again. I let him catch me after a good little game of cat and mouse, and when he finally did, we surfaced together in raucous laughter.

"Maybe you should stick to reading. You're not a very fast swimmer," I teased.

"Perhaps if I wasn't so distracted . . ." he replied, swimming backward until he reached the edge, never taking his eyes off me.

"You're too easy," I said.

"What can I say? I know what I like."

"It's only a naked body. I'm sure you've seen your fair share."

Kal raised an eyebrow and pulled off his shoes one by one, tossing them out onto the grass, then he unbuttoned his blouse, flinging it out as well.

"Is it my turn to be distracted?" I asked.

"It's only fair."

Butterflies fluttered through my belly, making me so light, I might have flown away. We stared at each other from across the river, the span of water between us seeming to thin now that he was promising me what was sure to be heaven with his eyes.

Voices broke through the fog of desire. Distant but approaching. Kal's ear twitched as he heard them too.

"Swim to the bottom of the river. I have a plan," he said.

I dove down and waited for him to join me. Kal followed, positioning himself directly above, shielding me from whoever was intruding on us. What would they think if they saw me out here among my elements? What of Kal's complicity in the act?

I tried to look past his shoulder when Kal stopped me, holding my face to his, and he kissed me. It was a kiss for distraction, but a kiss nonetheless.

And it was everything.

Weightlessly floating, the prince sucked my lip between his, his tongue sliding over mine to the roof of my mouth, linking us in a mind-numbing connection that sent lightning racing through me in all directions. The whole world fell away as our tongues and lips intertwined, ripples of heat racing across my skin, down my arms and legs, to the very tips of my fingers and toes, and all the way down my spine. Though he wasn't physically touching me beyond the lock of our lips and tongues tethering us together, it felt as though he were kissing me everywhere, all at once. No breath could sustain me as the magic of this kiss. Source power and something else flowed in and through me, charging me full of life. The water twirled around us, drawing us nearer one another as though approving of our bond.

Kal pulled away from the kiss, giving me a somewhat odd look, and I wondered if he'd felt it too. If the kiss had been as breathtaking and life-altering for him as it had been for me. If he'd felt the cold but delicious shock of it to his very bones, overcome by the rush of indescribable feelings.

Suddenly, I noticed the unfamiliar tone of my skin, streaked in silver, and the dark teal shade of my hair floating around me in the water.

"What is this?" I asked, my voice full of alarm as I stared wide-eyed at the unique, marbled pattern on my skin.

"A little glamour to change your coloring. Don't worry—you still look like yourself, though I doubt anyone but me would know it's you."

Kal wrapped his broad arms around me, swimming us up to the surface. He pressed me up against the riverbank, one of his hands over my head, the other gripping my thigh to wrap it tightly around him.

"As I see it, we have two options. One, we try to sneak away undetected," he whispered against my lips as a group of revelers approached. "Two, you play along and pretend to be Iris."

"Aren't they going to know as soon as I speak and I don't sound Iris?" I countered, my words pressed against his jaw.

Kal huffed a laugh. "You might keep your mouth busy elsewhere."

I gasped, raising my hand to slap him. But he caught my wrist, pinning it up above my head.

"Not here, little tempest," he said with a wink and the wickedest of grins. Sliding his knee up between my thighs, he captured my mouth in his again and then resumed kissing me all the way down my neck.

"But you need not play along if you do not want to. All you need do is blink twice," he said between kisses. "Blink twice if at any moment you're uncomfortable or if you change your mind, and I *will* stop."

I didn't know what to do, the desire to continue touching him, feeling him was so strong, I ached with it, but the fear of confronting the Iris was even more so. At least this way, I wouldn't have to speak, and maybe they'd just go away. I couldn't believe I was even considering going through with this, but their voices were growing louder and my time to decide was running out. I needed to make a choice. As crazy as it seemed, I couldn't think of a better alternative, and perhaps this would impress his friends enough to help me fulfill my end of the agreement. I could go along with it, at least until I didn't feel comfortable anymore. And I trusted his word enough that he'd stop if I asked. Didn't I?

"Do what you will with me," I said, my voice husky as I nodded.

Kal gave me the most devious smile, adding a sense of wariness to the thrill I felt over what I'd just agreed to. As though someone had doused me with a bucket of ice-cold water, I became painfully aware that I was practically naked with nothing more than an undergarment covering my lower half and the water's reflective surface to conceal me.

With one of my hands pinned overhead, Kal nuzzled his face against my neck, then began kissing me there. I suppressed a moan, my eyes fixed on the group of Iris who neared us. This kind of behavior was completely normal for them. This was what they did. If I were to show fear or inhibition, I would stand out, making them suspicious.

While I'd seen the Iris do worse in public, I'd never taken a lover out in the open before. This was new for me, and I burned with embarrassment at the idea of being watched or heard making such intimate noises. The feeling of wrongness engulfed my senses, but what surprised me was how it intensified my yearning for him and, worst of all, excited me.

"No need to be shy," Kal whispered as though sharing a secret, his breath hot over the delicate skin of my collarbone as he marked me with a trail of kisses. "There is nothing to be ashamed of, Tempest. This is beautiful." He took my other wrist, pinning it up above my head against the riverbank so I was now even more vulnerable and exposed, my skin going taut against the cool night breeze. "*You* are beautiful. Everything about you—from the taste of your skin to the melody of your voice."

My heart raced as I tested his firm hold on my wrists, finding myself completely defenseless against him.

"The Iris like being watched," he said, the timbre of his voice so deep, it rumbled through me. "And you are glorious when you sing for me."

Kal trailed kisses down my chest, taking a mouthful, summoning a wave of ecstasy that undulated through my very foundation. The sensation was so viciously good, it could very well have been enough to end me. His teeth raked over my skin, and when he gently bit down, tugging ever so slightly, I couldn't help the soft cry that escaped. Not knowing what he might do next was both thrilling and terrifying.

Kal looked up at me through thick lashes, his green gaze darkening with intensity as he held such a sensitive part of me between his teeth. Horrified and entranced all at once, I wanted more of him. I wanted to run. I wasn't sure why it hadn't hit me until that point, but in a sobering moment, the reality sunk in that he was a predator and I was his prey. Trapped in his clutches, I might never get out.

"Is that the prince?" a feminine voice said. "I wonder who he's with now?"

Kal continued kissing and nipping, holding me by my wrists, his knee between my thighs. As the prince endeavored to devour me, my body acted of its own volition, giving in to the need to arch my back and move with him. Kal made a deep, purring sound that resonated all the way down to my hips.

"There you are! Kaleidos, we've been looking all over for you. We have a little surprise for you but were told you weren't in your wing," came a deeper voice from just across the river.

Kal maintained eye contact with me, tongue and teeth teasing once more, daring me to make him stop. I went completely still in anticipation, my thighs flexed around him, wrists straining against his hands to be let free. I couldn't take it anymore, and he knew it. All it would take to get him to stop was a couple of blinks. He watched me, and I met his gaze, nervous but unwavering. Kal bit down, harder this time, making me cry out.

"Can't you see I'm quite occupied at the moment?" the prince drawled without turning his head to look at the intruders. He finally released my wrists, lacing his fingers with mine right when I needed it most. Our palms touching, I suddenly felt more in control, like we were in this together, and I relished that. He buried his face in my neck, which shot tingles down my spine all over again.

"As happy as we are to see you back to your old shenanigans, this surprise you won't want to wait for. It was Estrella's idea. It's for your . . . uhh . . . your bride," the Iris male said. "I'm sure Shelwin wouldn't mind taking over where you left off." He winked at me. Nothing about that sounded good. Nothing involving Estrella could be.

"Where are you from?" the Iris female said as she began stripping off her already barely there gown. "I don't recall seeing you before. Mind if I join?"

My eyes widened before I could help myself. *How would an Iris behave?* Jealous maybe? I kissed Kal possessively, pulling him down into the water with me. I could feel his lips form a smile even as he kissed me back, clearly amused by this game. The Iris female swam over to us as Kal and I surfaced again. Thankfully, he held up his hand to her.

"She's newly arrived from her family's outside station. A little on the possessive side though, aren't you, kitten?" he teased.

I kissed him in answer, biting his bottom lip hard enough to draw a drop of blood, which seemed to delight him even more. I gave him a look that told him he was going to pay for that nickname. He grabbed my rear, pulling me harder against him.

"If you wouldn't mind . . ." he said, using the water to push the female up and out of the river. She squealed as she was thrown onto the grass.

"Not nice, Kaleidos!" she protested.

The others giggled.

Kal formed a turbine beneath us and lifted us out of the water, depositing us gracefully on the opposite side of the river.

"How about I meet you back in my wing when the moon marks her descent," Kal offered his friends while I wrapped myself in his discarded shirt.

"Oh, Kaleidos. Always the showoff," the handsome Iris male said, then to me, "Don't let him wear you completely out. Some of us might enjoy a turn giving you a proper welcome to Prisma."

"I won't make any promises," Kal said with a wink, then threw me over his shoulder, running us back to his room.

CHAPTER 26
WEDDING GIFT

AELLA

My hand whipped through the air, smacking Kal across his chest playfully. "Call me kitten again . . ." I said, still laughing after he'd carried me back to the bedchamber half naked. My palm burned from the impact with the rock-hard muscles of his chest, my hand's unusual color fading back to silver and the rest following suit until the entire glamour was gone. Kal didn't flinch, nor did his marble skin redden in the slightest, but he avoided eye contact, which was odd.

"Punish me if you will, but save some of that heat for the bedroom." The words rolled off his tongue in that cheeky tone of his as he made his way over to his closet. "It appears my evening is not yet over. However, I will do my best to keep the courtiers away."

I followed him into the closet, which was one of the locked doors I'd been forbidden from entering until now. I took a moment to marvel at his seemingly endless collection of embellishments, from cufflinks, to rings, earrings, crowns, broaches, and more. Another door within the closet led to a bathing suite worthy of a king. Though it wasn't a deep, cavern-like spring as in my dream, the pool was wide and appeared to extend outdoors onto a terrace. I'd need to ask him for the key.

The prince paused rifling through his evenly spaced silk tunics and blouses and combed his fingers through his damp, tousled hair.

He groaned. "Stars, you are a tempest. You were . . ." He turned slightly toward where I stood at the door to the bathing suite with my arms folded across my chest. He seemed unable to finish his sentence and turned back to the mirror to admire himself in an oversized green shirt so dark, it was nearly black. It was a loose fit but fell just right, hanging open far enough in the front that it left little of his lean, muscled physique to the imagination. He then layered himself in an array of necklaces and rings, which, on anyone else, would have appeared a bizarre and chaotic combination. On him, the mismatched textures and metals looked both effortlessly alluring and curated to perfection. He finished his look, going for a simple, braided, mixed-metal crown that sat low on his brow. "Well, let's just say I don't think any of them have reason to suspect you."

"I've seen enough examples at the revels to play the part," I said, pushing a thick lock of my hair behind my ear.

"Of course . . . Remember how I once told you I live with more restrictions than you would think?" He stepped toward me, stroking his hand down my damp hair, but he kept his gaze fixed on my shoulder. "Every move I make is watched. Every action I take or withhold is a means for them to question my power, my authority, my ability to rule Esterra one day."

"If you can't prove to them you are as monstrous as your father, you could very well inspire a revolt," I said. I'd known going into this agreement that it was just a means to an end for him. Yet I silently wished there was more to it than that.

"Precisely. They want someone to condone their selfish acts, someone to inspire more of them. If I threaten any of that, I will lose every last ounce of their respect and adoration." Kaleidos rubbed his face. "I've made a name for myself by being the embodiment of the Iris spirit. What will they think if I suddenly change?"

I closed my eyes. I'd hoped he would've said something about what'd happened between us, but it felt like he was brushing off our connection, as if it had been nothing more than a ruse.

He's only talking about his reputation. I should take the hint.

Kal stepped toward me, holding the back of my head in his hands, and sank his forehead down to mine. "To be honest, I have no idea what to do. I have no model to follow. All I know is that suspicion on their part will only lead to more pain and suffering for you."

I wanted to melt against him, to believe what he was saying, but I was too disoriented by the idea that I seemed to have been the only one truly affected by that kiss.

"Tell me what to do, Tempest," he continued, voice softer this time. "Show me the way. I don't know how to be honorable except in the ways that you inspire me."

"Well, that show should have worked to fix your reputation, right? So, are we even?" I asked, refusing to show any emotion on the matter. I needed to distance myself from him, from this pathetic feeling in my chest.

Kal stepped back, appearing stunned by what I'd just said. "I never would have made you do something like that as a part of the agreement."

"So long as you don't require anything else from me at this moment, I think I'd better get dressed before anyone shows up." I waited only one second for an answer and then turned on my heel to march out of his closet.

"Are you angry with me?" he asked, following me out.

"No, Kal . . . I . . . I'm frustrated. My feelings are irrational. I can only blame myself." I scoffed. "But that's not your problem. I'll be fine. Now, go before your friends come looking." I pointed to the door.

Kal bunched his brows together.

"You wouldn't want them to figure out it was actually me glamoured as one of them, would you?" I asked.

"I'll make them leave. No one will come near you."

I took a deep breath, reminding myself what was most important. I had to stop letting my heart get in the way. "And undo all the effort we just put in? No. Allow me to play the part so you can get the power and respect you need to rule."

Kal squeezed his eyes shut. "Are you certain?"

"Yes."

"Then let us do it right." He reached out toward the wall, and a vine grew up from one of his many plants to wrap around and tug at the maids' bell cord beside the bed before shriveling up and withering away. The sight was so jarring, I couldn't help but shrug away from him.

"I'm curious to know why you didn't blink earlier?" he asked, his gaze finally meeting mine.

Because as terrified as I'd been, I hadn't wanted him to stop. Because it had meant more to me than just the little game we were playing. But I wouldn't tell him that when he'd just made it abundantly clear what his only motive was.

"I wanted to see how far you would go," I replied.

Kal stepped nearer again. "Did you like it?" He hummed into my ear, sending tingles all the way down my neck, my eyes fluttering shut. I inhaled deeply, his sea-salt-and-oak scent intoxicating me. But we both sensed someone coming, and when I pulled away from him, he did not follow. Even with the maids, it was best I wasn't caught still dripping from our illegal swim.

Although I'd spent time swimming under the stars, my powers weren't recovering as quickly as I'd wanted. It would probably take time to get my full strength back, though I wasn't sure if my source would ever be fully restored so long as I remained captive in Prisma. For appearance's sake, I willed the water to leave, and with every last drop removed, I fought the tears that threatened to escape. *I won't allow even one more drop of water to be taken from me without my permission.*

The door opened on silent hinges, and my maids returned, basket of brushes and beauty products in hand. They'd come to make me fit for whatever presentation Estrella had planned. My shoulders tightened at the reminder that, whatever it was, it couldn't possibly be good.

"Before you go," I said, as I walked Kal to the door. "I need one more agreement from you before you join your guests."

Kal raised a brow in question.

"I will play along with whatever games you need for the evening, but I need something in return."

"Name it."

"That when the time comes, you will not stop me from seeking revenge against Estrella."

Hardly any time had passed before the prince's wing was crawling with Iris revelers. Kal left me to join them in a bid to distract them away from me, but I was gripped by the unwanted feelings of jealousy after seeing the way his friends behaved among each other. I wondered who was on his arm or his lap, what Estrella's nefarious plan was, and what, if anything, Kal would do to stop her.

Though I had prevented him from taking revenge on Estrella for her hand in the games, I still loathed her. I feared that, despite his words, he might maintain a softer side for his cousin, but I knew we couldn't trust her. Estrella marched around the palatium like she was the true heir. I wouldn't be surprised if she had plans more devious than Kal credited her for.

The thumping of music and merriment came from the adjacent rooms as Kasha and Yulema made the finishing touches on my hair. My doors were locked, but it wasn't much consolation, as I was never sure someone wouldn't force their way in.

I had been waiting for them to enter at any moment but still jumped when the door swung open to the lavender-haired princess and her following. Her normally voluptuous curls were slicked back flat against her scalp in a shiny glaze. It was secured in a long ponytail so straight, it appeared razor sharp. She eyed me up and down with a sneer, then directed a long, pointed fingernail toward where I sat at the vanity.

"Is it safe without a collar?" Estrella asked aloud.

"I haven't seen her wear one in days," one of her followers said. "But she's nameless. What are you so afraid of?" The Iris laughed, which clearly irritated Estrella even more.

Estrella wrinkled her nose in disgust before stomping out, ponytail swinging behind her like a whip. "Bring her to the great hall," she commanded the guards.

Escorted by both of my handmaids and the guards, I made my entrance in the most magnificent, shimmering black gown that trailed behind me like a pool of starlight. Jaws dropped as we passed. My jet-black hair was swept back at the sides but fell like liquid silk down my back in a glorious cape of darkness, decorated in star-shaped jewels in every shade of blue and green. In place of the usual thick, false-iron chains, I wore a combination of precious metals to match Kal's look, welded of chains so fine, they would break if pulled on hard enough.

The great room was filled with most of Kal's "friends" and relatives, with a towering mass in the center of the hall covered in a heavy drape of red velvet. Kal was lounging on a divan, facing the concealed surprise. I tried not to stare at him, tried to school my face into namelessness—still, I noticed when he sprung up from his chair at the sight of me. In long, confident strides, he stood before me, holding his arm out for me to link with. His eyes sparkled, but something sinister lurked beneath, as though he knew Estrella's plan and was already two steps ahead of her. I raised my brow a fraction.

"How quaint," Estrella interrupted. "You've dressed her in such finery, as one might place a crown upon a hound." She chortled, but when Kal didn't join in her laughter, she continued, louder, "My dearest cousin, I don't believe I've given you a proper congratulations on your betrothal nor adequately welcomed your *bride*."

She turned to address the rest of the spectators. "After much planning and deliberation, I've designed the perfect wedding gift, and I'd like to present it to you early. A gift which will most certainly help her to feel a bit more . . . at home in the Palatium Crystalis."

Estrella and her posse giggled as though she were telling some hilarious inside joke. Then, without any further delay, she yanked on the fabric concealing her surprise. The velvet covering cascaded to the ground, revealing a massive, cylindrical tank that reached almost to the ceiling. Inside swam a variety of luminescent fish and eels that swirled around and around, trapped, unable to find their way out. And if that weren't bad enough, the glass tank was encased in what looked like a beautiful, decorative, wrought iron cage.

I wanted to laugh at the irony. For days, all I'd wanted was to submerge myself in water, and now she was threatening to make it my prison. How they'd turned what was once most comforting to me into a means of torture. *Only the Iris could be so cruel.*

I'd agreed to do anything, but already my insides were screaming. This was too much. I locked eyes with Kal, blinking twice. If this was just another game, he'd still honor it, right?

He clapped his hands slowly and dramatically.

"Nice try, cousin dearest, but silly of you to forget, water strengthens the Argenti. And according to the Faber Ludi, she is to be starved of it until my father decides the prophecy is no longer a threat."

My shoulders dropped in relief.

"But I've already run it by him. The tank is wrapped in iron bars, so even if she were able to somehow summon the strength to break through the glass, all her precious sea things would die in the process and she'd still wind up trapped within an iron cage. So you see, I doubt she would try anything that careless. She'll find more comfort occupying the water in her fishtank. Let's see her swim, shall we?"

The Iris cheered, and laughter surrounded us as the room became charged with anticipation.

I used to have to breathe to keep my powers under control, to keep them from starting up a hurricane. Now, what I really needed to control was my desire to kick Estrella in the throat. But I had to maintain my nameless act because there were far too many Iris in the room. So I took deep breaths, willing down the urges, and tucked my clenched fists into the folds of my voluptuous skirts.

"I'd rather not take the risk. Besides, how am I expected to sire an heir if she is in there?" Kal drawled.

Estrella leaned in closer to her cousin, speaking at a lower volume that was almost too difficult to hear above the clamor. Though she spoke with a false sweetness, her words were clearly laced with venom.

"Look how happy it makes them. You know, many suffered the loss of friends and family because of her. Because of her little show in the arena. Let them have this."

"I tire of your games, Estrella," Kal said. He took me by the hand, walking us over to the divan. She clung to his other arm, practically draping herself over him. "It's a curious effort on your part. If I didn't trust you, I'd say it almost appears as though you are making a jest of your prince. Are my choices laughable to you?" Kal made himself comfortable on the divan, bringing me to perch on one of his knees.

"My dearest Kaleidos, I would never dream of such a thing. I wish only to bring you joy. You've spent far too much time away from us these past months. All anyone desires is the return of our rakish prince of revels. You've done your duty and selected your bride, now it's time to rejoin your court." Estrella picked up a crystal decanter of clear wine from the low table in front of us, focusing on it for a moment until steam rose out of it.

"You won't have to worry about your little fish. She'll be safe, hydrated, and fed. No one will be able to touch or harm her in there, so you can come out assured of her well-being and enjoy yourself again." She poured some of the steaming liquid into small glasses for herself and Kal, then settled herself closer to him than I liked, leaning in closer still as she lowered her voice once more.

"At first, I considered, 'What's wrong with my cousin? Why has he become so protective over such an insignificant little elemental?' But then I realized, perhaps it's an heir you're worried about. It's only natural to have those types of feelings . . . so I've been told . . . and if that's the issue, your part in that is now done. Let Himmel and the Faber Ludi take over the burden of guarding her for you. Because if I'm being perfectly honest, your new demeanor is quite gloomy and tiresome. No one wants to see you traipsing around with your bride anymore. They grow restless and uncomfortable at the thought that perhaps you might be disillusioned, or worse. If you don't show the rest of the court there's nothing to worry about, it won't be long before talk of your replacement bears more weight. I may have even heard a few rumors already . . . but who am I to spread such gossip?"

"And I suppose that has nothing to do with this delightful little presentation of yours. A rather shameless attempt at gaining popularity, if you ask me," he replied.

"Ridiculous. It's nothing of the sort . . . This is all for *you,* cousin." She handed him the small glass, holding hers up to sniff the steam off the top. "I don't think I have a problem when it comes to the favor of the people. *You're* the one I'm concerned for."

She shot back her drink, then stood up. "Let's put them all to shame, show them how we party past dawn, just like the old days."

Kal glanced over at the tank thoughtfully for a moment. Then he gave Estrella the vilest of smiles that had her giggling naughtily and refilling her glass. She waved to the guards, who then wheeled over a ladder and set it against the side of the tank.

"Such a considerate and sensible gift, cousin." Kal now spoke with a raised voice, as though to address the entire room, and it fell silent in anticipation. "While I cannot in good faith accept this offering, I'd hate to see it go to waste. Why don't you show my bride just how comforting this prize is that you have so generously showered us with."

Estrella laughed, clearly expecting Kal to join in, but she was the only one laughing. Her face quickly changed to confusion and then annoyance. "You cannot be serious." The tension in her posture belied the confidence in her voice.

"Up you go," Kal encouraged with a smile. Though, it was clear by the tension between them, it was anything but a friendly smile. He was testing her, and she would be wise not to take it lightly.

"Kaleidos." Estrella gave a nervous laugh. "This isn't funny."

"Get in the tank, Estrella." This time, he didn't bother to hide the threat underlying his tone.

The room erupted into an excitement-fueled chant, "Get in the tank! Get in the tank! Get in the tank!"

Estrella tried to compose herself, then turned to leave the room. "I'm not doing this."

But before she could exit, Kal's suggestion had inspired a mob. The Iris went after Estrella while continuing their chant. My eyes widened as they carried her to the ladder, kicking and screaming all the way, ready to toss her inside.

"Get your hands off me," Estrella screamed. "I will do it myself!"

Kal raised a hand, and they set her down. With as much grace as she could afford herself, she smoothed out her dress, brushing a hand over her hair, and then climbed the ladder. Anger fumed off her with every rung she ascended. She glared at Kal as she kicked off her shoes in a huff and then slid her feet into the water. She shivered and then plunged inside, allowing herself to sink down into the tank without so much as another word. The moment she disappeared under the water, Iris crowded around, tapping on the glass.

Estrella attempted to maintain her dignity, but her entire body was ramrod straight. Her eyes widened as a crystal eel slithered past her ankle. A school of faerie fish swam by her head, and she flinched. When another eel darted by her neck, she began to utterly lose it. Air escaped her lungs in an endless cloud of bubbles as she started frantically twisting and turning, thrashing her arms and legs against the glass, her mouth open in a scream I could barely hear over the laughter of the Iris bystanders mocking her fear. The eels, feeling threatened, started attacking, and Estrella threw her fists at the encasement, screaming for help.

As much as she delighted in watching me suffer, I couldn't help but feel a little sorry for her, or perhaps I felt sorriest for the fish she was terrorizing in the tank. The difference between us was that I didn't take joy in witnessing the torment of others. Besides, it could have been me in that tank. Though it did serve her right for trying to embarrass Kal and me, I only feared what kind of revenge she might seek out when this was over.

I tried to turn away from the sight but found my eyes glued to her. I nudged Kal. "Are you not afraid of what she might do to retaliate?"

"She'd be wise to think twice before attempting another one of her schemes. Don't feel sorry for her. She brought this entirely upon herself."

Estrella continued her frenzied movements in the tall cylinder. Every time she attempted to swim toward the top, the eels would come at her face and she'd cower and scream. Soon, her cries were completely drowned out by the cheers and music as the revel continued on without her.

I winced at the sight, finally managing to peel my eyes away. "Do you think she's had enough?" I asked.

"She'd have locked you in there and thrown away the key," he replied. "And isn't this fun, Tempest?" Kal murmured, a glint of malice in his eyes that almost frightened me. "I promised you your revenge, didn't I?"

He turned me back toward the tank to watch Estrella struggle. I didn't want to admit that her suffering felt good. I'd spoken of revenge, but seeing it in action came with a whole confusing mix of emotions. Or perhaps it was more the fear that if I allowed myself to take part in it, I'd no longer be so different from monsters like her. But she was wicked and deserving of this humiliation, and the darker part of me won. And in those few moments, I watched, relishing it, claiming the double-edged reward.

Estrella seemed to tire, losing her fight against the eels.

"How much more can she take?" I asked.

"We're more resilient than you might think," Kal remarked. "But if you wish to show her mercy, I can let her out. Just give the word."

Fish and eels swirled around her in rapid, dizzying spirals, creating a mini cyclone that had water spilling from the openings in the metal grate at the top.

Estrella still had much to atone for, and she certainly didn't deserve my mercy. But the longer I watched her struggle, the more I feared losing myself to the monstrous desires within.

"Let her out," I whispered, "and return those poor creatures to the sea."

Kal nodded. "As you command, Tempest."

Kal eventually dismissed his friends and courtiers, and finally, as the sun rose, we were alone.

"Thank you," I said. "For a moment, I feared there wasn't a way out of it for me. I saw myself trapped in that cage."

"I'd have sooner shattered that tank and sent shards of glass flying at every last person in the room," Kal said, and a fierce rumble quaked the earth beneath our feet. The glass of the windows buzzed with the vibration of his anger.

I grabbed onto his shirt for stability, and the shaking stopped. In an instant, he swept me up into his arms and began walking us out of the great hall. I was too tired to fight him, so I let myself sink into his strong hold.

He carried me to his bedchamber, placing me delicately onto the bed, and then turned to leave.

"Stay," I said, and he paused. "Stay with me."

Kal eased himself onto the other side of the bed, head propped up on his hand as he rested on top of the bedding, facing me where I lay an arm's width from him. He reached for my hand and stroked his thumb over my knuckles, eyes on me, as though he was afraid to miss a single blink.

"Who knew Estrella's 'bath' would be the highlight of the evening?" I tried to make light of the thing that had scared me.

"And the irony of it all?" he said. "Her plan to embarrass me ended up winning me much favor in the end."

"You think so?"

"Oh, yes. I think it terrified them," Kal replied, "but they enjoyed it. That feeling of not knowing. That no one is truly safe."

"And am I safe with you?"

"That's a good question." He chuckled. "Though I suspect you're more of a danger to me than the other way around."

"Perhaps." I smiled, focusing on our connected hands, the heat of his gaze too much to take.

"And she finally admits to it."

"I don't know if it's an admission or more of a secret desire," I joked and found myself yawning.

"I'll keep you safe, Aella."

PART II

Evo & Nubia

Unknown Source

Although the Lux Verax had fled from Esterra, one rebellious youth remained behind.

Evo, the youngest of the Lux Verax, the last born in thousands of years, refused to return home without a mate for himself. He was tired of searching and waiting for a future he feared might never be.

Glamoured as an Adamas, Evo snuck into the alpine palatium, where he began waiting hand and foot on Princess Nubia, the fairest female he'd ever seen. His disguise as a simple servant made him appear harmless, so he was overlooked by her guards, enabling him to get close to her. He spent months earning her trust and attention, and they grew a friendship over that time as he captivated her with tales of worlds far beyond her own. Nubia was utterly charmed by this simple servant, and soon, she began inviting him into her bed.

"Tell me your secret, Evo. Please . . . Do you truly think I am so short of wit that I'd believe you to be a common male? Tell me, are you a prince in disguise? Are you from another star, as in so many of your fantastical tales?" She wove a ribbon of starbright hair through her fingers in the way she so often did. The rest of her long, silken hair doing a poor job at hiding the naked form Evo couldn't take his eyes off of.

"If I told you the truth, would you still love me?" He cocked a brow as he shoved the too-long ends of his tunic sloppily into his oversized trousers.

The princess leaped from the bed, using her air powers to draw him toward her. She kissed him passionately, stopping only to whisper, "What do you think?" She kissed him again. "Tell me, please. Who are you?"

Tired of the charade, Evo convinced himself that the princess truly did love him, that she would choose him and forget all of his lies.

"Fine, little diamond, I'll show you who I am," Evo said, stepping away from her a few feet before releasing the glamour.

Filled with anticipation for her to see his true face, Evo expected Nubia to leap right back into his arms and kiss him just as she had moments before, but when the glamour faded, his white hair sparking with color and his body practically doubling in size in muscle and in height, she recoiled from him. Her normally flirtatious grin was replaced by something else, something akin to terror or disgust. Evo stepped toward Nubia, but she backed away more, throwing a hand in front of herself.

"Stay away!"

"I don't understand. You asked me to show you who I am."

"I thought you were lying about your upbringing, not that you were a completely different species!"

"Why does it matter? Please, Nubia. I'm still the same person." He stepped toward her.

"One step closer and I'll scream," she warned.

"Nubia, my diamond." Evo closed the gap, thinking that if he just kissed her, she would sink back into him and everything would be as it had been.

Nubia screamed, a piercing shriek, enough to crack his heart in two. Evo stared back at her, hurt and rejection tainting his eyes as guards rushed into the room. But Evo was done groveling. He'd had enough of being desperate and alone. Evo killed the guards, massacring them with his bare hands, and when he turned back to find Nubia, she was cowering behind the bed. He stepped over her, watching her recoil as he reached a bloody hand toward her.

"You wanted stories? Come with me. We'll make our own."

She only sobbed, shrinking farther away from him in horror of what he had just done. "Please don't hurt me. Please."

"I thought you were the one." He scoffed. "My whole life, I've been alone. If anything, I thought you, with your protected life in the palatium, might have understood a little of what that's like. Clearly, I was wrong. Gone are my days of waiting. If fate won't give me what I want, then I will take it by force."

And so he stole the princess and headed back to the door in the mountain that would return him to his world. But when he arrived, weeping Adamas bride in tow, the Lux Verax rejected him.

Chapter 27
Stars Grant Their Blessing

WYNN

I was a stranger among friends. As if peering through glass, I watched but was not a part of it. It was bittersweet seeing Ari accepted back into the cabala as if she'd never left—especially by Helio and Rik. She hadn't had as much time to get to know the ladies, so Glint's occasional frostiness toward her did not surprise me, but seeing her laugh and smile for Helio or joke around with Rik? It hurt. Especially because it felt as if every time she looked at me, her eyes were filled with pity.

It had come as no surprise that she'd chosen not to fly with me—I didn't even think I could have handled it if she'd asked. I did feel slightly bad that she'd been traveling with Helio and didn't get the added protection from the wind that Rik or I could have provided, but she'd made her choice, and my Ari was stubborn.

Not your *Ari. Not* your *anything.*

The desire to throttle Helio, especially when he made jokes about me being a father, was strong. I had never been given the chance to try. Would Aella even want me in her life? Her mother had made it clear Aella already had a father. She didn't need me—grumpy, hardened wreck I'd become. But perhaps I could save her and that would be enough. I'd have done my duty to the child I didn't know—might never even have the chance to know.

I had to snap out of it; such morose thinking needed to end. If I remembered anything from all my years of leading missions, going into it expecting the worst possible outcome never helped. If anything, expecting the worst only brought more trouble. While I wasn't sure if there were any other feasible options to get Aella out of Prisma, my plan was to exhaust all other possibilities before moving to our last resort—me.

We waited up in the clouds while Rik went to make sure Concordia was safe for us. None of us had been to Concordia before. When my father had revealed the truth about the Iris, there'd been part of me that had been curious to visit, but considering how close it was to Prisma, we'd never wanted to take the risk. Funny how life had a way of taking a turn. After all that time, here we were, less than two days' flight from the Iris capitol.

Rik whistled an all clear from below, and we swiftly made our descent. I had no idea what kind of accommodations we were going to be looking at, but anything was better than sleeping downwind of Ari and having her scent torture me all night.

The stars must be laughing at me.

Why those fickle beings thought to bring her into my life, grant us a child, then keep us apart was beyond me. But perhaps I laid the blame in the wrong place. If only I had recognized what she was to me sooner.

The afternoon sun beat down on us as we gathered our supplies from the aquilas. Concordia was beautiful in an untamed way. The landscape had been left ravaged with the destruction of homes and buildings, but plant life had thrived, growing in and around the wreckage. A giant lake shimmered in the sunlight, and I just knew Ari was dying for a swim. I wondered how deep it was and if there had been any dwellings beneath. Perhaps it would be a good idea to find out.

"Arianwen," I called out briskly.

She turned, her skin flushed red and chapped from the wind, the marks from the goggles still evident around her eyes and nose. "Yes, Wynn? Is the scout here? Can we find out what's going on in Prisma?"

"I don't know . . . yet. In the meantime, make yourself useful and explore the lake. Let me know if there are any usable structures below," I commanded, instantly regretting I hadn't asked her politely instead when her eyes narrowed into annoyance.

She gave an overdramatic curtsy after shrugging out of her flying leathers. "As you wish, Your Majesty."

"Ari—"

She didn't even stop to listen as she took off in a run down to one of the rickety-looking docks and dove below.

Helio came up next to me, jostling my shoulder with his own. "Considering how tense things have been between you, you might not want to piss her off, *Your Majesty*."

I rolled my eyes and headed over to Rik, who was standing with one of our Aereus scouts. As soon as I approached, the scout sketched a quick bow.

"Your Majesty, we were able to set up a meeting space for you and whoever else you're expecting. We cleared out a large space in one of the less damaged buildings and added some extra structural support using the plant life within. There should be enough cover with all of the overgrown vines and trees, and any of the repairs made should blend in with the rest of the ruins."

"Thank you, and good work. Is there somewhere we can safely rest?"

"Yes, along this section over here. We managed to salvage a decent amount of what looked like old market stalls and homes and set them up for lodging. They're lacking in your typical comforts, but they'll be safe and dry until we secure and clear out that one over there." The scout pointed to a large building the size of a small castle. It was missing roofing and walls in some areas and was completely overgrown with ivy. Knowing the Aereus' skills, I was willing to bet it would be fit for a king by the time they finished with it. "It's a work in progress, and it'll take a little while to restore, but it's got good bones," the scout finished.

"Sounds perfect. Has anyone else arrived yet?"

"There is actually a group from Iveria already here."

I glanced over at Rik, wondering if it would be rude to make our guests wait or if we had time to rest. He raised his eyebrows, the tilt of his head letting me know he would handle anything that came up if I wanted him to. Before I could decide, a large Argenti male came out of one of the dwellings.

Faex. I recognized him immediately.

Arianwen's husband was here.

His stern features skimmed our group. "Is she here?" he asked without preamble.

"Is who here?" Rik asked, stepping in front of me, identifying the male in front of us as a threat.

"My wife. Is she here? I caught her scent," he said, starting to look around, concerned when he didn't see her anywhere.

Ah yes. That stars-damned scent.

"I asked her to investigate the lake," I responded, keeping my voice droll and unbothered.

"Alone?" he bit out.

"Do you see any other Argenti around here?" I asked, my voice dripping with sarcasm.

"You do now." He glowered before sizing me up, taking a few steps in my direction. "Do you always send people into unknown locations without backup?"

"In this case, yes," I replied. "You're welcome to join her and be her . . . *backup.*"

He growled at me. The male didn't even know who I was and he was growling at me. He strode down the dock, stripping off his tunic before diving into the water after his wife. I was sure they would have a happy reunion. I was glad I didn't have to watch.

Helio's eyes were round with surprise and amusement. "Yeah, I really don't think you want to piss off Ari. That husband of hers could tear you limb from limb."

"Shut up, Helio," Rik said.

Glint laughed. "Maybe I need to find myself an Argenti to tangle with. I love a muscular male with tattoos."

I scowled and stalked off toward the shelters, determined not to let the situation distract me from my purpose.

Rik quickly caught up with me and asked, "Should I meet with the Argenti rebel leaders?"

"Let's all eat together this evening. It will be the perfect opportunity to catch up and start making plans. Also, please check in with the aerial scouts and see what else they need to make sure the storm wall stays intact. I'd like to be made aware of anyone approaching from other courts or if there's any sign of the Iris," I replied. "Oh, and before I forget, if the scout from Prisma is here, send him my way. I want to debrief him myself."

"I'll take care of it," Rik said before heading in the opposite direction.

I needed some peace and quiet and time to think. As much as Ari's impassioned plea to finally rise up and defeat the Iris had stirred something in me this past week, I wasn't looking forward to dealing with the complexities of making it happen. Each court potentially had unique skills, connections, or information to offer in assisting us in this mission, but I wasn't sure if we could convince them to take the leap. The rebel leaders weren't exactly easy to persuade. The courts were very territorial, but we needed someone to lead them if we were going to get anything accomplished.

It had been years since I'd met with any of them, as I'd let my cabala handle all the rescue missions. Stars willing, my lack of presence in recent years wouldn't add to their wariness about working together.

Could we trust the other leaders? I wanted to, especially knowing we'd have to work together to build a new world if we managed to abdicate our Iris oppressors. I'd need to tread carefully.

CHAPTER 28
AN UNEXPECTED REUNION

ARIANWEN

The second my body was submerged beneath the chilly lake waters, I felt instantly refreshed. All the tension in my muscles and irritation at Wynn melted away as the water greeted me. Even though I hated how he'd ordered me around, as far as orders went, this had been the best possible one.

A school of fish flitted by, their scales catching the light of the afternoon sun as it breached the water. It felt amazing to stretch and kick my legs after all that flying. As much as I wanted to enjoy a relaxing swim, Wynn had sent me on a mission, and either way, I loved to explore. The lake grew cooler and deeper as I swam toward the center. I saw evidence of an underwater village with housing spaced out around it, so different from the overcrowded, smaller dwellings I was used to seeing in Iveria. Disappointment and sadness flooded me at the sight of so many destroyed and abandoned homes. A place that had once meant unity and hope had been completely ransacked, even down here. The Iris had spared no one. A righteous anger boiled inside me as I remembered what Wynn had told me years ago. We'd been taught the stars had destroyed Concordia, when, in reality, it had been the Iris, who feared the elementals becoming too powerful and the emergence of the one the prophecy spoke of—one born of united courts with the power to take them down.

Emotions warred within me when I considered the implications of Aella being the prophesied one. As a mother, the absolute last thing I wanted was for my child to be put at such great risk as the chosen one, but as an elemental fae who had been oppressed by the Iris her entire life and watched them abuse her people, I wanted nothing more than for Aella to step into her destiny and tear them down. As long as I could be there beside her to keep her safe, of course.

I wasn't quite sure what Wynn expected me to find down here. When we Argenti tethered our magic to the underwater dwellings to keep them dry and free from water damage, that tether only lasted as long as someone in the family line was alive. What was left of the homes had long been worn away by the lake's currents, fauna, and freshwater-dwelling creatures, though perhaps Wynn had no knowledge of that. Regardless, with the Iris having exterminated everyone in Concordia, the chances of there being anything usable was extremely slim.

The lake was gigantic. I could have spent days exploring, but the longer I stayed, the more depressed I felt. The destruction and devastation weighed heavily on me, the lump in my throat making it hard to breathe. I knew what I'd find if I tried to enter any of the homes, and the thought nearly broke me. Remnants of lives lived drifted by on gentle currents. I could envision the families who had dwelled here, almost hear the echoes of children's laughter as they discovered treasures in the sandy lakebed. The sheer number of lives lost was unfathomable.

Movement from the left caught my eye, and I darted behind a broken wall to hide. Who knew what predators lurked in these waters after so many years unchallenged and unchecked? Perhaps I should have waited for another Argenti to come with me.

What was it? Or worse, *who* was in this lake with me? My heartbeat picked up as fear of the unknown invaded my senses.

Surely it's just a large fish. There's no possible way there are Iris out here . . . right?

I peeked over the wall, looking around to find what had caught my attention. Among the wreckage of the ancient city were far too many hiding places. When nothing and no one appeared, I shook my head in relief.

You're way too jumpy, Ari.

Convinced I had imagined it, I quickly swam away from my hiding spot. I had completed my task; there was no reason for me to linger. As I swam back toward the surface, I saw something again in my peripheral vision. I whirled around, determined to not hide this time and face whatever it was head on, but nothing was there.

The water rippled around me, helping me sense the predator behind me. Closing my eyes, I sent up a prayer to the stars for luck, and in a quick, powerful move, I spun and slammed the heel of my palm into a solid—

"Verus?!"

My husband flew away from me due to the force of my blow.

"Damn, wife. Not the greeting I was expecting."

"Stars! Faex. Are you all right?" I rushed toward him, noting how he rubbed his chest.

Verus gave me a grin through the slight wince he couldn't hide from me as he met me halfway. "I'm fine. Glad to see those self-defense lessons I gave you all those years ago stayed fresh."

The biggest grin split my face, and I wrapped my arms and legs around his muscular body, pulling him in close. I was immediately overcome with emotion as I embraced my partner and my rock—the wonderful father of my children. It felt like we'd been separated forever.

Verus pressed his lips to mine in a passionate, toe-curling greeting. "Hello, my beautiful wife."

"Hello, dearest husband." I pulled him back in for another breathless kiss. "What in the stars are you doing here? Also, let me check your chest. I hit you pretty hard." I gently probed his torso and sent healing power to stop any bruising.

"Stop fussing over me," he said with a smile. "As for why I'm here, rumor had it my incredibly talented wife was exploring these waters alone, and I jumped at the opportunity for a nice private reunion."

My cheeks heated even as I squeezed my arms around him and laughed. "I missed you too, Verus. For a moment there, I thought you were a giant predator coming to eat me."

I pulled away and caught Verus smirking. "Don't be so sure I'm not, wife."

I sighed, rolling my eyes. Even after all these years, he loved to mess with me. "I don't know what Wynn was thinking by sending me down here. It would take far too much work to find any kind of usable space, not to mention, the Adamas can't see as well as we can down here in the dark."

Suddenly, I realized I had spoken freely about the Adamas to Verus after all this time, and I swam backward, covering my mouth with my hands. My shoulders scrunched, waiting for the inevitable pain, but nothing happened, and I heaved a sigh of relief. I truly was free.

Verus frowned. "Are you okay? Who's Wynn?"

"Wynn is the king of the Adamas, the one I went to for help."

"Wait—are you telling me the pale, sparkling male I met outside the lake is a king?"

"Stars, Verus, I have so much to tell you!" I swam back to him. "My oath, it's gone. He released me."

A glimmer of anger boiled in his eyes. "I should have punched him in the face before I knew who he was."

"Verus!" I exclaimed. "No need to punch anyone, okay?" I gently squeezed his shoulder, hoping to ease the tension rolling off of him.

"Understood, wife," he grumbled. "Am I not allowed to be angry at the male who kept you under that oath all these years? To imagine the king of the Adamas was so concerned about you sharing his secrets."

"You're allowed to be angry, but he was just trying to protect his people," I replied, scrunching my brow. "I saved his life at the beginning of my matri-ritus. The Iris shot him out of the sky, and he almost died, and then I sort of begged him to take me to see his court."

Verus cupped my cheek again and pressed a kiss to my forehead, his shoulders finally relaxing. "Why am I not surprised that you healed a wounded stranger and went on such an adventure?"

I laughed. "You know me well, husband."

He wrapped his arms around me, pulling me close again, spinning me around and causing my stomach to flutter. "Tell me *everything*. I want to know all of it—every part of you I couldn't know until now."

My heart flooded with warmth. It was all I'd ever wanted. "Of course, but first—what in the depths are you doing *here*, in Concordia?"

Verus sighed, his arms tightening around me. "When Lucris sent one of his servants to fetch me, I was terrified something horrible had happened. Lucris said travel was being arranged for me and the children, and you were safe and headed here."

His hold loosened as he slid his hands down to entwine our fingers, and I looked up at him. "I'm impressed he told you as much."

"I might have been a little extra persuasive." Verus smirked.

I blinked in surprise. "Poor Lucris. But where are the children? Are they okay?"

"They're okay . . . Definitely dealing with a lot of emotions about leaving their home and being scared about what the future holds, but they're on their way to Zephyria. Imagine my surprise when Lucris told me the Court of Air wasn't fully extinct. Mila took it the hardest. Leaving behind her entire life, her friends . . . She was—is—angry. It'll take some time for her to work through it."

My heart ached for our sweet second-born, and I buried my head into Verus' chest. "I can only imagine . . ." I replied, my voice muffled.

"Now before you ask, I had to twist his arm a little, but I was able to convince Lucris to let Leilani and her family go with them too. I also sent word to the rest of our family to lie low . . . to perhaps visit one of the outer villages or isles."

"Stars." I blinked as sudden tears filled my eyes. "I can't even fathom how intense this must be for them. I miss them so much. Also, I can't believe you dragged my sister into this! But I'm glad they're with her. There's no one I'd trust more."

"You'd be surprised what you're willing to do when your family's safety is on the line."

Memories of my journey and Fide curved my shoulders inward, and I sighed, looking down.

Verus gently cupped my cheek, turning my face back up to his. "Or maybe you wouldn't be."

"How are *you*?" I asked, changing the subject. I'd tell him the whole story soon.

Verus ran a soothing hand up and down my back, and if possible, I sank into him more. "I have so many questions, but I know you wouldn't have sent for us unless it was serious."

I nodded into his bare chest, his warmth and the familiar scent of him putting me at ease. How I'd missed him. "I didn't expect you to be here, but I *am* glad, mostly shocked that Lucris, the insufferable prick, just let you up and come to Concordia with him."

"Something along those lines," he agreed. "Anyway, you're not off the hook from questions. I still want to know everything . . . all the things you haven't been able to say over the years." His voice softened, and I pulled back to look up at him again and smiled.

"Of course. I can't wait to share it all with you, but we should probably head back to the surface. Wynn might have news of Aella."

"I still can't believe she's the daughter of a king," Verus remarked.

"I never said that." I looked up at him sheepishly. "How did you know?"

"You didn't have to. I am fairly intelligent, you know," he teased.

"That you are." I laughed, overflowing with joy at being reunited with the male I'd spent the last twenty-five years with, who'd helped heal my broken heart and always had my back. As we swam toward the surface, I looked back at the desolate, broken city. Maybe someday, elementals would return and rebuild this place, if the Iris were ever defeated for good.

CHAPTER 29
A BETTER WORLD

ARIANWEN

Standing on the dock, I siphoned the water out of my clothes and hair. The aquilas were gone, their size far too conspicuous to be waiting around for us. Their stealth and speed made them such a great mode of transportation, but they did like to stay close to the mountains so they could roost up high, where they were most comfortable. I remembered Wynn telling me about the nests they had in the various mountain ranges throughout Esterra. The mountains formed a sort of blockade between lands, making travel by horseback slow and difficult, if not impossible, in certain regions. The Iris usually journeyed by sea because of it.

A figure stepped out between two buildings, and if not for the movement, I would have missed them; their lookout position was perfect for spying and staying out of sight. I didn't recognize them, but they waved us over.

"The king has asked for everyone to join him for dinner in about an hour's time. Do you need me to show you the way to the central building?"

Verus spoke from beside me. "I know my way around. Thanks."

The scout nodded and returned to his position as Verus led me through the broken city to our lodgings, which he'd set up after his arrival the day before.

"I assume you want to stay with me," he said, waggling his eyebrows suggestively.

I laughed. "Why wouldn't I? I don't want to be separated for any length of time ever again."

Verus pulled me in, kissing the top of my head.

Moving aside some vines that covered the opening of what looked like an abandoned, rotted home, he ducked inside. I followed and was pleasantly surprised to find the space clean and welcoming. Verus told me the Aereus had used their powers to fill all the holes with plant life so that, from the outside, it would look like nature had won the battle, but the inside was dry and protected. The space was simple, offering a cot to sleep on, a small table and chairs, and a few gas lamps to light the space. The woodwork was practical and unembellished.

"I need to figure out where my pack is," I grumbled. "The cabala must have picked it up after I dove into the lake."

"Don't think I came empty-handed. You'll find some of your favorite seafruits in my pack." Verus pointed toward the corner of the room. "I bet you're hungry."

"You know me so well, husband." I smiled as I stretched up to kiss his cheek before heading over to rummage through his pack for the juicy fruit I was so fond of. "Aha! Here it is," I crowed before digging in and moaning with delight as the ripe flavor burst on my tastebuds. "Thank you."

"You're welcome," Verus said with a grin as he sat and made himself comfortable on the cot.

"As delicious as this is, I'd almost kill for a sticky bun from home." I leaned against the wall, popping another piece of fruit into my mouth.

Verus chuckled. "I promise we'll get you all the sticky buns you could ever dream of when we return to Iveria."

I froze, my appetite suddenly leaving. What if we never made it home? Or what if we made it back and everything was different? What if we didn't defeat the Iris? What would we do with Aella once she was free? Would we need to go into hiding?

Verus frowned as he noticed my mood shift. "Did the king come up with a plan to get Aella back?"

"He's waiting to hear from the scout he sent to Prisma before making any specific plans. I assume he also wants to find out what the other rebel leaders think and have to offer."

"What does he hope to accomplish by bringing them all together?" Verus pondered aloud.

"Perhaps it's my fault he summoned them all here," I replied, starting to pace the small room. "I told them about the prophecy and how I think Aella is the one we've been waiting for. The Adamas can't defeat the Iris on their own. We need all the courts to work together."

"And you want to rescue our daughter only to throw her into the rebellion as, what, a figurehead? We've tried to protect her and keep her safe all these years, and now you want her to start a war?" Verus asked incredulously.

"Of course I don't want to throw her into the front lines. I'm terrified of putting her into more danger, but ultimately, it's up to her if she will join the rebellion once we rescue her. Regardless of that, we can't stand by and let the Iris continue to destroy and control our lives. I've been bound by my oath for long enough, and now I'm free. We need to be more proactive. Think about Mila. Think about our other children who could have so easily ended up in Prisma if they'd remained in Iveria."

Verus pinched the bridge of his nose, his head tilted back against the wall. "I don't know, Ari. War? Is that really our best option?"

"Don't you want a better world, Verus? One where our children can be raised without fear? Where our daughter can embrace her power instead of being forced to stifle it? The stars blessed her for a reason. I have to believe there are greater powers at work."

Verus' eyebrows drew together. "You have always wanted to heal our world. That has been clear from the moment I first met you."

I stopped pacing and joined him on the bed, taking his hands in mine. "There is strength if we all work together. When I stayed in Zephyria for those months, it was amazing to see how the elementals lived in peace. Our powers can complement and strengthen each other. There are far more of us than there are Iris, and with the stars on our side, who can stop us?"

"I didn't realize I married such a revolutionary," Verus remarked while squeezing my hands, his eyes shining with pride. "You know you will always have my full support."

"That's all I need, Verus," I said, laying my head on his shoulder, grateful for his presence.

He patted my knee gently. "Now tell me your story, Ari. I want to hear it from the beginning."

A small smile wound its way onto my face. "Once upon a time, a young, female Argenti went on her matri-ritus, and a stranger fell out of the sky . . ."

CHAPTER 30
ONCE SEPARATE, NOW UNITED

WYNN

My eyes roved around the meeting room, taking everything in. From the large table surrounded by chairs to the living flames Glint had set up all over the room that emitted a warm glow. There were no windows, but the walls were covered in blooming vines, giving the room a pleasant, floral scent. As far as war rooms went, this one was a bit too pretty for my taste, but that was the least of my worries.

Enixus and Indre, the two rebel leaders from the Court of Earth, entered, observing the room and its inhabitants with a wariness about them. Relations between us had been strained ever since the mission with Arianwen twenty-five years ago. They had sworn they'd known nothing of the curfew that had been put in place nor did they have any idea why Arianwen's glamour had failed. Still, it had wounded the trust between us, and after that, I'd refused to send anyone down there except for Helio and Eden, and even that hadn't gone to plan. Eden's loss had devastated me and my cabala and had only made my responsibility to my court clearer.

"Your Highness," they greeted me, bowing their heads.

Helio sat to my left, twirling a dagger in one hand. "He's actually *king* of the Court of Air now."

"Apologies, Majesty," Indre replied in my direction. "We didn't mean to be disrespectful."

I waved my hand dismissively. "Let's not worry ourselves with formalities. Until Esterra is free from Iris rule, titles don't mean much outside of Zephyria."

Enixus looked thoughtful as he and Indre took seats at the table. "It is something to think about. What will become of the courts if the Iris are ever overthrown? The Court of Air is the only one that managed to maintain any kind of royal family. The Iris executed ours millennia ago—who even knows if any distant relations remain."

I nodded. "I suppose that is something we will need to consider, but I have no plans to rule all of Esterra, in case that was something you were concerned about."

"You could have fooled me, Your *Majesty*," a voice drawled from behind, and I turned to see Lucris enter the room. "The way you commanded us all to meet you here in abandoned Concordia, saying you had important news to share."

"Ah, welcome, Lucris. Lovely to see you, as always." *Prick.*

"I haven't seen your face in Iveria in decades," he sneered.

I curled my hands into fists and bit down on my tongue to prevent myself from countering with a rude statement.

Soft laughter and the sound of a male's low voice had me turning once more, and I almost wished I hadn't. Verus escorted Arianwen into the room, her face flushed with the most joy I'd seen on it since we'd been reunited. I couldn't help but note his hand around her waist and how she curled into his side.

Helio prodded me from the side. "You might want to fix your face, Wynn. That glare could cut diamonds."

I tried to smooth my features, annoyed I'd allowed myself to be shaken to begin with.

I turned to Rik on my right. "Have the Aurum arrived?"

"No, not yet."

"What a shame," I muttered quietly. Any buffer to ease the tension would be a good thing.

"Well, it looks like most of us are here," I said, looking around the room, purposely avoiding looking at Arianwen and Verus. "Let's eat, and then we can discuss why we brought you all here."

Lucris leaned forward. "Are we not waiting for the Aurum rebels to arrive?"

"We will fill them in as soon as they get here," I replied. I could only hope they *would* show up. Either way, we needed to move things along.

"Which will be when?" Lucris pressed.

"Do I look like an oracle to you?" I growled in irritation. "They'll get here when they get here."

"Speaking of oracles," Glint chimed in, ever the diplomat, "are you all familiar with the prophecy assumed to be about the Iris' downfall?"

Enixus snorted. "I don't put much weight on prophecy. No one ever truly interprets them correctly, and the study of them has been forbidden since the Iris came into power."

"I was planning on discussing this after dinner." I looked pointedly at Glint, who responded with a smirk. *Troublemaker.* "However, as you all know, Zephyrian libraries hold some of the oldest banned texts in Esterra. There is a prophecy some of you already seem familiar with." I pinned my eyes on Lucris. "We believe the one prophesied to take down the Iris has been born and the time to act has finally arrived."

Enixus and Indre whispered among themselves while Lucris leaned back in his chair, seemingly bored by the news.

"Is there something you'd like to add, Lucris?" I asked.

"I have contacts of my own in Prisma *and* in the palatium itself. Not to mention I have my own suspicions."

A sudden commotion outside the room had everyone pivoting in their seats. Our question was answered almost immediately as a travel-worn female walked through the door, flanked by two warriors.

"I'd apologize for my tardiness, but it doesn't look like you waited to get started, so never mind," the blonde female quipped as she lifted one delicate brow, her eyes piercing mine.

Glint stood and ran over to embrace her cousin. "It's about time you emerged from the ashes."

The female's posture loosened slightly as she returned the hug, giving Glint a warm smile.

"Please, take a seat." I motioned toward some empty chairs. "You're right on time, Ember. We just started discussing the forbidden prophecy."

Ember's eyes flashed with unhidden ire. "You should thank the stars we even showed up, Wynn. I have said it once and I will say it again, this fanciful idea of trying to take down the Iris is never going to happen. You might be safe in your small, hidden city up above, but our losses have been unbearable. Our Iris Guardians are far more restrictive than what we've heard from other courts. It's a miracle we even made it here for this meeting."

"We appreciate the effort," Glint said, her eyes softening. "We wouldn't have called you here if it wasn't important."

Volunteers started bringing food in, for which I was grateful. Ideally, everyone would be a little less irritable with a good meal in their bellies. Once we settled, I reopened the conversation.

"This might come as a surprise to some of you, it certainly was for me," I said, "but it was brought to my attention that I have a daughter, and she has been participating in the prince's Matri-Ludus. We believe she is the one who was foretold."

A hush fell over the room as the news sank in.

"That *is* shocking, considering you're basically a hermit in the alps," Ember quipped dryly, breaking the silence, and I heard Helio bite back a laugh. "What makes you think she has anything to do with the prophecy?"

"All the pieces fit." Arianwen spoke up, the confidence in her tone in front of so many strangers had me loosing a slow breath, and I couldn't help but let my gaze drag to hers. "Wynn and I had a child—born of two courts—twenty-five years ago. She wields water and air and is marked by the stars. I could go on."

"If the fated one is right under their noses in the competition, what do you need us for? Let her take care of them," Ember replied, her tone flat as she wrinkled her nose. "We risk enough already—let her shoulder the burden."

I saw Verus gripping Arianwen, as if to keep her from leaping across the table, and I couldn't help but find my lips twitching into a subtle smirk.

Arianwen rolled her shoulders back, her gaze burrowing into Ember's. "You said your people are under stricter watch than ours. I remember firsthand some of the cruel damage that was done to some of the Aurum refugees." She motioned around the room. "We have *all* seen the devastation the Iris' control has had on our lands and our people. Too many of our family members, children, friends, and lovers have been taken from us, and it will only get worse. If Aella is the prophesied one, as we believe she is, now more than ever is the time for us to be united and retake our world."

The silence in the room was deafening, and I watched as the leaders looked at each other uneasily. The passion in her voice was admirable, but I knew it would be hard to win over the ever stubborn Ember.

When no one responded, Ari twisted in her seat, her eyes meeting mine. "Wynn, what was the news from Prisma? You still haven't told us."

I took a large sip of my wine before answering. "I was about to get to that." I sighed, running a hand through my hair. "Would you like the good news or the bad news first?"

Arianwen's entire body tensed. "Just spit it out already."

"Aella is alive."

I watched her visibly melt as she turned and collapsed into Verus' arms. He whispered something into her ear, and I saw her shoulders shake with silent sobs. Verus looked up and caught my gaze, but I wasn't quite sure what he was trying to tell me.

Feeling as if I was intruding upon their moment, I looked away and brought my attention back to the rest of the group. "My contact confirmed what Arianwen said. Aella does wield both elements and nearly took out the entire arena where they hold their games. Thousands of Iris were killed in her outburst, and thousands more injured."

Shocked gasps filled the air along with murmured whispers. Lucris' pinched expression had me wondering what was going through his head.

"Stars," Ari said, wiping at her tear-filled eyes. "But she's alive? They didn't kill her after what she did?"

I folded my hands on the table, grimacing. "My contact thinks they are keeping her alive to show their dominance. They paraded her around Prisma clad in chains along with boasts that the king has defied a prophecy."

"But the prophecy isn't common knowledge, is it?" Ember asked with a raised brow.

"Not that I am aware of, but the Iris would likely have information not widely known to elementals," I replied. "Perhaps the biggest shock is that there are rumors they are moving forward with a royal wedding. Prince Kaleidos chose Aella despite the utter failure of his Matri-Ludus."

"What?" Ari looked stricken as the reality of the situation sunk in.

I nodded. "Hardly any of the contestants survived. I believe Aella was one of the few Argenti left."

Arianwen's head swiveled to Lucris, a look of grief on her face. "Viera?" she asked.

Lucris scowled, a choked quality to his voice as he replied, "Dead."

It did not surprise me that Lucris had his own intelligence in Prisma, but from the whispers around the room, others were taken aback.

I scrutinized him. "Do you have other news you'd like to share with the rest of us?"

He shrugged, a look of resentment coming over him. "I sent my son to spy for me in Prisma, and my daughter was supposed to kill the prince. She obviously failed." He looked over at Arianwen, his gaze accusing. "Before the final event, Viera sent word that the prince might be swayed to our side.

Apparently, your daughter had grown quite attached and was unwilling to help Viera kill him, despite her *many* opportunities to do so."

Arianwen jumped to her feet, slamming her hands onto the table, the glasses rattling at the sudden disturbance. "What in the depths are you implying, Lucris?" she growled. Verus leaned back in his chair, a somewhat bemused look on his face.

Lucris crossed his arms with a sneer. "I'm not *implying* anything. I'm saying if it weren't for your daughter, mine would probably still be alive and we'd be one step closer to taking down the Iris."

Arianwen bared her teeth before sending a stream of water from the table straight into Lucris' smug face. Helio started laughing but tried to cover it up with a cough. Lucris sputtered, then sent a giant orb right back at her, only to be blocked by a wall of water Verus threw up in front of it. The look on Lucris' face had me worried, so I stood, creating an impenetrable barrier of air between them.

"Enough! Hurling accusations will get us nowhere."

"She came after me!" Lucris complained as he siphoned the water from his clothes.

"Come on, Luc," Verus drawled. "You were baiting her and you know it."

I didn't want to admit it, but Verus was kind of growing on me. His levelheadedness and support of Ari seemed to be just what she needed. I knew it would take time, but I would try to be happy for her, even if it broke me. *She* was happy, and that was what truly mattered.

"I just thought everyone should know who we are putting our trust in before we risk our lives rising up against the Iris in her name," Lucris spat out.

Arianwen looked ready to claw his eyes out, but thankfully, Verus had an arm around her to keep her from launching herself at Lucris.

"I said *enough*!" I roared. "Unless you were there and saw it for yourself, you cannot possibly know all the reasons things happened the way they did. There is no guarantee *either* of them would be alive if they had made an assassination attempt. What we do know is Aella is marked by the stars and wields two elements. While the Iris might not have killed her yet, we cannot be sure how long they will wait or if she'll be safe."

"Couldn't we say her attack in the arena is a sign that she's the one?" Rik asked thoughtfully. "Just think. What she achieved—let alone survived—is evidence the stars are with her. We'd be fools not to consider that."

"She might also be nameless," Lucris said offhandedly, a heartless smile unfurling on his face.

Arianwen blanched, and I winced. *That arse.* Him offering that morsel of information seemed far too personal. Stars willing, he was wrong. Wouldn't the stars have protected her if she were the chosen one as we believed?

"That's just a bedtime story told to terrify children into behaving," Ember said as she picked up a piece of bread and examined it. "There's no evidence of its existence. The nameless key is just a fable."

Enixus frowned. "But if it's true, that changes things."

Rik sat forward in his chair, looking at Lucris with suspicion. "What have you heard?"

"Viera sent word through my son that some of the contestants had been made nameless. Complete shells of themselves. Most of the servants in the Palatium Crystalis are nameless as well. Why do you think we never hear from our family and friends who go to Prisma?"

"The king can't be making everyone nameless," Rik scoffed in disbelief.

Lucris shrugged. "You don't have to believe it for it to be true."

"If they had such a tool at their disposal, they certainly would have used it on her after her attack," Ember said coldly. "I can't imagine why they wouldn't, especially since they let her live and plan on wedding her to their prince. He's Solanos' only heir; I doubt they'd want to risk her killing him."

"Is it reversible?" Arianwen asked, clutching her hands in front of herself.

"If she is nameless," Lucris replied, tipping his head back and ignoring her question, "I don't see how she could be of any use to our rebellion."

Ember tapped her long nails on the table. "He makes a good point. What use is there in raising an army if the chosen one isn't fit to fight?"

"She's not just a chosen one—she's my daughter," Ari growled.

"And heir to the Adamas throne," Helio added.

Ember flinched so minutely, I would have missed it if I hadn't been looking at her.

I held up a hand in an attempt to silence everyone. "First of all, no one has any proof she has been made nameless, and secondly, we are not here to argue the merits of saving Aella. We will get her out and decide what happens after that, with or without your help."

"If you were just going to play dictator, why invite us to this meeting?" Ember asked, her eyes flickering with the fire of her element. "We have nothing to offer this mission of yours."

"Calm your blaze, cousin," Glint chimed in. "We need to be united if we want to have any chance of reducing the Iris to ashes, chosen one in hand or not."

"The Iris have been weakened," I continued. "If Aella took down thousands of them with no training whatsoever, just imagine what she could do if she had an army of elementals behind her. Not to mention, if we can bring all our people together, we can train them to combine and wield their various elements like we've done in Zephyria."

"That's all good and well, but we still can't be sure if she even knows who or what she is," Lucris spat.

"If the stars chose her, I have to believe they will protect her," Arianwen said, her eyes glistening.

Indre sat forward, breaking her silence. "While we also do not have anything to contribute to this rescue mission, we will support you, Wynn. Chosen one or not. It's high time we rise up against the Iris."

"Thank you," I said, nodding at them. Grateful for their support despite the tension that had lingered between us.

"The Aurum will wait until there is more information before making any decisions," Ember said, her gaze trained on the table before she glanced up at me. Her answer did not surprise me, but it was better than an outright no.

Everyone turned to look at Lucris, and he threw up his hands. "I want the Iris gone as much as anyone. You have our support."

I felt more than heard Ari's sigh of relief as she collapsed into Verus. This was only the first step. We still needed to get Aella out. Working together and raising our armies would only succeed if everyone agreed. Despite how weakened the Iris were after the attack, they were still stronger than us.

"So it's agreed. The first mission is to get Aella out of Prisma. After that, we can make plans for rallying all the courts' armies." I turned my focus to Lucris. "Since you appear to be so connected, what other sources or information might you bring to the table? Do you have any Iris allies in Prisma who could glamour us?" I asked.

"Yes, I can arrange that," he agreed. "But first, we should discuss my compensation for the intelligence I have risked and sacrificed so much to obtain."

I narrowed my eyes. "You and I can meet tomorrow morning and work out the particulars. As for everyone else, I would appreciate it if you could stay so we can discuss further details tomorrow when I'm done meeting with Lucris. It's been a long day of travel for most of you, and I think some rest could help us come together with clearer heads."

I looked around the table, satisfied to see nods of acquiescence. I was more than ready to escape to my small chamber and rest without Ari's proximity torturing me all night. Every moment in her presence reminded me of why I'd fallen for her—her strength in the face of adversity, her protectiveness, and even her quick wit. I'd been such a fool to let her go and not fight for her. Forcing myself to leave was almost harder than staying.

Taking a final gulp of my wine, I stood and said good night, heading out into the muggy evening. The meeting could have gone worse, I supposed, but I was looking forward to some quiet. My lips twitched in amusement as I recalled Ari shooting water at Lucris. Yes, it could have been much worse if we'd all let our elements get out of control.

I decided to stretch my legs before retiring and headed toward the lake. A slight breeze came in off the water, and I basked in the feeling of the air curling around me, allowing it to cool my body and the tension that had built up. Stopping to close my eyes for just a moment, I almost didn't hear her approach.

Golden hands slipped over my eyes from behind.

"Ember," I growled as my entire body tensed. "Don't you know it's not polite to touch someone without permission?" I turned around, noting her rosy lips twisted into a pout.

"Oh, come on, Wynn. It's just a bit of fun," she crooned, one hand playing with the intricate braids her long, cornsilk hair was pulled into. Her golden green eyes flared.

"Are you truly going to withhold your support if Aella ends up being nameless?"

She shrugged. "We'll see. My people have lost enough, and I won't raise their hopes for a coup destined to fail."

"Don't you think we have been sitting on our arses long enough?"

"Perhaps. But I, for one, have been actively trying to protect my people, and secondly, I like my arse and don't want to have it handed to me by the Iris if we are ill-prepared."

"Understood. I don't want to put my people in unnecessary danger either, you know."

She stepped closer, trailing a hand across my chest before I gripped it firmly in one of my own. "How about the two of us blow off some steam together? You look like you could use it, especially with the female you never got over getting all cozy with her husband right in front of you?" She bit her lip, looking at me suggestively.

Faex. If she picked up on that, who else did?

Taking my lack of rebuttal as an invitation, she pressed up against me.

"I can provide you with a distraction . . . just like before." She slid a hand toward my waistband.

I stepped back, letting go of her arm, putting space between us. "I am *not* in the mood for this, Ember. Find another male to satisfy your needs. One of your warriors perhaps."

She laughed, raising her hands in acceptance. "I understand, but the invitation is always open."

I pinched my nose between my fingers, the beginnings of a headache coming on. "Was it really that obvious?"

"Oh, I don't know . . ." she drawled. "Finding out you had a child with her? That tipped me off really quickly about who you'd been pining after all these years. I don't think you were *that* obvious."

She gave me one last lust-filled look before turning on her heel and sauntering away. "Come find me if you change your mind," she called out over her shoulder. "My warriors and I know how to share . . ."

"Not likely," I muttered under my breath. Yes, we'd had some fun together, but it hadn't been enough. Nothing had ever been enough.

Chapter 31

Torn

ARIANWEN

The hum and quiet conversations at the table droned on around me as I picked at the food on my plate. My appetite had fled after all of Lucris' accusations. Stars knew I needed my strength, and though Verus had prodded me to at least try, every bite tasted like dust in my mouth.

I pushed away from the large meeting table and rose to my feet. "That's it. I need to get out of here."

"Let's go for a swim," Verus suggested.

I managed a chuckle. "You didn't get enough of the lake today?"

"I just want to be with you . . ." His eyes softened. "I know the water always soothes you."

I leaned down, pressing a kiss to his lips, enjoying how they molded to mine. Despite everything going on, Verus' presence helped me to relax. When I was with him, I did not forget my worries, but I was at least able to compartmentalize the things I couldn't control right then and there. Verus was about to pull me onto his lap when the clatter of a dish and someone clearing their throat brought a flush to my face, and I quickly pulled away.

"Ari, as delighted as I am to see you in a happy relationship, there are other people here trying to finish their meals," Helio drawled.

Glint threw back her head and laughed. "Like you wouldn't be all over Rachell if she were here."

"You make a fair point," Helio said, downing the remainder of his drink. "All the more reason for her to stop. She's just making me miss Chells."

I smiled. "Sorry to remind you of what you're missing, Helio. We were just leaving." I reached over and tousled his copper hair when we walked past him. "We'll try to keep it down."

Helio's laughter followed us out, and I took a deep breath. I needed to hold on to these small moments of joy. When despair threatened to overtake me, these reminders of what we were fighting for were what mattered. A different world. A better world.

Verus slipped his hand into mine as we made our way back to the lake. I froze when I spotted Wynn and Ember practically embracing, her hands all over him. Despite my love for Verus, I felt the oddest pang of possessiveness overcome me.

What in the stars is wrong with me? I want Wynn to be happy. Though he could have chosen someone who didn't act like our daughter was an acceptable loss . . .

Unwilling to let them take up any more space in my mind, I turned to Verus. "Maybe we should just go back to the room. I don't want to interrupt."

"Whatever you need, Arianwen," he said, and we turned back. As the high stress of the evening started to wear off, a deep weariness overcame me. I just wanted to curl up and sleep forever, but there was still so much I needed to tell Verus.

"Did it feel strange seeing Wynn with Ember?" Verus asked after he closed the door. He leaned against it and crossed his arms.

"What? Why would you even say that?" I asked as I started to untie my hair.

Verus only looked at me, a brow quirked in question.

"Verus, no . . . I don't know. Maybe it was weird seeing them together."

"I can't imagine it would be easy seeing my former lover with another," Verus replied.

I laughed as I went to retrieve my comb. "She is quite beautiful, strong of spirit, and he deserves to be happy too. I only wish he'd chosen someone who wasn't so opposed to the idea of rescuing our daughter."

Verus walked over to me and sat on the small bed, reaching out for the comb. "Here. Let me."

I handed it to him and sat down. How I loved it when he combed my hair; there was something incredibly relaxing about it.

"You have nothing to worry about, husband. You are my one and only."

Verus hummed behind me as he deftly finished unbraiding my hair before using the comb to slowly work out the tangles in my mess of curls without hurting me. "I'm not worried about it, but can you really blame me for asking?" he said softly. "This is the male you were pining over when we got married, the one who left you as broken as I was when I lost my mate. I'd be foolish not to wonder if perhaps he had been yours. Plus, he's Aella's father and a king."

I closed my eyes, hating the hurt in his voice. "Yes, sometimes I am hit with an odd sense of jealousy or a possessive feeling, but he was my first love. And it's so odd seeing him after all these years. But there is one thing I am certain of: my love for you, Verus." Turning around to face him, I knelt and wrapped my arms around his neck. "You have my heart. That's all that matters."

His eyes softened, and his lips twitched into a small smile. "I love you too, Arianwen. Now turn back around. I need to finish your hair."

"All right, bossy." I pressed a quick kiss to his lips before turning around, tingles cascading down my spine as he gently worked on the knots. "What was it like? The mate bond?"

Verus sighed. "Do you really want to know?"

"I know you're not going anywhere," I replied. "What you had with Lyani was beautiful, and I want to know all of you. Your past included."

He paused his work on my hair. "I just don't want you to ever think you're not enough for me."

"So you're saying if she walked up to you in Prisma, you wouldn't leave me?"

Verus wrapped an arm around me, tugging me closer so I could relax my head on his chest, my hair suddenly forgotten. "The bond isn't quite like that . . . Yes, I'd be drawn to her. Being around her felt like being home. I could be fully myself, fully known. I'd like to think that, if our paths did cross, we could find a way to be friends. But, no, I wouldn't leave you. I think perhaps, if the stars were kind, they'd reunite us in the after."

I turned to look at him, my hand gently stroking his cheek. "Do you miss her terribly?"

"The pain has greatly lessened over the years, and I suspect she is no longer in this realm." He sighed, looking up at the ceiling. "It's hard to explain . . . but the physical need to be around one's mate is strong. Distance helps but doesn't fully diminish it."

"I'm sorry, Verus." I wrapped my arms around him.

"It's all right, wife. No need to worry about me." He pressed a kiss to the top of my head. Clearing his throat, he asked, "How do you think the meeting went?"

Sensing his need to change the subject, I shrugged. "I kind of hoped we'd have a more unanimous outcome, but I suppose it could have been worse."

"You were incredible. The way you stood up to all those strangers—I'm in awe of you."

I blinked to keep back the sudden tears that threatened to consume me. "I'm scared, Verus. What if I was too late and she's lost herself?"

He squeezed me tighter, his soothing voice rumbling through me. "I have faith she's all right. We'll get our girl back."

CHAPTER 32

POETRY

"Why is it that every morning when I awaken, you're gone?" I asked as I climbed into bed. We hadn't bothered with lamps once we'd come in from our swim since our eyes were already adjusted to the darkness outside.

The prince rolled onto his back, placing his hands behind his head. He let out a heavy sigh. "I stay because you asked me to stay. So I remain with you until your breathing slows, until the pained anguish leaves your brow, until I am certain you feel safe and are in a full, deep, and peaceful rest, but not a minute more."

I swallowed a painful lump at the idea. *Why, if he's so eager to leave, does he even bother staying at all?*

He turned to face me, taking my hand in his. "I leave the moment you no longer need me, because every minute I linger is another minute I have to hold myself back. The truth is, I do not want to keep my hands off you."

"And what if I wanted you to put your hands on me?" I breathed. "Where would you touch me?"

Kal's green eyes darkened and his grip tightened, his fingers and thumb exploring and working the muscles and tender flesh of my palm.

"The question should be where *wouldn't* I touch you . . . There isn't a single part of you I'd wish to neglect. I want it all, Tempest, even the parts you dislike, even the parts you most want to keep hidden. Especially those parts. I'd worship them all."

"And if I let you," I began, "would you show me what it feels like . . . to be worshiped?"

"Only for as long as you wish it to be so."

"Show me first, my prince. Show me where you would touch me so that I might make up my mind."

"As you command."

Kal released my hand, inching his body closer to mine. So close that I could feel the warmth of his breath as he lay next to me, propped up on one elbow. I closed my eyes the moment I felt him, the shadow of him that pulled me in, attracting me like opposite ends of a magnet.

He slowly glided his fingertips up my wrist, making his way to my shoulder, leaving a hot trail of goosebumps in their wake. His touch was so gentle, as though he wasn't quite making contact with my skin but only hovered close enough to channel an invisible current of electricity between us.

He retraced the path of his touch with his lips, tenderly kissing his way back down the length of my arm, stopping when he got to the tender area on my wrist that had once been scarred by the shadow fang. As though he too were thinking about it, a growl rose from his chest, the whole bed rumbling beneath us.

"Where else would you touch me, Kal?" I asked, returning his focus to the moment.

He nuzzled his face into the palm of my hand, then resumed his dreamy perusal of my body. Kal glided his fingers over the curve of my hip ever so slowly, sending more trails of delicious shivers, his hand making its way down my thigh. I shuddered as a wave of gentle thrills radiated through my core, making my skin tighten and contract. His unhurried approach served only to increase my longing and desire for him. Where most males were too eager to get to the prize, he acted as though he had all the time in the world, like this was prize enough for him, this slow and teasing dance, the moments between, like he savored them just as much.

My breaths became shorter, coming faster and faster the more he explored.

"Where else, Kal?"

"Turn onto your side," he murmured, sliding his nose across mine playfully, and I obeyed, turning away so my back was to him.

Kal sank his fingers into my hair, pulling it up to expose the entirety of my neck while giving my hair a gentle tug that made me gasp. He then traced my opalescent birthmark along the eight points of the elongated star, as though memorizing its shape. Tingles ran down my spine, and I shivered under his touch. I'd never felt more bare than I did now with that forbidden, condemning mark I had spent my entire life hiding, ashamed of on display for him. A source of so much fear and insecurity.

I wasn't prepared for the sensation that came next once his lips made contact with my neck. It felt so intimate, I wanted to simultaneously pull away and give in to it more. How could such a small place on my body generate such unfathomable heat? Flooding all my senses, I could feel everything and nothing at the same time. Like my body was humming, floating. I felt like I was glowing. Unable to resist any longer, I moaned, reaching for him.

"Yes, sing for me, my siren," he purred.

"Where else, Kal. Where else would you touch me?"

His hand wrapped around to my front where he explored the curves and slopes of my belly and ribs, where he most certainly noticed the increasingly rapid rise and fall of my breaths. His fingers grazed the sensitive skin over my ribs, and I arched into the warmth of his hand right below my breast. The movement scooted me deeper into his solid embrace. So close that I could feel the silent but impressive declaration of his desire.

"Where else?" My voice came out breathy as I challenged him one more time. Kal buried his face into the side of my neck and released a deep, approving sound that made my toes curl.

"Whatever you'd like, my tempest, my nymph. It shall be yours. Just please do me this one favor and kiss me the way you did that night when you made the stars fall from the sky and the earth come crashing up from below, when you brought me to my knees before you. Let me worship you until your limbs tremble and your head hangs heavy, until you can't take any more and you're drunk on the excess of pleasure."

I turned my head and chest back toward him, as much as our positions would allow, letting my lips brush against his. Kal captured the kiss with his own, locking us together, and with that, he sank his hand between my thighs.

The next morning, I awoke snuggled against him, my head on his chest, our legs tangled up in knots. I couldn't name the feeling stirring inside me, like I'd been filled with warmth and butterflies. It was delicious and terrifying, but it was coming from looking at him. All I knew was that it was more powerful than any surge of magic I'd ever experienced and that I wanted nothing more than to dive into it. I kissed him, and that strange sensation within my chest seemed to blossom even more. Rewarded by the behavior, I lingered over him.

Before his eyes opened, a languid smile curved the corners of his lips. He yawned and stretched his long limbs and then curled his body around mine, tugging me impossibly closer. *Stars, I could get high off the earthy scent of him.* I took a long, deep inhale as I nestled my head into the space between his shoulder and neck and traced my fingertips idly along the iridescent veins of marbling that decorated his skin. I followed a silver vein down the length of his arm, causing him to shiver and flex and then relax again beneath my fingertips. Following another vein, this one a golden color, I traced the snaking pattern that twisted around his forearm. Kal raised his hand, allowing me to continue my exploration of his skin all the way up to his palm. Before I could withdraw, his fingers hooked with mine, interlacing us. With our palms and hearts aligned, energy rippled through me.

Kal's eyes rolled back, and he breathed my name, beckoning. Stars, was I tempted to follow him. Surely if I tugged my hand free, the spell would be lost, perhaps to all eternity. But if I remained in his clutches, would I ever be the same?

The prince pulled me on top of him, and it was like drifting through water, our lips connecting, making everything freeze in place. Shiny specks of dust hung suspended in the air around us as though the world really did stand still in our presence. Power raced through our lips, through our tongues, binding us together. An infinity of light was spinning between us to the deepest reaches of consciousness and beyond. Overwhelmed with emotions both sweet and deadly, so expansive, I felt I might burst like a supernova.

Kal pulled back, breaking the connection. My eyes blinked open, and it took a moment to remember where I was, *who* I was if not connected to him.

I squeezed my eyes shut, replaying the night we'd had and our cozy moment upon waking, trying to sort out what had been real. What we'd just shared, it had been like charging with source power but so much stronger. For a moment, I could've been certain we'd been floating in and out of space.

"What was that?" I asked.

"We mustn't do that again." Kal sat up, his eyes unfocused as a look of bewilderment crossed his features. "It was careless of me."

"Do what?" I responded.

"You don't understand. It's . . . it's not meant for you."

"Not meant for me? What's that supposed to mean? I think I can decide that for myself."

"I mean, if that was what I think it was, we may have just tapped into each other's power. I could *taste* your magic."

I raised my brows at him, speechless. "Well . . . did you like it?" I asked.

He closed his eyes, a pained expression coating his features. "Stars, Aella, I did." He cupped my neck, pulling me in to kiss me again. "Almost as much as I like doing this," he said, peppering me with more kisses. "Wait, no, I like this more." He smiled a soft, lazy smile. "I so enjoy waking up next to you, my little sea nymph." He kissed the top of my head, taking a deep breath as though inhaling my essence. To be loved by him, it was like the sun shining only for me. But I couldn't let him distract me from the topic at hand, as addictive as his affections were.

"What makes you say it's not for me then?"

Kal sighed. "It's honestly so rare, I've only read about it or heard of it through rumors. I wasn't aware it could occur between Iris and elemental fae, so I didn't realize what was happening at first." He shook his head. "But I should have known better. It was highly irresponsible of me."

"Why? What could have happened?"

Kal stared at me blankly. "I don't know . . . I mean, what if it wasn't compatible with your elemental form? My aether, I mean." He furrowed his brow, considering for a moment, then continued, "When I poured it into Viera, it was a last resort. She was gone. And though it revived her, I'm not sure I know enough about it to test it with you. What if it harmed you, Aella? I'd never forgive myself."

"Oh." I shrugged. "Well, I don't think you need to worry about that. I think it liked me."

"Really?" He took me in with his big, green eyes. "Then I guess the better question is . . . did you like it?"

I opened my mouth to speak, only for Himmel to barge into the room unannounced.

Kal cursed.

Himmel curtsied with a false apology. "So late in the morning, I expected you to be in the sparring ring. I will be back shortly. Your bride has fittings today." She flitted out.

"Remind me why I haven't strangled that female already," Kal said.

"Oh, believe me, I wish you would, though I fear her replacement wouldn't be much better."

"Better to deal with the kraken you know," Kal murmured into my hair.

"Krakens aren't real." I huffed.

"Perhaps not in your world." Kal raised a mischievous eyebrow.

"Another one from your books?"

"Speaking of which, you've nearly cleared out my library," he teased.

"Only your informational texts. Besides, it's going to a good cause. But I've been meaning to ask if there is any way for you to get more?"

I wasn't sure if it was working, but I'd been getting books into as many nameless servants' hands as I could. Even if they couldn't remember their pasts, the idea was to give them something to believe in, and perhaps that would be all they needed to gain the will to fight back.

"More books on the elemental fae and surviving courts of Esterra. Consider it done. Anything else I might spoil you with, Tempest?"

"Well, if you're already going through the trouble of ordering, I might be interested in another book of *poetry*."

CHAPTER 33

TEMPERAMENTAL

WYNN

Massaging my temples, I closed my eyes to try to block out the rising volume of people speaking over one another. Not even the dense foliage and florals in our new meeting room in the restored castle did anything to muffle the sounds, and I sent up a silent prayer to the stars that we could agree on something, anything. Dealing with temperamental elementals was going to be the death of me.

It had been days of debate and discussion, ranging from questions of what courts were willing to contribute to the cause to who would run things if the Iris fell. I had the feeling no one was showing all their cards out of fear or selfishness, and it made working together quite challenging. To make things even more difficult, it had become evident Lucris was withholding significant details, seeming only to provide information when it benefited his personal agenda. We couldn't get around working with him though because he had the most connections and intel on the inner workings of Prisma and the Palatium Crystalis.

"Let's take a break," I said, amplifying my voice to cut through the noise. "Clearly we aren't getting anywhere, and I need to get some air." I rose and addressed Helio and Rik. "Would either of you like to spar? I need to move after sitting here debating for hours."

Helio sprang to his feet. "I thought you'd never ask."

Rik cracked a smile as he nodded in agreement.

I turned to the rest of the room. "We can reconvene later this evening. We do need to make some decisions though, as our time to plan for this event is limited. I think the wedding revels are our best chance to get in and out of Prisma in one piece." I pinned Lucris with a stare. "If you truly mean to help us, decide on your terms so we can move forward, with or without you."

He gave a subtle nod. I had a feeling I'd have to make a deal I'd regret to get his help, but I'd made a promise to Arianwen, and I wouldn't let that worm of a male stand in our way.

"I'd like to spar." A baritone voice came from my right.

I turned to look at Verus, who had risen from the table.

"Of course. We'd be happy for you to join us," I said somewhat stiffly. My workout regimen had increased over the years and I'd put on more muscle, but Verus definitely had an advantage.

"Oh, this should be good," Ember said, rubbing her hands together, an amused lilt in her voice bringing me back to the present.

"Come, cousin." Glint elbowed her. "Let's show these males how it's really done."

Ember rolled her eyes, but I didn't miss how they also lit up at the prospect.

Perhaps it would be good for all of us to work out some of the tension that had been building over the hours of discussion.

"Maybe you should come in case we need you, Ari?" Helio joked.

"I wouldn't miss it," she said with a laugh. "But please try not to kill each other."

"You better keep an eye on Helio then. He's known to get distracted by big muscles," I teased while flexing my bicep.

"One time, Wynn." Helio grinned, playfully punching my shoulder before winking at Ari. "With friends this good-looking, can you blame me?"

Laughter filled the air, and I couldn't help but feel lighter somehow. After years of closing myself off from the people I loved, the walls around my heart were beginning to crack. While there might always be an ache, I was starting to feel what it could be like to live in acceptance and peace.

The sun was high in the sky when we walked out to the sandy beach. The light rippled off the gentle waves of the lake, and I squinted as my eyes adjusted after being indoors for so long.

"No magic," Rik said, laying out the rules. "Let's try and keep things interesting." He winked.

We all grumbled our agreement. It would definitely make it a little more challenging, but those of us from Zephyria would have had an unfair advantage. We had experience sparring with different elementals, while most present did not.

I stripped off my shirt so it wouldn't get ruined and bounced on my heels while throwing a few practice jabs in the air, attempting to wake up my muscles. I couldn't help but puff out my chest and flex a bit. A little intimidation couldn't hurt. There hadn't been much time for sparring or exercise while traveling, and my body was feeling the lack of its usual routine, but Helio was right, we did look good.

Verus stepped into view. "Your Majesty, would you do me the honors?" He raised an eyebrow in challenge.

He had also removed his shirt, and the amount of muscle on him was impressive. This would be fun.

I nodded. "Weapons?"

He tilted his head. "If you think we need them."

I rolled my neck, sizing him up. "Hand to hand it is then, if you think you can take me," I replied with a cocky grin.

Verus nodded at the scars that mapped my chest. "I'd hate to add to your collection." He winked.

I huffed a laugh. "I'd love to see you try."

We both got into fighting stances, and I loosened up, dancing on the balls of my feet, waiting for him to strike. Verus looked as calm as the lake on a peaceful day as he slowly circled me, his eyes watching every movement as if picking out weaknesses.

Well, if he wasn't going to strike, I would. I feigned a right hook before coming at him with a left uppercut, which he deflected with ease.

"Already starting with the tricks, I see," Verus goaded.

Before I could respond, his right arm jabbed at me lightning fast, and I barely twisted out of the way in time. "Distraction tactic. Clever," I quipped as I swept out my right leg, attempting to knock him down. Verus leaped into the air while swinging a fist at me, which managed to clip my jaw. I spat blood into the sand and grinned. "Nice one, but you won't land another hit."

"We'll see, Your Majesty," Verus taunted.

What followed was a flurry of punches and strikes. We both got some good hits in but were evenly matched.

I wiped the sweat off my brow and held my hand out. "Shall we call this a tie?"

Verus stalked toward me, a mischievous glint in his eyes as he reached for my hand.

"Faex," I muttered as he grabbed my arm and used it as leverage to pull me off-balance and flip me to the ground.

Verus pressed an arm across my chest to hold me down and lowered his face toward mine. "She might not have accepted it, but I know."

I stiffened, my eyes not leaving his. "I don't know what you're talking about."

He loosened the pressure on my chest just slightly. I took my opportunity and launched myself up and over, rolling Verus to the ground. He laughed. "Nice move, Majesty."

"Just call me Wynn," I said as I jumped to my feet and reached down to help him up. "You're not going to flip me again, are you?" I asked.

"Tempting, but no," Verus quipped as he gripped my hand and quickly got to his feet. Without letting go, he pulled me in for a pat on the back. "Listen, I'm sorry for what you're going through, but I'm not going anywhere."

I swallowed and nodded before letting go and turning to look at the rest of the group. Helio and Rik were busy sparring, the clangs of their swords ringing through the air. Glint and Ember were sipping on water, watching them admiringly. As far as I could tell, no one had overheard Verus' words.

"That was quite the little show there," Ari said as she sauntered over.

"Did you like seeing me on my back, wife?" Verus joked.

Ari blushed, then looked at me. "Do you want me to heal your jaw, Wynn? Verus got you pretty good."

I shrugged. "I've had worse."

"Nonsense," she retorted before placing her hand on my face and flooding it with her power.

Verus' eyes caught mine, and I saw a sadness mixed with understanding in them.

"Is there anything you need, Verus?" Ari asked him.

"Nothing a dip in the water won't fix," he replied cockily.

I laughed. "Maybe you should check his ego, Ari."

She rolled her eyes. "I'm aware . . . Verus! I've got just the concoction for you."

"Faex no. Save that foul-smelling mixture for someone else," he threw over his shoulder as he jogged toward the lake.

"I added rosemary!" she yelled.

"Not enough!" he retorted.

Ari threw up her hands in exasperation, and I chuckled. "Do I want to know?"

"Oh, it's just something Liisa and I cooked up in Zephyria. It works amazingly on sore muscles, but the smell is . . . potent."

I shook my head and grinned. "Unfortunately, I've been a victim of said concoction. I have to agree with Verus. If only it didn't work so well, I'd have it banned."

Ari blew out a breath and crossed her arms. "You stubborn males."

"You've got yourself quite the husband, Ari. It's been really nice seeing you smile and laugh despite everything. I'm glad you're happy."

"Thank you . . . I know this must be so strange for you, Wynn, but I'm glad we're finding our way back to being friends," she replied with a smile, then turned and followed her husband into the lake.

"Always . . ." I said softly under my breath.

She's not yours, but that's okay. You're going to be okay.

CHAPTER 34

A Vulnerable Kingdom

"What if we take a tenth of the laborers and have them build new housing on the outer parts of Prisma?" Aella asked. She'd been pacing around my study with Rat perched on her shoulder. She stopped and leaned over the desk, bright-eyed as the idea came to her. "It shouldn't affect the progress of the arena by that much and would at least help take care of housing. You could even delegate a small portion to growing new crops and developing farmlands on the peripherals."

Our wedding had been delayed due to ongoing construction on the arena. To speed up the repairs, the king had ordered an influx of laborers, but it was becoming a disaster. Recruited en masse, we were facing a crisis of housing, feeding, and controlling the suddenly doubled population of workers. Not to mention the added cost of stipends we were expected to send home to all of their families.

Rat leapt from Aella's shoulder and burrowed into the pile of crumpled-up parchment with our cast-off ideas.

"That is a promising solution." I hummed. While my father cared not if elementals were given bare minimum living conditions, it weighed heavily on my conscience, knowing this was all being done for my nuptials. "So long as we can convince Solanos that they wouldn't be too far outside his watchful eye and control, this may be just the answer we need. He will not consider it otherwise." I tapped my fingers together. "He's shut down every idea I've brought to the council, but perhaps if we spin this in his favor . . ."

"Isn't this already in his favor? By doing this, he fares a lesser chance of the elementals turning against him. If anything, the way things are now, a revolt is just one straw short of happening."

I knew she was right, but Solanos would never see it that way. Against better advice, he had cut the elementals' stipends in half—*after* the tributes had signed up and boarded their ships, no less. What could they do? They'd get that or nothing at all, and grumblers were taken care of the old-fashioned way. Though I feared there was only so much they'd put up with before even that ceased working.

I stroked the hair back from Aella's lovely face. I imagined it must be difficult for the elemental fae to understand the depths of depravity Iris rulers would turn to rather than admit their vulnerability.

"My father has no tolerance for even the idea of a revolt. He would love the excuse to slaughter the whole lot of them to set an example. Better to not put ideas of revolt in his mind. He's acted on less than rumors before. I will present your original suggestion with the argument that it will increase their productivity so he only sees it as benefiting him."

"Do we stand so little a chance? Are we so little a threat to the king that he could wipe out such a large group of people without objection?" she asked, looking up at me with her big, blue eyes.

"For most elemental fae, yes," I said. "But not you, Tempest. You are the biggest threat he's ever faced. He's simply too proud to admit it."

She pursed her lips, suppressing a smile. I adored how she reacted to my words, as though she was never more than seconds away from either slapping me or falling into my arms. More than that, I loved her tenacity and her commitment to serving her people. Though perhaps most of all, I treasured her curious and brilliant mind. She was as fierce as she was vulnerable, and I was determined to cherish and support her, no matter the price.

CHAPTER 35

A Bad Feeling

ARIANWEN

After much debate, the time for action had finally come. Lucris had agreed to use his connections and intelligence gathered in the Palatium Crystalis in exchange for Wynn's support of his claim to the Argenti throne once the Iris were defeated. We also needed to get his son, Han, out of the city. The last thing I wanted was to see that self-serving male as king of the Argenti, but it was more important to rescue Aella. We could deal with the consequences of that bargain later.

Lucris had sent word to Lorin, one of his Iris allies, and he'd agreed to meet us in one of his establishments on the outskirts of Prisma, where he would glamour Wynn as Aurum fae and escort us onto the palatium grounds. Every Iris in Prisma had an open invitation to attend the revels celebrating the prince's upcoming wedding to my daughter. It had become the latest trend to bring their own elementals to these grand occasions, Lorin had explained, so no one would think twice when he brought a group of us into the palatium with him. Once we were inside, we could easily blend in with the other servants. We would never have another opportunity like this.

A shudder went through me at the thought of Aella being married to the prince of the Iris, and I hated to see her bound to one of them. We couldn't get her out of Prisma soon enough. As the chosen one, I could only pray the stars would be on her side. Without her, all our plans to unite the elementals would be for nothing.

Verus wrapped the long, leather straps of my sandals back and forth around my calves all the way up to my thighs before tying them off in a neat bow.

"I don't have a good feeling about this," he said.

"Verus," I hissed as I adjusted the skimpy dress I'd been given. "Can you try not to curse us before we even begin?"

Verus' eyes trailed up and down my body, lingering on the exposed skin of my thighs peeking through the dress' high slits. "I'm not sure I want you going in there looking like *that*, wife," he growled softly. I reached around to help him fasten the basic armor of an elemental guard on himself.

"Trust me, one look at Wynn and no one will be looking at me."

Helio's sudden laugh quickly turned to a cough as Wynn glared at him. His outfit was a lewd mimicry of a guard's attire, a decorative leather pauldron strapped across his bare shoulder and chest. His glamoured golden skin was on display in a way that reminded me the Iris only saw us as property to be ogled and used.

"Try not to drool, Helio," Wynn quipped.

Verus tried unsuccessfully to hide his smile as we gathered around to go over the final plans. Helio and Verus would escort our Iris ally as his guards, giving Wynn and me the opportunity to wander about the palatium unnoticed while they retrieved Lucris' son.

As we were preparing to leave, Lorin returned with a young Argenti female dressed the same as myself. Something about her seemed familiar, but I couldn't put my finger on it.

"My servant will go with you," he said.

I looked at Wynn, unsure what this meant. Could we trust this male? Was he using her to spy on us? I also didn't like the idea of putting anyone else at risk.

"We'd rather not bring any more into this mission than necessary," Wynn said from where he stood at the table, studying the patchwork of a map Lucris had given us. It wasn't perfect, but it gave us an idea of the grounds, halls, and wings. During the competition, Viera had been sending bits and pieces of the map of the palatium, which included some passageways we planned to locate.

Lorin eyed it speculatively. "It appears your map is unfinished and missing some important chunks of information."

"I was a contestant in the Matri-Ludus and might be able to help fill in some of those gaps," the female offered.

It hit me then why she looked so familiar, the similarities in her features.

"Lewenne?" I asked almost hesitantly.

She took a step back. "How do you know my name?"

I clapped my hand over my mouth and gasped. "You're alive! Thank the stars. Believe it or not, I know your mother. Oh, sweetheart. Are you sure you want to get into this? It'll be dangerous. I will never forgive myself if something goes wrong knowing you could've been safe here."

Lewenne shook her head. "I came to Prisma looking for revenge, but now all I want—all I can think of—is surviving. If I don't go in there with you and at least try to find my friends, I won't have a reason for that anymore. Please, I need to go back to the Palatium Crystalis."

"As long as you understand the risk," Wynn said.

"You may want to hurry up if you want to arrive before it gets too crowded," Lorin declared, waving his hands at us.

I took a deep breath. We were finally heading out. It was happening. I stretched up onto my toes and gave Verus a quick kiss. "We're going to get our girl back, okay? We won't fail."

Verus squeezed me tight before letting go. "I wish we weren't splitting up when we get in there."

"Remember the plan." I patted his chest. "Besides, there's no way you could pass for a servant. All those muscles? You'd be a guard for sure," I teased, hoping to put him at ease.

"I have muscles too," Wynn grumbled.

I bit back a laugh as we hopped onto the back of the carriage that would take us to the palatium.

As the carriage rolled toward the grand Palatium Crystalis, I clung to the hope that I would be holding Aella in my arms before I knew it. A small part of me was terrified I wouldn't recognize her after everything she had been through, but I silenced that thought immediately—I was her mother; I'd recognize her anywhere. I just prayed we weren't too late and we'd actually be able to find her. My biggest fear was that she had been made nameless and wouldn't know herself or any of us anymore.

I let out a breath after we finished crossing the narrow bridge and passed through the gates with no trouble. With the influx of Iris, the guards had just waved us through.

Doors wide open, the grand entrance to the palatium was more majestic than I could have imagined. Wynn, Lewenne, and I trailed behind Lorin into the luxurious entry, trying to keep our heads down as we passed through the crowded space. Even still, the glossy floors reflected the golden glow from the hanging glass orbs of light that appeared to float above our heads. I was grateful for the extra protection of Helio and Verus, as the Iris who flitted around were bold with their glances and even more daring with their hands.

I peeked back over my shoulder at Verus and immediately noticed the stiffened set of his shoulders and deep crease of his brow. There was a haunted look in his eyes as his gaze darted all around us. Faex. How could I have been so thoughtless to not realize what coming here would mean for him? Was he looking for her? The mate he'd lost twenty-five years ago? My heart ached, and I wanted to reach out and pull him into my arms, but we had to stay on task. When I finally caught his attention, I tilted my head, raising my brows, silently trying to communicate. He blinked once and gave a stiff nod. We'd talk later. I mouthed *"I love you,"* not missing the shimmer of unshed tears he quickly blinked away as he mouthed *"I love you too."*

We reached the end of the hall, which split in two directions. One side appeared to be inspired by the water court, and the other was a contrast with golden fire. We turned left, entering the water-themed corridor, with towering ceilings that seemed to reach the stars themselves and magnificent waterfalls that fell into shallow, glass-encased pools. Argenti performers danced and swam through them, their magic probably used to sustain the continuous flow of water pouring unnaturally into the decorative displays.

The entrance to the hall Lewenne had debriefed us on, which she'd assumed Aella would be held in, was closed off due to the celebration, but she thought we could find a way in through the gardens. Lorin led us out onto a terrace, where the revel was even more unrestrained than indoors. It was here I was able to see the disparities between palatial servants and visitors such as myself.

While some of the elementals seemed to be enjoying themselves, it was hard to ignore the glazed-over eyes of those whose bodies were used without consent, which only fanned the flames of anger I held toward the Iris. I had to remind myself I was here for one purpose only: get Aella and get out. This wasn't our time to free everyone, as much as it hurt to walk by and do nothing. I was already concerned about Lewenne trying to find her friends and how that could interfere with our escape.

There were small, silk canopies filled with lounge cushions set up all over the garden and terrace. My face flushed at the open debauchery taking place. The moans and cries of release managed to break through the incessant beat of music, making me wildly uncomfortable.

Lorin claimed one of the tents and motioned to Wynn and me. "I need wine and fruit," he demanded. "Go on then. Hurry up."

Lewenne gave us directions to the elementals' wing before rushing off while Verus and Helio casually slipped into the crowd in search of Lucris' son. Wynn grabbed a tray of spiky, green and magenta fruit from an unsuspecting elemental fae rushing by and was met with an angry look. Giving him a tight-lipped smile, Wynn said, "Apologies. I need this more than you do."

I quickly grabbed the elemental, pushing some calming energy into him. "Don't mind him. He's in a bad mood," I said soothingly.

The elemental shook his head, muttered a few curses, and turned back in the direction he had come from.

"I thought we were trying to keep a low profile," I hissed at Wynn after he set the tray in front of Lorin.

"Our time is limited," Wynn replied. "This is our chance."

I rolled my eyes and followed Wynn as he wove through the revelers back toward the palatium.

CHAPTER 36

VESPERA LUMINA

KALEIDOS

It was the eve before our wedding, and I was to celebrate the night away. Estrella had orchestrated a revel beyond imagining, coined the Vespera Lumina. The Palatium Crystalis would be open to all Iris, no invitation needed. By the time I arrived, the halls that encircled the palatium were already flooded with guests. She'd turned the entire circular hall into a continuous revel divided into three separately themed sections—fire, water, and earth—which expanded out into the gardens beyond with even more merriment and feasting. The halls felt almost like being outdoors, with their extravagant decor assisted by the magic of illusion and the lights sparkling above that mimicked the night sky.

Aella would be safe in my wing for most of the night, but I was expected to be out and about socializing, enjoying and partaking in the debauchery.

"So what do you think, cousin?" Estrella asked, clearly fishing for compliments.

"You've outdone yourself as expected," I obliged. I could play nice for now. Truthfully, I'd grown tired of her parties. After so many years of endless festivities, they'd all begun feeling the same. Just another means of passing the time, losing ourselves to life's pleasures, ignorant of the harsh realities we had placed the people we ruled in. I could hardly be dazzled by lights, music, or dancing when I'd seen them every night of my life. Although even I couldn't entirely deny it was an impressive feat to pull off something of this scale. I'd give her that.

"How's the little fish?" Estrella asked, the strain in her voice betraying the lightness she was trying to project.

"You really ought to be grateful to her, you know, or you'd still be inside that tank," I quipped. "If you'd like, I can have it sent to your rooms. You could do nightly performances."

"You wouldn't dare." Estrella narrowed her eyes at me.

"Isn't tonight supposed to be all about what pleases *me*, cousin?" She'd grown too comfortable and potentially dangerous with her power left unchecked, and she was clearly in need of another *gentle* reminder.

Estrella stiffened, and all pleasant pretenses fled. "Clearly you're in a foul mood this evening." She snatched a pair of glittering wine glasses off a serving platter, dumping them out haphazardly on the floor. "None of that cheap stuff," she spat and pulled out a small bottle of liquor from a pocket in her skirts, filling the glasses and then handing me one. "To your happiness, and whatever pleases you, my dearest cousin."

I couldn't drink it fast enough. Perhaps it would dull the gnawing desire to strangle her. After all she'd done to my Aella, being around her was a lesson in restraint. She'd had it coming after poisoning Viera, but it was Aella who still deserved to take revenge of her own. When the time was right, she would have her chance, and it couldn't come soon enough.

What had once been a friendship not unlike siblings had slowly rotted, revealing itself more and more for what it now was. Estrella had been using me to gain popularity and influence, and if I let her, she'd gladly destroy me if it brought her one step closer to her ultimate goal. It wasn't shocking, unfortunately, as Iris royalty had a long history of betrayal amongst ourselves. The only reason my Uncle Ventius had never challenged Solanos was because he had no desire for the responsibilities of ruling. But because of my closeness to Estrella, deep down, I'd always sensed there was a strong chance her life or mine would end at the edge of the other's blade.

I watched bemused as Estrella argued with any courtier who would listen. She had become preoccupied with one of the fire dancers performing above us, trying to convince us that he looked exactly like her former husband. She was in a heavy debate with another when I found my exit. I worked my way through the gilded, fire-themed halls, making my appearances as was my duty. There were so many guests in attendance, I had no idea how the Palatium Crystalis managed to control what went on. I could always tell who belonged by the apathetic looks on their faces. Lower-ranking Iris who hadn't been inundated with the constant revelry still had an unjaded appreciation for these delights, marked by their looks of excitement and awe. They did not yet need to intoxicate themselves to elicit those fanciful feelings.

Once I entered the earth-themed section, which had been transformed into a tropical paradise, the color of my blouse changed from gold to a rich bronze. I wove through the crowd, where not enough of the guests seemed to recognize who I was, failing to offer me the respectable distance I deserved. It had been a mistake not to have maintained my royal guards' presence.

Distracted and disoriented by the plant-covered walls and acrobats who swung from hanging vines overhead, I seemed to be going in circles trying to find the servants' passageway. My head grew fuzzy, dizzy even. *Strange.* I didn't recall drinking that much, but one thing was certain: I was about to be ill. One moment, I found myself leaning on a stranger only to stumble into a jog toward the outer wall the next, where I retched violently. The courtiers and nobles followed me with their eyes, and I could practically hear the whispers about the mad prince digging through layers of decor to unearth the hidden doors behind them. I didn't care. I was overheating and my brow was damp with sweat. I must have been drugged, and I needed to get out of there before I passed out.

Once inside the passageway, I realized I'd been going in the wrong direction and had ended up farther from my wing. I leaned against the cool wall for a moment to try to catch my bearings and then continued on. Something was off. Were those voices? Footsteps? I'd never even heard whispers in these passageways before. The servants were always like ghosts the way they passed through unnoticed. I pivoted to face the pair of suspected intruders behind me, but I must've turned too quickly. Everything spun around me, doubling my vision, making it impossible to focus on the figures down the hall.

"You aren't supposed to . . ." I began before my vision tunneled into darkness.

CHAPTER 37
A STROKE OF LUCK

ARIANWEN

The hall in front of us split into two paths, and I stared down at the map, trying to make sense of the twists and turns that would supposedly lead us to Aella's chambers. Lewenne had pointed us toward the elementals' wing from the gardens, which didn't seem to be that far, but based on the map, we'd need to go out of our way to reach the secret passageways. I could only pray we were on the right track.

There was a chance, of course, that Aella wouldn't even be there, but we couldn't wait. Our plan hinged on being able to sneak her out amid all the celebration and past the Iris who were most likely drunk off their arses and not paying attention to who was leaving the grand Palatium Crystalis.

The servants' hall was quiet, as most of the servants were out taking care of the excess of Iris guests, and a chill went down my spine as I worried whether or not we were walking into a giant trap. What if Lucris had somehow betrayed us? But no, he wouldn't risk his own son, would he?

"I think we go this way," I said, pointing to the left.

"Are you certain?" Wynn asked, his body tense and on high alert as he peeked over my shoulder at the map.

I could feel the tension rolling off him in waves and really wanted to send some soothing power into him, but he hadn't asked me to.

Holding up the map for him, he squinted in the dim light. "Yes, I think you're right."

Unable to stop my eye roll, I marched ahead. "You know, it will take us twice as long if you keep second-guessing every one of my decisions. If you'd rather decipher the map, have at it." I held it up in the air, waiting for him to snatch it out of my hands.

"Must you be so difficult?" Wynn groused as he caught up to me.

When he didn't grab the map, I lowered my arm and flicked my eyes down to check the directions once more.

"You're the one being difficult," I muttered under my breath.

Suddenly, Wynn grabbed me and pushed me into the wall, blocking my body with his.

"What in the everloving depths are you doing?" I whispered harshly.

"Quiet. I heard something," he replied.

My body stiffened in fear at being caught so close to our goal, and I held my breath as I waited for Wynn to say or do something.

"It's just one person," he whispered softly, pulling away from me and stealthily stalking toward whoever was in the passage up ahead.

I followed after him and watched as an Iris male spun around in surprise and gasped out, "You aren't supposed to—" before clutching at his throat as he dropped to the ground.

I'd seen Wynn do it before, but it still unnerved me when he used his powers in that way.

"Is he alive?" I asked in horror as I rushed forward to check his pulse. As much as I hated the Iris, I still didn't like the idea of taking a life; it went against everything I believed in as a healer.

"He's fine. He'll just wake up with a wicked headache," Wynn replied as he knelt beside me. "I wonder . . ." he pondered aloud. "Could this be the prince?"

Beside the young male's head on the ground was a silver crown. It was simple enough that it didn't immediately scream royalty, but woven in were bronze and gold metals, and the male did appear to match the description we'd received. But what was he doing in the servants' passages, and alone?

"This is perfect," I replied, satisfied that he was still breathing. If our plan failed, we'd now have something much bigger to barter with: the king's sole heir. "We can trade the prince of the Iris for Aella!"

"Or we could stash him somewhere and continue the plan," Wynn replied. "We came here for our daughter. Taking the Iris prince . . . Stars know what disaster that might unleash, if we could even manage to get him out unseen. We're lucky he was drunk when we found him, or I don't know that taking him out would have been so easy. I say we leave him and count our lucky stars he was alone."

"But what if he wakes up and sounds the alarm?"

A groan had me turning my attention back to the Iris male on the floor. I felt the pull of air, and I held up my hand. "Wait, Wynn . . . Maybe he can lead us to her."

"Lead you to whom?" the male said suddenly as he raised a hand to his head.

Before I could reply, he rolled onto his back. He tried to sit up, then gave up, letting his head drop back to the floor and closing his eyes again. A dopey smile stretched across his face.

How drunk is this male?

I could see Wynn shaking his head from the corner of my eye. Sadly, I was accustomed to dealing with this sort of thing, and it didn't even phase me.

"Summon Kasha or . . . Yulema, would you? They'll . . . they'll know what to do," the prince said, his voice and composure revealing his aloofness to the danger he was in.

"If you make any loud sounds or call for help, just know I can suck the air right out of your lungs in a heartbeat," Wynn said threateningly.

"Yes, of course . . . no, of course, whatever you need to do," the male said with a lazy wave of his hand, not even bothering to open his eyes again.

Wynn rifled through the prince's pockets, patting him down, looking for any hidden weapons, keys, or any other potentially useful objects on his person.

The prince's brows furrowed again, and he rubbed at the space between his eyes. "Wait, wait . . ." He grunted, blinking his eyes open. He stared at me as if he were looking at a specter. "Who *are* you?" He then focused his eyes on Wynn, then back on me, a puzzled look crossing his face. "Why do you look like my Aella?"

He said her name. Does that mean she isn't nameless?

I was almost too afraid to let myself believe it. I nudged Wynn. "It most definitely is the prince."

A dry chuckle came out of the male, and he nodded, flicking his hand in an irreverent manner. "Prince Kaleidos, at your service."

He attempted to sit up again, this time succeeding, which meant he was sobering up. Even his coloring was improving. That could mean one of two things: he would be a little more useful in finding Aella, or, more likely, he would cause major problems for us. I had no idea if we'd be able to defend ourselves against a sober Iris prince. I watched as he picked up the fallen crown, placing it sloppily on his brow.

A gust of wind pinned the prince's head against the wall, and he struggled against it.

"If you want to walk out of here alive, you will lead us to Aella immediately," Wynn growled.

Kaleidos' eyes glittered in the dim light. "No need for theatrics." His words sounded slightly sharper, and his eyes bounced between mine and Wynn's. "You're here to rescue her . . . aren't you?" When neither of us replied, he squeezed his eyes shut. "Release me, and I will help get your daughter back."

CHAPTER 38
AN EXERCISE IN TRUST

WYNN

This was too good to be true. There was no way it could be this easy to get Aella out of here.

"How do we know you're not going to betray us the second I let you go?" I asked calmly.

"Is she okay?" Ari asked, a note of desperation in her tone. "Does she know who she is?"

"She's fine for now, but I suppose you're going to have to trust me," Kaleidos replied, speaking slowly, as though it took a great deal of concentration to choose his words.

"Why did you call her *your* Aella?" Ari asked.

Ignoring her question, Kaleidos continued, "She *is* your daughter, isn't she? She looks just like you . . . both of you."

I stiffened. There was no way. Then I looked down. *Faex.*

The prince shook his head as if trying to rid himself of the effects of whatever had gotten him so intoxicated, a strangled laugh leaving him. Then, out of nowhere, his eyes shut, his body slumping against the wall.

In a second, Ari was on him, infusing healing magic into him.

"What are you doing?" I asked, slightly alarmed and tempted to pull her away.

"If there's even a chance he can—oh stars!" Her eyebrows knit together, her next words filled with shock. "He's been poisoned. Who would have poisoned the prince?"

"Nothing about this is right. Like I said before, I think we should leave him and get out of here. This can't be good."

Ari shook her head as she continued to work. "But he knows where Aella is."

"I don't like you wasting your source on him," I grumbled.

"Well it isn't going to take much—his body is fighting the poison better than I could. I just need to pull it from his brain."

Her hands hovered over him, repeatedly sweeping from his head toward his heart in rapid, rhythmic motions. The prince abruptly startled awake, and Ari lurched back.

"What did you do to me?" Kaleidos asked, staring up at me with an accusatory glare.

"You were poisoned. She healed you. Clearly you have enemies in the court. Why?" I asked.

"Enemies? Poison?" As though he had just figured it out, Kaleidos threw a hand to his face, muttering curses under his breath while a sinister laugh brewed beneath.

"You think this is funny?" I frowned.

"Petty revenge . . . That's what this is." He gave me a razor-sharp look, his eyes nearly black with intent, all traces of drink and poison gone. "But that does not concern you."

I growled, tempted to steal away his air supply again. "Of course it concerns us if you're involved with Aella. Tell us where she is, or I will cut off your breath and have her reverse the healing."

It was a bluff, as I wasn't sure Ari could even do such a thing, but the prince didn't need to know that.

"Your glamour is fading, *Adamas*. Might be challenging to sneak an extinct creature and *my* bride out of a palatium full of Iris without my help."

"She doesn't belong to you," Ari spat. "Take us to her. Now."

The prince held up a hand and tutted. "Believe it or not, I want her out of here just as much as you do, but there is one problem." He smoothed the creases in his shirt as though that were the solution. "Aella is to make an appearance at the revel at the stroke of midnight. If she's found missing, the palatium will be locked down, and you will never make it out of here alive."

"Do you think we can trust him?" Ari asked me hesitantly.

I shook my head. "I don't know . . . but I don't think we have a choice."

"I am still quite present . . ." the prince said with a hint of arrogance.

Ari's eyes glistened in the dim light. I could see her struggling not to move forward with the original plan and just get Aella out of here.

"There's at least an hour until midnight," I said. "If you truly mean to help, what do you have in mind?"

"Good, there is still time," Kaleidos mused, rising to his feet. "You must do exactly as I say if this is to work. Understood?"

I clenched my fists, hating that we were at the mercy of this Iris prick, but nodded in affirmation. Unable to stop myself, I let loose a gust of air, causing the prince to stumble, my lips quirking into a grin.

"This would be a lot easier if you stopped threatening me, Adamas. You may have knocked me out once, but I heal quickly," the prince said with a sneer.

I felt a slight rumble under my feet, and I raised my hands in surrender. I shouldn't have underestimated him.

"Aella is probably being dressed at this very moment for her appearance," Kaleidos continued, as if unphased by my actions. "To get her out, I will need to create a diversion for her handler and glamour one of her maids as a substitute. There will be a parade at midnight coinciding with her appearance. If she sneaks out then, everyone will be too preoccupied to notice, and you should be able to make a getaway from the storage room off the side of the palatium. Once you hear the fireworks start, that is your sign to go."

"So you expect us just to wait here for her to show up? What do you take us for, fools?" Ari quipped. "What guarantee do we have that you'll do any of these things and help her escape? For all we know, you will leave and immediately send guards to apprehend us."

A pained look swept over Kaleidos' face before hardening into a mask of something darker. "Do you think it is a simple thing for me to trust you, who I have only just met, with my Aella? You're right, there is no guarantee—for her safety or yours. But if there's even a chance she might be free again, I'm willing to take it. As her parents, I can only imagine you share the sentiment."

The earnestness in his tone gave me pause. Could he really mean what he was saying? Why would he care about Aella?

Ari gasped. "You're in love with her."

Impossible. The Iris only cared about themselves. With the exception of a few Iris allies we had made, they'd made it clear elementals were nothing more than a means to an end. But a prince? Even if he were capable, surely there was no way he would have fallen in love . . . Unthinkable.

When the prince showed no sign of denial, Ari turned to me. "I think we should trust him. He's the best chance we have of getting her out."

"Why don't you take us to her now and we can escort her to safety?" I argued.

"Are you prepared to eliminate her handler and all of her guards with a little air and water magic? They would sound the alarm before you even stepped near her," Kaleidos scoffed. "Wait here, and I will send my trusted maid, Yulema, to find you. She'll lead you to the storage room. After that, you're on your own."

"How will we know it's her? Yulema?"

He considered for a moment before lowering his voice to a whisper. "You'll know when she says, 'The stars are with us.'"

"We'll wait then," Ari agreed before I could argue further.

"Fine," I grumbled.

"Can you do anything about his glamour?" Ari asked.

Kaleidos narrowed his eyes in concentration, and I looked down as my skin once again gave off a golden hue. "I think you'll find this glamour lasts longer than the previous one, even if you do use some of your magic."

"Thanks," I muttered.

"Why did it fail?" Ari asked.

"Either the Iris who applied it became too drunk and lost his control over it, or you used too much source, which repelled it from you. Perhaps both . . . But never fear, I shall not betray you, and the aether in my royal blood will not fail you," the prince said with a smugness in his voice. He offered a slight incline of his head before he spun on his heel and sauntered off, leaving us to contemplate this new knowledge of Iris glamours.

I leaned against the wall and crossed my arms, the silence between Ari and me suddenly rife with tension. Before, we'd had a purpose in trying to find Aella, which had helped stem some of the awkwardness between us. But now? Stars knew how long we'd have to wait for this Yulema to appear.

Ari mirrored my stance on the wall across from me. "Can you believe the prince is in love with Aella?"

I snorted. "I'll believe it when I see him actually follow through. Though if she is anything like you, I understand why."

She rolled her eyes with a small smile. "It does make me feel a little better though, that maybe he was here protecting her even when I couldn't."

"Perhaps we'll let him live when this is all over."

"Wynn! Must you be so murderous?" She waved her hand at me, annoyance radiating off of her. "Your glamour almost completely faded due to your little power struggle with the prince. You're lucky he fixed it."

I sighed. "I still don't trust him."

"Back to your murderous tendencies," Ari continued. "If there's a chance *our* daughter loves him back, would you be so quick to take him from her?"

"To save my people? Absolutely. It's not as if they're fated by the stars. Imagine that, the stars pairing an elemental with an Iris . . ." I scoffed.

A pained look crossed her face. "Fated or not, we both know the devastation of losing someone you love."

My heart throbbed at the cruel reminder. She had no idea . . . or did she?

"Fine. Perhaps we'll let Aella decide his fate," I conceded.

"Wynn, I—"

I held up a hand as the soft shuffle of feet caught my attention, and Ari went silent. My body went on high alert, every muscle ready to spring into action in case it wasn't who we were waiting for, as an elemental fae came into view.

"The stars are with us." She spoke softly. "Please follow me."

She bustled past us, and I looked at Ari, seeing hope shine in her eyes. My heart skipped an uneven beat. I motioned for her to go ahead of me so I could watch her back, and she hurried after Yulema.

We passed a fork in the passage, veering in a direction that wasn't shown on our map. With torches fewer and farther between, just enough light cut through the dark, and the walls seemed to press in on us, adding to the sense of being trapped. The air was a stale mix of dust and stone and something faintly sweet like lillies. I kept moving, focused on reaching the storage room where I'd meet our daughter for the first time. Where we'd take her to freedom. How would she react? Would she even give me the chance to get to know her? I could only hope. A shiver of anticipation and nerves went down my spine. A longing to know this person I'd only recently learned about—someone who was a part of me that I didn't even know was missing—swept through me.

The path seemed never ending as we took multiple turns.

Stars, this better not be a trap.

"We're nearly there," Yulema said, seeming to sense our unease.

The passageway opened up into a larger room with wine barrels and crates filled with food and supplies.

"She will meet you here," Yulema explained. "No one else should be down this way, but perhaps try to stay out of sight if you can?"

We nodded in understanding and watched as Yulema disappeared back the way we'd come.

"I can't believe we're so close," Ari said, her eyes glistening with unshed tears. "Stars, I was honestly worried I might never see her again."

I couldn't help but squeeze her shoulder gently. "It's going to be all right, Ari. We'll get her out of here, I promise."

CHAPTER 39
You Will Not Hold Back

Aella

"Leave us," Kal ordered Himmel and Nephos as he stepped into the room.

I was being fitted for a gown that draped over my body, highlighting every curve. Its fine, silver chainmail clung to my flesh, and all I could think was how grateful I was that it was not made of real iron. Himmel gathered herself, the click of her heels reflecting her irritation as she made her way out of the room. She was probably worried about running out of time and opportunities to reprimand me before I was brought out in the crystal box, but she wouldn't argue with the prince.

The moment they left the room and it was just the two of us, Kal sprinted toward me with a sad, regretful smile. He swept me into his strong arms and kissed me desperately, heartachingly. *I love you*, his kisses said. *I need you, I want you.* He pulled back, taking me in with his deep green eyes, the gold and bronze ribbons like flames in his irises. His fingers traced along the curve of my jaw, gliding down my neck and chest.

"Kal?" Something was wrong. I could feel the swell of pained emotions radiating off him.

His lips turned up slightly at the corners. "My dearest, Aella. My tempest, my sea nymph. My siren, my water dancer." His hands rested behind my ears, and I searched his gorgeous, sorrowful face for answers. "I'm getting you out."

I stiffened. Surely I'd misheard. "What?"

"Your parents are here. They're waiting for you." He winced.

I stared at him blankly, too stunned to speak. Realization of what his words meant hit me slowly, and I looked toward the door from where he'd come.

"I've failed you in so much, Aella. Please, just let me do one right thing."

I whipped my head back to the prince. "I'm going home? They came for me? How is this even possible?" I took his hand to run with him to the door, but his feet were planted. I stopped. "Aren't you coming?"

Kal shook his head.

I huffed. "You're joking, obviously."

When he failed to affirm it, I drew in a breath. "You're coming with us." My voice dipped lower as my words became a demand.

"Aella," he said softly.

"Why?"

"If I don't stay here to create a distraction, you'll never get out, and neither will your parents."

I felt myself stretched in opposing directions—my heart splitting in two. I needed to go, yet I couldn't bring myself to leave this horrible place that had somehow become my own. This place I'd thought I would never escape. And what about the nameless? To abandon them now . . .

How could it be that, finally given the chance, I wasn't running for it?

I looked down at my hand that was still firmly gripped in Kal's, as though he was having just as hard a time letting me go. If I left, I might never see him again. I refused to give that sentiment any power. No. He needed me. We needed each other. We'd made so much progress together. I could even argue I needed to stay.

"Then I'm not going either," I forced the words out.

"I can't keep you here . . ." He broke off. "Not like this."

"But you wouldn't be *keeping* me here if I *chose* to remain."

"Look at you, Aella, at what this place has done to you. You're a shadow of your former self. You will only die here if you stay with me."

"But what about our plans? Don't I have a duty to finish what we've started?" Even as I was saying it, I knew they were only weightless, hopeful dreams with no guarantees.

"This is the best chance you'll have, Aella. You must take it."

"Please don't make me choose." I needed him to decide for me, I realized. "I don't want to go without you," I said, kissing him, claiming him.

"I can't leave, little nymph. I promised you I would find a way to end my father's rule."

I squeezed my eyes shut, burying my face into his chest. "And after I leave, what are the chances we'll meet again?"

He didn't answer, but he raised my hands to his lips, kissing them with so much reverence. He laced his fingers with mine, crossing them behind me as he backed me up against the wall. His forehead came down to mine, and a deep breath shuddered through him.

"I once told you that you were safe with me, but there's a limit to that. It's only a matter of time before my father takes you. So while we laze around in each other's arms, we are only biding our time. Knowing there is a possibility you can get out, there's no question in my mind—you must take it. I would never forgive myself if I did not press you to."

Kal released my hands and lowered himself down on one knee.

"How lucky I am to have been granted the honor of loving you. Even if only for a small moment in time, it was enough."

The meaning of his words made the air feel thick in my lungs, and I struggled to even my breaths.

He pulled his silver chained necklace up and over his head, offering it to me. "I have no ring to swear on, but I offer you this in parting. It is unbreakable, as is your spirit, as is my love for you."

My eyebrows scrunched together, but even as I opened my mouth to speak, I could find no words.

Kal's eyes pleaded with me, so I took the necklace from him. A surge of heat warped through me, and I grabbed his face with both hands, kissing him desperately. His lips were made sweeter in part by his words, only tainted by the salt of my tears.

I hate you, I need you, I can't live without you.

Chapter 40
A Little Violence

Arianwen

The silence of the large supply room was intimidating. Muffled music and chatter filtering in through the shuttered windows were not nearly loud enough to drown out our quiet conversation, and my anxiety was starting to get the better of me.

"How much time do we have to meet up with the others and return?" I whispered.

Wynn shifted uncomfortably on his feet as he took in the organized chaos of our surroundings. "We have less than an hour before we need to be back here, so we should go." We wove stealthily toward the exit, through barrels of wine and stacked crates of non-perishable goods, and he peeked his head outside.

"Do you really think we're going to be able to get everyone out safely?"

Wynn turned back to face me. "I wish I had an answer for you, but we have to trust the stars are on our side."

I bit my lip, wringing my hands. "Maybe I should stay here? Wait for Aella?"

He shook his head. "Let's stay together. We need to get everyone back here so we can leave—as long as the prince follows through with his distraction."

I sighed. "Fine. I just hate that we're so close to her. Regardless of what the prince says, I desperately need to make sure she's okay for myself."

Wynn put a gentle hand on my shoulder. "I get it, Ari. We *will* get her back." He glanced out again, and I noted the four-foot drop. "I don't see anyone, but let's keep our heads down so no one questions us," he said.

Wynn jumped down first, then offered a hand to assist my descent.

The music of the revel grew louder as we neared the south side of the palatium, and I couldn't help but gape at the beautiful, serpentine waterways that wound through the gardens. As we turned a corner, we almost collided with a group of Iris nobles, who reeked of alcohol. I muttered a soft apology and tried to pass them, keeping my head down, hoping against hope they would just ignore us.

One of them grabbed my arm, pulling me to a stop. "What are you doing so far from the party? Shouldn't you be attending your master?" he sneered. The others tittered to themselves, looking on with malicious glee, and I noticed a lone Aereus male being dragged along by a silver collar.

I pulled my arm out of the Iris' grasp, glaring at him. "We were sent on an important errand. We must be on our way."

The Iris noble looked me up and down. "Not so fast, Argenti." He turned to address his friends. "I can't imagine what errand they could have out here. I say they're lying. How shall we punish them?"

"Perhaps they can join our party," an Iris female tittered. "We'll have a whole set! I can't wait to play."

"Brilliant idea, Shelwin," one of the other Iris males replied as he pulled out two sets of chains with a smirk. "I knew these would prove useful. Our game is becoming all the more exciting . . ."

Trying to calm my nerves, I relaxed my posture and stepped forward, gently touching the Iris' arm. "There's nothing to worry about. We're headed back to serve our master. Go on and enjoy yourselves." I pushed some calming energy into him, praying to the stars it would work, even as my blood boiled at their behavior.

"What in the—release me at once!" The Iris noble looked enraged as he yanked his arm away before swinging a hand toward my face. Before it could make impact, it was blocked by Wynn's arm as he stepped in front of me.

"Do not lay a finger on her." His voice dropped to a low growl.

A flicker of fear shone in the Iris' eyes before he puffed out his chest, trying to regain control of the situation. "Perhaps we ought to teach you a lesson for wandering where you don't belong, slaves."

My eyes went to the Aereus male, who shook his head slightly, as if to warn us. I hated to imagine what game they had in mind.

"I'd like to see you try," I spat.

Wynn adjusted his stance, preparing for a fight. "You'll have to go through me, prick," he taunted.

The Iris noble looked spitting mad, the veins in his forehead bulging. "You dare speak to me like that? I would have your tongues cut out for such impertinence." He motioned to his friend. "Bring the chains."

Wynn took a step back and turned to look at me, tilting his head toward the large garden maze entrance about twenty yards away. Catching on to his plan, I didn't even wait for him to act and took off running in that direction.

I glanced over my shoulder and witnessed Wynn's fist smashing into the Iris' face before he ran after me. I bit my lip to keep myself from smiling. As much as I abhorred violence, that male had deserved it.

The other Iris nobles were in an uproar, even as their drunkenness made them sloppy and slower to respond. The ground rumbled beneath me, and I cursed, praying it wouldn't knock me off my feet. Wynn must have sent some wind to push me along—it felt like I was flying as I dashed into the maze. Wynn caught up to me and motioned to take the first right turn. We slid to a stop, the angry shouts of the Iris closing in.

"They should be here any second," he said. "I just needed to get them off the main path."

I nodded, catching my breath as we waited, my chest pounding as all my senses remained on high alert.

Two Iris nobles rushed around the corner, one of them holding a bejeweled dagger while the other swung the silver chains around. "You broke my nose, you flickering fool!" the first one shouted, throwing his dagger in our direction.

Wynn redirected it with a gust of wind, and their eyes widened in shock.

"What in the—"

Their bodies dropped to the ground as he pulled the air right out of their lungs.

I closed my eyes, turning away. Unlike what he'd done to the prince, these males would not be waking up. We couldn't leave witnesses, but I wished there could have been another way. If the king found out an Adamas had been here, it would compromise everything.

The rest of the Iris party turned the corner and cried out in shock at their fallen friends.

"You monsters!" the female named Shelwin screeched as she dropped to her knees in front of one of them. Another Iris female ran at us, swiping at Wynn with nails sharpened like talons.

He grunted as she left bloody trails down his arm before she collapsed. The Aereus male gaped at us in shock, and I hurried over to remove his collar as Wynn took care of the final Iris noble.

"Are you okay?" I asked the male softly.

He shuddered. "I don't know what I just saw, but thank you . . . You have no idea what they've been doing . . ."

"Come with us. We'll get you out."

He frowned. "What are you talking about? No one gets out of Prisma."

"We have a plan," I pleaded. I couldn't leave him behind—we'd make it work.

"Can you please help me move these Iris?" Wynn nodded toward the bodies.

"Of course," the Aereus replied, moving quickly to the first fallen Iris. He kicked at the body. "They're really dead?" he asked, almost in shock, before he started dragging him away.

Wynn bent down to grab another before I stopped him. "Hold on, Wynn. Let me take care of your arm first."

He straightened, holding it out toward me, and I summoned some water to clean it before letting my healing power get to work. When I was done, only faint lines remained.

"Thanks, Ari." He swallowed, looking down. "I'm sorry you had to see that."

"I know there will be casualties as we fight to free ourselves from the Iris, and they surely seemed wicked, but that doesn't make it hurt any less to see lives taken." I leaned against the hedge wall, taking a deep, cleansing breath. "Faex, Wynn. Why is everything so much more violent when you're around?" I tried to joke.

Wynn huffed a quiet laugh. "I can guarantee you my life has not been *this* violent in years. I think you're the one to blame." He looked over at me with sincerity in his eyes. "You know . . . I should thank you."

"What do you mean?" I asked with a raised brow.

"As angry as I was with you for showing up and turning my world upside down, it was just the kick in the arse I needed. You were right. I had been sitting up in my palatium, not doing everything I could have been doing. So thank you. Thank you for being a guiding star, for pushing me to fulfill my purpose."

My lips parted, his words so utterly unexpected, and yet they warmed my heart. Perhaps things could continue returning to some semblance of normal between us. Perhaps he could actually forgive me for keeping Aella from him and leaving all those years ago and I could let go of the guilt I had been carrying.

"Maybe you give me too much credit, Wynn, but you're welcome."

He stretched his hand out toward my face, then thought better of it, pulling away quickly. My heart ached a little knowing what he'd wanted to do—what had once felt so natural between us. I reached up and tucked the stray curl behind my ear myself. It was time to move forward and stop dwelling on the past.

Wynn went to help move the bodies further into the maze, depositing them at a dead end. Once our new Aereus friend concealed them in the earth, we quickly smoothed our hair and adjusted our clothing, making sure nothing looked amiss.

"Should we go out the way we came in?" I asked.

Wynn looked thoughtful before he closed his eyes and I felt a slight breeze sweep past me. "There's an exit closer to the revel," he replied. "I don't sense anyone else on the path, so we shouldn't run into any more trouble."

"That's a relief." I sighed.

"Who *are* you?" the Aereus male asked as he trailed behind.

"We'll explain everything once we get out of here," I replied, slowing so I could walk with him. "What's your name?"

He shrugged. "I honestly don't know . . . but you can call me Terran."

I gently squeezed his shoulder, wishing I could soothe the pain in his soul from losing something so essential—his identity.

As we followed Wynn, his power leading the way through the maze, I couldn't help but feel guilty that Aella had been disconnected from this other part of herself for so long. Would she be able to master the air element after stifling it her entire life? Maybe if I'd found a way to train her, she would have had an advantage during the trials—perhaps she wouldn't have become a prisoner.

As much as I wanted to wallow in my regrets, I'd made the decision to move forward. She would probably be very angry with me when we finally talked everything out. My oath had bound me to silence for so long, but I was finally free. I swore upon the stars I would make it up to her somehow.

Any worries I'd had about being noticed at the revel faded as soon as we stepped back onto the path. No one even gave us a second glance. There were so many bodies glistening in the starlight, writhing to the unfamiliar beat and melody of the music. As much as I tried to avert my eyes, it was difficult not to openly stare at how the debauchery had drastically intensified since we'd left. Clothing was sparse as activities that had been contained to the tents when we'd first arrived had spilled out into the open.

My nose wrinkled at the sour stench of wine mixed with sweat. I scanned the crowd, looking for the familiar shape of my husband. Stars willing, he and Helio had located Han without any trouble. We passed by the silk tent our Iris ally occupied, but I quickly looked away when I caught him engaged in his own flavor of indulgence, piles of fruit skins littering the floor.

"Do you see them?" I asked Wynn.

He shook his head. "Maybe we should stay here and wait for them to return?"

I jerked my head toward the tent and tried to hide a shudder. "I'd rather not listen to that."

Wynn laughed as he guided me around some dancers, Terran trailing behind us. "I can't say I blame you." Plucking a drink off a tray, he sniffed it before handing it to me. "This smells safe if you're thirsty."

"Thanks," I replied, knocking back half of it. The sparkling, fruity concoction tickled my throat on the way down, and I shivered slightly. "Maybe that will help me relax a little," I joked before handing the rest back to him.

Wynn grimaced after finishing the beverage. "Not as good as what we have back home, that's for sure."

"Ah, yes, glogg. There's nothing like it in Iveria, but we do boast a mean rum," I mused as I continued scanning the crowd for a familiar face.

My eyes caught on Lewenne, who looked to be having a heated conversation with another Argenti female while an Aereus and Aurum fae stood off to the side, looking around nervously.

"Faex," I said under my breath as I hurried over toward them. The last thing we needed was for Lewenne to draw unwanted attention, even if almost everyone present was highly intoxicated.

"Lewenne!" I exclaimed, noting that Wynn and Terran had followed me. "There you are. Our master is looking for you."

She looked up, her eyes darting between the three of us before her shoulders sagged in defeat. "Ilaria, please . . ." she said softly, turning back to the Argenti female.

"I'm done arguing with you. No one gets out of Prisma alive. You're a fool to even try," she replied under her breath, her nose turned up.

My heart ached for Lewenne. It was clear this friend meant a lot to her, but she wouldn't be persuaded, and we couldn't let it risk our entire plan.

I gently squeezed Lewenne's shoulder, pouring some soothing energy into her. "We need to go, sweetheart."

She nodded and went to join the other two females, leaving me with Ilaria. A light of recognition shone in her eyes as she looked me up and down.

"You came for her," she stated, almost in surprise. "You're Aella's mother."

I quickly glanced around, making sure no one was paying attention as I leaned in close and spoke into her ear. "You deserve more than this . . . If you change your mind, meet us at the supply entrance around the side of the palatium when the fireworks start. It's just below and to the right of the main entrance before the bridge."

Pulling away, I gave her one last look before I moved to join Wynn and the others.

"I'm pretty sure I spotted Verus and Helio," Wynn said. "We need to get them and head back."

My heart started beating faster, knowing I'd be reunited with Aella soon. I could only pray to the stars everything would go smoothly from here on out.

Chapter 41

Drink Up

Aella

"Look at you. You've ruined your makeup!" Himmel made no small show at how inconvenient it was to have lost so much time while Kal and I had been alone together. Kasha was wiping away dark smudges and reapplying my pearlescent makeup while I sat at the vanity at the back wall of the bedchamber. He'd left the room to grab something from his study before Himmel had arrived, assuring me he'd be right back, and I stared at the reflection of the open door, longingly waiting for his return. "You have been spoiled beyond measure in the prince's company," Himmel continued. "To think it would undo all of the progress we've made."

Her words used to scare me, but I found myself fearing her a little less. Possibly because I'd be leaving soon, or because there was little she could do before Kal returned.

"Perhaps you're in need of a little reminder," Himmel warned, and when I didn't immediately flinch at her words, as they'd so often come with sharp punishments to match, she repeated herself. "Yes, that's right, a reminder of your place would do you just right."

Knowing she'd be left unsatisfied without an answer, I bowed my head. "Yes, madam."

Himmel placed her hands on the shiny metal of the gown, transferring heat into it until I nearly yelped from the searing pain, reminding me of the similar infliction caused by the iron gowns I'd been forced to wear. I counted my breaths, willing myself not to scream. And with each breath and every second I endured, the pain transformed into something sharper inside me—a promise for revenge.

"Stop acting like such a spoiled brat. If it were up to me, I'd have you in chains again for such insolent behavior." She looked over to Kal, who was returning from his study, her voice instantly softening. "You'll have to excuse Nephos, Your Highness. He had another errand to attend to. The Faber Ludi will—"

"Take your hands off my bride," Kal said, his voice filled with malice as he realized what she had been doing.

The dim lighting by the door cast him in an ominous shadow, but all I felt was relief. So much that it numbed the pain of my ribs, the pain of losing him—even if only temporarily. And a small part of me relished the idea that I'd now get to watch him impose his cruel forms of punishment on her.

Hands shaking, Himmel stepped in front of me, as though to block the evidence of what she'd done. "It's nothing the balms can't soothe. I should remind you, the king has appointed me to her discipline, and it is well within my authority to do so."

"And it's within my authority to command you," he replied.

Himmel smoothed and fidgeted with the shoulders of her gown, refusing to maintain eye contact with the prince. It was clear she didn't enjoy being put in her place, her small power trip spoiled.

Kal pushed past her, and we shared a tender look. *Are you all right?* his eyes seemed to ask. When I nodded a shuddering *yes*, everything about him shifted, going cold and dark, and I braced myself for what he might do next.

"Aella, my bride, was there anything you'd like to say to your handler?"

Himmel scoffed. "Don't be ridiculous."

"She looks like she could use a drink," I suggested, keeping my voice meek and small.

"Excellent idea. A toast before the parade," Kal announced.

He brought forth a pitcher of wine, taking his time pouring two glasses. He raised his glass in salute, and when Himmel reached for the other glass, he stopped her. "That is for my bride."

Himmel gave a nervous laugh, clearly confused. Kal and I clinked our glasses and took a sip together. I wanted to giggle at the irony, but her fearful discomfort was too good to spoil.

"Whatever this game is you are playing, I want no part in it," Himmel said, eyeing the closed door and moving to back away.

"How thoughtless of me," Kal said, feigning sincerity before a darkness filled his eyes and his words took on a threatening edge. "You are not dismissed." He held the pitcher of wine to her lips and began pouring it down her throat.

She smiled nervously, afraid to further insult the future king, and took the wine in large gulps, but when he continued his pour without stopping, she began to cough, her eyes turning red and pleading. She tried to push the pitcher away, tried to pull herself back. The prince wouldn't let her though, holding her head in place with his free hand. He continued the slow pour, smothering her with wine. Himmel flailed her hands about, scratching and fighting. Her eyes met mine in confusion. In a last-ditch effort, she sought my assistance as she choked and sputtered on the wine that spilled over her face and down her throat.

"Drink up." I lifted my chin, letting all of the demure meekness melt away, allowing her to finally see the full extent of my defiance. Her bloodshot eyes widened impossibly farther as she failed to press away the jug.

The moment the wine pitcher emptied and Kal released her head, Himmel gasped for breath, doubling over. "Enough . . . Enough!" she panted.

"It's enough when my bride says it is," Kal countered.

I paused for a moment. Was this truly what I wanted? But when the prince nodded for me to continue, it was as though all fear and hesitation melted away. Yes, I wanted this. She deserved to suffer—for Ulli, Nickel, Jara, Rae, Elutha, Ramalia, Viera. For every fallen contestant in the games. For every drop of water she'd denied me. I'd repay them in kind. Make her choke on her own bitter poison.

I stepped forward with another pitcher of wine, standing before her and setting the almost full vessel onto the floor. She tried to back away, but Kal was behind her in an instant, restraining her. I cupped her chin in my hand, allowing the sharpened ends of my nails to press into her skin while tilting her head back up.

"There will be consequences," Himmel threatened.

I narrowed my eyes on her as a stream of bloodred wine traveled from the pitcher into her mouth at my command. She sputtered and gagged until she could resist no more. I directed the wine down into her lungs, drowning her right in front of me, continuing even as the fight left her eyes, not stopping until the pitcher was entirely empty. I released her face, and Kal allowed her body to fall to the ground with a sickening thud.

I swayed for a moment, and Kal was at my side in an instant, steadying me. I suddenly wanted to scream, surprised I had been capable of such a thing. That hadn't been me, had it? I'd told myself I wasn't like them.

Kal's head jerked at a shuffle of footsteps. He swiftly dragged Himmel's body behind the privacy screen, and I stood there, frozen in place, trying to forget all that had just transpired. As the Faber Ludi strolled into the room, I began combing my fingers through my hair, trying to look idle and nonchalant but probably failing terribly. The soft jingle of the keys that lay hidden between the thick, scratchy fabric of his robe wasn't loud enough to have alerted us sooner. My face fell as I spotted him carrying a box.

"Where is her handler?" He eyed Kal suspiciously. The Faber Ludi looked around the bedchamber, his gaze snagging on the wine spilled at our feet, then following its trail to Himmel's pointed shoes, which peeked out from behind the dressing screen. His eyes widened in disbelief.

"Whatever in the king's name—"

"She may have had a little too much to drink," Kal said with sinister amusement.

The Faber Ludi glanced back toward the room's entrance.

"No need. I already called for assistance," Kal lied. "Come. Do whatever it is that you came here to do."

The Faber Ludi cleared his throat, then spoke, his eyes shifting nervously. "King Solanos wanted me to place these on her for the parade this evening. There are so many visitors, you understand. We must keep up appearances—at least for this event."

"Of course," Kal agreed. "Though, perhaps you'd allow me to do the honors?"

"Certainly, Your Highness." He set the box down, opening it to reveal the cursed iron collar with matching wrist and ankle shackles, each with their own leashes—almost as though they wished to tether me like a puppet.

Kal donned the protective gloves with painstaking deliberation before removing and admiring the craftsmanship of the neck collar.

"It is rather beautiful, isn't it?" the Faber Ludi expressed, his eyes continuing to dart between Himmel's unmoving feet and the door.

"Your design, correct?"

"Yes, Your Highness."

"I think I'd like to see it clasped around your neck."

The Faber Ludi barely had a moment to react. Within seconds, Kal had squeezed the collar around the leech's spindly neck. The Faber Ludi dropped to a bow, sniveling at the prince.

"Please!" he whined, the sound like that of a squealing pig while his face contorted. "I can't bear it! I can't bear it!" He sputtered the words, drool and snot running from his orifices as he wept for mercy. Pathetic, his intolerance to pain while I had been expected to wear it showing none.

He incessantly begged the prince to remove it, but Kal only continued applying the shackles to each of his limbs.

"Suits you rather well. But alas, no more time for fun and games. Hand over the key so I can unchain you."

The Faber Ludi fumbled through his keys until he found the right one, handing it to Kal. Kal fidgeted with the collar's lock for a moment.

"Hmm . . . Are you sure this is the correct one?" he asked before reaching into the Faber Ludi's cloak and withdrawing the crystal dagger he'd used on Zaita to retrieve the nameless key. "Ah, this looks more like it."

The Faber Ludi opened his mouth to correct him but stopped, his head dropping to see his own crystal dagger embedded into his abdomen. Kal slid the dagger up in one smooth stroke, slicing right through the Faber Ludi's ribs, all the way up to his throat.

"My mistake. I must have *lost control of myself,*" Kal said without even a drop of remorse as he let the Faber Ludi fall to the ground in a pool of his own blood.

My mouth hung open. The prince was ruthless.

The chaos of what we'd just done faded away swiftly, as there was not enough time to dwell on such things when these minutes were all we had left. Still, a heaviness hung over our last moments together, the choice I needed to make, our inevitable goodbye.

"I'm not sure who I'm going to miss more," I said to Rat, giving her a good scratch under the chin. She made a soft, sad little reply. "Make sure he doesn't get too lonely, and don't cause too much chaos while I'm gone, all right?"

Kal called for Kasha, who nearly fainted at the sight of the Faber Ludi and Himmel. Despite her shock, she kept her lips sealed when she saw Kal's hands covered in blood, and she immediately agreed upon hearing our plan.

As much as I yearned for freedom, my heart ached knowing Kal and I were running out of time. I couldn't tear my eyes away from the prince, watching his every move, his every expression as though I might memorize them. Memories were all I would have left.

I held back tears while dressing Kasha in my wedding gown, apologizing profusely for the position I was putting her in. Knowing the suffering she might endure in my place, that my freedom came at the expense of her own was a heavy burden to bear. But hope sparkled in her eyes as she took my hands in hers.

"Don't apologize for anything, my lady. It is with great honor I wear the garments of the prophesied one. One day, our people will all be free. I do this with pride knowing that."

I laid the silver veil over her head, which would make it hard for the general population to know she wasn't me. Kal added final touches with a glamour. I couldn't help thinking how unfair it was that he'd be able to do that, to see "me" whenever he desired, while I'd be stuck with only a fading memory of him.

"I won't be able to escort you to your parents—the Iris will expect me to be present in the parade." He handed me the crystal dagger, which I stashed into the servants' pocket tied around my waist.

It felt weird to be dressed in the muted colors designed to blend in, even stranger to be leaving. It was all happening so fast, I had hardly enough time to think, let alone to grieve.

As we stood at the threshold to the passageway, a numbness fell over me. My future was decided. I wouldn't cry anymore. I sank into his arms one last time, my head pressed firmly into his chest, never wanting to let go. But his grip on me loosened, and I felt a cold emptiness where my heart was, as though I was leaving some part of myself behind with him. Kal pulled back just far enough to look me in the eye.

"You are the Tempest, the prophesied one. Go and call upon your people, build up your army. And promise me, Aella, that when the time comes to rise up against us, you will not hold back."

I nodded in agreement, unable to voice my reply, and then reached for the door to walk out. Kal placed his hand over mine. I waited, one breath, two breaths for him to stop me, to come with me, anything but what we were planning. One more breath, and he pushed the door all the way open. I bit my lip, peering out into the dimly lit hall to the future ahead of me—one that wouldn't include him. I couldn't look back, and I refused to say goodbye.

"Fly, Tempest," he said.

And I ran.

CHAPTER 42
No Other Choice

AELLA

As I raced down the passageway, my mind raced in equal measure. I had so many questions still, things we hadn't had time to discuss. Would Kasha spend the rest of her days glamoured to look like me? Would Estrella ever tire of torturing her? Would Kal grow to love and protect her the way he had me? An ugly feeling tightened in my ribs when I pictured him marrying her instead. Enough to make each step away from him harder. He would do what he had to do to protect her, to protect me. If I let myself think of him, I'd lose sight of the path ahead. But he'd stayed behind so I could break free . . . I gripped the necklace hanging from my neck, clinging to the only piece of him I could take with me.

I will not look back, only forward to the road that lies ahead.

Home. To my mother and father, my brothers and sisters. My parents were alive and safe, and they had come for me. My heart couldn't fathom what it meant, no matter how foolish or reckless coming into Prisma had been. To think they'd never once given up, that they'd risked so much to come here, that they'd done all of this just for me. They'd broken into the Palatium Crystalis for *me*.

A scream of joy bubbled up inside at the idea that, in a matter of minutes, I'd see my parents again and they'd be taking me home. I would never have believed it but for Kal's word.

Turning down another hallway, my heart rate picked up. I could almost feel freedom, taste it hanging in the air, waiting just ahead of me. I pictured the ocean surrounding me, the mighty current of the sea. Salt in my hair and sand beneath my feet, the comforting scent of home, and the little ones with soft hands and squishy cheeks. A tear escaped at the memories of my last moments with them. Their faces that had begun to fade, coming back—though soon, I wouldn't need to imagine them anymore. Soon, we could make new memories.

I'm coming home!

The air in the passage began to moisten, and the scent of lillies wafted by. Had I passed an exit to the gardens? I should have been getting closer to the storage room. Did this mean I'd gone the wrong way somehow, too distracted by my excitement? Kal had explained the route while we'd changed. It wasn't a short path, but it'd seemed simple enough to follow. I cursed myself. No, it had to be this way.

"Going somewhere?" a voice echoed through the silence.

I stopped dead in my tracks, the velocity of my run sending my hair flying into my face. I whipped around toward the voice, but in the darkness, no one was there. Only the steady click of heels . . . The scent of lilies suddenly made sense. I braced for what was coming, *who* was coming.

"Aren't you supposed to be out there?" She came into the light, pointing in the direction of the main halls of the palatium. Estrella eyed me up and down with a cocked brow and a smile that said, *gotcha.* I warred between continuing the nameless act and admitting the truth, but something told me she had already figured it out. Based on my servant clothes and the absence of a royal guard, there was no way to fake innocence. I sure as faex wasn't getting out of this without a fight.

"I always knew you were up to no good," Estrella said. "Smart not to run—you'd never outpace me."

I looked past her in the direction of Kal's room.

"Oh, my darling. I'm sure he's a few bottles deep already with your replacement draped over his lap. He's not coming for you. No one is." She stalked closer, slowly, eyeing me up and down. The fact that she hadn't been surprised to find me like this spoke volumes—it was almost as if she'd known she'd find me here.

I had one thing on my side—Estrella was still afraid of me. And though she tried to hide it, I could sense it in the way she kept her distance. I could work with that.

"You win, Estrella."

She folded her arms, staring me down. "Well, it looks like the stars favor me tonight . . . I couldn't have planned this better myself. Game's over for you, little fish."

I put my hands out in surrender. Estrella smirked as she cautiously crossed the distance. She huffed a laugh and paced around me with the smooth precision of a shark. I stared right back at her, doing my best not to show even a drop of fear.

"I almost thought you might do something silly, like put up a fight," she chided.

"That *would* be silly, wouldn't it? What chance could I possibly have against you after all of the torture and source starvation I've endured? No, I'd rather save the humiliation and go with you willingly. But I do have one question."

"How sweet. Of course you think I have nothing better to do than answer you." Estrella tutted.

"You could have sent guards after me, but you must not want anyone else to know I'm here. Or rather, you don't want Kaleidos to know you caught me. What do you plan to do with me?"

Estrella stopped her pacing and narrowed her eyes on me. "You want to know what I think? I think the king has gotten what he needs from you. He's proven his point to the people, the prophecy defeated. Keeping you around is becoming more of a liability every day you spend near the prince. I don't intend to torture you, humiliate you, or even keep you alive."

"Except the prince has chosen me to be his bride. It's not for you to decide whether I live or die, now is it, Estrella?"

She laughed, high-pitched and maniacal. "I could take care of you right here and the prince would never know. If you think for one minute I will stand by and watch you further ruin Kaleidos . . . ruin everything we have built here, you are wrong."

I let her see fear, let her see the slow realization overcome me, of what she might do, what she might get away with.

"You think he's different from the rest of us?" Estrella continued. "You don't know him the way I do. I was here before you, and I will be here long after you're gone."

"You're right." I dipped my chin in submission, kneeling before her, tucking my hand into my pocket. "You won't have to stand by watching me with your cousin anymore." I wrapped my fingers around the hilt of the crystal dagger. "You won't be standing at all."

I slammed the dagger into her heel, yanking it back with such force that it nearly severed her foot. Estrella let out a bloodcurdling scream as she crumpled in pain. I stood over her, and she looked up at me through disheveled, lavender hair, her gaze as cold as the sea's trenches.

"You filthy Argenti whore. You're going to pay for that!" she spewed, all the fake pleasantness in her voice gone. She looked at her foot, to the ribbons of flesh and bones that remained, and cried a guttural roar. "You should have learned your place by now." She went on cursing and hissing, and I couldn't hear it for a second more.

"Choke on one, Estrella!"

Her eyes widened for a split second before cutting into a sneer. "Such a foul tongue for such a pretty mouth." She seethed with painful rasps. "In another life, we could have been friends, you and I."

I couldn't help but laugh as I looked down on her where she lay, crumpled on the ground, her ankle bleeding out. "I would sooner trust an anglerfish."

I turned to leave, but she called after me. "Tell me—why would my cousin do so much for someone as insignificant as *you*? What hold could you possibly have over him?"

I shook my head. As much as I'd love to rub the answers in her face, I couldn't waste any more time. "I guess you'll never find out, will you?"

Hoping I wasn't too late, I darted in the direction of the loading area, taking off into a sprint.

"I wonder what your parents will think when you don't show up." Her sing-song voice chased me down the passageway. "Your mother was so desperate to see you, she blindly accepted Kaleidos' offer to lead you into my trap."

At the mention of my parents, I stopped, the passageway seeming to close in around me, my heartbeat pounding in my ears.

"Shouldn't you have been there by now?" Estrella cackled in a hysterical fit.

"What have you done?" I stalked toward her.

If she knew about my parents, could she have killed or captured them already? Had we ever stood a chance of getting out of here alive? My hands began sweating, my hope dwindling to seafoam.

Estrella took another deep breath, her entire body stilling before she unfolded, coming up to stand on one spindly heel. She smiled, and it unnerved me, the way her injury seemed to bring out an even darker side of her that had a tolerance for, or perhaps even enjoyed, pain and the challenge it presented. A sign that maybe she wouldn't be quite so easy to defeat.

"I have to say, I wasn't expecting to hear they were your parents, but when the male used his air powers on my cousin, it explained how you called upon the storm in the arena. You're not the star-blessed, prophesied one—there's nothing special about you. Your father is just Adamas."

Adamas?

At my look of confusion, she continued, "Oh, were you expecting someone else?" Estrella's laughter became shrill and snorting. She could hardly contain herself, and then she abruptly stopped. "You didn't know, did you?" she pried, tapping a finger over her lips as though she'd just uncovered the juiciest gossip and her leg wasn't leaking blood all over the floor. "Could it be that your mother is even more of a harlot than yourself? Perhaps not even she knows who your true father is."

"My mother would never . . ." I shook my head. She wouldn't have kept that from me, *would she*? She did have so many secrets.

"You're an abomination. To think my cousin could have made an heir with your polluted blood." She nearly gagged on the words.

I charged into her and swung the crystal dagger, aiming for her throat. But even with her injury, her reflexes were too fast, and she jerked back, my dagger only managing to scrape from her cheekbone to the corner of her lips. Her hands gripped tightly around my wrist, and with more force, she angled the dagger toward me.

I pushed against Estrella, straining against her terrible strength, the dagger pressed against my sternum.

"Did you harm them?"

Estrella smiled, her long tongue licking at the blood that dripped from her cheek. "Does it matter?"

I stood firm in the face of wickedness until her hands began to shake and the dagger began angling back toward her. Estrella gave me a surprised, almost impressed expression. Then, without warning, she threw me back with a force that had me crashing into the wall behind me, the wind knocked out of me.

"You're never getting out of here, little fish."

I lay there, curled on my side, gasping uselessly for air as my muscles spasmed within my chest. Even if my birth had been the result of some deep, dark secret my mother had kept, Estrella had been goading me, and I'd been foolish to fall into her trap.

Fire rushed toward me, a blaze of heat blasting my face. I just barely managed to roll out of the way before she shot more at me.

There was no water here, but I had two elements, and fire needed oxygen. Just as the flames were about to consume me, I took a deep, forceful breath, sucking all the oxygen from the space, the fire winking out. Estrella choked for a moment, holding one hand around her throat, the other gripping the wall for balance.

The floor began to shake beneath us, stones overhead loosening with the intense vibration, threatening to topple down over us, bury us alive. I leaped out of the way as a large brick fell, nearly hitting my head. I charged at Estrella again, pinning her against the wall with all my strength and a gust of wind. I swung my fists at her face, but Estrella caught both my hands in hers, my diminished source powers no match against her strength. I slammed my forehead into her nose with a crack and fought with everything in me to release my hands from her grip.

Estrella grinned through her smashed nose and bloodied teeth. "Funny how you still think you have a chance." She pressed back, making the walls and ceiling shake again, more bricks falling into the passage up ahead.

"What makes you so certain I don't? You Iris think you're so much better than us." I focused on her wounds, on the moisture within, keeping the blood from clotting, draining as much blood as I could from them. "I used to think you were the stronger race, but after living with you, watching you, I think that with every new generation, you're becoming more like us."

I eyed the passageway I needed to escape, which was now almost completely caved in, and growled. "Your blood is thin with the mix of my kind. It's only a matter of time before our powers equal. So whether I beat you today or we beat you tomorrow, we *will* defeat you, Estrella, and there's nothing you can do about it."

Her grip loosened, allowing me to finally yank my hands free from her grasp. But as I stumbled back a few steps, weeds grew up through the cracks in the stone, snaking their way around my feet, crawling up my body in a mesh of thorns and leaves. I ripped one foot away, but within seconds, the weeds climbed back up and over it, tethering me in place. Estrella was in front of me in a blink and shoved me with both hands, making me fall back.

"Cute theory," Estrella said, "but you're wrong." Finishing the job, she collapsed a few more stones, sealing off my escape route. "It doesn't matter how many times we breed with your kind, only Iris have aether. In fact, we have it on record that you elementals don't even live as long as you used to. Your powers have weakened, and your life spans may as well be that of fireflies. Proof that even the stars agree we are more valuable than you." She bent, picking up the fallen dagger as the weeds grew over and around me, strapping me down. "Keep struggling, little fish. You'll never break free. Neither you nor your people. Freedom will soon become a long-forgotten concept. Not a single Argenti will know of it." She held the dagger to my throat.

"Kaleidos will never forgive you for this."

Estrella scoffed, "There is no room for a soft-hearted prince on the Iris throne."

I cried out as she pulled back and drove the crystal dagger into my left hand, the escaping blood slowed only by the pressure of the weeds wrapped tightly around my wrists.

"You want to know the best part of all this? You've somehow deluded yourself into believing you're better than us." She laughed, yanking free the crystal dagger. "As much as you'd like to think otherwise, you've proven *exactly* why we must keep your kind separated and controlled. You'd try to kill us all if you could, wouldn't you? Make a graveyard of Prisma like you did in the arena."

She smoothed a hand over her lavender hair. "We've been so gracious to share this tiny world with you, allowing you to live peacefully in your respective courts, letting you keep your little lives, families, and even your traditions." Her face hardened. "But perhaps we have been too lenient. If we wanted, we could take it all away, make every last one of you a slave. We don't have to be so kind."

As she spoke, the restraints grew thicker. My struggles seemed only to aggravate the vines, causing them to tighten more. Blood pounded in my ears, drowning out the muffled booms and pops of fireworks outside.

Estrella leaned down, trailing the dagger along the creases of my other hand, taunting me with her intent to stab it as well, but she sheathed the dagger instead.

"Enough fighting," she snarled as she wrapped the bulk of my hair around her hand several times, pulling it taut. "I was going to leave you here, make it look like an accident, like you tried taking your own life. But look at the mess you've made. You've left me no choice but to take you to the king."

I watched in horror as weeds wrapped around her foot and ankle, splinting the partially severed limb back in place. Estrella sliced through the base of the thick vines that anchored my hands and feet, then dragged me by my hair. I tested the restraints again, but the more I fought, the tighter they became, threatening to cut off circulation altogether. Estrella limped us toward an exit. Soon, I'd be right back where I'd started, locked in a cell. Only this time, I feared not even Kal would be able to save me.

I've come too far to give up now.

Searching deep within myself, I said a prayer to the water, to the air, and to the stars that had blessed me with both. I'd thought I'd been too weak, that I hadn't had everything I'd needed. But there was no more time to wait or plan. Maybe I just hadn't been looking in the right place. What if all I'd ever needed was myself?

"There is no limit to the lies you tell yourselves," I uttered as I felt the electrical rush of power surging through me.

Estrella craned her neck to look back at me, the portentous expression of triumph melting from her face.

I pulled and pulled, drawing source from every direction. I'd been warned not to let it consume me. But it was a little late for me to play righteous.

Estrella panicked, tangling her hand as she tried to swiftly unravel it from my hair.

Lightning danced over my skin, the weeds and vines wilting away from my body. I forced myself to stand.

"If the stars still believed in you, they wouldn't have made me."

Terror shone in her eyes as she reached a hand to feel her puckered-in cheeks and the skin that tightened and shrunk over her bones, her lips pulling away from her teeth. She let out one last gasping croak before collapsing to the ground, nothing more than a dried up husk.

Sometimes, you have to become the thing you fear most to overcome the monsters that plague you. Sometimes, they leave you no other choice.

CHAPTER 43

OVER THE BRIDGE

ARIANWEN

The booms of the fireworks grew louder and closer together as our group approached the loading area. We had made introductions on our walk over, and I tried to keep track of who was who despite my racing thoughts. We were so close to reuniting with Aella, it almost felt like I would be sick with anticipation.

Verus seemed to be struggling to keep all his emotions in check too, and I squeezed his hand tightly.

"Are you sure you're okay?" I asked quietly.

He squeezed my hand back. "I will be. I just didn't expect to see *her* everywhere." His voice sounded almost choked.

"What can I do?" I asked, hating that I didn't know how to help.

"Let's just focus on getting Aella out of here. Worry about me later."

I squeezed his hand again as we finally made it to the loading area.

"Helio and Verus, go secure a wagon big enough for all of us," Wynn commanded. "Han, go with Lewenne to get the horses. Jara and Ona, stay here with Terran and keep watch. If anyone else approaches, try to stay out of sight and signal us with two sharp whistles. We don't have much room for error. Ari and I will retrieve Aella from the storage room."

The group scattered, and I took off into the storage room with Wynn close on my heels.

"Aella!" I called out softly, looking around the empty room, checking behind the large barrels and crates that filled the space. "Shouldn't she be here by now?" I asked, tension building within me.

"Try to breathe, Ari," Wynn said. "It's going to be okay. There's still time."

Pacing, I strained my ears for the sound of footsteps, something—anything—to signal her approach. I wrapped my arms around myself, the cool, damp air sending a chill through me.

This is all my fault. This is all my fault.

My racing thoughts consumed me, fear overwhelming me.

"Ari, stop," Wynn commanded in a voice some primal part of me knew I had to listen to. He tilted my chin up with a finger, his touch firm but gentle. "This is not your fault. This is on the Iris. You're not responsible for what happened."

I bit my lip, blinking rapidly to clear the tears that had started to form. How had he known what thoughts were plaguing me? "I would die for her. I would have taken her place if I could have," I rasped.

"I know you would have." Wynn dropped his hand, letting out a sigh. "I wish—"

The ground rumbled beneath us, and a piercing scream echoed down the passageway we had come out of earlier. Without hesitation, I raced in, only to be met with a wall of rocks and debris blocking the path. I screamed in frustration as I tried to claw my way through, rocks digging into my fingers, making me bleed. A cool breeze rushed by, and I could feel Wynn's approach.

"Ari, we can't get through." Wynn's voice sounded pained. "The collapse is at least twelve feet deep from what I can sense. We've already waited too long, and the prince's distraction won't last forever. We need to go."

"No!" I cried, looking at him over my shoulder. "Help me! We have to get her. What if they're hurting her? What if she's dying? Go get Helio and

Terran—they can use their earth element!" I pulled frantically at a large boulder.

Wynn firmly but gently pulled me away from the immovable rock, shaking his head as he forced me to meet his pain-filled eyes. "There's no time. The Iris could be swarming these halls as we speak, and if we don't leave now, there's a good chance none of us are getting out. If we want to have any chance of rescuing her later, we have to go. Now."

"I can't leave her," I sobbed. Wynn pulled me into his arms, and I buried my face in his chest.

"My—Ari, we have to go. If the prince loves her, he will keep her safe."

"Arianwen!" Verus called out, startling me. I pulled away from Wynn to see my husband running toward us. "Where is she? Where's my Aella?"

Tears cascaded down my cheeks as I shook my head in defeat. "We can't get to her," I cried, gesturing toward the debris.

Verus' eyes shuttered with pain as he reached me and cupped my face in his hands before pulling me close. "Stars . . . There's nothing we can do? Helio and Terran?" he asked Wynn.

"There's no time. There's too much in the way. We need to go while we still can."

Verus swept me up into his arms with one last look at the rubble and carried me toward the exit, as if knowing I couldn't physically bring myself to leave Aella behind. "The wagon is ready and we need to go. We felt that quake all the way outside. It won't be long until someone comes to investigate."

Sinking my head in Verus' chest, I tried to center myself with the familiar scent and feel of him. I tried to breathe, but all I could think about was the fact that I had failed her once again. I was leaving her to whatever fate befell her behind that wall of stone.

"I've got you," Verus murmured against my head. "I promise we won't give up. We will come back for her."

Taking a deep, shuddering breath, I nodded in agreement, even as my heart broke with each step away from the palatium. Verus set me on my feet, and I met the questioning gazes of the others, only shaking my head in response. Lewenne's shoulders drooped, and she held out a hand to help me climb into the back of the covered wagon as Wynn and Helio ran around to the front.

I settled down onto the wooden wagon bed. It felt sticky under my fingers, and my nose crinkled at the sweet and sour odors of rotten fruit and spilled wine that must have worked their scents in over the years. We were all crouched and huddled together, Verus' arms wrapped around me, and my body lurched as we started rolling toward the bridge. Lewenne and Terran kept a lookout through corner gaps in the wood paneling to watch for Iris guards until Lewenne's entire body tensed.

"Stop the wagon!" she yelled, fumbling to open the back.

A strangled cry came from my right, and Han launched himself toward the back of the wagon, calling, "Slow down! We need to stop!"

The wagon finally slowed, and I rubbed at my tear-stained eyes, unsure of what I was seeing. Ilaria ran toward us, dragging another Argenti female with short-cropped hair behind her.

No. It can't be.

"Viera?" I asked, meeting the familiar eyes of my daughter's best friend. "But we were told . . ." I shook my head in disbelief before reality crashed in—there would be time for explanations later. We needed to get out of there.

Han reached down and pulled Viera and Ilaria into the back of our wagon before wrapping his arms around his sister.

"I'm so glad you're here," I said to her as I gave her arm a squeeze.

"We're good to go," Verus called out to Wynn, and I braced myself as we took off.

Viera straightened suddenly. "Aella?"

Lewenne shook her head, eyes brimming with tears while Viera let out a choked sob.

"Faex. I was hoping," Viera said.

Taking a deep breath, my gaze swept over Terran and the five girls we were getting out. Knowing Aella, she would be grateful we saved them. I looked back toward the palatium as the wagon rolled further away.

We're coming back for you. Just hold on.

"You came," Lewenne breathed as we all settled after Terran finished securing the covering. "What changed your mind, Ilaria?"

Ilaria looked down at her hands, picking at her nails before looking up defiantly. "We're not out of here yet . . ." She shrugged before nodding at me. "But . . . hope. Something gave me hope."

I braced myself on the side of the wagon as it lurched to a stop again.

Faex. The guards must have stopped us before the bridge.

I signaled for everyone to be quiet, and strained to listen to what was happening up front. If they searched the back, we were done for. There was no way Helio and Wynn could explain the presence of so many fae back here.

"Where are you off to so late?" The disgruntled voice of an Iris guard filtered back to me. They must have pulled the short end of the stick to be stuck on guard duty while every other Iris was partaking in the revelry.

"The steward sent us out for more wine. Apparently there was an altercation and hundreds of barrels were destroyed. Didn't you feel that quake earlier?" Wynn replied.

I held my breath, wondering if they'd buy his story.

"That's what that was?" the Iris guard asked, sounding uncertain. His footsteps crunched on the gravel as he walked around the wagon. "Let me just check the back and you can be on your way."

"We're really in a hurry," Wynn continued. "Can't let anyone get too thirsty now, can we?"

The guard opened the back flap and peered in at us. "Hey! There are other fae back here. Don't let them pass!"

The crack of the reins sounded, and the wagon lurched forward amid shouts of alarm. I grasped the side again to steady myself, listening to the pounding of our horses' hooves until the sound indicated we had made it onto the narrow stone bridge that connected the Palatium Crystalis to the rest of Prisma.

The angry shouts of the Iris guards grabbed my attention, and I felt the searing heat of a fireball as it hit the wagon's fabric covering and it went up in flames.

"No use hiding now!" I yelled as I summoned water from the sea far below to put out the flames.

One of the guards continued shooting fireballs in our direction, waiting for the other guard to retrieve their horses to chase after us, and Verus and I surrounded the back of the wagon with a water shield.

"Can we go any faster?" Verus called out to Wynn, who was skillfully guiding the horses over the bridge crossing the steep chasm.

"Not if we want to make it off this bridge in one piece," Wynn gritted out.

"Faex! It's only a matter of time until they catch up to us," I said, straining to keep the water shield in place against the onslaught of fire.

Suddenly, a blazing firebolt breached the shield, and Verus hissed as it grazed his shoulder before it pierced the back of the wagon behind him.

I threw him a worried glance. "Are you all right?"

"Don't worry about me, wife," he grunted out, sweat beading his forehead.

"Drop the shield so we can fight back!" Jara pointed toward the water. "They're going to breach it in seconds anyway."

I could see the Iris closing in on us and looked over at Verus.

"Ready?" I asked.

He nodded, and as one, we let go of the water shield so Jara could send some flames of her own toward them. The guards' horses' eyes shone with fear at the fiery darts heading their way, rearing up and nearly throwing the Iris from their backs.

"Way to go, Jara!" Lewenne cried out in encouragement, but one of the Iris guards quickly threw up a wave of water, extinguishing the darts before they could hit them.

Ona crept over to the side and called forth tiny rocks that she flung toward the Iris with precision. Little spots of red bloomed over their faces, and they cried out in aggravation as the rocks cut into their skin.

The Iris guards glared at us across the short distance we were managing to keep, when suddenly, they both threw out their hands, mocking smiles gracing their faces. I braced myself for an attack, but nothing came.

What in the stars was that?

Suddenly, our wagon lurched to a stop, the horses at the front snorting in distress.

"What's going on?" I cried out.

"The bridge is gone!" Helio yelled.

What in the depths?

"That's not possible," I muttered under my breath as I stood to look. Surely we would have felt it if the bridge had collapsed.

"A glamour!" Viera exclaimed.

"Faexing Iris," Wynn ground out as he tried to coax the horses to walk on the invisible bridge, but they wouldn't budge.

The Iris guards thundered after us, and we were trapped if our stars-damned horses wouldn't move.

Han leaped over the side of the wagon and mounted one of them, leaning forward to cover its eyes. "Helio, come get the other one," he shouted.

Helio jumped onto the other horse, covering her eyes gently with his hands. "Come on, girl," he coaxed. "It's all in your head."

Slowly but surely, the wagon started forward again as the horses moved across the invisible bridge. I shuddered as I looked ahead. The illusion felt more real than I wanted to admit.

Jara kept throwing fire darts at the Iris, which only served to slow them down a bit, as they kept dousing them with their water shields.

"This is never going to work," Ilaria spat out. "Even if we get to the other side of the bridge, they'll be right on us. And backup is likely already on the way. We'll never get away."

"Do you have any better ideas?" Lewenne asked as Jara and Ona continued throwing their elements at the Iris guards.

"How about we give them a taste of their own poison, but for real. If we can get to the other side, maybe we can take down the bridge," Ona gritted out.

"But how do we keep them from catching up to us?" Viera asked.

Before anyone could answer, Ilaria launched herself off the back of the wagon, hitting the ground and rolling before leaping to her feet.

"I've got this!" she cried out, summoning a mighty vortex of water to form a barricade between her and the Iris.

"Ilaria!" Lewenne screamed as the distance between us grew further and further. "We can't leave her!"

My heart crumbled as Lewenne cried out for her friend.

Viera pulled Lewenne into her arms, holding her close even as tears rolled down her own cheeks. "She knows what she's doing. Don't let her sacrifice be in vain."

The Iris threw everything they had at the vortex, letting the glamour slip. As the bridge reappeared, Han, Helio, and Wynn coaxed the horses to pick up speed. The wagon shook and rattled with their galloping pace as we flew across the narrow bridge.

"Helio! Terran!" Ona cried out. "When we get to the other side, we need to collapse the bridge."

The wagon careened to a sudden stop once we were over, and Ona and Terran jumped out, running to the edge of the bridge. Placing their hands on the ground, everything began to shake as Helio joined them, and I watched in horror as the bridge started to collapse.

Ilaria released the giant wall of water and turned to salute us one last time, then looked up to the stars, surrendering to the chasm as the bridge dropped from beneath her.

"No!" Lewenne screamed. "Why?" Her entire body shook with sobs as Ilaria disappeared.

The Iris turned their horses around and raced off the bridge, barely making it before it crumbled behind them.

Helio, Ona, and Terran leaped back into the wagon, and we darted off into the night, our hearts heavy from the failure to save Aella and the sacrifice of one of her friends.

CHAPTER 44

Missing Iris

KALEIDOS

"A carriage full of slaves has escaped, collapsing a section of the bridge near the city. Water, fire, and earth elementals, all working together," Pavel, one of King Solanos' advisors, reported. "And Himmel and the Faber Ludi are still missing."

They got out.

I fussed idly with the collar of my shirt to hide my relief. Barely an hour had passed since Aella had left, and I'd been anxiously expecting to learn something had gone wrong. When this emergency hearing had been called not too long after, I'd braced myself for the worst—that she'd been captured or killed—but she was free. Finally.

Solanos sat in silence. The only sign of his rage, a subtle ticking of a muscle in his jaw.

"My daughter was found *desiccated* in the servants' passages!" Spittle flew from Ventius' mouth as he shouted. "I want her dead!" My uncle turned and glared at me, his eyes bloodshot and face swollen and contorted.

I flinched. Was she truly dead? Estrella was once my closest confidant, making it a thick piece of knowledge to swallow. Whether or not it had been by Aella's hand, I would not stand for her taking the blame. I had given her permission to take revenge, and if that'd been how she'd seen fit to best my cousin, who was I to judge?

"Is this my reward? Have I not been a worthy uncle, guiding you, standing as your counselor and offering my support through the years?" Ventius seethed. "Or is this *her* doing, that elemental of yours, poisoning your mind against your own blood?"

"That is my bride you are making such accusations of—on the eve of my wedding, no less."

"There isn't going to be a wedding, Kaleidos," Solanos said, pronouncing my name with every syllable as though it were a threat.

"Surely you don't think a nameless would be capable of doing all of this. Any of this, really," Nephos jumped in with a forced, light-hearted chuckle, attempting to ease the tension in the room.

"Can't you see? All of this is her fault." Ventius seethed. "In confidence, Estrella expressed her disapproval of this matrimony, and look what's happened now."

"As much as it brings me no joy to admit it, there is no possible way the nameless bride could have done any of it," Nephos said. "As everyone saw, she was parading with the prince through the revels at the time we were called for this meeting."

"Nephos speaks true. She was in my care," I added. "Nothing in relation to that girl goes on that I am not implicitly aware of."

"It matters not whether *she* was the one to physically do it. Her very existence has emboldened the slaves. Can't you see?" Ventius gestured with his hands, rallying the rest of the council to agree with him. "It seems the ridiculous plan to use her as a display of victory has backfired. If word were to get out about this . . ." Ventius trailed off, shaking his head as though lost. But I was certain he knew full well what he was doing, planting seeds of doubt in Solanos' mind.

The king stood, demanding silence and everyone's attention. "The elementals have been given far too many privileges in our world. Perhaps it's time for a change, time to remind them *why* they serve us and what happens when they disobey."

Councilmembers leaned forward in their seats, hanging on his next words.

"From this day forward, there shall be no more marriages between elemental and Iris, no more titles or ranks bestowed upon them, no more benefits or rewards. They shall only be used as slaves and heir-makers." He focused his cold, citrine eyes on me. "Kaleidos, tomorrow, you will choose an Iris bride for yourself instead. And the festivities shall continue on . . . in celebration of the commencement of our new monthly games."

He was mad to try such a thing. More than ever, he was giving cause for a rebellion. As though the mere idea of Aella's existence could be the very thing to fulfill the feared prophecy.

He might think himself untouchable, but perhaps he'll crumble under the weight of his own pride.

"I have already chosen a bride."

"I want new rules, new games, new stakes," Solanos continued without so much as an acknowledgement that I had spoken. He then turned to the remaining elemental handlers. "Ladies, find some contestants. I don't care where you get them—male, female, whatever you can get your hands on. Nephos, you'll be taking over the Faber Ludi's role until we can locate him. I want three game suggestions by nightfall tomorrow." The king raised his chalice. "The elementals think they can challenge us? We'll show them how we play." He laughed, and the room joined him in chorus.

"This still doesn't take care of my grievance," Ventius muttered. "Someone needs to pay for what was done to my daughter."

"Yes, of course, brother. I shall take care of it." He directed his attention back to me, his voice nonchalant as he spoke. "Kaleidos, my son, bring me the water fae. I should very much like to see for myself what all the fuss is about before she's tossed back into the games."

It was clear that nothing I said or did would hold weight so long as I argued against them. It was as good as shouting into a void.

"She has not yet fulfilled her duty to the throne," I gritted out in a last attempt. My hands made fists in my pockets as I fought to hold back my rage.

Though Aella was gone, safe with the party that had escaped, I couldn't let Kasha suffer whatever fate he planned for Aella. My blood simmered, knowing he would take her from me as he had my mother. I'd always feared this day would come, which was why I had urged her to go, even if it'd meant giving up the one thing I wanted most.

Thank the stars she got out. Thank the stars I was strong enough to help her.

"Never mind that. You're young. We'll find you another. It took me seven hundred years to sire you," he said with a wave of his hand.

"Just before the parade, Himmel herself confirmed the elemental was with child," I lied, clawing for any excuse that might sway him. If for no other reason but to protect Kasha.

"Stars' teeth! He thinks he's something special," the king ridiculed before narrowing his eyes. "You may keep the water fae until she produces the heir. However, as soon as her duty is completed, she will be cycled back into the games. Until then, keep her behind closed doors. We don't need her presence inspiring any more petty rebellions." He held out his hands in show to Ventius. "What is it with these water fae, birthing offspring at every turn?"

As I strolled back through the halls to my wing, revelers were still going strong, oblivious to everything that had just taken place. The festivities would go on until I said my vows. *Faex.* I needed to choose a new bride. At a time like this, how could I possibly bring myself to even consider something like that? None of that mattered anyway. Aella had gotten away safely. That was all I cared about. She was finally free, and I needed to move on. I needed to think of something else, or better, think of nothing at all. Numb the pain that had tormented me ever since I'd sent her off and my soul had been severed in two. I slowed my pace near a server, who offered me a pour, and I took the bottle instead. Lifting it to my lips, I downed the wine before handing it back.

"Have you watered it down so early in the night?" I muttered. Perhaps wine was not the solution. I needed something stronger.

The server shook his head nervously, grasping for another bottle with shaking hands, but I waved him off, reaching instead for a long pipe.

Moments later, as I waded through the ongoing revels back toward my wing, I assessed the Iris females of the crowd. I let myself really look at them, trying to find something I liked. They'd all started to look the same to me—same pointed noses, puckered expressions, disdainful eyes. What had once been a favorite pastime now seemed meaningless and empty, and I dreaded the idea of bestowing upon one of them the title and rank they all so clearly aspired to. I couldn't do this. Not now. Not ever.

About halfway back to my wing, I developed a tail of Iris females. *Word travels fast.* I had never been one to tour the palatium's vast halls by means of palanquin, but now that the secret passages were sealed off for investigation, I decided to catch a ride.

By the time they'd hoisted me up, it was too late. The revelers had seen me already, and the crystal palanquin was practically at a standstill as the bearers struggled to move through the growing crowd of Iris swarming around me. Ambitious females and curious onlookers practically formed a blockade between me and the path to my wing as they batted their eyes seductively and danced in various states of undress before me. They became more and more desperate for attention, and when they couldn't get mine, they reached for each other in a frenzy, their gazes and moans directed toward me. When that didn't work, they resorted to fighting each other, ripping and tearing at each other's flesh with the same sharpened nails and decorative, elongated canines my cousin used to wear.

Oh, Estrella. If only you could see this. That conniving, traitorous husk. Served her right to meet her end at the hands of my Aella. But what had Estrella been doing in the passageway? My back stiffened. Unless . . . Had she followed me there? To what end?

My heart stopped as I thought through her potential motives.

They'd said a carriage full of elementals had made it out, but there was no way to confirm Aella had been on it. Could Estrella have managed to sabotage Aella's escape in some way?

I could no longer sit in this box moving at a snail's pace while the females around me fought over me, especially with the line of thought my mind was taking me down. I tapped on the roof, signaling to the palanquin bearers I wanted to step out.

The celebratory cheers and seductive gasps and moans had been replaced by breaking glass and the shrieks of brawls. They would tear themselves apart for my attention.

I stepped out of the palanquin to see a female grab a serving girl by the hair. My hand was around the female's neck so fast, I hadn't even the time to consider what I was doing. It snapped. Limp body fell. Wide eyes. Everything stopped as the crowd took in what their prince had just done.

"Enough," I said, turning in a full circle, taking inventory of the females in my vicinity while making eye contact with each and every one of them. "Is this what a queen looks like . . . ? How a queen behaves?" I raised my brows. "Perhaps *you* should be the ones competing in tomorrow's games."

A mix of terror and indignation crossed their faces as they surely wondered if I would really subject an Iris to such a demonstration. If gossip of Estrella's "bath" had spread wide enough, they could be sure nothing was off the table.

"I didn't think so. Now clear a path. I am bored of this."

The crowd parted but did not leave as they watched me pass. They would likely camp outside my door for a chance at being chosen, utterly shameless in their pursuits.

"So how will you choose?" One female strode forward, breaking through the line. Completely nude, the scratches and tears healed themselves as she stood before me, leaving only streaks of blood on her rainbow-colored skin.

"You want to make this a competition of flesh, but I think I've seen enough of that tonight. Win me with your words. Give me *one* reason I should choose you."

Furious whispers and gasps and groans of exasperation followed.

"In the next hour, scribes will be sent out to collect your petitions. Until then, you can plan your statements."

I marched on with long, determined strides, signaling I was done with them, but that one female refused to step out of my way, standing there until the last second, until she realized I wasn't stopping for her. Disappointed murmurs and cries rose behind me, and I held back a laugh. The idea of using their brains to compete had most certainly flabbergasted the boldest of them. That I'd choose based on wit over beauty or seduction was beyond their reckoning.

Once the doors slammed shut behind me, I braced myself for the emptiness of my room, my bed. I waited for that cavernous ache to recur inside my chest, that terrible feeling I'd chosen to numb earlier. I wanted it back now because it was her I'd felt, and perhaps it was all I had left. I needed to feel her absence to know it was real—that she was truly gone.

As hard as it had been to let her go, like tearing my heart from my chest and telling it to go beat all on its own, I'd do it again a thousand times over. I'd never know if she was happy. I was left with no comfort but to tell myself she was free. At long last, she was free and, stars willing, safe. A carriage of elementals had escaped. Estrella had been found dead. No word of Aella. She had to have been in it. I wouldn't accept any alternative.

I pulled a cord to summon Yulema and Kasha and awaited them at my desk. I didn't imagine I'd be getting restful sleep with all that plagued me, so I'd get started on the task at hand. I needed scribes to amass and sort through a list of eligible females.

"Yulema? Kasha?" I called when they didn't come right away.

Still no reply. I strode through the chambers of my wing, calling them again. *Strange.* They were normally so quick to respond. Finally, in the bathing chamber, I found Yulema and my decoy bride attending to . . . Deep blue eyes bright as sapphires with stars like diamonds peeked up at me through thick, dark lashes. Her clothes were a tattered mess, and she was bleeding. I crossed the divide, lifting her into my arms without hesitation.

She wasn't supposed to be here. She was supposed to be gone. She was supposed to be safe. What had happened? Selfishly, all I could think was that she was here in my arms. She was home, and I hadn't lost her. Icy terror seized me. But the games. He'd threatened to throw her back into the games. I set her back down gently.

"You shouldn't be here." I shook my head. "Stars, Aella, why didn't you escape?"

"Estrella." She winced. "She stopped me. I killed her, Kal. I tried not to, but she left me no other choice. I'm sorry."

"Don't be sorry," I said.

"I know she meant a lot to you."

"No, Aella. I think . . . she was important to me, because I had no one else. I thought her to be the only one who knew me. But she knew only the version she wanted me to be. And when I stopped playing her games, it became clear how truly selfish and calculating she was. How our friendship was never more than a means for her to control me. I am glad you did it. Glad to be free of her." I leaned closer to my Aella, needing to touch her, to feel the soft skin of her cheek. I needed to convince myself this was real. Still, I could hardly believe she was actually before me. "But why did you come back? Why didn't you run?"

"My exits were sealed off. And like this"—she gestured to her appearance—"I'm lucky I made it back to the rooms. Do you know if my parents . . ." She broke off as though afraid to say the words. "Do you know if they made it out safely?"

I nodded. "There was report of a group of elemental fae who escaped. They aren't sure who yet, but they said there were fire, water, and earth elementals amongst them."

Aella visibly softened, relief washing over her features.

Yulema shook her head as she worked a balm over Aella's injuries. "We should continue to use Kasha as the decoy until Aella is fully healed," she suggested. "Your bride can stay hidden away with me until then."

"No," Aella and I responded together.

"What if she needs to make an appearance?" Kasha asked.

"There won't be any more appearances," I said. "If you ladies could please excuse us. Aella, we need to talk about the wedding."

After Kasha and Yulema left the room, Aella assessed me with that star-filled gaze of hers.

"Whatever it is, I can already tell it isn't good based on your expression," she said. "Though I suppose it can't be much worse than my failure of an escape."

"Remember how I told you my biggest fear? The reason I needed you to leave with your parents?"

She squeezed her eyes shut. "How much time do I have?"

"I'm not sure . . . He's only allowing you to live because I told him you're carrying my heir." I blushed slightly at the admission, then cleared my throat before continuing. "So I don't know . . . Maybe a few months, give or take, until it's discovered that isn't the case? But, Aella, if your parents took that risk coming for you once, I don't doubt they'd do whatever it takes to get you back. They're not giving up on you."

Her eyes glistened with tears, and she nodded before seeking refuge in my arms once more.

"I was so close," she said. "But somehow, I was glad to come back to you. In whatever sad, twisted way, I think maybe I can learn to be more like you, learn to share your people's depraved culture. After the things I've done, taken part in, can I still say I'm so different? Perhaps this is where I'm meant to be."

"You are the Tempest. You will do great and terrible things, but there is nothing you could do that would make you any less of a star in my eyes."

She hugged me tighter in reply, stifling a yawn, and considering she had probably expended a great deal of energy during her fight with Estrella, she would need a good sleep.

"Come, have a rest. We can figure out our next steps in the morning."

CHAPTER 45

LIBRARY LADDER LESSON

Dear Mom, Please spare us the humiliation and refrain from making direct eye contact with this chapter. Nothing to see here . . . You won't miss anything important. Promise!

AELLA

"You can't be serious." Before he could respond, I got up from the bed, marching out of the room and into the library. "You do realize what you're asking of me?" I shouted from the other room. All my emotions threatened to burst through the seams, and a wild laugh erupted from my chest. I took a moment to ground myself and then marched back into the bedchamber to face him. "After thoughtful consideration, my answer is still no, absolutely faexing not."

"Understandable," he replied, scratching the back of his head.

Kal looked good lying there in his relaxed state. So good, I was tempted to give in just to make him happy. I had to snap myself out of it. I shook my head, reminding myself just how ridiculously unthinkable his idea was. What else could I have expected from him? It's not as though they gave lessons on morality to the Iris.

"Tell me, Tempest, might you suggest an alternative plan?" he drawled, and again, I found myself compelled to please him.

What kind of spell had he cast over me? Yes, he may have let me sleep and drool all over him like he was a giant body pillow last night. Yes, he may have woken me up with the most thoughtful display of all of my favorite foods this morning. Yes, he was only making a suggestion to include me in something he was being forced to do—as unhinged as it was. But I could not allow myself to be persuaded by the charm of this dumb, beautiful male.

"Um, while I sincerely appreciate you asking for my input, I'd rather not have *anything* to do with it," I said, spinning back around to resume my pacing in the library.

Kal jumped up from the bed and followed me to the other room, where he leaned casually against the doorframe to watch me. "I just thought maybe you'd be able to make a better choice than I could—see through their games and weed out the most wicked appeals."

I continued my aimless laps around the room so as not to become ensnared within the trap of his deep green eyes.

"It could be fun," he suggested.

I squinted at him. "For you, maybe."

"I meant more for you, but I can't say I wouldn't enjoy watching." He winked.

"You're so vain," I scoffed but couldn't help the smile that tugged at my lips.

"You're imagining it, aren't you?" he teased.

"It would never work. Not to mention, I'm lacking the necessary *equipment* for that," I declared in my best impression of the proper-sounding Iris accent—which I'd probably completely botched. "But truly—though I don't fully understand the limits of glamours—I do fear that if I dared open my mouth to speak, everyone would know I wasn't really you!"

"Well, Tempest, I am more than happy to give you lessons on how to use that tongue of yours."

"Is that so?" I asked, the pitch of my voice undoubtedly higher and breathier. While I wasn't inexperienced, I'd never been on the receiving end of *that* kind of lesson. "Would you care to show me?" I challenged.

"Oh, Aella," he purred, prowling toward me. "I thought you'd never ask."

A thrill coursed through me in response to his voice, and I moved slowly away from him until my back was flush against the rolling ladder along the bookshelves. In seconds, I was pinned, my chest expanding against Kal's as breaths came in rapid succession. Tilting my chin up with his thumb and forefinger, his gaze captured mine.

"May I?" he asked.

I nodded and swallowed.

He stroked a hand up and down the smooth, wooden side rail, a curious look on his face. Glancing between the ladder and me, he treated me to a wicked smile that sent shivers up my spine. He stepped back and offered me a hand. When I placed mine in his, he spun me away from him, confirming what he intended for me to do. While I had challenged him to this, he'd found a way to take it one step further. It filled me with a mix of giddiness and suspense not knowing what he would do next.

I stepped up one rung of the ladder and then another and another, my arms and legs tingling. Anticipation bloomed with each step until the heat of his breath warmed my thighs. I knew he was good with his hands, but this was certainly a new angle. I turned my head, looking for his reaction, and caught him shameless in his desire, dreamily admiring my rear, his teeth slowly grazing and tugging at his lower lip.

"Is this where you want me?" I asked.

He replied by making a circular motion with his finger for me to turn around. I followed his instruction and braced my hands on one of the higher rungs.

Kal gazed up at me with those carnivorous green eyes of his and trailed his fingers from the inside of my ankle all the way up to my inner thigh. His hand disappeared under the hem of my silk robe, bringing with it a wave of fire. I gasped in anticipation, but he stopped just before reaching my very center. He then tugged at the tie of my robe, allowing it to fall open, revealing gauzy, lace undergarments, which, by the look he was giving me, wouldn't last very long. Cool air and a pleasant chill danced over my skin in delightful contrast to the burning heat simmering just below.

Kal took one leg and then the other, hanging them over his shoulders as he settled between my thighs. His hands cradled the tender flesh of my rear, pulling me closer to him. The damp heat of his lips had me gripping the ladder harder, and I reached for my own pleasure with the roll of my hips and the squeezing of my thighs. Soon, the teasing wasn't enough—I wanted more. I hooked my legs behind his neck, pulling him closer, and he huffed a hot, steamy laugh that diffused across my center.

"Mmm . . ." he purred. "I want you to do that again, but first, let me remove these." Kal withdrew a dagger, and before I could even flinch, my undergarments were drifting to the floor in shreds, the dagger safely tucked back into his trousers.

Now completely bare before him, I could do nothing but surrender to the prince's torturously slow but luxurious lesson. I could feel it all—from the soft cushion of his lips to the sharp points of his teeth and the flexing, fluid motion of his tongue. I secured my legs back around him, and as my longing surged, I squeezed harder, moving my hips in a primal rhythm of swirls and jerks against him.

"I'm so close," I breathed. I didn't want to stop, even as my arms began to fatigue from hanging on to the ladder and as the muscles in my legs threatened to give out. But I was at a breaking point, unfounded fear and hesitation weighing me down.

"Don't hold back, Tempest," he rumbled.

"I don't know if I can hold on any longer," I whimpered.

"Let go, Aella." The vibrations of his deep voice pushed me dangerously closer to the edge. It was more than I'd felt before, more than I'd thought I could feel.

"That's it, little nymph. Claim it," he said, and everything inside me came to a sharpened peak. The motions of his skillful tongue blurred into one synchronous wave as he increased in speed. One moment longer, and I'd burst. It was too good. It was too much.

"I want to hear you scream," he growled.

I held my breath as I flexed my trembling thighs with one last desperate struggle. Shaking, squeezing until I could no more. And then, at the moment of defeat, I relented, turning myself over to the whims and follies of pleasure. I cried out, helpless, delirious, overcome as the flood of sensations engulfed me, giving every last drop of myself to it. But in my falling apart, his thirst for me seemed only to grow. Kal took me higher and higher, pleasure surging through me, swell after swell, a thrill of waves rippling up and throughout my body, destroying me, renewing me. For a moment, all else ceased to exist as I floated in a space of all-consuming release.

I gasped for air, the muscles in my legs twitching around the prince's shoulders as I drifted down from those heights. My fingers had become entangled in his dark mess of curls, and when I reached back for the ladder, I realized we'd somehow drifted to the center of the room. I yelped, squeezing my quivering thighs to keep from falling backward, but Kal stabilized me with the firm grasp of his hands.

He then shifted his hold on me, letting me slide down his chest until we were at eye level. "I've hardly gotten started on you," he said as he carried me back to his room. "If you'll allow me, I will push you beyond the limits you thought possible. I want to ring every last bit of pleasure from your body until you are so thoroughly wrought out, you don't even remember your name." He lowered me onto the bed. "Does that sound good to you, little nymph?"

I nodded feebly.

He spread my legs wide as he knelt between them, and I shivered with nerves, unsure how I could possibly take any more.

"I want to hear you say it," he said, pulling slightly away.

"Yes." My voice was thick with yearning.

Kal removed his shirt, revealing the deep bronze, lean muscles of his chest. Iridescent, marbled veins pulsed and shimmered as I trailed my fingers over him. The sight was entrancing, but what was more was the way he seemed to shiver and almost purr beneath my touch. He wasted no time as he kicked off his trousers and climbed over me—hearts centered, warm skin coasting over mine with each of our uneven breaths.

What we'd done before had only been an appetizer of what was to come, and his dark gaze seemed to awaken something inside me. I pulled him closer, drawn to him like he was the answer to everything, like he could cure all my pain.

Kal slid deft fingers along my bare skin with smooth and gentle precision. He took hold of me, his thumb against my center. His grasp was firm, tethering me to him as though staking his claim.

His eyes locked with mine, searching. But more than that, he was letting me in, opening his soul up to mine. I held my breath in anticipation as he slid his solid length over me until we were angled just right.

"Are you sure you want this?" Kal guided my hand down to grab hold of him. He groaned into my shoulder at the contact, and my heart stuttered in my chest. He then lifted his head and kissed me tenderly, nuzzling his nose along mine, as though he endeavored only to breathe my air, leaving heartbeat kisses so fleeting, I found myself reaching for more. My grip tightened on him as I pulled him impossibly closer to me, drawing forth a deep moan of pleasure from his lips.

"Yes, Kaleidos," I breathed. "Have your way with me."

"Aella," he purred, then eased forward.

I whimpered a muffled cry against his lips, and he stopped abruptly.

"Are you all right?" he asked, his voice full of concern.

"Don't stop." I inhaled sharply. We both knew he would ruin me with his size, but I didn't care. I wanted all of this blessed torture and all of its release. Just as he began again, I moved along with him. Urging him to go deeper. "I want all of you."

And with that, he finally obliged, anchoring himself inside me.

"Yes!" I cried, my voice distorting into a strangled moan at the sensation of him reshaping me from within. I held on to him like I would fall straight through the bed and into another universe if I let go. Kal stilled, giving me time to acclimate. He was visibly shaking, sweat beading his brow, as though the simple act of restraining himself was pure torture as he waited for me to relax.

But as I stared into his eyes, offering myself to him, I took his mouth with mine in a devouring, ravenous kiss. With it, I released every bit of my longing and sadness. For that was all I had to give—it would have to be enough. In my moment of vulnerability, he met me with a fierce acceptance. My emotional pain did not deter him—more, it seemed to draw him in further.

Everything hummed as energy zipped through our connection. With every motion, an exchange of power, allowing me to taste and feel every part of his essence—so much, I could have gotten lost.

"Aella," he said, reeling me back in. Kal sat back on his heels, holding me by the waist and kissing me as he guided and helped lift me over him.

"This is everything," he murmured between kisses. "*You* are everything."

My eyes rolled back as I lit up with more waves coursing through me, each thrust claiming me, taking me higher. It was like we had been made for each other, perfectly in tune to each other's wants and needs.

And it went on and on, drawing forth unholy screams of pleasure, vows and promises pouring from both of our lips.

Kal continued sending me back into that fathomless place over and over and over again until the sun went down, until my body was a quivering mess, soaked in sweat, plastered to the bed, until I could neither speak nor scream anymore. Until the only thoughts left were, *take me, claim me, I am yours.*

CHAPTER 46
PRINCELY DUTY

KALEIDOS

Collapsing beside her on the bed, I tugged her tiny body into the hollow of mine. I buried my face into her neck and the pile of hair gathered there. She smelled of salt and sea along with the honeyed fragrance of plumeria blossom. I took a deep inhale to memorize her scent mixed with the essence of sweat and desire.

I'd sealed every door shut to keep people out while I took my time pleasuring my bride. I didn't care that I had duties to attend to, expectations. Nothing else had mattered the moment she'd given me that singular challenge. How I'd been dreaming of such things, but never in my life had I been rewarded with such unfettered release.

It was as though, with every wave, bonds had unraveled, one layer after another until she'd been truly free, and the freedom had pulsed through her like a cataclysm of flexing and trembling hips and thighs. And it had coursed through me by extension, a pleasant fluttering in my chest and an insatiable thirst for more. I could think of nothing else but giving her more, as though it were my sole purpose just to bring her ecstasy.

I'd felt every tug of pleasure, every pinch of pain through the way she'd moved, even the way the pitch of her voice had changed, the rhythm of her breathing, the pounding of her heart, and the throbbing of her blood flow, drawn forth soley for me. I'd been encouraged by her moans and by the way she'd tensed and flexed, the signals that had let me know when she'd wanted more or when she'd been close to breaking. Oh, how I'd wanted her to break free. I wanted to mold her to the shape of me so she couldn't even think of pleasure without calling my name. The way I couldn't think of anything but her. I'd been compelled to test those limits. My Aella deserved nothing less.

The soft, rhythmic sounds of her breath lulled my senses, and a quiet stillness came over me, carrying me into the peaceful dark.

"What is the meaning of this?" King Solanos exclaimed.

I squinted my eyes against the glaring light streaming through clerestory windows.

"You were supposed to choose a bride yesterday. I sent for you multiple times. Useless cowards said you'd made the place impenetrable. I had to come see for myself."

I threw my forearm over my face, silently willing him to depart.

How in the stars' light did he break through the wards sealing my wing?

"Get up now. You've had your fun with the slave. We promised the court a bride—now go out there and make your selection. Perform your duty to the crown. Don't make me tell you again!"

Faex.

I sat up and heartily chugged half a pitcher of water from my bedside table. "You can hardly expect me to make such a grave choice in so little time."

Solanos stepped closer to the bed, casting a shadow over us. His proximity set off subconscious alerts that he was threatening the safety of my bride. I threw a dome of protection over her and leapt out of the bed to place myself between the two of them as an extra measure.

He eyed me up and down with a grimace, then turned toward the window, muttering a string of curses. "Put some bloody clothes on."

Stepping into my hastily discarded trousers, I winced slightly as I fastened them, sore from overuse. Aella's moans came crashing back, and I could still taste her on my lips. I fought to keep my grin from spreading, but it was hard knowing I'd soon get to tuck her back in against me . . . feel the softness of her skin again. If only I could get Solanos to leave. My features relaxed back to bored disinterest.

"From which house are you choosing?"

"None," I stated.

"Don't be ridiculous."

"If you had seen their desperate attempts, you'd agree with my decision. They were no better than the elementals—like animals, all of them." The words, which previously would have spilled from my lips with no shame, sent an ugly twinge through my stomach. She wouldn't hear me through the barrier, but I hated saying them next to her, like they came at some moral cost. I'd do much worse if I had to though—to keep her safe.

"Are you not aware that your comrades would spill blood for a mere fraction of such attention?"

"It's not me they're after—it's the throne. I have no interest in wedding a status-seeking opportunist."

"You seem to have forgotten who *you* are," Solanos said.

From the corner of my eye, I noticed Aella shift in the bed behind me. I clenched my jaw, forcing myself to look elsewhere so as not to draw attention to her, but to no avail.

"It appears you have been awfully lenient with the girl." He shook his head, stepping around to the foot of the bed.

A low snarl erupted from my chest as Solanos reached for Aella. She had rolled onto her belly but still appeared to be in a very deep, blissful state. Good, the dome of protection appeared to be working, sealing out the sound and commotion of our discussion. Better she slept through this. Though, after the night we'd shared, it was little wonder my father's arrival hadn't awoken her.

Solanos scoffed. "Need I remind you why we make them nameless?"

"For control," I said.

"So they don't try to manipulate their way back *into* control."

"Imagine that, a world where elementals rule over themselves!" I masked my true feelings with a laugh.

"You think this is a game? What do you think would happen if we allowed that?" he spat.

"'If we relinquish control, they will rise up against us and take back their immortality,'" I recited. "'There can only be one dominant race, just as there can only be one immortal creature on Esterra.' If you can even believe any of that. How many times have we rewritten history when it was convenient for us?"

"And you would risk finding out? We came to this forsaken world as a means of survival. You owe it to your fellow Iris to ensure the continuation of our species, and if hosting games and playing by the rules is the price, then you'll pay it. I will not have you risking my legacy for an elemental whore. You do not let your heart get in the way. Do you understand? Don't think I won't replace you with your heir if you can't get your priorities straight."

I remained stoic, guarding myself from showing my true thoughts as he spoke, lest he read them from my expression.

"Now put her back in chains, or I'll make sure she's locked up in the fish tank in my throne room until she births the next heir."

"I will not have her in chains again," I said.

The king laughed at my defiance, reminding me that nothing I said or did mattered.

"I am at a loss to understand how—even now, after she's been made nameless—she still holds such sway over you."

"The same way my mother once held sway over you?"

"Do not dare speak of her again," he warned. Solanos started to turn, but something made him pause. The set of his jaw sent a jolt of regret through me. I'd gone too far. "I've permitted her presence for too long," he said, the words all too familiar.

My mind was a haze as I sifted through memories of past and present. The one thing I'd feared he'd do, I'd somehow managed to hasten. Bringing this upon Aella, myself.

Without warning, the king grabbed Aella by the ankle, cutting through my protective barrier like it had been nothing, and pulled her off the bed toward himself.

"Do not touch her!" I exploded, a cataclysm of powers threatening to obliterate everything in my vicinity, yet for her safety, I restrained myself. I would kill him.

Aella's screams were drowned out, and soon, all I could hear was Solanos' laughter. Once again, I was a child in the stands, watching my mother fight for her life. The crowd jeered, and guards held me in place, making me watch her last moments. I choked down metallic, briny tears as the tang of blood misted through the air and a piercing sense of failure and blame coursed through my chest. My fault. It was all my fault.

"There is no room for weakness on the throne," his voice boomed through my head.

The illusion played over and over. I was Iris—I should have been able to resist it, see through it—but it struck such a nerve, throwing me back into the trauma. Splintering through the fragile parts of my mind and filling in the gory details. I thrashed against it, blood boiling, but even I couldn't contend with his terrible influence—this never-ending means of torture he used to threaten and control me. Hate wasn't strong enough a word.

I strained against the hands holding me in place, but even as the fog of my vision cleared, I was still being held by Iris kingsguards, and now, the king was holding Aella, who lay limp in his arms.

"What have you done?" I cried.

"Spare me the theatrics—she's only dreaming. I've spun a sweet tale for her from which she shall not wake until I release her."

"She belongs to me," I snarled, struggling with the six guards. Normally, I could have thrown them off me in an instant, but every time the king used his illusion on me, my powers were drained and I was inexplicably as weak as a child again. Another reminder of how utterly unrealistic my aspirations of defeating him were. Pure delusion. I would never be able to fulfill that promise to Aella. Just as he'd showed me time and time again, I was as good as powerless against him. We all were. No wonder he didn't fear the prophecy. He truly was omnipotent.

"You're lucky I don't have you whipped for your insolence. I've been lenient for far too long. The elemental is coming with me to become a fixture in the tank in the throne room. If you care about your heir, you will do as I say. Find yourself an Iris female to bond with and start behaving like the superior being that you are." He turned and marched toward the door.

No.

"I will do it!" I gasped, using what was left of my strength in a final attempt to throw the guards off of me. The king waved a hand, and they released me. I collapsed to my hands and knees. "I will do it," I repeated as I tried to catch my breath. "Bring me the chains. I will do it myself. Let me prove myself to you."

She would hate me for this, but I could not let him take her.

"At last, you've come to your senses." The king smiled as he laid Aella back onto the bed and raised his brows, waiting for me to complete the task.

I dropped my shield on the door and called for my guards. As I began applying the crude restraints, the king allowed Aella to wake up. Her eyes darted between the guards and me, confusion and fear contorting her expression. She winced with each application, her body trembling from pain as her eyes welled with tears, but I couldn't stop. My father was watching so intently.

"Take her to the elemental rooms," I said, rising to my feet. "And ready my wing for my new Iris bride."

Disappointment and betrayal thundered through her—so strong, I could feel it, even as I kept my gaze distant. She would hate me for this, but she would live.

"You are alive for one purpose, and that is to give me an heir. Now go. Fulfill your duty. I am tired of you."

I gritted my teeth, watching helplessly as the guards dragged her out of my room, naked and in chains. I'd promised her better than this, but I could not allow my father to take her. If he did, it would all be over. As long as I played my part, there was still a chance I'd get her back, and then I'd find a way to make her understand.

"Very good, son. I knew you had it in you," Solanos said, and his face softened. "You look ill, child. Best go back to sleep."

I climbed back into my bed, the weight of my utter failure and the shame of my weakness weighing each movement. I'd warded the room, sealed it against all entry, yet my father had broken through without even waking me up. And then, when I'd placed the barrier of protection over Aella, my father had reached through it. He hadn't even flinched or shown any sign that it was there at all. Were my powers so useless against him?

"Perhaps I shall give you a week to decide on your next bride, but nothing more, or I'll choose for you. Understood?" Solanos said as though he was making a generous offer.

I closed my eyes, turning away from him, and I could sense he was miffed I hadn't graciously accepted. Though perhaps if he was now in a benevolent mood . . . I turned my head back to look, and just as he reached the door, he vanished into nothing.

I blinked and rubbed at my eyes. *What is this?*

The walls stretched and morphed around me as I tried to piece it all together from the moment I'd joined her in bed, watching her blissfully sleep. My Aella, my fierce and unyielding love. I reached for understanding, for proof that should have been clear. Each action from the moment my father had arrived . . . Had it all been part of some cruel game, or had it spun even farther than that? A wave of sickness churned within.

The picture of her in the king's arms began unraveling. It was hollow, unlike the visceral nature of a real memory. That hadn't been the face of the one I loved but a projection from the king. Had he even been here at all?

I leapt from the bed and ran out of my room after the king, after the guards, after Aella. Through the halls of my wing, I shouted as I sprinted to the main palatium's halls. But I was too late and they were gone. Just as I'd predicted, females were camped outside my wing, blocking the exit, fighting to get in. So many of them, I could not push past them as they pressed the doors in. I could do nothing as Aella's crystal box drifted farther and farther out of sight.

Soon, my wing was swarming with uninvited guests, so I retreated to my bedchamber. But when I arrived, it was already filled with maids stripping the bed, clearing out the books and the vanity and all her things. I crashed to my knees, the raw weight of it all sinking in, worse than any illusion. Shame twisted in my chest.

What have I done?

CHAPTER 47

A KING'S DECISION

WYNN

"Enough!" I called out, silencing the meeting room as I rose to my feet. My eyes swept across the room, noting the clear lines that had been drawn between courts except for my cabala.

Despite rescuing the contestants and Lucris' children the week before, the mood in Concordia was somber. There was talk of the Aurum and Aereus leaders getting restless. The failure to rescue Aella had people questioning if the stars were truly on our side.

"I know our mission to retrieve Aella failed, but it was not a complete loss. We are stronger when we work together, which was never more evident than when a group of untrained elementals used their various gifts to get us out. The Iris have been fighting to keep us separated for millennia, and even now, in this very room, we are separated by our courts. Imagine what we could do if we trained as one people, combining our skills. The Iris wouldn't stand a chance."

"That might *sound* well and good," Lucris drawled, "but you'll find the courts need more than pretty words and ideals to raise armies. You need the prophesied one to bring people together. Without Aella, you have nothing."

My eyes drifted toward Ari, who sat with her head bowed, defeat written all over her. Seeing her break had been one of the hardest things to witness. I was grateful she had Verus to comfort her and keep her together, grateful she wasn't alone. The guilt of failing to deliver on what I'd promised was eating me alive.

"I know. That is why I sent word to King Solanos before we left Prisma and proposed a trade."

"You did what?" Helio yelled, jumping to his feet and pacing the length of the room, muttering curses under his breath.

"Damn you and your bleeding heart," Glint blurted out before turning to whisper something to Ember.

Rik's eyes smoldered, and the look he gave me expressed his anger that I hadn't given him a heads up.

The rest of the leaders shifted uncomfortably in their seats at the lack of unity between my cabala and me, but sometimes, hard decisions had to be made.

"Solanos has been after me for as long as I can remember. It is the only way to get her back. If the spies are to be believed, he still thinks she's nameless and not a threat," I stated. "I, on the other hand, have been a threat to him for years. There is nothing he wants more than to remove me from the playing field."

"But *we* need you," Valerik argued. "Our people need you. We already discussed this back in Zephyria—it is not a viable option."

I slammed my hands onto the table in front of me. "Enough arguing. I am your king," I said, looking directly at my friends. I pulled a rolled-up parchment from my back pocket and threw it onto the table. "It's already been agreed upon. We are meeting the king on the cliffs outside Prisma in two days' time."

A soft gasp came from Arianwen's direction, and I turned to meet her gaze, her eyes brimming with tears. She bobbed her head in acknowledgement of what this decision meant. I had made her a promise, and I was going to get our daughter to safety, even if it meant I might never have the chance to know her.

"The deal is done," I reiterated to the room, "but that doesn't mean we can trust the king to uphold his end of the bargain. Our number one priority is to get her out, so we need to make sure we cover all our bases. That is what we are here to discuss. We leave at dawn, so we cannot waste any more time."

Sparks shot up into the air as I turned the spit full of game over the crackling fire. My stomach rumbled as the scent wafted to my nose.

"Faex, that smells delicious," Helio said as he made his way out of the small shelter we were staying in for the night.

"Nothing quite like eating beneath the stars, huh?"

"There is something oddly satisfying about eating food we had to hunt and prepare for ourselves," he mused. "Not sure if the stars have anything to do with it."

I laughed, nodding at Rik as he walked out of the woods to join us.

"I, for one, am glad we don't need to sleep out here at least," he said with a grin.

"Eavesdropping on us, Rik?" Helio teased.

Rik gave him a deadpan look. "Always."

A snort came out of me as I turned the meat one final time. "How do the shelters look, Helio?"

He shrugged. "Pretty basic." He pointed toward one of the small stone huts. "That one has two rooms we can use. I already set up our travel cots." He gestured to the other. "I think Ari and Verus claimed that one over there."

"Perfect," I replied. "Okay, food's ready. Rik, can you gather the others please?"

He nodded and disappeared into the small shelter. Our group had left in two waves to avoid detection. The other half wouldn't be arriving until later this evening.

Lucris' contact had clued us in on deserted shelters they'd discovered outside of Prisma. Perhaps the Iris had wanted to build a settlement out here, but the terrain was unfavorable. Either way, we'd take advantage of it. Being this close to Prisma sent a chill down my spine, but at least we weren't at the mercy of an Iris host who could betray us.

Tomorrow was the big day. We'd either rescue Aella or die trying.

"How are you feeling about the trade?" Helio nudged me with his elbow as he reached over and helped himself to a portion of meat from the spit.

"Our plan will either go smoothly or fall to pieces the moment Solanos shows up." I sighed, running a hand through my hair.

"Do you really think we can fool him into thinking we brought a whole fleet?" he asked.

I shrugged. "Our air power is the biggest advantage we have. If we do it right, there's no way he'll be able to tell without calling our bluff. Thank the stars the Iris never found a way to capture and use aquilas for their own aerial force."

"No kidding," Helio said with a laugh.

Ari and Verus appeared with Rik on their heels. "Already started without us?" Rik teased.

"Unlike Helio, I have manners," I replied with a wink. "Come, join us. Nothing like sharing a meal before heading into battle."

"Battle?" Ari squeaked.

"Metaphorically speaking, of course," Verus said, pressing a kiss to the top of her head.

"Any confrontation with the Iris makes me want to be battle ready." Rik groaned. "I don't trust them one bit."

"And you shouldn't," Verus agreed.

"Well, what's for supper?" Ari asked.

"My personal favorite." Helio grinned. "Nothing like some freshly roasted bird and a good bottle of ale."

"Better not let Lunaya hear that," Glint said cheekily as she appeared behind him and gently smacked him upside the head.

Helio rolled his eyes and dug into his meat.

"I don't know if I *can* eat," Ari grumbled. "I'm a bundle of nerves waiting for tomorrow."

Verus gently squeezed her into his side. "It's going to be all right, Ari."

Was it? I could only hope and pray to the stars that he was right.

We sat around the crackling fire, quietly eating our fill, the mood solemn.

Helio passed around a bottle of ale he'd brought, which seemed to loosen tongues.

"Are you all normally so laid back before such a big mission?" Verus asked, quirking a brow.

As much as I hadn't planned on it, Verus had grown on me, and I respected him. While I suspected we'd never be close friends, perhaps if we had lived another life, things would have been different.

Helio laughed, slapping him on the shoulder. "We've found it's in our best interest to let off some steam before heading out. Showing up all tense never served anyone."

Ari straightened. "Is that why we stopped for a swim on the way to our mission in Ilithania?"

I chuckled. "Well, that certainly didn't hurt, but no, we stopped for you. I knew how much you were aching to get into the water."

Verus turned to Ari. "You went swimming in the Court of Earth waters?" A look of awe crossed his features.

She blushed at the attention. "I hadn't gotten to that story yet," she said demurely. "But yes, early on, we traveled there, and I hadn't been to the sea in what felt like ages."

Helio grinned. "Ari invited us to ride dolphins."

Rik raised a brow at me, and I hid a smile as I threw back the bottle. I would *never* forget that day.

Verus guffawed. "I bet she did. You might not know it, but she can make friends with any sea creature."

"Okay, so tell me," Glint jumped in, "are there kraken in our waters?"

"Wouldn't you like to know," Ari teased.

"I wouldn't ask if I didn't mean it." Glint rolled her eyes.

"Lighten up, would you?" Rik gave Glint a pointed look. She glared at him, grabbed the bottle of ale out of my hand, and took a large swig.

"Yes, do tell us tales of the mighty kraken," I cut in, unable to hold back my grin.

"Ahh, those are only fairy tales told to young Argenti to make them behave," Verus said smoothly.

Ari nodded. "If there are kraken in our waters, I have yet to meet one."

Glint shuddered. "Yeah, no thanks. I'm happy staying on dry land." Her posture softened as a wistful look overtook her face. "As much as I adore Zephyria, I miss home. There's nothing quite like entire cities built into the trees of the Easthen Forest."

"Would you describe it for us?" Ari said softly. "I wish I could visit."

"Maybe someday. You can visit once we take back our lands," I mused.

"Someday," Ari agreed.

Glint smiled. "Picture intricately crafted bridges that softly sway between treetops. Hollowed-out trees lit with eternal flames. Detailed woodwork unlike anything you've ever seen. The forest seems to glow, not just with the fireflies."

"Sounds beautiful." Ari smiled.

"It's more beautiful than you can imagine," Glint said, staring off into the trees behind me.

"Still waiting for one of your cutting remarks," Helio teased.

Glint smacked him upside the head again. "I'm allowed to be nice sometimes. I've lived around you sorry lot long enough, haven't I?"

The teasing and laughter soon fell back into stagnant silence fraught with emotion. It was an eerily dark night with only a few stars visible in the sky.

I watched Ari curl into Verus as Rik sat rigidly. Helio was half sprawled on the log and half on the ground as he finished off the ale. Tomorrow wasn't promised, but I'd do everything in my power to make sure every single one of them made it out and we'd have many more evenings of food and fellowship.

All too soon, we dispersed to our rooms to settle in for the night. As each of my friends disappeared into their huts, an ache settled deep in my gut. Taking a final look at the pitch-black sky, I prayed the stars might still hear me. We needed them with us as we faced one of our greatest challenges yet.

CHAPTER 48

THE TRADE

ARIANWEN

The sun hung low on the horizon as we flew in on our aquilas, the morning rays casting a blinding light over the jagged cliffside and obscuring our view. My heart pounded as we quickly dismounted, sending our birds into the sky before marching up to the meeting point. As we'd made our approach, we'd seen the first group arriving. Practically sprinting toward them, I urged the others to keep up. I needed to get closer—I needed to see her. Waves crashed violently against the rocks below as I came to a cool halt, my breath catching when I laid eyes on my daughter a few hundred paces away.

Aella stood before us, smothered in iron chains beside Prince Kaleidos, a host of Iris standing guard behind them. She was pale and had lost weight, and I shuddered at the thought of the burns she must have under the iron they'd adorned her with.

As much as I loathed the idea of harming another, seeing my daughter in chains evoked a rage deep within me. My blood burned in my veins and my heart thundered in my chest as I reconsidered my sacred healer's oath.

They need to pay for what they've done.

The king's party made their way up to the cliffs outside of Prisma with all the pomp and circumstance I'd expected from the vain Iris. King Solanos approached, seated upon an elaborate crystal throne carried on the shoulders of twenty elementals. Those carrying it looked void of hope and filled with resignation as they struggled up the mountain. When they reached our meeting point, he made them continue to hold him aloft, guaranteeing we'd have to look up at him, showing us exactly where he thought we belonged.

King Solanos was treacherously beautiful, his citrine eyes glimmering with malice and glee. He was dripping with opulence, draped in gemstones that rivaled his glowing facade, but I glimpsed the monster beneath. The king's beauty made him almost too painful to look at, his skin vibrant with its swirls of gold, silver, and bronze. With a goblet of wine in one hand, he couldn't even be bothered to get off his elevated throne and greet Wynn, ruler to ruler.

Wynn approached the king, no crown on his head, adorned only in his flying leathers with a sword at his hip.

"You will disarm," came the command from a nasally sounding Iris commander standing to the right of the king.

Wynn tilted his head, showing no fear or trepidation as he challenged back, "You first . . . in a show of good faith, of course."

My entire body tensed, waiting for the king to change his mind or refuse to comply, but I released a shaky breath when he flicked his hand and his commander gave the order. The clanking of swords dropping to the ground grated my ears, and I couldn't help but worry as Wynn laid down his. Some of the guards were armed with crossbows, but they remained slung across their backs.

As we stood before the Iris king and his many guards, fear washed over me. The Iris prince gave me a quick shake of the head—a warning? Something was wrong. Had it been a mistake coming here? A trap as we'd suspected? What if the Iris had lied? What if they didn't let any of us leave? Verus had been so worried when I'd insisted on coming to this exchange, but I'd promised him I'd come back to him—we both would.

Everything was going to be fine. They would give us Aella, and we would leave. Even though Wynn was bartering himself, there was no way we'd let them keep him. Verus had been confident Wynn would make it out. He and the cabala were working with our Iris allies. They had a plan, and it was going to work. If Solanos betrayed us during this meeting today, we had a contingency plan for that too. I accepted no outcome other than success.

We had been promised safe passage, but standing before the Iris king felt anything but safe. Rik, Helio, Glint, and I positioned ourselves behind Wynn. We'd needed to keep our party small, partially to allow Solanos to think he had the upper hand, and because the rest of our small group of people would be hidden above the clouds in the event that the king planned anything nefarious.

I hadn't seen Verus this morning, as he'd left early to head out with the other team, and my heart ached that I had not been able to say a proper goodbye. The night before, he'd held me extra tight, as if he never wanted to let me go. Having so many people I cared about putting themselves in harm's way had my heart beating painfully in my chest.

"Your Majesty." Wynn sketched a bow before King Solanos. "Thank you for agreeing to my terms."

King Solanos ignored Wynn's address, speaking over him while summoning a slave girl to sit upon his lap like he was attending a revel instead of a political exchange. "The last Sorensen, is it? After all this time, I am surprised you would turn yourself in for a female." His voice was nonchalant as he scoffed. "Oh, I know, she's not just any female . . . I know all about the prophecy. She might hold a certain allure, it's true. I should have demanded more in exchange, but I am a reasonable male."

"Let it be known," a royal herald cried, "the prophesied one is no match for our mighty king!"

The king's guards cheered, and Solanos snickered to himself. Wynn's body tensed at the words, his hands balled into fists, but he seemed to soften when he glanced at Aella. I regretted that I hadn't had a chance to speak with him this morning either—a chance to thank him for his sacrifice and all he was risking.

Overwhelming grief lanced through me as I fixed my eyes on Aella. I wanted to run across the open space and pull her into my arms. She was an echo of her usual self.

What have they done to her? How could the prince have allowed this?

Magic thrummed beneath my skin, screaming to be let out as my anger built within and a roaring filled my ears.

"Come along now. Turn yourself in," the king said.

"Not until you hand over the girl," Wynn replied. "And before you even think about betraying us, I'll have you know that I have one thousand aquila riders circling overhead, ready to rain their wrath down upon you."

Beside me, Rik whistled, and on cue, the sky thundered overhead with the magically amplified wingbeats and cries of our small aerial fleet. Not the massive army we were bluffing, as there hadn't been enough time to assemble with such short notice, but the Iris would never know with the thick cloud cover blocking out the sight. A strong gust of wind blew through Solanos' army, and some of the younger-looking guards cowered in fear of being outnumbered.

A muscle ticked in Solanos' jaw, a sign he didn't like being outmaneuvered.

"You've made it very clear she is no threat to you," Wynn continued. "Let her go to my people, then I will turn myself in." He motioned toward where we stood.

I kept staring at Aella, begging her to look at me. I needed to know if she was okay, but she stood there, unmoving, her eyes glued to the ground.

Finally, King Solanos relented. Lifting a hand, he flicked it toward her. "I have no interest in battling you today, Sorensen. I presented myself before you with my son and only two hundred guards. Do you think I'd risk my own legacy for foolish games? But now that we are showing all of our cards, I will admit, she is nameless, merely a shell. The girl you're after is long gone, but take her body if you'd like."

I held back a gasp. My heart splintered. I'd tried to prepare myself for the worst, but even knowing it was a possibility, nothing could have prepared me to hear those words from his lips. Was it our fault? Had our failed rescue caused this to happen? Was that why the prince had shaken his head?

No. Not my Aella. She is stronger than that. I refuse to believe it.

"I agreed to trade my life for hers, and you just admitted she is gone," Wynn growled. "Restore her name."

King Solanos' lips turned into a wicked grin. "We agreed to a trade, yes, but her name was never a part of the deal. You couldn't expect me to give her back whole. She's the *chosen one*, after all. Take her as she is or not at all. We still have many ways we might use her if you change your mind." He held his hand out as though to stop the guard from leading her toward Wynn.

My eyes darted back to Aella, hoping I'd see some spark of life in her to prove him wrong. I didn't care if it was true; I just wanted her back. We could figure out the rest later. We needed to get her away from these wretched people. I glanced at the Iris prince, whose facial expression appeared bored, but his body was tense, contradicting it.

"I'm not backing out," Wynn snapped. "Release her."

"That's what I thought."

The Iris guard tugged on Aella's chain and dragged her toward us. She followed as though used to the treatment, her head bowed. Wynn's eyes tracked her movement, looking pained. Was he saddened he'd never get to know his daughter as she'd been? Was there any way to return her name to her? I didn't know enough about the fabled nameless key.

Each clank of the heavy iron chains only served to enrage me further. I desired to see the Iris Kingdom drown for what they'd done. Aella would barely be able to summon a raindrop with how weak she looked. I was grateful for the water nearby, crashing against the cliffs. Once she was free, it would help revive her. If not her identity, at least her physical wellbeing.

As Aella approached the middle ground, the Iris guard jerked at the chain before tossing it so she stumbled and fell. Wynn hurried toward her, helping her to her feet, and whispered something into her ear. A look of confusion filtered through her expression, and I finally caught her eye. The spark of recognition had my breath hitching in my chest.

She knew me. She was still in there.

I held back a sob, unwilling to expose her. Perhaps the stars truly were with us and we could make it out of here.

"Not so fast. Stay with the prisoner," the king commanded the guard. "Until he's in chains, we can't trust the birdstain not to fly out of here."

Wynn held his hands up in surrender as he walked toward the king while the Iris guard retrieved Aella's chain, keeping her from coming to us.

The guards flanking the king pulled the crossbows from their backs and pointed them at Wynn as he approached.

It took everything in me not to run to Aella and throw my arms around her, but revealing our connection was a risk I was unwilling to take. She was so close, but it still felt as if there was an ocean between us.

"Looks like you have me," Wynn drawled as an Iris guard clamped irons around his wrists. "Now let my people go, unharmed, like you promised."

King Solanos leaned down and whispered to one of his guards. The guard walked over and threw a punch right into Wynn's face, shattering his cheek and nose. The Iris in attendance cheered and laughed, rallying him on.

I gasped, helplessly watching as more guards joined in, taking turns beating him to the ground. Helio and Rik flinched when a guard kicked his side, his ribs cracking with the impact of the metal boot. We all knew if we acted, none of us would get out of here. Glint let out a soft cry as Wynn grunted in pain. He had expected torture, but this? It was cruel and unnecessary, as if the king were taunting us, waiting for one of us to act. My fingernails dug into my palms, the pain the only thing distracting me from screaming at them to stop. Wynn didn't deserve this. He was good and just.

One of the guards lifted him up just for another Iris to spit in his face before landing another blow to his already bloodied and shattered cheek. He slumped in their arms.

Monsters. All of them.

A crack of thunder shot through the sky, the cries of the aquilas amplifying and growing near again.

Solanos looked down his nose at Wynn. "Your little birds don't scare me."

Wynn spat blood onto the ground before raising his swelling face to look up at King Solanos. "Are you satisfied?"

"We have only just begun." King Solanos let out a brutal laugh and pointed in our direction. "Seize them!"

Arrows were let loose as the guards picked up their swords and charged toward us. A sob caught in my throat at the realization that he'd called our bluff and we might not make it out of here. The cabala stepped in front of me, their weapons back in their hands, ready to fight back, and I couldn't help but feel useless. I wasn't a warrior.

"You didn't really think I was going to let them walk away with the girl, did you?" the king taunted. "Where are the one thousand aquilas you threatened me with? Have they abandoned you?"

Wynn dropped his head in defeat, his broken and battered body straining with the effort to remain standing. Suddenly, he let out a fierce roar, as if summoning the strength of one with nothing left to lose, and flung out his arms.

The Iris guards around him stumbled back, dropping the chains as he used their surprise to his advantage. Wynn whipped the chains dangling from his limbs around the throats of two of his tormentors, jerking them to the ground.

Arrows rained down from the clouds, but despite their precision and speed, they were only enough to distract the king and his guards for a moment.

Rik split the Iris' arrows from our path with a blast of wind just before they struck while Helio rumbled the earth beneath the charging guards' feet to slow them down.

Aella. I needed to get Aella.

My gaze darted toward her, her eyes wide with fear. We had not come this far to lose her again. I broke through the cabala's protective line to run toward her.

Glint caught my arm, trying to stop me. "You're going to get yourself killed!"

I ripped my arm away from her. "Are you going to let his sacrifice be in vain?"

"He'll never forgive me if I let you die." Glint shook her head, then signaled to Rik. "Just stay behind me."

The cloud cover broke, and the sun beat down mercilessly as a dozen aquilas dove in, fighting and holding off the enemy line so we could get to Aella.

Glint sprinted toward the Iris guard holding Aella's chain, and Helio raised the earth beneath her feet like steps, boosting her for a running leap. She pulled out a matching pair of long daggers, setting them alight as she jumped and twisted her body through the air like a tornado of flaming blades. A gust of wind hurtled her toward the guard with so much speed, she sliced him to bloody ribbons before he could even react.

When I finally caught up, I grabbed Aella's hand and turned to look at Wynn. A pair of aquilas dove toward him. They would get him, just as we'd planned. Three others shot down crossbow bearers from above as the two approached. Nearly there. I counted the wing beats. The one on the left tumbled into a fall, and I nearly choked. One more. There was one more. Seconds later, it too came crashing down in a spray of feathers, dust, and blood. Aquilas cried. They wouldn't stop trying. We had backup. They would come for their king. The three flew down at hurtling speeds in tight formation toward him. *Come on, Wynn. Just hold on.*

It happened in an instant; if I'd blinked, I would have missed it. He stood, chest heaving with effort as he looked toward us. His mouth formed words that looked like "*I love you*," when suddenly, his body went rigid.

A blade was thrust into him from behind, right through his heart.

The world went utterly soundless as I screamed.

This couldn't be happening. We needed him . . . *I* needed him to be okay.

"No!" I screamed over and over. No, this couldn't be happening.

Uniting their powers with our small aerial fleet, Helio, Valerik, and Glint held off the onslaught of guards.

"Too many of them," Rik shouted.

"We'll all die here if we don't run," Helio cried.

"Take the girls. Rik and I will hold them off," Glint said, creating a wall of fire as Rik fueled and blasted it toward the line of guards.

Helio grabbed me from behind, dragging me away as Aella followed. "I'm so sorry, Ari. We need to go."

It wasn't supposed to be like this. *No. No. No. No.* Tears streamed down my face as I watched Wynn collapse onto the ground, his blood pooling around him.

"What is this? *What is this*!" the king screamed.

Ringing, something was ringing, or was it screaming? Something was breaking. Shattering.

Wynn's body rippled—his white hair turned black, his alabaster skin now silver.

As if suddenly returning to my body, every sense crashed back into me, the metallic scent of blood most overpowering of all. My throat was on fire, and I realized screams were still coming out of me.

No. No. No. No.

I started screaming anew as I recognized my husband bleeding out on the ground. It wasn't possible. No. Why would he have done that? Why?

I wrenched myself out of Helio's arms, my body flooded with grief and rage. I ran toward him, unafraid of the king, unafraid of the guards. How dare they cut him down? This was not how it was supposed to be. All my hopes were dashed on the rocky cliffs below. I cursed the stars. I'd thought they would save us.

Calling upon my element, the tempestuous waves crashed below, heeding my call, and I let out another feral cry as I let it take over. Unending rage as powerful as the sea itself poured out of me. They would pay. I'd make them pay.

Throwing my hands out, I screamed louder as I called on the water, tunneling as deep into my source as I dared . . . They'd been fools to meet here with my element so close and quick to command.

The roar of a tidal wave rose up, gathering behind me. It would destroy anything in its path, but I no longer cared. Let them drown in the sea of my despair.

CHAPTER 49

TIDAL WAVE

AELLA

The sky dimmed, the morning sun blotted out by burgeoning clouds and an enormous wave on the horizon. A harbinger of mass destruction, but it would be our salvation. A stillness came over me, muting the surrounding cries of terror. In the midst of so much chaos, I should have been screaming, crying, or at the very least, shaking. I was numb, my heart frosted over, my mind clear as the calm before a storm.

My mother's vengeance was so fierce, the king fled like a coward, his guards retreating after him. She had run toward them. My mother, the healer, had run fearlessly, straight through the throng to my father. Nothing could withstand the crush of a wave of this magnitude—large enough to take out a coastline.

Legends would be written of this day.

Assessing my surroundings, our only option for escape was clear. I needed to grab Father and dive over the cliff with him. Mother could heal him. That's why she'd run to him. All would be well. It had to be. As the disaster unfolded around me, I almost forgot I was still in chains.

I ran toward my parents as fast as I could with the restriction of the shackles that bound my wrists and ankles. The Aurum female warrior rummaged through the Iris guard's bloody remains for a key, and the Aereus male stood over my parents, mouth and eyes wide at the approaching wave, shaking his head.

"There isn't enough time. We need to get out of here!" he said.

"May I?" the warrior asked, her voice surprisingly gentle. I nodded, and she unlocked the restraints one by one. The iron's oppressive weight lifted, allowing me to finally draw source from my surroundings again. A surge of strength coursed through me as I set my eyes on the horizon—the male was right.

"Take your birds and go," I commanded after she'd unchained my father's wrists. "You won't survive the water like we can." He hesitated, and I screamed, "Go! You're running out of time. I'll handle my parents."

He nodded and raced off toward the aquilas, shouting commands for their Adamas and Aurum companions to join him.

I turned my attention back to my parents. My mother was curled over my father in a trancelike state, her body glowing, pulses of brightest light beaming off of her like rings in water spreading out from a tossed stone.

I grabbed her shoulder, trying to shake her out of it. "We need to go!" She didn't budge, as though she couldn't even hear me. "Mama! Please!"

It didn't matter that we were water fae—I had lied to the male. The impact of the wave would throw us against land and stone, but I didn't want my mother to worry about anyone else. She needed to focus all her strength and healing on my father.

The water below was receding fast, and we had minutes, possibly less, until it would be too late to jump. I took her face in my hands, forcing her to look at me. She blinked, and then recognition flickered across her anguished brow.

"Aella?"

"Help me carry him," I said. "We need to jump!"

She nodded, then grunted as she attempted to lift him with me. Each of us taking one of his shoulders, we managed to sit him up, his head lolling forward. But he was too heavy, all dead weight, and we could hardly budge him further. I roared as I pulled with all my strength. I would not leave him here.

Suddenly, Kaleidos was there. I flinched at the sight of him, the jagged edges of his betrayal tearing me apart. My first instinct was to scream at him to leave us, but there was no time. We needed his help.

"Let me do this," Kaleidos offered.

He took my place, wrapping my father's arm over his neck, heaving the brunt of his weight up onto his shoulder. My mother and I supported my father from the other side as we hobbled hurriedly to the edge of the cliff. The water was waning too fast and I didn't know if we could jump far enough to avoid catching on anything, but our choices were to definitely die here or possibly die on our way down. Kaleidos shifted the ground beneath our feet, making the ledge hang farther over the cliffside, giving us a better platform to jump from.

"On the count of three," Kaleidos shouted. "One."

One breath.

"Two."

Two breaths.

"Three."

We ran out onto the ledge until our feet left the earth.

And we were falling.

Falling.

In the middle of the drop that lasted only seconds, time seemed to freeze the moment I realized we were short one person. I had too many questions for him. Too much unresolved between us. Looking up, I reached my hand toward Kaleidos, my gaze sharpening, studying him. His face changed, a new mask falling over it just before he disappeared behind the ledge.

My breath caught in my throat, threatening to strangle me. I'd been fighting not to believe it, hoping against doubt for an explanation from him, that his actions would all make sense. But even now, even though he'd helped us jump out to sea, this one act didn't absolve him of his actions.

From the very beginning, he'd shown me who he was. It had been my own reckless desire that had led me to put my trust in an Iris prince. Bitterness took root as the distance stretched between us. The male up there, the one I had clung to in my most vulnerable and exposed state, was a stranger, a coward. He was nothing more than my captor wrapped in the pretty illusion of safety.

And just like that, time sped up again, and the sea swallowed us, pulling us to safety beneath the waves, our bodies carried on a stream that cradled and held us together, my father, mother, and me.

My parents. They were here. We were together.

My father.

A wave of panic washed over me as reality forced its way in.

My mother had her hand over Father's open wound. Her eyes squeezed shut, brows furrowed in focus, in prayer. Uncertain what else to do, I placed my hand opposite hers, silencing my hiss as the briny water stung my iron-ravaged skin.

"Show me. Tell me what to do . . ." I begged, my chest cracked wide open, all of my bottled up emotions leaking out of me. She placed a hand over mine and murmured over and over again, prayers, petitions, offerings to the stars.

Why isn't it working? I lifted my head to the heavens, to the stars not visible in the light of day, and screamed a strangled, pleading cry.

Why have you abandoned us?

Without warning, the sea spit us out onto a sandy beach far from Prisma. Father coughed, blood mixing with the clear, shallow water that gently washed over us. My mother shook so violently, she looked ready to collapse, pouring so much into him. She'd deplete all of her source if she wasn't careful.

"Verus, you have to stay with me," she cried, tears streaming down her face as she pressed her hands over his gaping wound. "We need you—the children need you—you can't leave us." Her voice cracked.

Blood continued to ooze from his open wound, staining the sand, and my magic wasn't helping either, drained by the iron that had bound me. No matter how hard I tried, I couldn't help close the laceration, I couldn't stop the bleeding. No matter how much I wanted it, it just wasn't enough.

"I'm so sorry, Mama. This is all my fault." My chest was caving in on itself. I hated that this was because of me. He was dying *for* me.

Verus fluttered his eyes. "Ari . . ." he rasped. She immediately sank her forehead to his, her tears falling onto his cheeks. His head lolled toward me, his battered face pallid as he sought me.

"We got her out," my mother cried into his neck. "She's free because of you."

His laugh was choked, but his eyes were a pair of crescents. I swallowed tears and kissed his cheek, squeezing his limp, calloused hand in mine.

"I'm so proud of you, Aella." He struggled the words out between agonal breaths. "Do not hide. Do not be afraid of your purpose."

Despite the ache in my throat, I nodded, forcing myself to smile as brightly as I could. These were the words of a dying male, and more than anything, I wanted to let him know I was okay because of him.

"Thank you for being the best father, for never making me feel unwanted or unworthy of your love . . ."

"You will always be my daughter, my little whirlwind," he said, his words filled with love.

The emptiness in my chest flooded, and I was suffocating on grief, gasping for breath between sobs.

He looked back up at my mother. "We've had a beautiful life . . ."

"No! No, no, no, no, no. You stay right here, you hear me? I won't give up on you. I won't!" she sobbed, clutching at his bloodied leathers. "Our life isn't over. We will have many more days together."

"She's free . . . My purpose here is complete." He coughed, eyes fluttering again—his vibrant light fading before us—but he fought to get the last words out. "Now live."

"Please, Verus. Please don't leave us," she wept, utterly broken.

"I love you with every piece of my tattered soul . . . This is my fate. Follow yours."

CHAPTER 50
Too Much Rum

WYNN

The night before the trade

My ears twitched at the approach of footsteps just before a knock at the door brought me to my feet—a curious but welcome escape from my thoughts after pouring over maps of Prisma and studying the best escape routes. Even with our small fleet of aquila riders, the chances of me getting out were slim, but I wasn't going to give up without a fight.

"Come in," I called out.

I blinked in shock when Verus appeared, a bottle of liquor and a pair of tin mugs in hand.

"Your Majesty, would you mind if we had a chat and perhaps a drink?" he asked.

I motioned for him to have a seat on the dusty floor as I lowered myself across from him. His presence filled the space, making the room feel all the smaller. He uncorked the bottle with his teeth and poured us a set of drinks, placing them onto the floor between us.

"How can I help you, Verus?" I asked, raising an eyebrow as I leaned against the wall. "You're the last person I expected to see . . . alone."

Verus laughed softly, raising his cup in a silent toast before tossing it back. "I wanted a chance to thank you for what you're willing to do for my daughter."

I lifted my cup and did the same, shrugging as I tried to ignore the sudden possessiveness I felt over someone I'd never even met.

"I owed her . . . Arianwen, I mean. I don't know if she explained now that the oath is gone."

Verus crossed his arms, leaning back casually. "Yes, she finally filled me in. I'll admit, I was very tempted to knock your teeth out."

I laughed. "Well, I'm glad you didn't, but I understand. I was a fool then. She deserved better . . . and it looks like she is happy. I suppose I have you to thank for that."

"We've had many happy years together. I'm grateful to the stars for every moment."

I couldn't help rolling my eyes. "As if the stars have anything to do with our happiness."

Verus' eyes glinted in the low lamp light. "You'd be surprised."

I shrugged in answer.

"You know, Your Majesty—"

"Stop. I told you to call me Wynn," I interrupted. "We're something akin to family now, I suppose." It was my turn to offer a pour, and I did so generously.

Verus flashed his teeth. "All right, Wynn . . . You know this plan of yours tomorrow is most likely going to end in your death, right?"

I sighed and pinched the bridge of my nose. "So everyone keeps telling me. But we have plans to get me out. Stars willing, one of them works, but if all else fails, I might be able to convince them to keep me alive long enough for the rebellion to stage a coup."

Verus shook his head, his eyes wide as he leaned forward. "There's no guarantee of that, and are you prepared for the very real threat of torture as they interrogate you? You'd really be willing to endure that for a daughter you've never even met?"

"If Aella is the one the prophecy speaks of, it's not even a question. We need to rescue her for the good of all fae kind. I'm willing to endure anything for a chance at our freedom. And even if, against all reason, she isn't the prophesied one, I made Ari a promise, and I intend to keep it."

"There's got to be another option," Verus said. "The courts need you to lead them. You have the strongest army right now, and they answer to you. Do you really think we can unite everyone without you? Even if we save Aella?" Verus shook his head. "I can't believe I'm saying this, but as much as I hate to admit it, Aella is going to need you to teach her things—things I'm not capable of."

My answering laugh came out strained. "Don't you worry. I've put measures in place in case I can't get out."

"Do you still love her?" he asked.

His candor caused my heart to stutter. I hesitated. Verus could still easily knock me on my arse.

"A part of me will always care for her," I admitted. "I had thought she might—never mind. I know she is happy, and for that, I am grateful." I shook my head. "You know . . . before she met you, she was so worried you'd be an awful match."

Verus threw his head back in laughter. "Sounds like my wife. It did take us a while to open up to each other."

I raised an eyebrow as Verus poured from the bottle of Iverian rum, topping off our cups.

He tossed it back again in one swallow. Setting the tin mug down onto the floor, his eyes had a far-off look in them. "It took her over a year to let go of you."

My eyes widened. Ari had hinted they hadn't truly been together right away, but hearing it from Verus . . .

"There was no time to meet before we married. When she returned, her parents immediately sent word, requesting the marriage continue as planned. My family just wanted me to up our status and fulfill my duty to the Iris. I had little desire to be wed, but I wasn't about to back out of my word. When I saw her at the lagoon, looking simultaneously terrified and determined, I knew she was going to be trouble."

I knocked back my drink and quickly poured us another set. While part of me couldn't bear listening to Ari and Verus' love story, another part of me wanted, no, needed to know.

"Go on . . ."

Verus continued, "I admit I was a real arse the first year of our marriage. I wasn't exactly ready for a relationship after losing my mate to the marriage drafts, and I didn't think I had anything left to offer her."

"You had a mate?" I interrupted. "Damn. The stars sure have a sick sense of humor."

Verus nodded and gave a wry laugh. "I've said the same thing many times. Our arrangement seemed fated by the stars. She was already expecting a child, so I figured we could get by living as strangers while fulfilling what was expected of us."

The thought of what Ari must have gone through with the oath binding her made me sick. I hated that I'd been the cause of so much pain for her.

I nodded for Verus to continue.

"It wasn't until I thought I might lose her and Aella that I realized how much she meant to me."

"Lose them? What happened?"

Verus shook his head. "Blame it on my ego." He knocked back the rest of his rum. "I'm just lucky she didn't give up on me. There was a time I feared she'd leave, but not anymore." He relaxed into the wall, crossing his legs out in front of him. "I'm not threatened by your history with her. I'm grateful it brought her—brought them—into my life. I have no regrets."

"That's exactly why I have to do this, Verus. This isn't just about duty." I ran my fingers through my hair and blew out a breath. "The truth is, if I hadn't driven Ari away all those years ago . . . if I hadn't chosen my stars-damned duty over my heart, our daugh—Aella would have never been in this situation."

Verus reached over and squeezed my shoulder. "There is no point in playing out the 'what ifs' and 'could have beens.' As much as I have cursed the stars, perhaps there is a purpose beyond what we can understand."

"You're right. I can't live in the past, but I can try to atone for my mistakes. I can make it up to them the only way I know how. I made Ari a promise, and I won't let her down again."

Verus leaned his head against the wall. "You know she doesn't blame you for this."

"Be that as it may, I'm doing this for her. For your family." I played with the tin mug in my hand before looking up, hoping he could see how much I meant these words. "I can never thank you enough, Verus, for taking care of Ari all these years, for loving her how she deserved to be loved—choosing her. And for loving my daughter, for raising her and being her father. My only regret is I might not have the chance to know her."

"She really is amazing," Verus said, his voice tinged with awe. "You should be so proud."

I reached over, gripping his shoulder, an understanding passing between us. "I'm happy for you. I really am." I let go and knocked back my third—or was it fourth?—drink.

"I'm glad we had the chance to talk," Verus said. "I wanted you to know I've had a wonderful life, filled with love and family. My stars-given purpose is clear, but you haven't fulfilled yours yet. And, Wynn? I know what she is to you."

"Verus, I would never—"

"No, I know," he interrupted. "I just need you to know it's okay to love her."

The room started to spin. How much had I had to drink? I tried to sit up straighter, shaking my head in an effort to clear it.

"Was there something in that drink?"

Verus looked apologetic. "I'm sorry, Wynn. I know you feel like you need to atone for your mistakes, but like I said before, we can't let you do this tomorrow."

We? Who's we?

"It'll wear off in a few hours."

"What in the stars are you talking about? And why . . . why aren't you on your arse?"

Verus smiled sadly as he stood and went to the door. "The Iverian herb in the rum doesn't affect me." He paused before continuing. "You're a good male, Wynn. Take care of them." He opened the door, and my jaw slackened when Rik and Helio walked in holding rope.

I tried to stand, but I couldn't get my legs under me and the room kept spinning. "Faex," I mumbled. "Whatinthestars are you two doing co'spiring against me? Whadoyou think you're doing?"

"It's for your own good, Wynn," Helio said as he tied my hands behind my back.

"I couldaveyou ex'cuted for this," I growled, my words slurring.

"Hate us today, but this way, you'll at least live tomorrow." Rik tightened the rope around my legs.

I wanted to argue. I was their stars-damned king. How dare they defy me? Before I could say another word, my world turned black.

Present

I fought against my restraints, but they had been tied way too tight. If something happened to Verus, Arianwen would kill me. It was my duty, my place to go—even if I knew I might not have made it out alive. If they'd done what I thought they'd planned, if Verus' glamour fell, there was no telling how long the Iris would let him live. I roared in anger.

Why has no one come to free me?

Faex. Either they're all at the trade, or Rik must have put up a sound barrier. I was furious at all of them, how they had plotted and planned behind my back.

"Faex! Let me out!" I shouted again, despite the futility. I had no idea what time it was or how long I'd been bound. Damn them and their supposed good intentions. I was going to have some serious words with them if they managed to return. Idiots. Fools. I growled in frustration as I glared at the offensive bottle of rum left on the floor.

Did they have to tie the ropes so damned tight? Yes . . . they did, or I would have been out of these bindings and throttling them before they left for the exchange.

I supposed it was my fault, drinking far too much the night before a mission.

Seemingly out of nowhere, Glint burst into the room, blood-splattered and wild-eyed.

"That better be Iris blood. Tell me you didn't do what I think you did!" I glared at her as she cut the ropes. My body ached, and I stood and stretched, which elicited a groan after being bound in that position for hours. "I could have all your heads for this, or at the very least, throw you in the Zephyrian dungeons," I spat. "I haven't yet decided I won't."

Glint's eyes were serious as she put her hand on my shoulder. "You might be angry with us now, but I just witnessed the Iris stab you through the heart. I knew it wasn't you, but I never want to see that happen again."

"What did you do?" I commanded as shock and anger pulsed through me.

Glint ran her hand through her windswept hair. "No time to waste. Ari summoned a tidal wave that could take out half of Prisma. We barely made it out in time."

My jaw dropped. "Explain."

"We had Verus glamoured to look like you. He took your place in the exchange. Our contingency plan failed . . . Solanos . . . he called our bluff and chaos ensued. Verus went down trying to give us time to escape."

"Fools."

"That could have been you," Glint argued.

"It was my choice to go! I knew the risks. That was my call to make, not yours."

Glint's shoulders softened. "We need you to end this. It was for your own good and for the good of all elementals. You can hate us all you want, but I'm *not* sorry you're still alive."

"Faex . . ." I paused. "Did you get her? My . . . daughter?"

"Yes. Last I saw her, she and Ari had jumped into the sea. Helio and Rik are going to find them and head straight for Concordia."

"Verus?" I was almost afraid to ask.

Glint shook her head. "He was with Ari, but I can't imagine he survived."

A deep ache worked its way through me—for the female who would always have my heart and for the daughter I didn't even know. Loss of a loved one was not a pain that easily faded. It was ever present, ever lingering. One had to learn how to live with it.

"I've got Luminara and the others waiting outside," Glint said. "We need to fly."

CHAPTER 51
NOT ONCE BUT TWICE

AELLA

We hadn't moved from where we'd said our final goodbyes to Father before the water had swept in to claim his body. Not a word had been spoken since he'd passed. We'd only sat, watching the shadows travel over the sand, our bodies a sundial as the hours slipped by. I had no tears left to shed, no feeling in my hollowed-out chest. All that had been taken from me had shredded my soul into a fragile, leaking thing. The wounds left gaping had hemorrhaged all that was good. The only cure, to bury or seal it back up with anger and revenge.

Aquilas the size of horses flew in, landing near us on the beach. It was a sight that, any other time, I would have marveled at, but in my current state, I had no emotion left to spare. The ivory-skinned male accompanied by the darker male with bright copper hair dismounted and ran toward us, slowing to a stride as they neared.

"Oh, Ari," the Aereus said, pulling her up into an embrace. She struck his solid chest with trembling fists while crying big, choking sobs.

"He took his place! How could you let him . . . How could you let him? How could you let him!" She cried so hard, practically collapsing, and he scooped her into his deep bronze arms. The two males shared a quick glance and a nod before he carried her over to one of the large, hawk-like birds, leaving me alone with the handsome, fair-skinned male.

Cropped short to his head, his white hair emphasized his striking, blue eyes. With crystalline skin so fair, he had to be Adamas, just like the male my father had been glamoured to look like.

"Where are you taking us?" I asked. These people had colluded with my father in a trade that had cost him his life. Against my mother's knowledge.

Dropping to his knee before me so he was at eye level, he spoke with a smooth and relaxed cadence, as though we had all the time in the world.

"We're going to an encampment in the ruins of Concordia. It's safe—I swear this to you."

"Excuse my reservation, but I just left one prison, and I'm not about to go willingly to another."

The male chuckled, giving me a look as though what I'd just said was adorable.

"Who are you?" I asked.

"My name is Valerik, and that's Helio over there. We're good friends of your mother's . . . from way back," he said.

I reached for the star on the back of my neck, remembering what Estrella had told me about my father in the servants' passages.

"I should probably give your mother the chance to explain everything to you first . . . uh . . . but we need to head back to camp. Everyone is waiting for you there." Valerik's eyes crinkled at the corners in a sad smile. He could probably read all of the mixed emotions storming through me as I tried to make sense of everything. All the secrets my mother had kept from me.

Stars, was this the Adamas male Estrella had called my father?

"By the way you're looking at me right now, let me just make one thing clear, your mother and I . . . we were never like that." He raised his palms up in mock surrender.

I forced myself onto shaky feet and walked in the opposite direction. I needed space. This was all too much to take in.

"W-wait!" he stammered. "What I meant to say is, I am *not* your father."

I kept walking, putting more distance between us.

"Holy birdstains. This is why I'll never have kids," Valerik muttered before *flying over me* and landing just a few feet away.

My eyes widened with a mix of shock and reluctant awe as I witnessed someone else wield air powers for the first time, but I quickly steeled myself.

"I'm going to make this really easy for you. I don't know you. I don't trust you. I'm not going with you." I bared my teeth. My father had sacrificed himself for me, and they had let him, I reminded myself.

"Look, I get it. You're mad, you're hurt, you're probably confused about so much. I don't want to step on anyone's toes here—I just want to bring you to safety. That's all. And then you can have at it, ask any question you'd like, and I'm sure they'll be happy to clarify things for you. I just don't think your mother would appreciate me being the one to fill you in on everything."

I scoffed. "Asking her has worked really well for me in the past."

"That was before she had her blood oath released."

"A blood oath?"

Valerik nodded.

I stared cooly at him. I couldn't argue what he'd said.

"If it makes you feel any better, I'll tell you something about me?" he offered.

"I don't think there is a thing in the world that could make me feel better," I said.

His brows furrowed. "I know."

"Do you want to know the worst part?"

"What's that?"

"I already grieved the loss of my parents. I came to terms with the fate I was dealt. Then I let a tiny morsel of hope in, and even knowing the risk, knowing the uncertainty, I let it take hold . . . only for it to let me down again. Just like everything else. And what am I supposed to do now? Shatter again after all he did to rescue me? I won't be that person. I refuse.

I am so tired of having no control over what happens to me or the people I love! I am so tired of being the victim! This is my life. It's my story. *I'll* decide what happens to me after this. Are we clear on that?"

"Yes, Your High—"

"You don't need to call me that. I never actually married the prince."

"Right . . ." He sifted his fingers through his hair. "Will you please let me take you back to camp, and then *you* can decide where to go from there? I'll personally escort you out if you choose to leave. No one will keep you there against your will."

I nodded with resignation.

Valerik's shoulders slumped in relief and he sighed. He held his hand out toward the birds with a smile. "Ever dreamed of riding an aquila?"

"Has my mother been to Zephyria? Is that where you met? In Zephyria?" I asked yet again.

Despite his earlier offer, he'd been cleverly evading my inquiries, managing to avoid answering any of the questions about my mother I'd hammered him with. For all I knew, my mother had threatened her friends not to say anything. She could be persuasive when she wanted to be.

I still couldn't get over the fact that she was friends with Adamas and Aereus fae, that she'd had this whole other life I'd known nothing about. Perhaps the worst part was that it made Estrella's revelation all the more believable . . .

All this time, I'd been dreaming of the Adamas, wondering what it would be like to meet one, to have the chance to learn more about my powers. And now, to come face to face with them . . .

I observed the male, wondering why, if I were half Adamas, I didn't look like him. So fair his skin was, he could blend right into the clouds we passed through. No wonder the Adamas had been able to stay hidden all these years.

But there always *had been* something different about me. The reason I'd been taught to keep my head down, not to draw attention. The birthmark.

Could it be that it was just a patch of Adamas skin? What a wonder that it was in a location I could easily hide. Had it been more obvious, perhaps my life would have ended long ago.

The lack of physical similarities aside, it was like a dive in the icy deep, the reminder of just how much I'd been lied to by the Iris and how little I'd been told by my own family, blood oath or not.

The entire flight, my mind kept drifting to the male my father had been glamoured to look like. The one they'd meant to trade for me. The king of the Adamas. Why would he have been willing to do that for me? Had it been because he too believed me to be the fulfillment of that damned prophecy? Though it hadn't truly been him, my mother must've believed he would sacrifice himself for me.

Any answer I came up with made me feel worse, and I couldn't keep thinking about it. Not so soon after losing my father. His face flashed in my mind, and I felt myself harden even more, my heart freezing over protectively.

I wouldn't let myself wallow in the pain. I'd been in that place far too much in far too little time, and I wasn't ready to go back to it. I'd bury every crushing feeling. They didn't serve me. If I'd broken after every trauma, there'd be nothing left of me. Prisma had taught me what weakness could do to a person. I would not let myself become that. Numbness would be my strength.

While our journey was long, the daylight came and went in a flash compared to the lingering hours in the Palatium Crystalis. The sky was a deep, dark blue as the last slivers of light began to disappear into the horizon. Stars traced the sky above us as we flew over mountain and plane, and my head had nodded into Valerik's back, the air thin in my lungs. Exhaustion was creeping in, but I didn't want to fall asleep not knowing where we were. I feared waking up in an unfamiliar place.

With a layer of air surrounding and protecting us against the cold whip of the wind, a part of me wished the protection would fall, even if only for a second. Perhaps the icy wind would numb my heart a little more and take the rest of my pain away. Or, at the very least, keep me awake.

"Do you always use a wind shield?" I asked, trying to force my eyes to stay open. "It seems so . . . unnatural for an air elemental."

"I thought it might help make you more comfortable. I don't need it, but you might get cold or have a hard time breathing since you're not used to the air at these altitudes and speeds."

I mumbled something unintelligible, yet he seemed to have heard me perfectly.

"Okay, fine. I'm going to let the shield down, but if it becomes too much for you or you change your mind, just . . . squeeze my hand." He reached back for my hand, and I gripped his, bracing myself, ready for anything.

"Lean forward. It will help." He curled over the front of the saddle, angling his body to practically lie flat on the bird's neck, just like in the illustrations I'd seen in Kaleidos' book. I copied him, laying my head and chest on his back.

"Ready?" he asked.

I nodded, ensuring I still had a good grasp on his hand and that my body was as flat as possible. *I can do this.*

All at once, the wind pelted against my face, cold as a shock of ice. It wasn't terrible, but he'd been right, it was a lot harder than I'd expected, and I wasn't sure how long I could last being this exhausted. I' hate to admit it to him though, so I tried sticking it out for as long as possible, breathing in short, sharp gasps.

"You doin' all right?" he drawled.

"Yes!" I replied just as the wind shield came back up, making my reply sound way louder than I had intended, like I was screaming. I'd expected my air powers to somehow kick in and strengthen in the wind's presence, the way I always felt strongest near water, but perhaps it was too much to ask so soon after removing the iron chains.

"Nice job. Baby steps, all right?"

"I could've lasted a little longer. I was just getting used to it," I said, my ego bruised.

"The squeezed imprints on my hand would beg to differ."

I quickly released his hand.

"How does *he* take it? He's not even Adamas!" I gestured toward the Aereus flying with my mother.

"Not everyone's built like Helio, I'm telling you . . ." He laughed.

"And my mother? Can she ride an aquila on her own?"

Again, the silent treatment. I stared at her like she was a complete stranger, passed out on the aquila with Helio.

At last, we'd made it to the camp. My mother had slept the entire way to Concordia. Valerik said she must've nearly exhausted herself from all of her source and could sleep for days to recover.

The camp was almost impossible to see. Completely camouflaged by the old city ruins and rough terrain surrounding the lake, I'd never have spotted it if it hadn't been for Valerik pointing it out to me.

Upon our arrival, Helio had carefully removed my debilitated mother from his aquila and escorted us, her passed out his arms, to a room in an overgrown ruin with a sweeping view of the lake. Stars glittered within its reflective surface. Even with all the old, broken buildings surrounding it, it was breathtaking.

Behind me, a healer checked on my mother as she lay unconscious. The healer tried to come and assess me next, but I flinched away from her, shaking my head.

"That's all right. We'll be back in the morning to check on her. Please let us know if there's anything you need. Try to get some rest, okay?"

I nodded, shock washing over me as it suddenly hit me that I wasn't in the Palatium Crystalis anymore. That my choices were respected. That I'd no longer need to submit to the Iris.

I was free.

The healer left the room, so it was just me and my mother in the big, empty space, save for a modest bed.

I strode over to my mother, still asleep, and crept into the firm bed, snuggling up in the lightweight cotton blanket next to her. Combing her unruly curls out of her face, I felt the pinch of tears threatening to escape. A face I'd thought I'd never get to see again. So many things I wanted to tell her, things I needed to ask. But none of them truly mattered as much as the fact that we were together again, even if I was still angry with her.

Though I'd been through hell and back, in her presence, I was still just a lost little girl who needed her mother. Now, we shared this trauma, and she'd need me too. My mother, who had come for me, who had risked everything in facing the king. Who had come to find me in Prisma, not once but twice.

My dearest Arianwen, my partner, my wife,

What I'm planning is unforgivable, I know. I should have told you, and for that, I am most sorry. I can't risk saying a word—knowing you will convince me otherwise, as you are always so persuasive—but what kind of male would I be to keep our daughter from meeting or knowing her true father?

Ever since stepping foot in the Palatium Crystalis, I have been haunted by the memory of my mate. I could sense her there. She was in the flowers, the waterways . . . Somehow, she managed to leave her mark, however insignificant she should have been. Being there ripped those wounds raw, flooding me with feelings of losing her all over again. To walk the grounds she once walked, to stand within the very walls where she spent her last days . . . Seeing the way elementals were treated there and knowing that was how she had been treated made me sick with grief. I cannot bear for that to be our daughter's fate if we do not rescue her. My motivation for getting Aella out of Prisma has never been stronger.

I know this plan is foolish, but what would be more foolish still is to allow Wynn—the leader of the rebellion and Aella's father—to sacrifice himself; we all know he would not come out of there alive. There are things Aella needs to learn about herself and her powers that I cannot teach her, and she will need them for the days ahead. You must not blame Wynn or his cabala for their parts in this— it was my idea, my choice. I've instructed them to give you this letter in case the worst happens. You must believe me when I say this is the only way, Arianwen. I want you to know that I go willingly in his place.

Now, this is perhaps most important for you to hear: what kind of male would I be to keep you from your true mate? While our love may have patched the holes in our hearts, it was only ever a temporary relief—enough to soothe each other's aches. It was exactly what both of us needed, but perhaps it wasn't meant to last forever. You're my best friend and have brought me true happiness, but a piece of me has remained forever lost, sucked under on a swift undertow. I know you must feel this way too. There is a cost, being separated from your mate. There is a part of you that never feels whole, an ache that not even distance can quell.

I can't pretend to understand the stars' design and why they've allowed things to happen the way they have, but none of that matters. Do not fault yourself for caring about your mate. It is only natural. It does not change what we had, nor does it diminish it.

I love you, Arianwen, with all of the torn-up and shredded pieces of my heart. While I believe you can have more than one love in your life, there is only one soul that might make yours whole again. Who am I to keep that from you? You deserve to be whole, as I so long to be.

Yours in this lifetime,
Verus

P.S. You know there is nothing I wouldn't do for you and our children, and with help from the cabala, I have set things in motion so you will not want for food or shelter in my absence. I love you, wife.

PART III

THE IRIS

UNKNOWN SOURCE

"This is wrong!" the Lux Verax elder cried. "You have taken the choice away from the elementals. We cannot start a new generation based on such things. You would curse our people."

Evo stood tall amidst the rebuke for taking the Adamas princess against her will. "I stayed in that wretched land after you fled. After so much searching, you gave up too quickly, almost as if you didn't really care about the cause you stated was so important to us. I risked my own neck to find a way for our people. Can you not at least recognize my willingness?"

"We will find another way, an honest way."

"Forgive me if I am not eager to wait another five hundred years to find another people to fail in negotiations with."

"Enough!" the elder said. "We will not let him spew any more evil from his deceptive mouth, lest it infect our pure and truthful spirits."

Evo did not lose the confidence in his stance nor the look of triumph in his eyes, even as they wrapped him in a silencing bubble that shrank in on him until it became invisible. Even without sound, he did not miss the moment the elders sensed the spark of life pulsing within the princess, glowing with a combination of both aether and source.

Torn over the dilemma, the Lux council, debated for days. The prize was tempting but too dangerous. The general consensus was that keeping the Adamas female was wrong and they could not allow it, but what would they do with her? With the child? What would they do with their tarnished son who had done something so wicked and cruel?

A decision was made. They would send him back to Esterra as punishment for his crimes, never to return home. They could not allow his wrongdoings to spoil all the good and honesty the Lux Verax prided themselves on. His sin was deemed so unforgivable, they had to do away with him—their youngest, their last thread of survival. They refused to allow their knowledge to be passed on to the spawn of such deception.

While he was imprisoned and awaiting their decision, Evo made promises to his guards too good to deny—that they'd be rulers and kings in Esterra. They'd shine brighter with him than their current fates would ever allow. Because of his charisma and his way with words, his promises spread like a virus amongst them.

The moment Evo was thrown back through the door between worlds with his elemental bride, he was followed by a rush of guards. Chaos erupted as Evo's new followers stormed through the portal, desperate for the power and dreams he had offered them. Desperate for more meaning than they had been given in their dying world. Against the elders' protestations and screams, they were willing to take a chance, even if it meant parting with their morals, even if it meant they would never return to their beloved home.

The Lux Verax were met by an army of Adamas, who, out of good will, asked only for the return of Princess Nubia so they could avoid war, but Evo refused. And in this deadly battle, which cost so much life, Evo and his people emerged triumphant. His pregnant bride, Nubia, was a symbol of hope to his Lux followers, and he would have done anything to protect her.

Shedding their former identities as the Lux Verax, the now-called Iris left the mountains in search of a more hospitable climate, one more similar to their own. Once they discovered the other elementals in Esterra, they preyed on their innocence using glamours and lies, pretending they had been sent from the stars *to get what they wanted. They spread far and wide to collect elemental brides and grooms as their leader had, demanding tribute when not offered freely.*

Away from their home, shut off from all that had made them good, their truths and knowledge were forgotten, their hearts withered as they filled their souls with vanity, greed, and a hunger for power. And in each generation after, compounded by their parents' rejection of home and thence everything good, only wickedness thrived.

CHAPTER 52

TOGETHER

Taking off my slippers, my feet squished into the soggy shoreline. The peaceful lake stretched before me like an ocean of sorts, a gentle current scattering the sun's rays silver across its surface.

The water swirled around me as I waded deeper. It had been too long since I'd been in a natural source, felt liquid freedom surrounding and carrying me. After noticing how dirty and disheveled I was in the lake's crystalline reflection, I splashed its cool water onto my face. My arms still bore remnants of the shimmering makeup the Iris had adorned me with for the exchange, and I suddenly felt the need to wash all of Prisma off me. I painstakingly scrubbed—aggressively rubbing at my face and arms in an attempt to rid them of every last fleck of glitter—until my skin was nearly raw.

"If you rub any harder, there won't be any skin left."

I froze at the familiar voice, unsure if I could trust my own ears. I turned to find the most beautiful female dashing through the shallows toward me.

"Viera?" I called out, half expecting her image to fade.

"Aella!" she called back, tripping forward with a splash. "Got caught on a root!" she laughed.

Laughter bubbled out of me as I waded through a patch of dense vegetation to reach her. My foot got stuck too, sucking me under, and we continued on like that, screaming and laughing as we fought our way toward each other.

"I tell you, whoever's genius idea it was to set up camp on this stars cursed lake . . ." Viera trailed off as we finally reached each other.

My eyes scanned over her, looking for injuries as I stretched out to touch her, to confirm she was actually real. Her fingers threaded with mine, our palms pressing together. She looked so different with her hair cut short—her formerly long waves chopped to a short, bouncy mop—and darker with all the lightened ends trimmed away. But her wide, aquamarine eyes still held in them all the memories and love we'd always shared.

We hugged, hearts close, laughing. *Together.*

"Kaleidos told me . . . Still, after seeing you fall in the arena . . . it's hard to believe my eyes. How did you get here?"

"We're here too, Aella," came another voice from the shoreline.

Looking past Viera, my eyes widened at the sight of Jara, Lewenne, and Ona. While Lewenne and Ona ran toward us into the water, Jara held back.

"I don't do lakes. Sorry."

We crashed into each other in a big hug.

"Come on in, Jara. Wash the Prisma off of ya," Viera said.

"Oh, trust me, I burnt it off days ago," she joked, then returned her attention to me. "Thank you, Aella. None of us would be here without you." She wiped away a tear, then turned to walk back toward the ruins. At the top of the small hill, another Aurum female with a smile as big as the sun's golden rays waved to her. Jara gave us a final salute before smoothing out her cornsilk hair and walking eagerly up the hill.

"Actually, Lewenne deserves some credit for getting us out of there too," Ona said. "Though this lake is a bit much."

"And Ilaria," Viera said.

Everyone went silent, and I searched along the coast for her.

"Ilaria? Is she here?" I asked.

Lewenne shook her head. "She didn't make it. But she found Viera. And she helped us escape. And so did Ona."

"It was a group effort." Ona sniffed. "All right, you all can stay in this swampy water, but I'm heading back up."

"Not a swamp!" Lewenne exclaimed. "None of you seem to have any respect for the delicate ecosystem you're tromping around in. Come, Ona. I'll show you how to maneuver without waging war on the lake."

"To be fair, it was perfectly tame when first I got here," I said.

"Sure, blame it on me." Viera laughed.

Once we were alone again, Viera's laughter fell, and her face became more serious as she took me in again. My shoulders tensed in anticipation. She then plastered on the flawless, composed smile she'd inherited from her mother for times when nothing was right but she had to pretend otherwise. "What do you say we head back for a bite to eat?"

I let out a tremendous sigh of relief, nodding with a smile. "Please tell me they feed us real food here."

Her eyes widened. "Oh, Aella, we have food. But not just Iverian. There are cooks from each court here! And wait until you try this stuff called coffee!"

CHAPTER 53
UNCHANGING FATE

ARIANWEN

My body ached as I slowly regained consciousness. My throat was as dry as Ilithania's desert—a pounding headache making me want to pull the blanket over my face to block out the dim light. Completely disoriented, I tried to remember where I was.

It was far too quiet. I took a deep breath, inhaling the lingering scent of sandalwood and plumeria. Memories crashed into me, and I sat up too quickly, the sudden movement flooding me with nausea. I leaned over the side of the bed and retched until there was nothing left.

He's gone.

I sobbed. My shoulders shook with grief as I remembered holding my husband in my arms for the last time.

Aella. Where was she? I needed to see her, to make sure she was all right. There were too many things unspoken between us.

My eyes were drawn to a glass of water that had been left for me, and I eagerly grabbed it, gulping it down. How long had I been out? I tried summoning a small orb, but my hands shook as the water barely retained its shape before splashing into a small puddle on the floor. Clearly, it hadn't been long enough for my body to recover from the immense amount of source power I had used.

I needed to get out to the lake. I needed to find myself somehow, even though everything I had known for the last twenty-five years had been stolen from me by the cruel Iris king. Had he survived the reckoning I'd poured out on Prisma? Stars, I hoped not. I felt a twinge of remorse when I considered the innocents who might have been caught in the wake, but it was completely overpowered by the overwhelming grief that flooded me.

Suddenly, my body stiffened.

The letter.

I frantically tore through the bedding, fumbling through my pockets, searching for that last remaining piece of Verus. As soon as my fingers felt the crumpled-up paper, another sob wrenched itself from my body. With care, I removed it and smoothed it out on the bed. My eyes hungrily took in his words again, even as despair threatened to drown me. It was too much. It hurt too much.

Stumbling out of bed, I took a moment to breathe, holding myself up on the wall.

A soft knock at the door startled me, and I tried to call out, but my voice was raw and hoarse.

The door flew open, and I was met with icy blue eyes filled with concern and devastation. "Arianwen, are you all right?"

Unable to answer other than with a brief shake of my head, I took a step toward the door, meaning to ignore the male whose choices had led to my husband's death. If he'd not initiated the trade . . .

When my knees buckled, Wynn was there, scooping me up into his arms. "I am so sorry—I never wanted this to happen," he said, his voice low and filled with sorrow.

Giant tears slid from my eyes. I was surprised I had any left. "How could you?" I rasped. "How could you let him take your place?" I tucked my head into his chest, unwilling to look him in the eye, unwilling to forgive him for what had transpired. I wanted someone to blame, my grief looking for an outlet.

"My—" He sighed deeply, his chest rising under my cheek, the sound of his heartbeat oddly soothing. "Ari, be angry with me. I can take it. It is my fault. I let my guard down. It should have been me."

His response surprised me. I had almost expected him to lay the blame on Verus or his cabala.

I knew it had been Verus' choice. His letter had explained it all, but still, I wanted to hate him for leaving me, for leaving our family. I wanted to hate that he chose the good of all people over us—but he'd wanted to see a better world just as much as I did. How many nights had we lain under the stars, dreaming of a better world for our children?

"Take me to the water . . . please," I whispered.

"Of course," Wynn said softly before he carried me through the camp and toward the dark, glistening lake. The sun had started to set, but I closed my eyes—unwilling to gaze at the beauty around me when all I could feel was the desolation of my shredded heart.

The water splashed as Wynn strode straight in, carrying me until my body floated on its surface.

"Where's Aella?" I tried speaking again, my throat aching with each word. "Is she okay?"

"She's here. She's safe," Wynn replied. "I believe she's eating dinner with her friends. Would you like me to get her?"

I shook my head, finally meeting his eyes. "I'm sure she has many questions, but it hurts to speak," I said in a strained whisper.

Alarm shone in his eyes. "Let me find you a healer!"

I shook my head again. "No, I just need my element."

My fingers loosened as I realized I'd been holding tightly to Wynn's tunic even though the water buoyed my body. Letting go, I relaxed into its embrace, floating away from him.

"Ari," he said, his voice hesitant, "if there's anything I can do . . ."

"Can you change fate?" I whispered.

His silence was deafening. Even as I drifted away from him, I could sense his presence as he stood watch, the connection between us coaxing me to return.

Verus had not sacrificed himself merely for the fate of Esterra or for the safety of our daughter—he had sacrificed himself for me. He'd known the pain of losing a mate, and he'd discovered Wynn was mine.

CHAPTER 54

DRIFTING

ARIANWEN

I lost myself in the water. For hours, I drifted—long after campfires had fizzled out and the evening buzz had died down, replaced by the chirping of crickets and other midnight sounds. Stars twinkled above as the well of my power refilled itself oh so slowly.

A disturbance in the water startled me, and all I could think was that I wanted to be left alone in my grief. My anger had expended itself after the tidal wave, but now I felt lost in a pit of despair. The thought of having to explain what had happened to the little ones was overwhelming.

"Mama?" Aella's voice was muffled with my ears below the water.

Relief coursed through me as I splashed my way to standing in the chest-deep water.

She's safe. She's here.

My eyes flew from her to Wynn, who stood at another part of the shoreline, wondering if she'd figured out who he was.

"Wait there," Aella said, then began tearing off her shoes. "I'm coming!"

I shook my head, taking a moment to breathe. I didn't quite understand what was happening to me—I had never felt so completely lost and alone, even while standing in front of my daughter who meant everything to me.

Wading through the water, I pulled Aella into my arms, needing to feel her and know she truly was safe, even if just in this moment. "I'm so sorry . . . I've failed you in so many ways." I sobbed as tears fell anew.

Aella pulled back, resting her forehead against mine. "Do *not* blame yourself." Her voice neared breaking as we held each other. Aella's stiff, guarded posture softened just the slightest.

Even if she didn't blame me, I would carry that weight forever.

"You came for me." Aella took deep, trembling breaths, her body shaking with months of pent-up pain and suffering trying to break free.

"I couldn't leave you there." I sniffed.

"I never thought I'd see you again . . . and then after your first attempt . . . I—"

Waves of grief washed over me, even as the water tried to soothe us with its embrace. She would never be the same Aella we'd said goodbye to that day on the docks. She was safe now but not unharmed. It might take years for her to heal from what she'd been through. I only hoped she'd feel secure enough to share with me when she was ready.

"It's okay, Aella. I've got you."

We floated silently next to each other on the lake's gentle current, our hands entwined. There was so much I wanted to say, but I waited, giving her time, giving her a chance to take control. After so many months in Prisma, it was probably a foreign concept to her but a gift I needed to give back. The stars shone down upon us, and part of me wanted to shake my fist at them. It was impossible not to lay blame. They had stolen so much from me, my family, and my people—they did not deserve our worship.

My element moved around me as Aella straightened and stood in the waist-deep water and began slowly walking, sifting through and inspecting the lily pads in an idle but introspective manner. Getting the sense that she had something important to say, I let my feet sink to the sandy lakebed and joined her, trailing my fingers through the water's surface to create gentle ripples.

"Valerik told me about an oath," she said, finally breaking the silence. "All those times you shut me out . . ." Her brows bunched together as she drew her attention away from the floating botanicals. "I could never understand. I thought . . . I thought you didn't trust me. That I would forever be a child in your eyes."

She wrapped her arms around her middle and continued, "It hurts to know you had this whole other life before, like I don't even know you." Her eyes sought mine. "The world I grew up in is falling apart all around me. Everything I thought I knew has changed. I don't know what to believe anymore. I don't know who I am. You're not even the person I thought you were, and now to hear people say I had another father? That my father—" She took a sharp inhale. "Please tell me you have answers. Because right now, it's like the water has slipped out from beneath me and I'm falling to the ocean floor. I need the truth."

"My darling," I said with a sigh, "I've wanted to tell you. You have no idea how heavy a burden the oath was for all those years."

"Is it true then? I mean, it must be." She shook her head in disbelief. "It's just, all this time, I've pictured you as my mother and a healer, and nothing else." She looked down. "I'm sorry. I didn't mean to make that sound small. I simply mean that it's hard to believe you've been on adventures and had a whole other life before. I'm happy for it, that you've had a chance to live and experience all of those things, but I guess I feel saddened to know there's this other side of you that's been kept from us, lost to the past."

"I never wanted any of this to come between us, and I mourn the time we've lost . . . My past may have been hidden—and it may not feel this way now—but you *do* know me, and all of those things I couldn't tell you about your origins and my past, they don't change who I am at the core. I hope you will give me a chance to share them with you now that I finally can," I said, brushing a thick strand of wet hair behind her ear. "I'm free of that oath now, and I can finally answer all your questions. I would love to show you who I was—even the parts I'm not proud of—if you want me to. I want you to know all of me."

She nodded, her fingers finding their way to the back of her neck the way she'd always done. "I'd like that."

Aella was trying so hard to be strong. I wanted her to know she didn't have to be in this moment, but she wasn't asking that of me. She wanted answers, and I needed to earn her trust.

She looked over to the shore, where Wynn lounged with a mixed group of elemental fae, and it was clear what she wanted, no, needed to know most.

"Perhaps you've figured it out by now, but Wynn is your biological father."

"So, it's true." Aella blinked, then began wading and sifting through the water idly again. "I heard he was Adamas . . . and I guess a part of me hoped there was some other explanation, but after coming here, meeting them . . . learning you had a secret past . . . it was the only thing that made sense." She paused for a moment, then spun back around to face me, her head slightly tilted. "But you're telling me you went off and fell in love with not just any mythical Adamas male, but an Adamas king?" Her face paled. "Wait, what does that make me?"

"I didn't know he was royalty when I found him." I shrugged. "As far as titles go, I honestly don't know what his plan is. That's probably a question you'll have to ask him . . ."

"I—I can't ask him that," she stammered.

"Listen, I know this is a lot of new information, and I understand if you need some time to process." I paused, trying to gather my thoughts. "My relationship with Wynn is complicated. I resented him for so long for preventing me from sharing such important things with you, with your father."

"Why would he do that? How could he do that to you? To us?" Aella asked.

"Wynn didn't know about you when I left, and we didn't fully realize what consequences the oath would have. Please don't blame him. I willingly made that oath because I wanted to see his world. I wanted more than the life my parents had arranged for me."

"Was that the scandal I overheard Aunt Lani talking about?"

A soft laugh escaped me. "Ah, yes. The scandal of my disappearance was the talk of the Coral District. Your father and I had to put on quite a show in the early days—he didn't want anyone to doubt who you belonged to." I looked over at Aella, her eyes brimming with love and pain. "He claimed you from the moment he knew of your existence. You were always his daughter—you always will be."

Aella took a deep breath and looked back up at the stars, as though it was too painful to continue holding my gaze. "So he knew and didn't care."

"You captured his heart before you were even born, little whirlwind," I said softly.

A small smile curled her lips before a flash of pain crossed her face. She cleared her throat, changing the subject. "Why did you leave Zephyria?"

I shook my head. "Our love, mine and Wynn's, it was a complex thing, and there were too many forces against us. Perhaps we were too young, too impetuous, too bound by our ideas of duty. He made choices that hurt me, and instead of trying to work things out with him, I fled."

"Did you ever regret leaving?"

"There may have been times when things were hard, but if I had to do it all over again, I would have made the same choice a thousand times over. Was it perfect? No. But I would never choose to give up the life I had with your father."

Her shoulders seemed to drop a little, as though relieved. "It feels like a betrayal," she said, "to get to know *him*."

I nodded. "It makes sense you would feel that way, but I want you to know it's *your* choice, Aella. For all his faults, Wynn is a good and honorable male, and I know your Papa would not have wanted you to stay away from him for his sake—he made that very clear in his letter. Even as he rests with the stars, he knows you love him. Death will never change that."

Aella took a deep, shuddering breath and lay back in the water. Sensing she was done talking, I squeezed her hand and joined her. We still had a long way to go to restore trust between us, but I was thankful we would have the chance.

CHAPTER 55

FIRST FLIGHT

AELLA

I pushed through the doors leading out of my bedchamber to find an Adamas male—*the* Adamas male—walking down the hall. Flooded with instant regret that I'd even considered leaving my room, I spun around to go back inside. It had only been a week since I'd found out who he was. *I'm not ready for this.*

"Wait," came his voice from behind me.

I closed my eyes, taking a deep breath for *one, two, three.*

"Aella?" he said, his voice unsure.

Turning back around slowly, I took in the male standing before me, the king of the Court of Air, my biological father.

A pained smile cracked through his sorrowful expression.

There were so many questions I wanted to ask him, so many things I wanted to say, but I found myself frozen, speechless. We stared at each other for a long moment, looking for the familiarities between us. It was a good thing he hadn't pressured me into speaking before I'd been ready, because I'd have blurted out something terrible or accusatory. But in the silence, I could read that there really was nothing to blame him for, only questions to be asked and possibly a very long history to be revealed.

At last, I sighed, allowing my shoulders to settle just a bit lower, not having realized I'd been clenching them up to my ears when I'd first discovered him. I stood a little taller, willing composure in preparation to speak.

"I won't pretend not to know who you are, but . . . I hardly know anything about you." *And I'm not sure I want to.*

The male stepped forward before giving a subtle nod. "I'd like to remedy that if you'd let me. Wynn Sorensen." He held out a hand for me to shake, opening his mouth to say something else.

I flinched back at the gesture as though he'd pulled out a weapon, stopping him. My mother had said my father hadn't wanted me to avoid him. He'd wanted me to learn from him and thought he might help me find my true purpose. I couldn't imagine sitting down for a talk with him . . . but maybe I didn't have to.

"Can you teach me how to fly?" I blurted, the words practically flying out of my mouth. I didn't have to like him, but I could use the distraction.

The king, *my father*, laughed, dropping his hand, the awkward tension between us seeming to fade just a little. "It would be my pleasure," he replied.

I loosed a breath. "Really? I mean, you think it's possible? I'm not . . . too old to learn?"

He tilted his head as if to consider. "It might not be easy. But coming from someone who's had to learn things the hard way, I'd like to think it's never too late."

"Okay. Hold on tight," Wynn said as I interlaced my fingers behind his neck. "Do you trust me?"

I nodded a quick yes, though I wasn't sure if I could actually ever have been ready for this. My mouth was dry with nerves and excitement, and I could hardly feel my arms as the thrill of what was about to happen coursed through me. I'd had dreams of flying, but now that it was about to happen, I couldn't explain the sweating of my palms, the jumpiness, the way my muscles had gone numb and weak and ready to give out at a moment's notice. It was almost as if they didn't even belong to me anymore, so loose and wobbly, like they would've swum off without me if they could have.

"You've got this," he said in that smooth, amber voice of his.

I took one last deep breath to try to prepare myself, and we were off, shooting high up into the sky as though we'd caught a high-speed current. The earth fell away from us as we flew higher and higher. I wanted to laugh. I wanted to scream. It was incredible, even better than I'd imagined. Once we made it above the clouds, Wynn slowed down.

"We're still a little too close to Prisma for my comfort to risk flying at lower altitudes. It will also be safer for you in case you fall."

"Really? I'd imagine it would be the opposite." I curled a brow.

"Think of it this way—at this elevation, I'll have more time to catch you before you go splat."

"That's reassuring."

"Look, I wouldn't be doing this if I didn't think you had it in you. From what I heard you did in the arena, you have a lot more of my powers in you than you may realize."

"You mean my epic failure."

"I'm not going to argue whether that was a failure or a feat. My point is, you have a lot of potential, and I'm going to teach you how to use it."

"If I *am* your daughter, why don't I look like you?"

"Honestly, I'm not completely sure how it all works, but some elemental forms seem to show up more dominantly than others."

"How is it even possible? I thought only Iris could . . ." I trailed off, realizing I probably needed to scrap everything I'd learned about the world, since most of it was controlled or had been rewritten by the Iris.

"In Zephyria, we don't have laws that keep elemental fae separate. Don't you think it's strange that you were around other elementals in the capital and no stars fell from the sky?"

"It's because . . . I thought . . ." All of my logic was Iris propaganda. I gave up. "The lies they told us are so ingrained, I can't trust anything I know about how the world works anymore."

Wynn chuckled. "This reminds me of the first time I met your mother. She struggled with many of the same feelings." He smiled as if thinking back to their first encounters. "You're half Adamas, so I have no doubt you'll be able to fly. Even if you don't have my fair complexion, you have it in you," Wynn said. "Now, close your eyes and tell me, how does it feel to be up here—to feel the wind carrying us, tempting us to drift away on it? How does it feel to be surrounded by so much of your air element, far from the sea, just the vastness of wind and sky around you? Can you feel it?"

It was so different from the enveloping pressure of water, in fact, almost the reverse, which was terrifying. I couldn't see it, couldn't feel it unless there was movement in the air, so elusive and unguaranteed. If it didn't like me, it could just let me plummet to the earth. The idea had me tightening my grip around his neck.

"I'm not going to let you fall," Wynn reassured me. "Now, why don't we try a gentle glide? It won't take much source, but it should help you get comfortable with the idea of flying. I'll hold your hand, and if for any reason you start to slip, I'm right here."

A layer of air formed a fluffy sort of cushion beneath my feet, and I was able to take a step back. I forced myself to loosen my grip on his neck, reaching for his hands instead, one hand at a time. A giggle erupted from my chest as I took in our surroundings, it was as though we were standing right on top of the clouds.

"Now this is—" I began, then looked back up at Wynn, who watched me with a smile filled with so much emotion, I couldn't even begin to unpack it.

Afraid to be caught staring, I looked away. I didn't know if I could ever get used to the idea that I was related to him. As much as I didn't want to admit it, there were similarities between us. In the shape of our noses, or was it the cheekbones, or the eyebrows? I'd always thought I looked like my father. Perhaps I'd earned his smile and his demeanor. I pushed those thoughts away as they began choking me with a sadness I didn't want to feel.

"Okay, so what next?" I forced myself to say.

"All right. You're going to need to let go of one hand so we can glide side by side."

I closed my eyes, trying to trick myself into thinking I wasn't standing high up in the clouds, before letting go of his hand, and before my eyes could open again, we were tearing down through the cool mist of clouds, layer after layer. I screamed, and then it all stopped and we began climbing up up up, back through the clouds.

"Open your eyes, sunshine."

"I thought you said we were going to glide? That felt like free-falling!"

"Because we *were* free-falling. Look, try holding your other arm out and starfishing your legs a little, like this." He showed me with his own limbs. "And keep your eyes open this time. You ready?"

"Not really*yyyahhhhh*!" The puff of air beneath my feet disappeared again, and our bodies angled down, heads first toward the ground. Remembering what he had said, I threw my arms and legs out, imagining I was a bird or a sail catching the wind. And just like that, we were gliding. Stars, it was miraculous. Wind still whipped at my hair and clothes, but I could feel the protective lift of the air beneath me as it slowed and guided our fall.

"You doing all right?" he asked.

I nodded, a huge smile spreading across my face. And we continued on like that, gaining height and then gliding down together, hand in hand in a slow and controlled manner until I was confident enough to let go and do it on my own.

"Remember, if you start to feel like you're falling, just let me know. But you're doing great!"

"Really?"

"I mean, considering you've never flown before and this is your first day, I'm impressed."

That's right, I'm a grown adult and I've never done this before, so I should feel proud of myself. I'm a freaking badass. Letting the confidence go to my head, I let go.

Viera and the girls were waiting for me down at the lake. Big smiles greeted me, and I ran to them, even after I'd bounced on my arse on the landing, nearly eating it as I came in with a little too much speed.

"I'm getting better!" I exclaimed.

"You sure are!" Viera laughed while hugging me to her chest.

"It's so different." I shook my head. "But he says I'm doing really well, considering it's only been a week of flying lessons."

"You still look like a fledgling leaving the nest for the first time," Jara teased. "With your arms and legs out at awkward angles." She did a little mock impression to show me how I looked, and I laughed at the ridiculousness of it. "Not bad though, for a new trick."

"I'm just glad I don't have to worry about trying to impress you." I waved her off. My spirits were so high after flying, nothing could bring me down except . . . No. I refused to think about what I'd lost. "As long as you're not too embarrassed to be seen with me."

Jara linked an arm with mine as we walked back toward the main camp. "And risk losing my connection to ancient fae royalty? I think I can deal with a little humiliation." She winked.

That title still felt wrong, like it didn't belong to me. I'd always be a Kalani, no matter what they wanted to call me.

"I almost forgot how jarring Aurum fae decorum is." Viera sighed. "I honestly can't tell if you're joking or serious half the time, and I don't know if I should hit you for talking to my friend like that."

"Oh, if I didn't like you, you would know," Jara said.

"And how's that exactly?" asked Viera.

"I wouldn't even bother speaking with you. You see, for an Aurum to make fun shows we've been thinking about you, watching you. It's actually the highest form of a compliment. Far from the indulgent platitudes the Iris are so fond of."

Viera gave her a long, appraising look, and I could tell she still wasn't sure she bought anything Jara said.

"Right, princess?" Jara said, and I winced at the title.

"Hey, I'm feeling a bit wiped after flying. I'll see you all later . . . At dinner, maybe?" I waved them off and walked briskly in the direction of the old castle ruin.

"A, wait," Viera called as she hurried behind me.

I didn't slow my pace, even knowing she was there. I couldn't bear to face her with the weight of guilt and shame upon me. All of the time I'd spent training my air element with Wynn this week, the fact I was staying in the old castle among the leaders of the rebellion, and now being referred to as a princess—it was as though my father had disappeared and meant nothing. As if I had replaced him with another. I swallowed it down. He had wanted me to learn from him. It was a part of his last wishes.

"What's going on?"

"Nothing. I'm just tired," I said, but my voice cracked, giving me away. Deep breaths, I needed deep breaths. But I found myself struggling, hyperventilation taking over.

Viera caught up and wrapped an arm around my side, keeping with my pace, and soon, her breathing modeled the slow, deep breaths my parents had taught me, and I breathed along with her.

CHAPTER 56

FABER LUDI

KALEIDOS

My stomach turned at the sight and sickly scent of elemental blood and source power that coated the ballroom floor—it seemed to follow me wherever I dared walk throughout the Palatium Crystalis since Aella had left. The violent bloodshed was no longer limited to the games. No elemental fae was safe.

With the arena's restoration delayed by the flooding several weeks ago, the ballroom had become a temporary stage for the more exclusive nightly games. At first, they were nothing more than crude, fight-to-the-death matches held between three elemental fae sourced from wherever my people deemed fit. The blood-hungry attendees were given permission, encouraged even, to step in and *remind* the elementals how powerless they were. Motivated by the false prize of freedom in exchange for their brutality, the victors were crowned in wreaths made of foxglove, only to be handed over to the highest bidder at the end of the night.

I could hardly stand to watch, let alone be a part of it, but duty required I partake in the sport, or at the very minimum, show my support by attending at least one game a week. Though I'd have rather eaten glass, I saw no escape. I had a role to play, particularly as I was already treading on thin ice with my father. He hadn't missed the disgust in my eyes when I'd witnessed the depths of depravity he'd been willing to stoop to during the tidal wave.

My only reprieve was that he'd let go of the notion that I must be immediately married off to another Iris noble. Considering the extensive destruction of Prisma, rebuilding was a priority.

"Let me preface this by saying the role of the Faber Ludi could not have gone to a more deserving servant of the king," Nephos announced, dressed in a moody ensemble of aubergine feathers. His near black attire was a striking contrast to his usual showy display of colors, and his eyes seemed to flick nervously to mine every so often as he continued his speech. "As of this day, he has dedicated his life in service to the most noble of causes, Iris entertainment. Without further adieu, twelfth in line to the throne, son of Eranis . . . Gaelor Manus, our new Faber Ludi!"

Gaelor strode out in heavy robes onto the balcony that overlooked the ballroom, head shaven, skin gleaming in the newfound attention and power.

I rolled my eyes at the idea of my cousin holding such a title, tossing back my wine before making my way toward the exit.

Gaelor had the audacity to turn and hurry over to me, blocking my way, a look of defiance in his eyes as he greeted me.

"The dress suits you," I said with a pointed, lingering stare where the nubs of his hands remained hidden beneath heavy sleeves.

"I take it you've been enjoying the games?" Gaelor asked, ignoring my remark, though I could see the twinge in his eyes with his false smile.

"I enjoy violence as much as any Iris. But I'm sure you've got that well in *hand*." I made a show of cracking my knuckles while laughing in his face.

Gaelor bristled, then raised his chin as he attempted to rectify his state. "In that case, I think you'll enjoy this evening's entertainment especially." He snickered triumphantly before turning and sneaking off into the crowd of Iris behind me.

My eyes followed him as he tried to put as much distance between us as he could, but the whispers and erupting laughter soon drew my attention back to the ballroom floor below. Courtiers parted as I stalked to the balcony's edge. Every muscle in my body roared as I suppressed the disaster my powers drove me to inflict at the sight. On the ballroom floor below was an Argenti female clad in an iron gown with a transparent veil atop her head.

They had dressed the contestant in Aella's clothes. Though I'd been trying to feign indifference, the fury that rose within me must have been palpable, because the courtiers around me shrank even farther away. It took only seconds before I reached Gaelor, my hand wrapped around his throat and his feet dangling off the ground. Rather than fear in his eyes, he had a crazed, humor-filled expression.

"You can't kill me," he wheezed.

"Care to wager?" I growled. Screams pierced the silence as the ballroom floor fractured at the center, sending a web of fine-seamed cracks radiating out, ready to split the ground open at a moment's notice. I'd kill everyone in this room to prove my point.

"I wouldn't do that if I were you," said Solanos from behind, his voice unworried but stern. His very existence served as a cold reminder of my mistake. Of why such a rash outburst had been foolish.

Iron-tipped spears pointed at me from all angles, only inches from my skin. I dropped Gaelor to the ground and turned to face the king.

"I've chosen him myself, and I like his ideas. Any harm done to him will be considered treason, as it has been for all Faber Ludi before him."

"You would allow him to make a mockery of me?"

"Certainly you don't still associate yourself with that pathetic slave? Look around at the Iris in attendance tonight, each one a victim of her attack. The least you can do is allow them this entertainment."

"You will not make me watch," I said through gritted teeth. I pleaded with my eyes.

"Oh, I will, and if you do not, I will make sure we have a 'Silver Bride' in every event from this day forward."

The nights were long, as I could not sleep. I couldn't dream without seeing her in the event. Though it hadn't been Aella in those clothes, the images of her violent deaths worked themselves deeper and deeper into my subconscious.

And my dreams weren't only of the death matches. The courtiers had become bored with simple violence, and the monsters had been brought back in. A shadow fang, starved and isolated in a cell, had been released into the ballroom to hunt the defenseless contestants as spectators cheered at their demise from balconies above.

So I stayed up with the moon, not resting until it was bright out, until sleep took me without permission. Exhaustion wrestled me into the terrors of what I'd seen, now blending into the nightmares I'd had since childhood, Aella's and my mother's faces merged into one.

And then there were the bodies. The mass grave of elemental fae sacrificed in my name. It grew every night as more innocent lives were added to the weight on my conscience.

The last I'd seen of my Aella was her falling from the cliff into the waning sea below. I couldn't explain why I hadn't gone with her, why I'd stayed behind. It hadn't been logic or fear; it had been as though some invisible force had tethered me, leaving no other choice. Perhaps it had been some primal instinct, self-preservation, or perhaps the stars themselves had willed it. Whatever the reason, I'd fought it, strained against it, but eventually, I'd given in.

Tidal wave incoming, I had seconds to flee before the wave thundered down upon us. Nowhere to hide. I ran after the king and his guards, my feet hardly touching the ground as I sprinted, shifting sand and earth to hasten my escape.

I stumbled, nearly falling on my face the moment I witnessed my father harness the source of every elemental guard around him. One hundred elementals bowed, forming a circle around him, their bodies going slack as one hundred beams of light raced toward him. Our eyes connected, but it was too late. The towering wall of water struck the side of the cliff with a thunderous crash that shook the earth.

"More! More!" Solanos screamed, his voice strained with the effort of whatever illusion he was spinning to manipulate the guards. In the seconds before the wave swept over us, another hundred guards bowed in a circle around him, offering up their source at his command. The wave spat salt and spray at my back as it came racing toward us.

I leapt through the air, tumbling upon landing near the king just as Solanos put up a shield of protection curving up and over me, sealing me in with him and some of the two hundred guards who now lay wasting at our feet. Turbulent waters, torn up trees, stone, massive boulders, pieces of wrecked ships, sand and silt, and all manner of sea beast pelted against the shield, but it held firm.

"Now you know," Solanos said.

So this was the secret to his power. This gift I'd once unknowingly used on Aella. What had been a beautiful moment between us, my father used with such greed.

"They are dying. Give it back to them!" I shouted.

"They would die anyway. This way, we live."

I tried to stand but doubled over, retching. "This is wrong," I said.

"This is what true power looks like, Kaleidos. It's so much sweeter when they are nameless . . . as I'm sure you know. They give it up so freely. Not like this mess. If they'd been nameless, I wouldn't have needed so many of them." He picked at his nails, filed long like that of an animal as he held the forcefield without strain. "It matters not—they would have died in the wave regardless. A wave one of their kind inflicted upon us, no less."

A wave that was meant to kill him, that would have killed him if not for this terrible power.

As though reading my thoughts, the king stepped down from his pedestal and strolled toward me. He lifted my face in his hand so we could see eye to eye.

"It is who you are. There's no sense in denying it."

Though the damage to Prisma and number of lives lost had been immeasurable, the king had declared it was time to move forward with his revenge. Beyond the new nightly games, he'd become suspicious and paranoid and had taken arms and armor from every elemental soldier, making them nameless too. Across the continent, elementals were being stripped of their ranks, removed from their homes, and brought to the capital as slaves.

Too many elementals were being shipped in to rebuild and restore the city, and no provisions had been made for the influx of people. All attempts I'd made at pitching Aella's ideas had been tossed aside. The king could not be reasoned with. The elementals could eat dirt and sleep in the rubble for all he cared.

Along with the guards, he'd begun making every elemental in Prisma nameless, no longer just the disobedient or troublemakers. So much so, he'd forgone hiding the key in the bodies of his servants. He'd had a special glove and secret hiding places made for him that allowed him to use the key frequently and safely. But also so he could bring it out to wave it around and threaten whoever dared question him.

Madness. My father, the king, had descended into utter madness. I could not stop him. I could not stop any of it.

What would she have me do if she were still here? I endeavored to imagine the world she dreamed of, the kind of ruler she'd have me be. I'd poured over books for answers, for stories of kings before and how they'd been surpassed, how I might stand a chance at removing Solanos from his throne.

Despite my best attempts at filling the role my father expected of me, courtiers had continued their snickering and sneering, making outward their disfavor. I wasn't convincing anyone. Already, I could feel them plotting against me. Even if I found a way to defeat Solanos, I had no guarantee they wouldn't dethrone me. The literature was clear. Without a following—without respect, admiration, or fear—no Iris king was safe. I'd need to remove all of his supporters and anyone who opposed me as well. But then who would be left to support my vision for a fairer world?

A knock sounded at the door. I looked to find Nephos poking his head into my study.

"Oh, good. I'm so glad to catch you awake." He strolled into the room.

I stared at him blankly.

"I have a message for you," he said, placing a rolled-up piece of parchment on my desk.

"What is this?" I raised a brow.

"It's a peace offering."

"Excuse me?"

"I know what you've been searching for . . . in the records. I'm not sure how much good it will do you, but I can understand your need to know."

I glanced down at it warily before looking back up at him. I'd gone down too many disappointing paths in my search to trust this would be any different.

"Th-there is talk," Nephos stuttered. "What your father demands . . . it's too much. He's gone too far."

"I'm not sure why you're coming to me for this," I said dismissively.

"I'm not asking for myself, I mean, it's not only about the games." So unlike his usual boisterous self, Nephos, who could speak before thousands without a shred of fear, was utterly nerve-stricken in my presence as he bared his intentions before me. "There is unrest in the city. With so many elementals coming in to help rebuild, a rebellion is forming right beneath the king's nose, yet he is too proud to recognize it. And there are others like me, other Iris who are tired of violence and bloodshed. We want to help, but we need *your* help."

"You need *my* help?" I nearly laughed. "You do realize if the elementals come for Solanos, they will come for us all."

"Yes, but we thought that perhaps with your assistance, we might fight alongside them. We are not all wicked." He stood taller.

"Your name is practically synonymous with the games, Nephos."

"I understand. I just—never mind." He seemed to shrink, his shoulders curling in.

"Wait." I stopped him. "Of all people, you, with your fame and title, with so much to lose . . . why would you risk it all, coming to me?"

"We all do what we must to survive. Not everyone is brave enough to stand up against the mob. Some of us do small things, the only things we feel we can do."

"You're telling me you've been against it for all these years?"

"Not from the beginning, no," he said regretfully. "But sometimes it takes a personal blow to open your eyes. For some of us at least, we don't learn things the simple way. We have to take it like a knife to the chest, have our hearts sliced open before we even know we had one."

"And what was yours?"

"He was my Danny." He teared up. "A faithful elemental guard in the Palatium Crystalis for over thirty years. He should have been safe." He took a shuddering breath and continued, "I have not come here seeking your pity." He turned to leave.

"We should have done something long ago," I said, and he stopped, turning back to face me. "Though, if the stars are real, I already know there's no redemption for us."

"I wouldn't blame the stars," he said. "I thought of the elementals as little more than animals once, it's true. But they *are* better than us, aren't they? With their ability to love, their ability to live, and I mean truly live. Because even in their short, seemingly meaningless lives, they manage to fill them with so much more than we could even if we spent a thousand years trying. Isn't *that* worth risking everything for?"

Nephos had left me with so much to consider, I'd almost forgot about the scroll he'd given me. I cradled it in my hands, afraid to crush it but also too afraid to believe. I'd had too many disappointments, too many false hopes until now. Perhaps he was right, that it would do nothing for me, the knowledge of who my mother had been, her name before it had been taken. And there was little if anything I could do to verify this was reliable information.

I stared and stared at the scroll, unable to bring myself to open it. Was it just another dead end, or was it truly what I'd sought after all this time?

I opened a drawer of my bureau in haste, tossing the scroll inside before curiosity could drive me any further.

But before I could slam the drawer shut, Viera's note caught my eye. Blood-stained and torn, haphazardly left inside where anyone might have found it if they'd cared to look. I picked it up delicately, reading the message again.

> *A storm comes to defeat the Iris.*
> *Our marked one, daughter of wind and sea.*
> *The prophecy comes to fruition.*
> *The end of the Stellaris line is near.*
> *Ready yourselves. The stars are with us.*

Viera had been carrying this, communicating with the rebels from within this very palatium. My eyes widened, and I began pacing around the room. This entire time, I'd been so blind. I'd been doing everything wrong. Perhaps I didn't need to put my efforts into defeating the king but rather on raising an army from within Prisma, from within the Palatium Crystalis itself.

No time to waste, I headed straight for my closet, stripping off the jeweled ornaments that lined my fingers and dropping them hastily onto the ground.

My people were more powerful than elemental fae, more trained and equipped for battle. But we'd had a rapid growth of nameless, far too many to really pay close attention to, and more disgruntled Iris, if Nephos had spoken true. Aella had made great strides to educate the nameless, who might now be able to pass that information on to newcomers.

What the king didn't realize was that his own actions were brewing the perfect storm. He was leading the rebellion right to us, and he'd end up crumbling his very own kingdom all by his damned self.

I dressed in the plainest garments I could find, finishing off the look with a glamour and a deep-hooded cloak for extra measure. I couldn't give my people reason to doubt I was on their side or suspect what I might be doing, so I'd become someone else in the shadows. Before heading to the servants' passage, I grabbed my mother's book.

Rat squeaked behind me.

"Are you sure you want in on this?" I said, trying to hide my Iris accent.

Rat scurried ahead, and we were off, swiftly making our way down the restored passageway my Aella had been meant to flee from.

As prophesied one, Aella had a very important role to play in all of this, and though I'd told her not to hold back, I couldn't give her any reason to doubt what she needed to do. If Aella was to rally her people against me, I needed to become her villain.

This is who she needs me to be.

I was the prince of Esterra. Countless had died in my name. I was the perfect target for her hatred. I would spread the word myself. Let it get back to her through the rebellion. Let her hear of my wickedness. Let her unleash her fury upon me.

This is my destiny.

CHAPTER 57

TRAINING

ARIANWEN

Thwack! The spear flew through the air, embedding itself in the target. While it had missed the center, her attempts had been getting better with each pass.

"Nicely done, Aella!" Rik shouted.

"Stars, that's harder than it looks," Aella lamented as she pulled her arm across her chest in a stretch.

In the blink of an eye, Rik threw two spears back to back, the first one hitting the bullseye dead on and the second splitting the first spear in half.

"Show off." I laughed, almost surprised at the sound as it left me. Stars, my emotions were all over the place. Rik turned to wink at me before he went to assist Aella, reviewing the different air techniques she could use to guide the spear where she wanted it to go.

"She's working really hard," Wynn said, joining me where I stood watch.

I turned and acknowledged him with a slight nod. We'd cleared a training ground within the nearby forest to prepare for the battle to come. Elementals from other courts were showing up daily, and I worried our army would grow too large to conceal. Though, fortunate for us, from the reports coming in, it seemed Solanos' attentions were focused elsewhere.

It had been a month since we'd rescued Aella from the Iris, one month without Verus. A deep-seated ache surfaced whenever I thought about his sacrifice, and while the tears might be fewer, the grief was still fresh. He might not have been my mate, but our love had etched itself into my heart.

After Aella's rescue, Wynn had met with the other rebellion leaders, and they'd finally agreed it was time to move on the Iris.

"We did it, Ari!" His eyes shone with hope. "The courts are finally coming together. Thank you."

I remembered standing there, feeling the weight of his gratitude, when all I'd wanted to do was hide in my room and cry over my loss. If it hadn't been for Verus, Aella would have still been in Prisma. None of this would have been possible. Was he watching from the stars? He would have been so proud of her and how hard she was working.

A cool breeze tickled the back of my neck, a reminder of the changing seasons. I glanced over at Wynn. His eyes were closed and his head tilted back, a slight smile curving his lips as he enjoyed the gentle kiss of his element. Was it whispering secrets to him? His fighting leathers clung to him like a second skin, and I imagined he was grateful for the cooler weather—Concordia's humidity was surely a vast change from the eternal winter of Zephyria. His skin had a rosier hue, and small beads of sweat gathered on his neck. He must have been training in the ring. Another gust of wind swept by, and the fine lines around his eyes softened, his shoulders seeming to relax just a little. I couldn't even fathom the amount of pressure he was facing putting this army together.

One might have thought the silence between us would have been uncomfortable, but it seemed to be exactly what I needed. I was tired of the overused platitudes and condolences. No matter how well-intentioned, they did nothing to soothe the pain of loss. Wynn's calm, quiet presence made me feel less alone.

We still had not discussed the bond between us, and I was grateful

Wynn was giving me the space I needed to grieve and come to terms with my new reality. While he had never said the words to me, I knew he had to know. I felt foolish for not having recognized it sooner. Perhaps I'd been blinded by the blood oath and thought that was what had pulled us together, or perhaps I'd just never considered that a mate bond was possible between two courts. When I recalled the conversation I'd had with Verus about mate bonds now, it all made sense.

Deep in my heart, I knew he would want me to be happy and that he would not want me to separate myself from my mate—his letter had confirmed that—but I also couldn't help but carry the guilt that he'd sacrificed himself not just for the greater good, not just for Aella, but because of me.

As I grieved for him, all I could do was wish him that final happiness—to be reunited with his mate, Lyani.

"Yes!" Aella's excited cry broke me from my thoughts. She flew down to inspect the target with the perfect bullseye and yanked out her spear. "All right. I'm calling it a day."

"That's amazing, Aella! I'm so proud of you!" I said, my cheeks hurting from my wide smile. Seeing her come alive with training and discovering what she was capable of had been the most healing of balms for my broken soul.

"Great job," Wynn said. Aella gave him a reserved smile and a slight nod. She hadn't fully warmed up to him, though she appeared to be trying.

"Uh-uh-uh, not so fast." Rik tutted. "Now you need to learn how to do it without looking." He pulled Aella's attention back to him.

"Or you could just let me have this win." She squinted her eyes at him before begrudgingly flying off to another target.

Wynn let out a chuckle, and I couldn't help but join in. "Rik is tough to please. But she really is doing well," he said.

"I'm so glad she's connecting with the other half of herself . . . She'll be a force to be reckoned with."

"I wager she already is," he replied.

"Better watch out with wagers," I teased.

"I don't know—I think I have a pretty decent record."

I jabbed him with my elbow, and he laughed before we fell back into a comfortable silence.

CHAPTER 58

RISE

"It's hard to believe this is just a lake," Lewenne said. "It feels like an ocean compared to Lakehaven's."

"I could spend years exploring its depths . . . Stars, it's incredible." Viera sighed.

"Nothing like an early morning swim for a good stretch." I groaned with the painful but also sort of pleasant sensation, my muscles pulling taut and releasing all the tension built up in them from the day before. Time had flown by as we'd spent every waking moment training and preparing for war. It was hard to imagine we'd be flying into battle in a month's time.

I whipped my hair back, allowing the spray of water to fly through the air with it, and willed the water away as we made our way to the lake's shore. It had taken a while for me to be comfortable doing that again, getting used to the idea that nothing was withheld from me, that I didn't have to hoard or cling to the tiny drops of water like they might be taken. In a way, we'd all been starved of our element in Prisma with no natural source to swim in. At least I'd had the little canals in the gardens, but Lewenne and Viera hadn't even had that when they'd been confined to the houses they'd served.

"Wanna train with us today?" I asked Viera.

"Nah, I'd rather check in with Liisa and your mom in the apothecary. I'm still sore from sparring last week."

"Whatever you do, don't let her convince you to use that potion . . . unless you want to reek like the back of a fishmonger's stall."

"Don't knock it till you try it," Liisa said from behind, and I cringed before turning to wave at my mom's friend.

Viera hugged us goodbye, and we were off to the sparring ring.

Already working up a sweat, Ona deflected an oncoming attack from Terran, rising up on a pillar of earth high above. She came slamming back down and knocked him right off his feet in a blurred combat sequence Helio must have taught her.

"And I thought her moves in Prisma were impressive," I mused.

"Wait till you see what we can do when we combine our elements now," Lewenne said.

Just as Ona was taking a prideful bow, Terran manipulated the earth below her, making her disappear in a poof of dirt only to reappear a few yards away. He gave a little mock bow, and Helio turned his belly laugh into a cough the moment he caught Ona's glare.

I muffled my own laughter, skirting away before they caught me watching.

Rik and Wynn were further down, in a private discussion by the looks of it. They always looked so serious.

"Hey, Rik, any chance you'll let me train with the other elementals today?" I already knew what his answer would be.

"I've only got about a month left to teach what you could learn in a lifetime."

"Was worth a shot." Lewenne shrugged. "See you at lunch?"

I nodded, and she jogged to one of the mixed elemental rings, where she'd get to practice combination moves.

"So what is it today, fight or flight?" I asked Rik.

"I was just telling Rik we'll be flying out to the aeries today," Wynn interjected. "It's about time you bonded with an aquila of your own."

I stared blankly at him.

"This is the part where you thank me for letting you take time off from training today," Rik said, and I ignored him, all of my focus on what Wynn had just said.

"You think I'm ready for that?" I asked, my eyes darting between the two of them as I searched for confirmation.

"No!" Rik exclaimed, shaking his head. "But, bury me alive, this is war . . ."

"Sink or swim, huh?" I raised my brows.

"Fly or go splat." Rik winked.

"I think she's ready." Wynn narrowed his eyes at Rik, who raised his hands in mock surrender and backed away from us.

"His confidence in me is astounding," I commented, my words laced with dry amusement.

"Look, you've been Adamas your whole life," Wynn said. "And though most of your energy has been focused on suppressing your powers, you have accomplished extraordinary feats. You've done things most Adamas can't do, even in their prime years. But don't let that go to your head." He tapped my temple with his forefinger. "If you're going to be the figurehead to lead us into battle, we still have some work to do. I believe in you. All right?"

I nodded.

"It's remarkable, really, how your parents managed to keep your identity safe in Iveria with raw powers like yours." He huffed in bemused astonishment.

"They were really there for me," I said.

Wynn's demeanor shifted slightly. He looked away for a moment, then said, "They really did an amazing job. I can see where you get your strength and resilience—your bravery."

"Thank you," I said, "for not trying to replace him."

"I would never . . . Your father . . . he was someone I really grew to respect and admire. I'm so glad you and your mother had him in your lives."

I swallowed against the aching lump in my throat. "So, how exactly does the bonding process work?"

"Remember what I said and don't give up too easily. It's usually right when you think you're done for that they make their choice," Wynn said.

"And if they decide against me?"

"You've been practicing crash landings with Rik, right?"

"Yeah, sure. Plenty." My nerves filled me with a sense of infiniteness and terror that could have fueled me to the stars and back. We'd only ever practiced over water, and I still cringed at the memory of my many failed attempts to halt my dives with a blast of wind. I couldn't be great at everything, but to be fair, I was still partially convinced my two elements warred against each other on that one, making it harder than if I were to do it over land. That's what I kept telling myself anyway.

Breathe in, one, two, three . . .

"Hey." Wynn cut through the chaos of my mind. "I know you can do it, but you need to believe it too."

"The sky is at my command."

"That's the mindset." He patted me on the back awkwardly, and I gave him a weak smile. "You ready?"

No.

"Yes."

Wynn went into the mountainside aerie while I flew in slow circles higher up, awaiting the rush of birds that would soon fly out. I was nervous and excited and afraid . . . So, so many feelings. *He wouldn't have me doing this if I wasn't ready for it yet, would he?* Before I could work myself into another spiral of fear, there was a piercing shriek, and a dozen aquilas tore out of the cave and flew straight in my direction.

One.

Two.

Three.

All twelve of them shot past me while I hovered there, wide-eyed like a stunned minnow.

Faex.

My delayed reaction would cost me. I chased after them for all of a minute before I realized how useless that would be. It didn't matter how high I could fly, there was no way I could've matched the speed of our winged friends. Out of self-doubt or desperation, I searched for Wynn for guidance, but just as he'd told me, he wouldn't hover around and risk the aquilas losing their respect for me, or something along those lines.

No matter. I wasn't about to give up just because I'd missed my chance to leap onto one while they'd exited the cave. I needed to let them come to me or put myself in their path somehow. The clouds thickened, darkening, and it was getting harder to scout where the birds had flown off to. Would they come back? Had I already lost my chance?

Thunder crackled in the distant weather wall the Adamas had put up to discourage the Iris from patrolling the barren lands between Prisma and Concordia, and an idea sparked. It was either terrible or genius, but I was going with it because it was all I had.

I waited by the mouth of the aerie while focusing on the sky and clouds above. Rain began to pelt down, but still the clouds thickened as I called in more. The aquilas still didn't return, so I whipped up the winds. Maybe that would bring them back? I waited and waited until finally I called upon the storm, summoning a flash of lightning. I'd gotten pretty good with that, and I smirked with pride at how second nature it had become.

An aquila's cry answered and then another. It was working.

Okay, this is my chance.

Aquilas broke through the dark cloud cover and flew for the aerie in a neat row. One after another, they darted into the cave, faster than I could reach for them. I counted—that was eleven. One was still out there. I looked back up, and blending in and out of the rumbling clouds, a brave aquila faced the storm, weathering it alone as he made a circle around a mountain peak. That had to be my bird.

"You're not going to make this easy, are you?" I flew up to his level. The bird gave me an assessing gaze as he continued to circle the mountain. I tried to fly into his path, but just as I thought I was about to catch him, he took a dive.

This is it.

I dove after him, my body streamlined to hasten my fall. I was gaining on the aquila, but the earth was rushing closer by the second, and I didn't know if I'd catch up in time. Tempted by the urge to use wind to speed up my fall, I resisted briefly, remembering Wynn's caution against it. Better to not risk killing myself and the bird in the process of bonding. But hadn't he also said it might come down to that?

Come on, come on, come on.

We were nearly the same level but losing altitude rapidly, only seconds to change course. I would not give up. I reached for his feathers, but at the speed we were diving, I could barely control my arms. *The sky is mine.*

"You are at my command!" I screamed as I used the wind to launch myself at the bird.

Three hundred.

Two hundred.

One hundred.

The aquila blinked, and then I was on his back and we were gliding just feet from the earth. Showing me how close we'd just come, the aquila let out an irritated shriek. I screamed with joy and fell into laughter as he flapped his wings, taking us higher.

"You stubborn, stubborn bird!"

"He's probably thinking the same thing about you!" Wynn projected across the distance as he flew toward us on Luminara.

"I thought you weren't supposed to watch?"

"And risk letting you get yourself killed?" He waved me off. "I didn't want to be a distraction."

"And what would you call what just happened?"

"I've been around aquilas enough to know he wasn't going to let you fall."

"Uh-huh." I was still dazed by the rush of adrenaline.

We climbed up over the clouds, where the sky was blue and the sun was shining, which felt good on my skin after being cold and drenched below. "That was . . . incredible."

"Nothing compares," he said. "Smart thinking, using the storm to get them to come back so quickly. Some Adamas are gone for weeks trying to bond with an aquila. I wasn't going to tell you this or your mother would have had my head, but there's a stigma around those who come back without bonding. They say your chances are cut in half each time you fail."

"And you're telling me this because?"

"I'm just glad you bonded one quickly, or we'd be stuck out here until you did." He laughed, presumably at my horrified expression. "So what are you going to name him?"

I studied the white bird for a moment. His feathers shone so brightly, they were blinding in the sunlight. His wings faded from white to silver to a sliver of black at the outermost tips. Sharp like blades.

"He's strong-willed—fearless in the storm. I think I'll call him Ferathor."

"And why is her presence necessary in this meeting?" Lucris pointed at Viera, who sat next to me in the meeting room.

"Because we need to discuss the prophecy," Wynn said, gritting his teeth.

Lucris laughed, clapping his hands. "Oh, this is too good. You think she can help convince '*the chosen one*?'"

"Viera and I know more about the king and the way he operates than anyone in this room, so you may want to take the wax out of your ears and listen for once," I snapped.

Lucris was affronted, but he shut his mouth as I shared all I'd learned from Kaleidos when we'd been planning Solanos' demise. This meeting had been long in coming, and with our impending attack on Prisma, Viera and I had been preparing for this for months.

Reports had come in about the madness that had befallen the king in Prisma. There was nothing good to say of Kaleidos and little proof of his efforts to help us. The general consensus was that he was an active participant in the killing and corruption happening in the Palatium Crystalis. The Iris were chanting his name in the streets, singing songs of their prince's wickedness, glorifying his role in the horrific changes that had taken place. Nothing I said could prove otherwise, and I'd begun doubting myself, my memories, my feelings for him. He was good. I knew him, didn't I?

"After everything he did to help me escape Prisma, I'm finding it hard to believe he's as wicked as the reports are saying," I pleaded with the council, even as it felt like my stomach was filled with rocks. "Knowing him, he must be doing it for show."

"Aella, these reports . . ." My mother squeezed her eyes shut as if she were just as sorry to say it. "We owe him our gratitude for helping us escape that day, but the new prophecy . . ."

I whipped my head toward Viera, catching her guilt-stricken look. "You told them?"

Biting her lip, she nodded. "I wish I was wrong, but it's fairly clear that only one of you can survive—*yours or hers, the choice is made*—and I will always pick you, A."

"And you all agree?" Too betrayed by her admission, I asked the others in the room.

"The Iris are a plague upon our lands," Viera continued. "What other choice is there?"

Rik and Helio avoided my gaze while Wynn shook his head slightly, as if he couldn't undo what had already been done. A malicious glee spread across Lucris' face, making me want to slap the expression right off. The Aurum leader, Ember, bored her green-gold eyes into me, testing me, waiting for me to explode. My mother had warned me that the Aurum were the most hesitant to help our cause. The Aereus leaders had nodded in agreement at Viera's statement.

Not even my best friend was on my side.

I was alone.

Wynn cleared his throat. "I know this isn't what you wanted to hear, but we need to trust the stars' commands. If we have any hope of taking back Esterra, there can be no room for error. Solanos *and* Kaleidos must die. The Stellaris line *must* end."

Viera reached over and squeezed my shoulder, but I flinched away from her. I didn't want to believe the things they had been telling me about Kaleidos. They had to be wrong about the prophecy, but it was clear how far my role as chosen one extended when no one would listen to me.

"If there were any other way . . ." my mother reiterated.

"I see your choice is made," I gritted out. "Now give me the space to come to terms with it."

Wynn nodded, and the dismissal was clear.

The ringing in my ears rose to a level that blocked out the voices in the room, and I squeezed my eyes shut, wrapping my arms around my middle as though it might help dull the aching, vacant feeling inside. For once, I wanted to breathe without the weight of the world resting on my shoulders. It felt as though they were asking me to tear out my own heart in sacrifice. Even though no one had said as much in words, I knew it, felt it to be true.

The prophecy stated I had a choice to make, and it only made sense this was it. *Shouldn't the cost of freedom be high? Wouldn't it also be worth it? For my family, for Iveria, for all of Esterra?*

I curled my fingers around his silver chained necklace as I walked out of the meeting.

"Wait for me," Viera called, catching up to me.

Grabbing her hand, I pulled her into the closest room, some kind of sitting area, closing the door behind us. I walked around, checking to see if anyone else was there.

"Is this about the prophecy?" Viera asked.

I closed my eyes, taking a deep breath, reeling in my hurt. "It was yours to share—I can't fault you for that." I tried to steady myself. "But now . . . I'm not sure I can stand beside you in this. I've done things, Viera. Things that make me no better than the Iris. How can I suddenly turn around and condemn them without condemning myself?"

"You've seen what they're capable of. You're nothing like them, Aella."

"Are you so sure?" I asked. "You've seen me these last months. Am I the same person you knew in Iveria?"

"None of us are." She became more serious. "The prophecy says—"

"Enough with the prophecy!" Most of the time, it brought me reassurance to think I was part of something greater, to make sense of all I'd been through, but in this moment, I could think only of myself, of Kaleidos.

"It's giving people hope, Aella. It's the reason we're all here. The reason any of this is happening."

"I know, I know. I agreed to be that person, to fill that role as the figurehead. I will even fly into battle . . . but what they're asking of me . . .?" I shook my head.

"I know it seems like a lot, but it's not all on you. Forces are gathering from every corner of Esterra. My father and others have been planning for this their entire lives, some for generations. This is our chance to take Esterra back, and it's real. It's already set into motion because of the prophecy, because of you. Can't you see how incredible this is?" She took my hands in hers. "Aella, you have the power to end this. It's written in the stars, but remember, you have the world behind you. You're not in this alone."

I took her hand, pressing it to my chest. "Will you also hold my hand while I plunge a dagger through the prince's heart, even as it pierces mine as well? It's not so wet and dry for me, Viera, whether we should kill him or not—"

"No one is asking you to be the one to do it!" Viera cut in.

I shook my head, my voice thick as I tried to hold back tears. "I've grown to care deeply for Kaleidos. I'm afraid I would do terrible things if it meant keeping him safe. So that begs the question, is the fate of Esterra worth more than my love for him? And I hate that I can't immediately say yes. I hate that a sick and selfish part of me wishes I were still there, chained in iron, just to be near him again." My voice finally broke, and I struggled to get the words out between sobs. "And the truth is . . . with the way things ended between us, I should agree with you . . . When he chained me up and tossed me away like I was nothing . . . I just kept telling myself it was an act. I needed to believe that what we shared was real. That he loved me. That he was good."

"Oh, Aella," Viera said, pulling me into a hug. "Our minds will do a great many things in order to survive, and if that means clinging to the one person who gave you a sliver of reprieve during your time in captivity, that's only natural." She pulled back so she could look me in the eye. "I need you to see him for what he truly is. A dark star, a deceiver. He could never love you, even if he wanted to."

I pulled away. "You would say this even after he saved you?"

"He is Iris, Aella. They are tarnished souls, cursed even. They cannot be good even if they want to be."

"And the elemental sympathizers?"

"Yes, Aella, even the sympathizers. They might find interest in helping us because of some perceived slight or unfairness against them, but they can never truly be trusted. An Iris' loyalty remains only to themselves. Didn't you hear what they said about Kaleidos in the meeting?"

"That's not the Kaleidos I know. He is good. He wanted to change things. I know him. I . . ." I hadn't wanted to believe it. Had been blocking out the truth, even when the truth had been plain as day. There were too many signs, and I'd chosen to ignore them.

Viera spoke as if speaking my own thoughts aloud. "If he was so capable of change, why did he chain you up again? Who was he performing for then? And why didn't he jump off the cliff with you? Why did he stay behind in Prisma? Iris are masters of manipulation. You knew only what he wanted you to see. You can't trust him."

"But there has to be a reason for it. Maybe he stayed to continue our work, to defy his father, to prepare the Iris for change," I pleaded with her.

"Every report has confirmed otherwise." She shook her head.

"But the connection we shared . . . there was no mistaking it."

Unless it truly all had been just a contest for him like Estrella had implied. That he'd take what he wanted and then tire of me and move on. A trick of the Iris illusion or a glamour to make me believe there was more to him, more to us. Like there was a bottomless pit in my stomach, I felt myself crushing inward.

Unable to physically stand anymore, I slid down the wall to sit with my back against it. "I don't know if I have it in me to allow it."

Viera joined me. "We can't let that much power remain unchecked . . . Sometimes it's hard to see the stars' plans even when they are right in front of us. But even more so when being misguided by the dark."

I leaned my head onto her shoulder.

"You can't blame yourself for letting your feelings get in the way of the true mission," Viera said. "You did what you had to do to survive. We all did."

"What's ridiculous is that I'm supposed to be the chosen one, but I already tried killing Solanos and failed miserably. With everything in me, all of my rage, and it didn't work. He still lives. Not even my mother's wrath defeated him. Do we really stand a chance against him in this war?"

"Maybe rage isn't enough. Maybe it's not about that. Maybe it's faith." Viera stood and held out her hand, helping me up. "We're free now, and we will not run and hide. The end of the Stellaris line is near. Rise in your power, Aella. Become the storm. Help us take back what is ours."

CHAPTER 59

RAISE AN ARMY

WYNN

Luminara shot through the clouds at a speed that almost made my eyes blur, but I needed this. The world was hazy and the air cool as I allowed the wind to whisper its secrets to me. Elemental armies were on the move, and we'd be advancing on Prisma in a few days' time.

My aquila let out a trilling call, and a response came flying along the wind.

Finally.

Luminara and I broke through the clouds, and Rik's aquila swooped by before banking and pulling up beside us.

"Fancy meeting you up here," Rik called out.

I snorted. "It's the closest I've come to feeling at home since we left."

It had taken some time to get over my anger at my cabala's underhanded plan, but deep down, I knew they only did what they did to protect me.

"Your mother sends greetings." He winked.

"I'm sure she does."

"She wants to know when you are planning on leaving this 'rebellion nonsense' behind you."

"Oh yeah? Did she have anything else to say?"

"She asks that you come home and see to your responsibilities as king." Rik paused. "You never told her, did you?"

I ran a hand through my wind-ruffled hair and shrugged. "She was too busy grieving. Besides, I couldn't take the risk that she'd blame Aella if I didn't make it out alive."

Rik shook his head. "You were planning on sacrificing yourself from day one, weren't you?"

"I knew it was a real possibility."

"Do you intend for her to rule after you?"

"I intend to give her a choice. She didn't ask for any of this, but I believe she has the potential to rule if she wants to. Her parents raised her well, and I can see the leader she could become if she accepts it."

Aella had been working her arse off these last months, taking everything thrown at her with grace and strength. While she still had some things to learn, I felt confident letting her fly into battle with us—not just as a figurehead but as a warrior in her own right. Pride warmed my heart as I remembered her first solo flight and how she'd taken to the wind like she'd been born for it.

Rik huffed a laugh. "I agree with you. And it's not like you have any other heirs running around."

"To my mother's eternal chagrin." I sighed. "Do you think we're truly ready for this? Am I leading our armies into a battle we cannot win? I must believe we can defeat the Iris, but I'm also afraid I'm leading our people into Prisma to be slaughtered."

"Prisma has never been weaker and Esterra never more united. You must have faith and hope. Faith that the stars have guided us here and hope for a better future." He shrugged and blew out a breath. "Without hope, what is there to live or die for? I'd rather go down clinging to it with my last breath than go into battle expecting the worst."

"And that is why you are my right hand. Don't ever change, Rik. I don't know what I'd do without you."

"Are you sure you're all right? Why so sentimental?"

"The guilt of initiating the trade weighs heavily . . . It was supposed to be me. How can I live knowing he died in my place? How can I possibly allow myself to dream of a future with Ari—"

"Stop," Rik interrupted. "What's done is done. Verus made his choice. Let the cabala carry this burden for you."

"It kills me that she's hurting. I'd love nothing more than to comfort her and be a safe place, but I also have to be okay with the fact that she might never accept the mate bond between us."

"You wouldn't fight for her?" Rik asked.

My heart ached as I looked up to the heavens soaring above us. Even after Verus had essentially given me his blessing, I was still afraid to broach the subject with her. Had she finally realized what we were to each other? I would never forget that cloudless day in Iveria when I'd discovered what she was to me. The pain and self-control it had taken to walk away . . . Could I really do that again?

"I am willing to let her go if that's what she wants, but I won't give up on her. Regardless, now is not the time. We need to set all of our attention on this battle and finally free our lands from our oppressors."

"Is everything in position?" Rik asked.

"The winds have confirmed we're on schedule. With the Capitol still in chaos after the tidal wave and the king's descent into madness, this is our best shot. Elementals from all across Esterra are on the move, ready to converge on Prisma."

The atmosphere in the war camp was buzzing with energy as we prepared for the additional incoming troops. We were less than a day's flight to Prisma and on high alert.

I strode through the camp, inspecting the assembly of temporary housing. It warmed my heart to see elementals from each court working together as I made my way toward Arianwen's field hospitium. She really should have been running the one in Iveria with the skill she had, but she'd lived a humble life, helping those who had needed her most. She was extraordinary.

Some healers from Iveria had arrived, and I'd overheard them speaking of her; my heart had grown in my chest upon learning more about the selfless female I was irrevocably in love with. Sometimes, I thought the stars were torturing me for my choices by putting us here together while keeping us so impossibly apart.

Pushing back a curtained doorway, I ducked into the tent. Ari was hard at work, ordering healers around while preparing healing concoctions. Her hair was twisted up on top of her head in a braided knot, stubborn strands sticking to the sides of her face. I shoved my hands into my pockets so I wouldn't be tempted to touch her, as I had been so many times in the past weeks. The air smelled of lavender and rosemary, and I shuddered at the thought of what smells would assault my nose when this place was filled with our wounded.

Ari looked up and caught me staring, giving me a small smile even as her eyes bore a haunted look. And yet . . . when she saw me, the stiffness in her shoulders seemed to soften, like a weight had been lifted, and it filled me with hope. Perhaps she recognized the connection between us. Perhaps with time . . .

"Is something wrong?" she asked. "Is there news?"

I shook my head and stepped closer. "Everything is fine. We should be moving out in the next day or so. Unfortunately, we can't wait too long, but we'll make do with whoever else arrives in time."

She nodded in understanding as she continued grinding up herbs. "I wish I knew what to expect." She bit her lip. "I mean, I know there will be plenty of wounded to care for, but the idea of flying into battle is somewhat terrifying."

"We're in this together. You won't be facing this alone." I gave her what I hoped was a reassuring smile. "You are one of the most gifted healers I have ever known," I continued, meaning every word. "You'll save many lives, and we'll need you with us."

She closed her eyes as if trying to gather strength. "You have no idea how many times I've gone over those moments on the cliffside. If I hadn't used up all my source calling that tidal wave, maybe I could have—"

"Ari," I interrupted, reaching out a hand, not knowing if she was even willing to accept comfort from me. "It wasn't your fault."

Ari closed the distance between us, bypassing my hand and wrapping her arms around me. I closed my eyes as I held her tight, hating this defeated side of her. Everything within me wanted to help, and I sent a quick prayer up that my words would bring her comfort. "Because of you, Aella got out. If you hadn't called that wave, Solanos would have surely killed or imprisoned you all. Even still, I am so, so sorry . . ." I murmured into her hair.

"I tell myself that if I just stay busy and focus on the tasks at hand, it will stop hurting, even though I know grief doesn't work like that."

Loosening my hold, I stepped back, not wanting to cross any boundaries by mistake.

She met my gaze and shrugged. "You'd think that after everything I've seen as a healer, I'd know the best way to heal myself, but it's just not the same."

"Grief isn't linear . . . and perhaps we all need to find our own ways to do so. But you are stronger than you think you are."

"Thanks, Wynn," she said softly. "Thank you for being here."

"Always."

CHAPTER 60

THE FINAL BATTLE

ARIANWEN

Rummaging through my field pack, I double- and triple-checked my supplies. I had no idea what to expect going into this battle, and the thought simultaneously thrilled and terrified me. I couldn't believe we were finally here. All the planning and training had led to this moment. Were we ready? Was *I* ready?

"Where's your armor?" Aella called out as she breezed into my tent with all the confidence in the world. "You might want to hurry up. Dusk is coming, and it's about an hour's flight from here."

I blew out a breath. "Fine. All right. Hopefully I'm not forgetting something important."

"Knowing you, you're overpacked and overprepared," Aella teased.

Turning, I pulled her into a quick, tight embrace. "How are *you* feeling, sweetheart? I understand it's been hard for you to accept the council's decision about Kaleidos, but I want you to know I've been considering every possible alternative. I've gone over the prophecy a thousand times, but I just can't find a way around it. My heart hurts for you, and I realize this is extremely difficult, but know I'm here. We're going to make it through this, and it's all going to be okay in the end. I promise. The stars wouldn't have commanded it otherwise. I have to believe that."

Aella tensed up in my arms and quickly pulled back, looking away. "I know, Mama. I've come to terms with it." She took a deep breath, then stared me straight in the eye. "I didn't want to. I wanted to believe he was good. But there are still too many lingering doubts." Her face hardened. "He promised I was safe with him, but after he got what he wanted from me, he chained me up again. You don't do that to someone you love. I just wish I had answers, that's all."

My heart ached with the pain radiating off of her. "I know, sweetheart, and I wish I could give them to you. When I met the prince all those months ago, I could have sworn he truly cared for you." I shrugged. "But I still don't fully understand the extent of Iris illusion, and perhaps I was wrong."

"Viera said they are incapable of true love."

"I find it hard to believe he couldn't love *you*." I took her hand in mine. "But then I also used to believe—"

"Even if he did love me, our short romance doesn't make up for all the wrong he and his father are responsible for. We're flying into battle tonight to stop that—to save our people—and that's all that matters now."

"You're right. The Stellaris line must end, even if I wish there were another way."

Aella seemed to swallow her emotions as she straightened, rolling her shoulders back. "I understand my role in this, Mother, and I'm ready to do whatever it takes to free Esterra from Iris rule."

I reached out and tucked a stray strand of hair behind her ear. "I'm so proud of you, Aella. Your father would be too."

She blinked, and I took a deep breath to hold back my own tears.

She made her way back to the door. "I'm gonna go check on the others."

"Be safe."

"You too, Mama."

Taking another cleansing breath after watching her leave, I turned toward the neat pile of armor Wynn had sent earlier.

Picking up the largest part, I slipped it over my head, twisting and turning, trying to figure out how to fasten it. The armor was stiff and unwieldy, completely unlike what I was used to wearing.

"Do you need some help with that?" a deep, soothing voice asked.

"Is it so obvious I don't know what I'm doing?" I laughed awkwardly, turning to see Wynn. "Do I really need to wear all of this?"

Wynn returned my smile and leaned forward, gently flicking my nose. "Yes, Ari. We need to make sure you're safe when tending to the wounded."

My heart fluttered wildly in my chest at the casual touch along with a twinge of guilt for enjoying his presence.

It's just the bond . . .

He motioned for me to turn and buckled the straps of armor that protected my chest and back.

"That's a bit tight, Wynn."

"I'm sorry, my . . . um, we just need to make sure there are no gaps. So no stray bolts or arrows find their way in."

"Well, I appreciate how thorough you're being."

Wynn gently tugged on my braid, and I turned, raising an eyebrow. As hard as this was for me, I imagined it was even harder for him.

"I have something for you," he said.

"Oh?"

"I know you're going into this battle as a healer, and I know you can handle yourself—you've proved that time and time again—but just in case the need arises, I want you to be prepared."

He pulled out a jeweled dagger and handed it to me. I admired how the opals embedded in the hilt caught the light, the shimmering reds and blues winking as I turned it around.

"I don't know what to say."

Wynn frowned. "If you're not comfortable carrying it—"

"No! That's not it. It just looks incredibly valuable, and I'm afraid I might lose it."

He smiled. "It was my sister's. She believed in a better world just as much as you do, and I'd be honored if you carried this piece of her into battle."

I was choked with emotion, but I nodded. "The honor would be all mine."

Wynn pulled out a sheath and held it up. "If you'll allow me?"

I nodded again, and he knelt on one knee. Gently lifting my foot so it rested on his other knee, he let go as he wrapped the sheath around my thigh, pulling the straps tight. His eyes lifted to mine, and so many unspoken words made the air thick and heavy with tension. He reached for the dagger, and I handed it over, allowing him to slide it into place.

"Wynn?"

"Yes?"

"Do you think we'll make it out of this? Are *you* afraid?" I asked.

His hands tightened around my thigh before he gently set my foot back onto the ground and rose to his feet. "I'd be lying if I said I wasn't afraid. Battle is not without its losses, and pretty much everyone I care about is heading straight into it. I also worry about what this world will look like at the end of it all."

A light shudder went through my body, and I tucked a stubborn tendril of hair behind my ear. "What if we fail?"

Wynn straightened his shoulders, the warrior in him rising to the surface. "Whether we win or lose this battle, we won't stop fighting for a better world."

Warmth and pride rushed through my heart.

"No matter what happens, Ari, I am honored to fly into battle with you."

⚜

Wind whipped around us as we made our approach on our aquilas. My power surged within me, heavy like the thickening clouds in the night sky, a torrent of rain about to break free at any moment.

The Iris had stolen so much, and now was their time to pay for what they'd done.

Aella rode next to us astride Ferathor; she looked fiercely unafraid of what came next. The way she was willing to return to Prisma and fight filled me with awe. She'd been beaten down, but she was stronger for it.

Wynn's voice echoed all around as he used his power to amplify and spread it throughout the ranks. "I realize so many of us thought this day would never come, but here we are."

Cheers erupted around us as the atmosphere filled with anticipation.

"The courts are united to fight for a just cause—our freedom," Wynn continued. "Do not falter. Do not waver. The stars are with us, and we will see victory with the morning light." He paused before roaring, "For Esterra!"

"For Esterra!" the cries of our people reverberated through the air, bringing a sense of hope.

Luminara let out a fierce battle cry, echoed by the ranks of birds flying with us. Some of us flew in pairs, Adamas and Argenti working together to create a hailstorm that would rain down upon the city, giving us an advantage in battle.

On the horizon, an armada of ships sailed in. That the Argenti had been able to commandeer so many was a testament to the numbers we had on our side.

The Aurum blazed in from the north on horseback and were followed by a pride of shadow fangs ready to scorch a patch through enemy lines. The beat of horse hooves thundering across the plains as the sky brimmed with mighty storm clouds above so thick that they blotted out the stars, surely struck fear into the city below. From the south, the earth thrummed and quaked with the incoming Aereus, who rode in with war elephanti dragging catapults. There was no turning back. This was our moment to reclaim our world.

My stomach was filled with rocks, the dread and anticipation of what we might face weighing heavily.

"Arianwen," Wynn rumbled from behind me, his arm gently pressing into my waist. While I was strapped in, having the extra support of his arm made me feel more secure, but I knew it couldn't last.

I turned my head slightly. "Yes?"

"Are you all right?"

"As all right as I can be, but thanks for checking in."

He gently squeezed my shoulder. Once again, so much left unsaid between us.

The clouds overhead were charged with lightning held back by the Adamas to unleash at the right moment, and my own element surged with the volume of rainwater waiting to be let loose. We wanted to release it over Prisma to blind our enemies, to distract them from the ground offensive. Our plan was to land at the northen side of the Palatium Crystalis and take it by storm.

Like a beacon, the brightly lit city came into view, and I could see the horses and shadow fangs cresting the hills below. They would be at the city walls in moments, and we would attack from the skies. That was our greatest advantage. We had the higher ground, and the Iris would, with any luck, be taken by surprise by our late evening attack when they were most vulnerable—their bellies full of wine and rich food.

I caught the glint of something metallic reflecting moonlight off the top of the city walls, and our view of below became blurred by a wave of iron-tipped bolts shooting in our direction.

"Shields!" Wynn cried out, and the Adamas used a combined force of air to shield us and the aquilas before the bolts could strike. They bounced off the invisible walls below us. A triumphant battle cry resounded, and I let out my own whoop, rejoicing in this one small victory.

"Release!" Wynn shouted, and the Adamas retaliated with arrows of their own. The wind guided them in odd patterns toward indirect targets to throw off the Iris defenses.

As the walls of the city shone with their excessive use of eternal flames, more volleys of bolts shot toward us, and once again, they bounced off the Adamas' shields. I was starting to feel hopeful we would have very few casualties on our side.

With a signal, sheets of rain flowed from the skies, turning the streets to rivers, followed by a hailstorm that smashed through the crystal domes and rooftops. Lightning cracked the sky around us as Adamas directed veins of electricity toward the wall's defenses.

Pride surged within at the sight of Aella at the head of the fleet, coming into her power, lightning bolt in hand, a fierce strength and determination shining in her star-speckled eyes like she was meant for this. We were some-what protected by the shields of air the Adamas blasted against incoming projectiles, but it was too soon to declare victory, as we would need to get down and fight to secure the palatium.

A piercing shriek came from our left, and an aquila flapped desperately with only one wing as it spiraled to the earth. Its riders were forced to abandon it and make landfall just outside of the city gates. Seemingly out of nowhere, another was struck, and this time, the riders were not so lucky. I felt and heard the near-silent whistle of an invisible bolt as it flew right past our heads, chilling me to the core.

"They must be glamouring the bolts and firing them at random to throw us off!" I cried.

"Hold on tight, Ari!" was all the warning I received before we dove out of range, but to my horror, more screams erupted from behind us.

Stars, that could have been us.

Whistles of alarm fired through the winged host, cut with aquilas' screeches and pained screams that called to the healer side of me. I'd known war was horrific, but nothing could have prepared me for this, and I feared it was only the beginning.

Luminara shot back up at an almost ninety degree incline, sending my stomach into my throat as we climbed rapidly above the clouds, where we took a momentary reprieve before diverting back down toward the frontlines. The sky was a mix of smoke, wind, and turbulent rainfall, making it hard to see.

Where was Aella? I searched for a shock of black hair among the remaining fleet of silvery white birds and could not find her.

Wynn went rigid behind me as a familiar form pierced the clouds. Valerik had been struck with a bolt through the abdomen and was in a freefall.

"Where's his aquila?" I gasped.

With a command from Wynn, Luminara shot toward Rik, scooping him up in her talons. Feeling helpless from my position, I searched desperately for a solution, but Wynn was already on it, sending out a whistling call to fall back. We reared and surfaced up above the clouds again, where the bolts could not reach, meeting with Wynn's cabala to regroup. Luminara deposited Valerik onto the back of another large aquila who had lost their rider, and as if we were on the same wavelength, Wynn started loosening the safety buckles that secured me into the harness.

"You're going to need to jump." His hand momentarily hovered near my face, but he stopped himself. "Don't worry. I won't let you fall."

Our eyes locked briefly and then broke as I gave him a determined nod. Before I could talk myself out of it, I stood and leaped off Luminara. It was almost as if time had slowed—I felt weightless before the feeling of falling took over and my stomach lurched into my throat. Wynn's power enveloped me, the sage-and-pine scent of him putting me at ease as he guided me safely onto the other aquila's back. After strapping Valerik and myself in, I immediately pressed my hands over his stomach, infusing him with healing energy, trying to ignore the flashes of memory. I could do this. I would not fail him. Valerik's bloodshot eyes fluttered open.

"Arianwen," he murmured. "Tell me—how bad is it? Am I going to die?"

"Not if I have anything to say about it. Do you really think I'd be bird hopping if you didn't have a chance?"

"Aella . . . I was on her tail like Wynn and you asked . . ." He groaned.

I wanted to tell him to conserve his energy, but I needed to know. "Is she safe?"

"No one is safe going into battle . . ." His eyes fluttered again as he started drifting into a delirium. I pressed another wave of healing power into him.

"Was she struck?"

"She's a real windwhip, that girl of yours. You should have seen it, the way she commanded Ferathor through a series of rolls and turns." His forehead creased. "She ditched the fleet. She was headed for the palatium. The last I saw her before . . ." He gestured at his bloody abdomen. "She's on her own."

CHAPTER 61

DAUGHTER OF STORM AND SEA

AELLA

The Palatium Crystalis loomed ahead, unbreached by the rebel forces. I was taking a risk by going alone, but I had to find him. I needed to get to him first. My heart pounded in my chest in tune with the thundering sky as lightning struck all around me, scorching the earth. If he was going to die, it had to be by *my* blade.

Below, plants grew wild in a destructive frenzy, and the ocean's waves collided in a menacing dance. I tucked my head as Ferathor careened and heavy winds whipped fronds of palm and other loose objects in a torrent of flying devastation. Aquilas cried in the distance alongside the bellows of elephanti and roars of the shadow fangs.

Circling back over the palatium, thick, heavy smoke permeated the air, making it a challenge to navigate. I took deep, focused breaths, charging myself full of my elements. This was the closest I was going to get to the palatium on an aquila without being struck down by the Iris defenses. Grabbing my spear from its holster, I leaped from Ferathor's back and shot with the force of lightning through the glass ceiling of the atrium in Kal's wing before halting my landing with a blast of wind.

I always knew I'd do better under pressure.

The din of battle was quieted within the palatium's thick, marble walls. Slick floors rocked beneath my feet as I stepped over crushed glass. It was an odd sensation, seeing his wing in this state. These rooms I'd spent so many months in that had somehow become my own, the place I'd thought I'd spend my last days, now unrecognizable through all the dust and smoke. I bolted through it in search of him as the floor tilted and shook with the earthquakes. But his wing was deserted, awakening a thunderous torrent of emotions within me.

"Where are you?" I screamed, panting as I held back my fury, attempting to save it for the moment I'd need it most. "Will you not even bother to show your face in the great battle?"

Determined not to let it crush me, I gritted my teeth and departed the forsaken place. I'd find him . . . or at least I'd know I'd tried.

As I ran out of Kal's wing into the massive, circular hall, the sudden impact of a projectile outside vibrated through me, the wall splintering and cracking all the way up to the ceiling. A chandelier crashed to the floor ahead of me, shooting shards of crystal in all directions. I held out my arm, and the sharp objects bounced away from me with a shock of wind, impaling the ceiling and walls.

Another heavy quake nearly sent me careening, but I balanced myself with a lift of air, powering my speed with a bit of flight as I looked for signs of Kal. I'd search every room and every hall if I had to. The palatium was desolate and dark, as though there were no longer elemental slaves powering its magnificence. No water features running, hanging glass orbs now empty vessels without their inner flames, no twinkling lights down the sweeping halls. What had happened to the nameless? Had they been sent out to fight against us? Or had they all been turned to fodder for the nightly games I'd heard of? Abandoned palanquins clustered near the familiar courtyards, vintage bottles dropped in haste.

There was a sticky slick patch, and next, there were bodies and limbs. I'd thought I'd been the first to breach the palatium. Who or what could have done this?

Following the trail of gore, I found myself at the massive doors to King Solanos' wing. They hung crooked from the hinges, split apart with a narrow gap just large enough for a small person to fit through. Royal guards lay in pieces just outside the wing. Before entering, I called again on my elements, letting them fill me with wind and rain for the task ahead. Lightning crackled through my veins and danced across my skin. Though I had yet to face my biggest foe, I felt invincible. I was ready.

I cleared the smoke ahead of me with a gust of wind. The heavy doors wouldn't budge further, so I squeezed through the constrictive crack, gaining entry into the mostly undisturbed space. Somehow, while so much of the palatium was in ruins, these royal wings had managed to remain mostly intact beyond the doors, except for the layer of soot, dust, and ash that had settled over the furniture and floors, leaving a trail of footprints behind me as I walked. The city on fire cast the hall in an orange glow, and flashes of light brightened it with a shuttering effect. The air was eerily still. I searched with my new element for a whisper or hint of another living being.

Show yourself! I wanted to scream, but something held me back.

Passing through the seemingly endless hall, I jumped back when a bright light caught on a figure slumped against the wall, her chest torn open, then another and another—shredded apart, their flesh in bloody ribbons. Bodies, gutted and destroyed, littered the floor the closer I got to the bedchamber. Shadow fang wounds from the looks of them.

My heart was in my throat and goosebumps raced up my arms as I stepped over viscera. Was the beast still inside? I gripped my spear as I continued on, readying the defensive techniques my father had taught me and blocking out the flashes of memory and flickering distortions of lightning interspersed with Ulli's screams that seemed to echo around me. I fought the urge to curl up and hide, all confidence gone, but I shook my head, trying to clear it, reaching deep within for the strength I needed to keep on—reaching for the memory of Father's smile and his belief in me.

My sight was clouded by smoke and visions of my fellow contestants in the arena. And suddenly, it was their faces I was seeing on the bodies. Nickel, Ulli, and every last one of the other eleven girls who'd been slain that night. But it was more than that. As they all came flooding back, I saw Elutha dead in the sand, killed by my own doing. I saw Viera next, then last of all, myself.

I choked on the sickening feeling, shaking my head again, willing the visions to clear. It was too much to bear, the memories, trauma, and fear overwhelming me, but I could not stop here. I could not break down. *This isn't real.*

Taking a gasping breath of dusty, smoky air, I willed myself to hold still, to calm down, squeezing my nails into my palm and tightening my grip on the spear. I centered myself once more, focusing on the power buzzing inside me.

Waves of source coursed through me, strengthening me, reassuring me. I would not be crushed by the traumas of my past. My power stores abounding, I marched on, leaving a wind tunnel of destruction in my wake. Books and jewels hurtled through the air, crashing through windows, and curtains ripped from their poles.

When I made it down the long hall to the final set of double doors, I used my vortex of wind to burst through, sending the large doors flying and shattering against the far wall. All curtains were drawn, shrouding the room in darkness, lit only by the silver glow coming from my lightning-charged skin. Below my feet, a trail of sticky, red blood led to the oversized, canopied bed in the center of the room. I sensed for a movement of air, something, but neither heard nor felt anything but a sickening *drip, drip, drip* from the bed.

A flashing light flickered in through the open doors, dimly revealing my reflection in the vast, mirrored walls. At once, I was reminded of what this place had made me. A prisoner, a slave, a monster.

But I was the prophesied one, a princess of sky and sea. I was the tempest, and I would not be intimidated or diminished. No one would take my power away from me again. All of my hurt and all of my anger made me a force to be reckoned with. Overflowing with unnatural strength of storm and sea, I would not be afraid—I would be feared.

"Show yourself," I commanded, my voice full of unbridled authority.

My steps landed with assertion and defiance. Lights flashed again, revealing the heaping mound of a shadow fang atop the bed, deathly still. I aimed my spear, ready to strike as I inched closer.

Where is he? Has he run like a coward?

Visions forced their way back into my mind, like traveling back in time.

"How is it that an Argenti, of all beings, managed to defy the power of the nameless key?" a voice rumbled through me.

I spun around to find the origin but instead found myself once again in chains, being led to the throne room, naked and caked in blood. Brought to the king after my failed assassination attempt in the arena. I'd just lost everything.

"Tell me, girl!"

"How do you know it was me?" I struggled through strained breaths, trying not to give in to the illusion. "Maybe it was just another way the stars chose me instead of you."

Time sped up and then came to a stop the moment I grabbed onto the key.

"I saw the want in your eyes as you reached for it."

Kal's hand dug firmly into my hair. The king gasped as though it had only just occurred to him. "My son is responsible for this."

Searing pain lanced through the side of my skull, and the king's council swirled and faded away as his control infected my thoughts now with false sights of my mother falling through the sky, my friends, all dead, struck down, the rebel camp up in flames, elementals losing the war, enslaved. So much blood, so much death.

"We gave you a peaceful existence."

His voice boomed as I found myself standing in the heart of Iveria.

"We gave you little freedoms. We even gave you honors and ranks."

I ran through the empty, dilapidated market in search of the voice that seemed to echo through and around me.

"We asked only for a small tribute. Did we not spoil you enough?"

I turned again, and I was standing in the rubble of Iveria, the sea dried out like a desert.

"Look at what you have done!"

Blood poured from my hands, and I choked on the dryness of the air as I struggled to understand what was happening. *This isn't real. None of this is real.* I rubbed my eyes, willing the vision away, but it was like being stuck in a dream I couldn't wake from.

Breath crawled over my neck. I spun toward the source, stabbing my spear blindly, but was met only with a proud chuckle.

"Have we been too lenient? Too generous? The lack of fear in you is incomprehensible."

Hands slithered over mine, controlling them like a puppet's, making me drop the spear. I screamed and, with it, released a surge of lightning in a powerful blast. The vision flickered.

"I will have to remind your people why they serve us, a reminder they will not forget as easily as you have . . . Whatever is left of your people, that is."

"Even if you defeat us today, the stars will save us. You'd be a fool to think the elemental fae would submit to you again after their taste of vengeance," I snarled.

The king stepped into my vision then, pacing a slow circle around me where we now stood at the center of a plateau in the midst of a vast wasteland.

"I've already defied the prophecy. There are no gods in the sky, and if there were, it's clear they care little for this world." He rolled up his sleeves. "What makes you think you'll get lucky this time?"

"That's funny—I was about to ask you the same."

In a flash, lightning shot from my palms straight for him, but he was faster, misdirecting it with a cloud of dirt. I fought back with more power, more streams of crackling light and wind, targeting him from every angle. The king deflected just as fast, his laughter echoing around me the entire time.

I paused my attack, pulling in the source I'd just expended, wrenching it out of him and his surroundings. His laughter paused, giving way to surprise when he realized what I was doing. Not only willing back the power I'd just spent but also taking from him.

"An upside of the iron," I mused. "I hadn't realized what it was that first time . . . when I drained Estrella into a husk. But I guess I should thank you. All that time wrapped up in those leeching chains taught me how to seek out the source . . . by any means necessary." I tugged at his powers even more, hearing him grunt as the illusion began to flicker again. "And I'm afraid it likes me more than you." I pulled harder, preparing to attack him again now that he was evidently weaker.

But before I could strike, I was distracted by a small noise, the piercing cries of my little sister, Mila. Too long since I'd heard the sound of her voice. I was sinking, my feet disappearing into quicksand. It had been another illusion to catch me off guard, and I should have known better than to have let it distract me, but it was too late. The king paced around me again.

"All right, now that you're done showing off your parlor tricks, why don't we get to the part where you beg for your pathetic little life?"

"Never," I roared, whipping up a sand storm around us that I could see but somehow couldn't feel. Sand swallowed me up until I was neck-deep, the king circling me, laughter echoing all around, but I kept fighting.

"Enough of this defiance!" he snarled, patience clearly wearing thin. "Stop clinging to your hopeless cause. Accept your fate and surrender. It's over for you and your people. Give up. Let go."

His words reached into my mind, taunting, tempting, even as the sand covered me, filling my mouth, burying me alive. He was trying to manipulate me by using fear and flooding all of my senses with lies. If only I could find a way to see through them so I could truly fight him.

But wait. Why hadn't he killed me already? Why go through so much trouble to disarm me only to trap me in my own mind? Why did he want me to give up? What did he still need me for? Then it came to me.

What if his perceived power and strength were only as real as this illusion? What if this was his last defense against me?

"I cannot fathom why you continue to fight. It's a waste of your source power. You'll drain yourself to nothing. Submit to me and accept your defeat," he taunted.

This isn't real.

My surroundings changed to a blur of colors as I resisted the illusion with all my might. My body moved in slow motion, like swimming against a powerful current, like being caught in a tangle of sea kelp, unable to kick free. I fought and I fought until I could no more, exhaustion taking over, reminding me of my limits. Perhaps my powers weren't infinite. Perhaps I'd been a fool to come here all by myself.

As I strained to reclaim my source, I suddenly realized the only way out was to do exactly as he'd asked—to stop fighting, to give in.

Releasing the last bit of control, I let myself fall into the enemy's arms. Everything rippled and pulsed around me as though I was being pulled from a dream.

"See? Obedience becomes you." His words were soft and enchanting as he lured me back into his chamber. "Now, to me," he said, his voice betraying a hint of urgency that filled me with alarm. Still, I was compelled to follow.

He walked me over to the bed, my mind and body obeying him as though under his spell. My eyes widened when I finally beheld the king, the true king, not the phantom of him I'd been wrestling. There he lay, resting beneath the darkness of a limp shadow fang's lifeless body—the shreds of velvet bedding and black mane matted and coated in blood. The fit figure beside me flickered out, just an illusion, the last of the king's consciousness as he clung to the final threads of life. The bed was soaked in so much blood, how the fading king managed to still hold on was astounding.

"Give it to me," he rasped, his voice barely hiding the truth. Standing over him, I held out my palm, summoning my elements in a spinning orb.

"Is this what you want?" I asked, watching him lick his greedy, parched lips, his once glowing, citrine eyes now a sickly shade of yellow. His face so similar yet so different from the one I knew. Handsome in the same strong angle of his jawline as Kaleidos but crueler without any of the softness in his lips or eyes. "You want me to give you my source so you can heal yourself."

He glared at me impatiently, his control over me waning by the second, only shadows of claws grasping for power now. He'd used too much of it trying to ensnare my mind.

"Give me your source, and I'll let you have my son. That's what you want, isn't it? Who you came alone in search of. I'll return your status as his bride, and you'll be the first elemental princess we've had in centuries."

"You can keep him," I spat. "What about my family and friends, my people? There's a war being fought out there to destroy you."

"You believe you're winning?" He laughed. "This ramshackle uprising of yours is no match for my trained Iris soldiers."

I let the orb fade back into my hand, and he sneered. "Very well—I'll guarantee your family's safety and call an end to this war if that's what it takes. But come now. How much blood will you let stain your hands while you make up your mind?"

I stepped back, surprised by my draw to his offer. Would it be worth it to end the war now? To stop all the bloodshed? Perhaps that way, Kaleidos wouldn't have to die.

"You'll free my people and stop the games too?"

"Whatever you'd like, it shall be yours," he said.

His desire mingled with mine, wrapping around my mind, enticing me, making me want to agree.

"Why should I trust you to uphold your end of the agreement?" I challenged.

"You've proven yourself not so easy to manipulate. I respect that."

"Your respect means nothing to me. Prove your value. Give me something I might hold over you."

He snarled in my mind. *I'm still alive, am I not? Why linger, hovering over me, if killing me is what you intended?*

"I suggest you keep your illusion from my mind if you intend on coming to any form of agreement."

"Ask me anything. Could it be wisdom or secrets that you seek?"

"Tell me how the nameless key works. Tell me how to restore their names."

He blinked, surprised by my request. "It's not possible."

"Don't lie to me," I threatened. "Now answer my question. What's the cure?" I used my wind powers to fly my spear back into my hand, angling it for his throat.

"I swear," he spat. "I've tried! Believe me, I've tried . . . There is no cure." A longing sadness took over his face. What was left of his controlling powers had completely vanished from my mind. So it was true then.

I shook my head. "And you would use it so indiscriminately knowing this?"

The king's despondency was quickly replaced by an icy cold. "I've made more than enough offers to you. If you don't intend on taking any of them, then leave." He coughed up blood, and his breathing became more ragged. I almost felt bad for him. Almost enough to give him a drop of source in exchange for more answers, but he did not deserve my mercy.

"Solanos Stellaris, Son of Parthalos, Defier of Prophecy, King of Esterra and all surrounding seas, I came here to destroy you." I tutted. "You thought you could defy me. So much power you claim, yet here I stand. You're no god, Solanos. You couldn't even take on a shadow fang."

"Kill me and be done with it already," he rasped. "Don't force me to sit here and listen to your goading . . . unless . . . you want another taste of the aether?" A hint of confidence shone in his fading eyes as he latched on to the enticement he saw in mine. "I can smell it on you."

The hair rose at the nape of my neck.

"My son's reckless lack of control must have bled into you—it's no wonder you managed to resist me for as long as you did. I could give you more of it. Make you as powerful as an Iris queen."

I would not allow his words to persuade me.

He panicked, speaking quickly. "With whatever blood that's left in my body, I swear it to you . . . I'll even swear an oath to the stars."

"No."

"Then get out!" he screamed through bloody teeth, but I stood my ground.

"You do not get to tell me what to do. You do not get to tell anyone what to do again. You will die here, helpless and weak with not even aether at your command."

"Where *is* my coward son anyway? And don't even pretend to deny it. I saw the temptation in your eyes when I spoke his name before. It's laughable you still want him after everything he's done while you've been away. Was the chaining not enough to deter you from him? You've come crawling back, hoping for breadcrumbs? Perhaps you think he cares for you because he helped you over the cliff. Don't you see that was only so he could return to the pleasures of the court? He's been free to fall back to his old ways since you left. I'm sure you've heard the gossip."

I gritted my teeth to keep myself from strangling him, but more than anything, I wanted not to give in to a single one of his requests. Let him die in the face of my defiance. Let his last thoughts be of how he'd failed. How he'd lost to me.

"Please!" the king began to cry, begging, pleading with his final breaths.

"You want mercy, but where was yours when the elementals cried out in the arena? Where was your mercy for the mother of your own child?"

"You know nothing," he rattled through his strained last breaths. "You will regret this choice . . ."

Then the breath left him for good.

CHAPTER 62
YOUR LAST BREATH

The earth was rumbling again, the squalls of battle outside becoming louder, closer. The elementals were finally breaching the palatium. Solanos was dead, fitting as it was, by his own pet. I removed his sovereign ring that bore the Iris symbol, looping it onto the silver chain hanging from my neck. If only this were enough to end the war and halt the bloodshed, but it had been agreed that the stars demanded Kal's life as well.

Time was slipping away. I still had questions that needed answers, and I feared I wouldn't reach him before the rebellion did. He'd once planned for this day. Told me not to hold back. He'd also betrayed me. I wanted so badly to believe there was an explanation, but it was impossible to ignore all the reports, making it seem unlikely he would fight alongside us to bring down his own family. Though, regardless of where his loyalties lay, it had already been decided, and I'd needed to accept that for the fate of our world.

I had a prophecy to fulfill. This final task would be the hardest, and I wasn't sure how I could go on living after, but it had to be done. For every child who had lost a parent, for every lover, for every friend. We had all lost too much, and it needed to stop. This was the only way. For Esterra.

Full of resolve, I left the king's chamber. Glass crunched underfoot as I made my way back out through the long corridor that led to the main hall. Gone was the glamour of blood and gore I'd stepped over on my way in to face him, only the damage from the wind tunnel I'd created remained. Running through the hall, I halted when the doors at the end blew open with a blast.

Through a plume of dust and smoke, the dark silhouette of a figure stormed in.

It was not a shadow fang, not a soldier nor a guard that I beheld marching in, weapon in hand, clothes splattered in thick layers of dust and blood, hair damp and wild. Black embers and orange flames flickered behind him. Prince of earth and fire, water and air, prince of the Iris, now king of Esterra. Kaleidos, my enemy, my undoing.

Kaleidos froze the moment he recognized me, relief mixed with a profound sadness portrayed across his stunning features. Amid so much death and destruction, smoke and blood, he radiated beauty, was enhanced by it even.

Spear in hand, all my resolve melted at the sight of him. My heart leaped for him. I squeezed my fist around the spear's shaft, reminding myself what I'd come to do, but the rush of tingles that shot through me in his presence almost made me weak, my hands shaking. And it was clear he could read it all, every turmoiled thought, as if they were his own.

"Don't make me fight you," I gritted. The spear became hot in my hand, sweat coating my palm. The prophecy made it clear, he needed to die. He was our enemy. He was Iris. He was wicked.

Yet he was mine.

With long strides, Kal closed the gap between us and pulled me into his broad arms. I dropped my spear, sucking in a ragged breath, and I melted into him, my safe place, my only comfort in my darkest days. He kissed then rested his head atop mine, holding me tightly, and I held on tighter still. If only it could save us. If only it were enough.

Kal pulled back slightly to cradle my face in his hands. Foreheads together, breaths heavy, our noses grazed as we inhaled each other's air. A muscle flickered in the prince's jaw, and he tore off his armored vest.

"What are you doing?" I asked.

"If our lives are tied to the outcome of this battle, it's not my choice to make. But you . . . you need to live, Aella."

He held my face with one hand and slid the other down to withdraw a dagger. With calm assurance, he placed it in my hand, wrapping his around mine before positioning it at the base of his heart.

"I will never be able to rectify all I have taken part in. There is no redemption for what I have done."

While I could feel the slow, steady rhythm of his pulse, mine was firing rapidly. One of his steady hands was folded over my trembling fingers, his other was wrapped behind my neck. Looking into my eyes, he nodded slightly to let me know it was okay, that he understood, and that he didn't blame me.

"No," I whispered as my whole body shook with the grief of what I was being made to do.

"But you must," he murmured over my lips as he kissed me. "It's all right, my love. My tempest. My Aella." He kissed me over and over again, soft, confirming kisses, each a gift of love and adoration, an ode to what we'd had, to what we'd been. To what we'd never be.

"Please don't make me do this." I looked up at him, pleading through heavy, tear-laden eyes.

"I don't think I could make you do anything even if I wanted to," he said with a sad smile. "But I think you know as well as I do that it was always going to end this way."

"But I can't do it." My voice broke off.

"Yes, you can," he said, his grip tightening around my hand, tipping the point into his flesh, a deep crimson spreading through the silk of his shirt.

How can this be the right thing?

"There has to be another way—there needs to be," I said, shaking my head. "We will leave, never come back to Esterra, find a brand new land to live in."

Kal shook his head. "I will not run from this."

"Then fight beside us. If you die, I die with you," I said, and I yanked my hand out of his. "Even if we are defeated . . ." I threw the dagger across the room like a dart, getting it as far away from us as I possibly could.

"What are you doing?" he asked, eyes wild.

"I don't exist in a world without you, Kal. You have worked yourself in and through the very fabric of my soul. I need you just as I need the breath in my lungs and the blood in my veins. I don't care what the prophecy says, I don't care what anyone says about you, because I know who you are. And I'm willing to test the stars. Let's choose our own fates."

Kal brushed away my tears as he stared into my eyes for a moment so long, it felt as though time stood still, the world disappearing around us.

"I forgive you, Kaleidos Stellaris, for what you took part in and for the things you did not do. You are not to blame for the world you grew up in or for your father's crimes. I forgive you for all of it, because you are worthy, and because . . . I love you."

And as though I'd broken some kind of spell, the prince groaned, drawing me back into his arms, kissing me with an intensity unlike ever before, his hand reaching into my hair, our bodies molded into one.

"Then we will face them together," he murmured through gasps for air between kisses, "if that is what you choose."

"Together," I said over and over again, claiming him, kissing him with an urgency that rushed through us, like we were still living on borrowed time.

Glass crashed behind the prince, and I opened my eyes just in time to see Henri, an Adamas soldier, aiming his bow, but it was too late. By the time I registered what was happening, Kal's body jolted with the impact, a feathered arrow deeply embedded into his back. The soldier was drawing up to shoot another when I screamed, putting myself between him and Kal protectively.

"No!" My magic whipped across the room, knocking Henri off his feet.

Henri counteracted the winds, getting back up and aiming another arrow at the prince, as though to protect *me*, while giving me a confused look.

"I command you to stand down!" I said, my voice breaking.

"It's better this way," Kal grunted as he attempted to mask the pain. "Now the prophecy will be fulfilled and your conscience will remain clear."

"No," I whimpered. I rushed back to his side, frantically trying to recall the little I'd learned about the healing arts in Concordia. If I removed the arrow, he could bleed out, but if I left it in, the iron tip would prevent him from healing. He was Iris though, so his wound would heal faster if I removed it. I broke the feathered end of the arrow, then let out a feral scream as I pressed on it with all my might until it punctured through his chest.

Kal grabbed the tip of the arrowhead, yanking it the rest of the way out. Blood poured out of him from both sides, and he dropped to his knees.

"No!" I cried as I pressed shaking hands over both wound sites, trying to staunch the bleeding. I tried to will healing magic into him, but I couldn't focus as I devolved into panic. All I managed to do was fiercen the storm inside the room, the air whipping around us like a tornado. My lips wobbled uncontrollably as I watched Kal's eyes slowly shut, his body slumping further.

I don't know how to fix this.

"Stay with me," I commanded, this time to the prince, who opened his eyes again but rested his head against mine as though it was too heavy to hold up on his own.

"What's wrong with him? What did you do to him?" I accused.

"It's a fire-iron arrow, Your Highness," Henri said softly, pointing to the bloody pieces on the ground, the pointed arrow tip nearly gone. "It was designed with an inner flame that melts the alloy upon contact with flesh. He has iron poisoning in his blood, so he won't be able to heal himself."

"It's all right," Kal murmured.

"No, it's not!" I said more to Henri than to Kal. "We need to get out of here." I attempted to heft the prince over my shoulder to help him stand. Any elemental who saw an Iris was sure to try to kill him, especially if he was the crowned prince. I needed a way to get him help while remaining out of sight. I couldn't trust he wouldn't be struck down by another elemental warrior or that they would even let us escape.

I scanned the walls, looking for a servants' door. The earth shifted, and I wobbled under Kal's added weight, threatening to drop him as he became heavier and more unstable by the second. A bewildered Henri helped me lift him from the other side. Kal was too heavy to carry alone, and I had a feeling he wouldn't be able to support any of his own weight for much longer as blood sputtered from his lips.

"Escape. How do we escape?" I choked out through tears. "There has to be a secret passage. Come on, Kal. Show me how to get us out of here."

He lifted a heavy hand to point to a long bookcase that spanned the inner wall, trying to speak, but more blood bubbled up. Leaving Kal with Henri, I felt along the shelves for something, anything.

A familiar little squeak came from behind the wall.

"Rat?"

She squeaked again, and I followed the sound, pulling the books out one by one, tossing them to the side until, finally, the bookcase swung inward, revealing a secret passageway that led to a set of spiral stairs.

I ran back toward Kal, placing one of his arms over my shoulders. Kal's head hung limp, his feet dragging behind him. Between the two of us, we were barely able to continue on.

"Do the Iris have lead in their bones?" Henri grumbled.

"Come on . . . Can we try to use our air element to help lift some of his weight?" I asked. Henri grunted and did as I asked. Rat ran down the stairs, looking back at us every so often to make sure we were keeping up. The staircase spiraled down so deep, the pressure in my ears built with our descent. Kal's eyes fluttered open as he momentarily regained consciousness while we floated him down.

Another blast from the outside sent a spray of stone tumbling down, and my fear of the stairwell caving in on us became a very real threat.

"We're almost there," I lied. "Stay with me." I forced a smile.

I had no idea where we were going or how much farther until we found help. I just had to keep hoping we'd be out of the palatium soon. I needed to find my mother—she would know what to do. Last I'd seen her, she'd been flying with Wynn, but by now, she'd probably gone back to camp with the injured. I'd never find her in battle. The field hospitium was our best option.

Finally at the bottom, we made it to an underwater cavern. We'd need to dive down into it to find a way out, and I had no idea how far it would be or if this Adamas soldier was any good at swimming.

Rat sniffed the air, then scurried back up the stairwell. I wished the tiny creature safety, silently praying I'd see her again once this was all over.

Suddenly, from under the water, Uncle Tal burst forth, a spear in his hand. He nearly thrust it at Kaleidos before I blocked him with my body. A look of shock distorted my father's best friend's features when he realized exactly which Iris I was protecting.

"Please, I need your help. He's dying . . . I can't let him die . . . Please," I urged. Then, looking back at Kaleidos' pallid face, the bleak reality threatened my resolve. "I can't . . . I can't."

Uncle Tal gave me a look of disbelief that I was helping the prince, that I was asking him to be a part of it. Time folded in on itself as he stood there, appearing to contemplate his choices. Then, with a look of frustration and a clenching of his jaw, he said, "If only for your father, who I know would spurn me from the heavens if I didn't help you. Please don't make me regret this."

◬

When we finally made it out of the cave, Tal helped me lug Kaleidos up into a small boat with the help of the water. We'd had to leave Henri behind.

"If I know your mother, she's back at camp already, healing the injured as they're brought in. I'll try to get us there as fast as possible, but . . ." He gave Kal a bleak glance. "I'll try my best."

"My mother will know exactly what to do. She'll know," I mumbled to Kal with false reassurance. Trying to convince myself that she would be there, that we'd make it in time, that we wouldn't be stopped by other, less sympathetic elementals. But I felt my own strength and powers fading as hope seemed to drift farther and farther out of reach.

The boat sped along the bumpy water, dodging massive waves as Uncle Tal guided us through the turbulent swells.

"My mother can heal you. She'll make everything better. You just need to hold on a little bit longer." Kal's breathing became irregular, and I willed the boat to move faster. "We're running out of time. Please, Uncle, hurry!"

I pressed my hands to Kal's chest, whispering prayers, sobbing, and begging him not to leave me. Pleading and bargaining with the stars.

Let this not be the end.

The boat sped faster, this time going right through a wave instead of around it, the water lifting our bodies up in a turbulent, floating state before we met the surface again, slamming back down onto the hardwood floor of the boat.

"Stay with me," I repeated. "Stay with me," I whispered like a chant, over and over. "I need you. Stay with me."

Kal's breathing stalled. I stared at him, holding my own breath, willing him to inhale. This was all my fault. I'd led the attack. I'd meant to kill him, but I couldn't. I'd thought I could follow through with the stars' destined path for me. I'd thought I was strong enough to fulfill the prophecy, but I wasn't.

I didn't know how or why, but I loved him. I forgave him. I didn't want him dead. He could change—he'd shown me that. He *had* changed.

I leaned down, whispering a choked, "Stay with me" one last time, my lips right over his. His body was so still beneath mine, an emptiness filled my chest, and it felt like the world had ended. It was ending. And I was fading. Then my breath was sucked right out of my lungs, and I closed my eyes, collapsing over him as my world tumbled into darkness.

CHAPTER 63

FOR A BETTER WORLD

WYNN

"To the palatium!" I called out, letting the wind carry my orders to my remaining cabala and the group of trusted warriors that flew alongside us.

Kairi and Glint soared ahead on an aquila, letting out a whoop of excitement.

"For Rik!" Helio cried.

"For Rik!" I agreed. A pang went through me. Stars willing, Ari would be able to patch him up. He hadn't looked good when they'd flown off, but he couldn't have been in better hands.

We flew over the canyon that separated the Palatium Crystalis from the rest of Prisma, and in an instant, Helio catapulted himself off his bird and hit the ground running. "Time to kick some Iris arse!"

"Show off!" Glint yelled as she and Kairi unbuckled their harnesses, flying down together.

I couldn't help the laugh that burst out of me at his antics. After jumping off Luminara's back, I unsheathed my sword and ran into the fray. It was a chaotic free-for-all as my cabala started to fight through the line of Iris guards blocking the entrance to the palatium.

"That's two down," Helio crowed as he stomped his foot, sending the earth rippling outward in one direction and summoning a wall of earth in the other, cutting off a blast of fire.

"You're slacking, Helio," Glint taunted. Wielding her flaming blades, she sliced through the Iris defenses like butter. "I've taken out five."

"Now who's the show off," I countered as Kairi and I knocked a group of Iris off their feet with a strong gust of wind, trying to even the playing field. "Thanks for the assist, Kairi!"

"At your service." She grinned from the sky as she pulled shots at the fallen guards with her bow.

The Iris, though stronger and with more powers, had clearly been unprepared and couldn't keep up with my cabala's synchronized precision, proof of our years of training together. When one faltered, another was there to lift them up. We had each other's backs, no matter the cost.

"Wynn! Behind you!" Helio shouted.

I spun around just in time to see a guard charging at my back. The Iris gave a malicious grin as he swung his sword at me.

"Not today, you sparkling arse," I spat as I met his sword with my own.

"You don't like pretty things, do you?" He sneered. And from one moment to the next, all the smoke and dirt in the air suddenly glittered, partially blinding me to another near-fatal blow.

I ducked just in time to avoid the sword swung at my head and threw mine between his thighs, slicing upward with a leap, severing him in half. The illusion mercifully faded, and I was able to find the others again.

More of our fighters arrived, including a group of Argenti led by Lucris' son, Han, but the Iris still blocked our entrance into the palatium.

I'd have sucked the air out of all their lungs to break in, but there were far too many so I used the power sparingly. I continued on, meeting every strike with my own, calling down lightning that shot through their ranks, attracted to their shiny, metal armor.

The Iris fell back as we made ground, but the moment my feet hit the marble pavement of the forecourt, I was struck with an illusion. The Iris guards before me appeared as unarmed elemental fae begging for mercy. I'd seen them change—still, it was jarring. How could I believe my eyes? I felt the air shift with the oncoming assault, even though the sight before me remained the same. A blade cut through the air, and I swung my sword to block it. The illusion flickered a moment, just enough to see the Iris pricks laughing while we struggled with our senses.

"It's only an illusion!" I shouted. "Don't be fooled."

Aella had told us of their spells and tricks. She'd said weapons had been spelled in the arena to trick contestants into seeing each other as enemies. Perhaps this was similar. I closed my eyes to block out the horrific images they played—to make us fight our own as though we were in one of their arenas.

Needing to gain perspective, I flew upward, and within moments, the illusion began to fade. My fighters on the marble forecourt seemed to be aiming their elements and swinging their weapons blindly, missing blows and succumbing to the Iris guards. They were being slaughtered. Those fighting on the grass, however, were having no issue defending against the onslaught of Iris attacks.

"Fall back! Get off the forecourt!" I shouted. "The illusion is triggered by the marble stone!"

We needed a way to eliminate or neutralize the illusion, or we'd never advance on the palatium. Diving back down, I blasted a row of Iris guards, who were obstructing some struggling rebel soldiers from leaving the marble steps.

The grunts and cries of battle surrounded me as I ducked and spun, moving through the forecourt like a whirlwind, my element swirling and sensing the danger around me as it guided my movements while I hovered over the marble.

"Take out the general and the illusion will fall," Han grunted out next to me as he thrust his spear toward a guard.

"Traitorous Argenti filth," the guard spat.

My blade sliced through him a moment later, and Han gave me a thankful nod before moving on to the next target. He was new to fighting with us, but he'd been a valuable asset in our battle planning, teaching us the common fighting methods and techniques the guards used and how to recognize them.

"Fall back!" I shouted again. Kairi and other Adamas assisted from above to guide our ground soldiers out and off the marble steps so we could regroup. I flew over to my cabala, where they fought side by side, maintaining the front line against the Iris.

"We need to take him out!" I pointed.

"I'll hold the line and keep them distracted over here," Kairi said, leaping and sending out a wave of arrows as she spun and rolled through the air.

"Let's get his shiny, pompous arse!" Helio rallied.

I threw out my arm, the air splitting a path through the Iris guards as they were knocked atop each other while Helio simultaneously cracked the marble, bringing up pillars of earth in a series of steps to launch Glint into the sky for her signature move. In a running leap, she tore through the air, slicing the Iris in her path to shreds as I made her spin so fast, she was untouchable. Not even their general could clear her path fast enough, and within moments, the illusion was gone.

Attack!" I cried out, and as I gave Han the signal, he called down buckets of rain from the skies, directing it at the guards. Glint boiled the rain to scalding temperatures and steam. The guards screamed curses but had no clue what was coming as Kairi and I summoned a storm upon them. Lightning struck, taking out a dozen of them where they stood in floods of water. The sickening scent of burnt flesh filled my nose, and I quickly summoned wind to clear the air. Helio sent vines after stragglers, and those tethered by his vines were also singed as the electricity ran through them.

I signaled again, and a fresh flood of water poured from the skies in sheets so thick, I could barely see through them. This time, however, the temperature dropped, and icy wind kissed my skin as my Adamas soldiers and I turned the drenched guards to solid ice. A wave of bolts from the aerial fleet came down on them and shattered the frozen Iris guards into pieces.

Each slash of my sword cut through our enemies, but it'd started to feel as if their reinforcements were never ending. I shook my head, wondering how much of our fight was being tampered with illusion. The Iris seemed to have caught on to our methods and were countering with their own elements.

We'd almost cleared a path to the palatium when the earth rose up in a wave and shoved a line of our soldiers off the side of the mountain, their falling screams echoing in the canyon. Before I could react, aquilas swooped down from above and dove into the chasm. Stars willing, they could save some of them.

We were surrounded. The Iris guards had managed to box my cabala and me in, and we stood back to back, the clang of our swords and spears ringing through the air. A fresh wave of Iris emerged from the palatium, and for each soldier we cut down, two took their place. They had completely blocked us off from reinforcements of our own. We were not going to make it out of this.

"I hate to be the bearer of bad news, but we're kind of outnumbered here," Helio grunted as he threw up walls of earth to block the Iris, hoping for a short reprieve. He wiped at the sweat dripping into his eyes as he strained to keep the Iris from crumbling the wall.

"It's been an honor, my friends," Kairi replied as she blocked blows from above with a shield of air.

"If we're going down, you can count on me taking out as many as I can before it's over," Helio said through gritted teeth.

"I love you, guys," Glint said, her voice cracking uncharacteristically.

"I couldn't be more proud to fight next to each one of you," I choked out. "We're not down yet. Let's give 'em everything we've got."

With rallying cries, we dropped our elemental shields and started swinging. As though renewed by each other's strength, we tore through countless Iris, a feat of strength in the midst of our demise. Sparks flew as metal met armor. Fire, water, earth, wind, and lightning collided in flashes of light as we fought for our freedom—fought for Esterra.

"Kairi!" Glint screamed as our friend went down. Glint's golden face burned with unholy rage as she lit her body aflame and crashed into the Iris guards. The smell of burnt flesh filled the air along with the guards' agonized screams.

I roared, summoning every last breath of source in my body, and sent an electrical blast toward the first line of guards as I rushed toward Kairi, who was attempting to crawl to safety. Kneeling beside her, I gripped her bloody hands in mine, trying to ignore how blue her lips were from loss of blood.

"Don't you dare give up now," I commanded.

She let out a gasp, and her eyes widened as she looked past me. I spun almost a moment too late as a spear meant for my heart pierced my left shoulder. The pain burned through me, but I bellowed and rushed the guard, who still held the end of the spear, sinking it deeper into my shoulder, my left arm hanging uselessly at my side. Using the force of my element, my right fist made contact with the guard's face. The sickening crunch of bone reverberated through my arm, crushing his skull inward into his brain.

The butt of the spear still embedded into my shoulder, I let out a grunt as I pushed it with my right hand. I needed to get it out. Stars knew what poisons or spells it was coated with.

Glint rushed over and helped pull the rest of the spear out from the back, and I curled forward in a mix of relief and agonizing pain.

"I'm sorry, Wynn, but this is going to hurt even more."

"Just do it," I grunted.

She placed her hands on both sides of my shoulder. Burning pain licked through my entire body as she cauterized the wound.

"Thanks," I panted. "See if you can help Kairi. I'll try to hold them off."

Glint's brow furrowed, but she didn't argue, and I gripped my sword, trying to ignore my useless arm as I readied my stance to meet the Iris reinforcements. There were too many of them—without Kairi and with my injury, there was no way we were flying out of here.

If this was it, I'd make it count. My only regret was that I hadn't once told Ari I loved her. I'd wanted to give her space to heal, to wait and see if she'd give us another chance, but perhaps it was not meant to be.

I let out a growl as the first guard swung his sword at me and I parried. Before he could make his next move, the ground began to shake beneath us. Another earthquake?

No, it was the rumbling of feet pounding the earth and a thousand voices rallying toward us. It was the sound of an army. Had the rest of our forces finally pushed through?

The roar of shadow fangs pierced the air, and I looked to the destroyed arena. A thousand elementals charged toward us across the narrow bridge. My eyes widened in disbelief. Was this the nameless army Aella had been trying to raise? She'd been so convinced that all the work she'd done had been for nothing. A giant swell of pride rose within me.

Fearlessly, they charged toward the Iris, slamming into their ranks. Helio let out a loud whoop as he used the earth to direct the remaining Iris toward the oncoming horde.

I threw up a quick thank you to the stars and to my brilliant daughter for unknowingly saving our arses at the final moment.

With renewed strength, we pushed back. The Iris' gleeful expressions turned to terror as an Aereus on a giant basilisk crashed into the ranks. The acid-tipped fangs of the giant serpent tore into the Iris guards while a shadow fang made quick work of another. The sight was gruesome, but there was an irony to seeing the Iris cut down by the very beasts they had used to torment and murder elementals.

Crashing to my knees, my sword hit the ground. It was almost over. The Palatium Crystalis would be ours—we just needed to take care of So-lanos and Kaleidos. A wave of dizziness swept over me, and I blinked. *Faex.* My shoulder was bleeding again, and I'd lost more blood than I'd thought. My heart raced as I looked around for my cabala. Helio and Glint were charging into the palatium's crumbled doors with the hoards of elementals, shouting commands to search for the king, the prince, and every last Iris courtier lest they try to escape. I froze. If Glint wasn't with Kairi . . . My gaze swept to where she lay still on the ground. *No.* I needed to get back to her—I wouldn't lose another one of my cabala. I refused. Groaning, I shoved myself back to my feet and staggered toward her.

"Kairi," I choked. She didn't move. "Kairi!" I cried louder. Nothing. Tears flooded my vision as I knelt next to her and gently pushed her matted hair out of her face. She almost looked peaceful, as if she were asleep. I wept at the loss—another friend taken too soon.

Everything hurt, and black spots danced in front of my eyes. I tried blinking them away along with the tears, but my body was heavy and useless. Suddenly, I was staring up at the night sky. Had I fallen? My racing heart slowed as though it too were tired. So tired. Sluggish in my chest. Perhaps this was the end.

It's okay. We won. Our people will be free. Ari and Aella will make it out of this.

Darkness fell, and I knew no more.

"Wynn! Wynn. Come on. Please." A familiar voice pulled me out of the darkness. "Don't you dare leave me," the voice commanded.

I blinked, groaning as everything came rushing back. The searing pain in my shoulder had dulled to an ache. The sky was still blanketed with stars—I must not have been out too long—but the forecourt was eerily silent. I blinked again, and the most beautiful face came into focus.

"Still sure you're not a star in disguise?" I rasped, my throat dry.

A strangled sob came out of her as she threw herself onto me, burying her face in my chest. "Faex, Wynn. I thought I'd lost you. Again."

My right arm snaked around her waist, and I held her as she cried, her nearness a soothing balm to my soul. I didn't want to let her go.

When she pulled away, I mourned the loss of her touch but allowed her to help me sit up.

"What happened? Rik? Is he all right?" I asked.

"He'll survive. He's mad he's 'missing out on all the fun,'" she said with a sigh. "I'm so sorry about Kairi."

I winced, the loss too raw. "Me too . . ."

Ari gently probed at my shoulder, sending healing energy into it. "The king is dead."

My eyes widened. "Did I hear you correctly?"

"Helio and Glint breached the palatium after the battle and found Solanos dead underneath one of his giant cats."

"Huh. I have to admit, I'm a little disappointed."

Ari frowned. "Why in the depths would you say that?"

"I was looking forward to beating that monster."

"You're in absolutely no shape to be beating anyone right now."

"If you say so." I grimaced as I stood. "Any word on Aella? I thought she was headed this way."

Ari bit her lip and frowned. "She's not in the palatium as far as we can tell, though someone said they spotted Ferathor circling above."

I gently brushed her hair behind her ear. "We'll find her."

CHAPTER 64

THE ABYSS

AELLA

Weightless, I opened my eyes to find I was floating alone in an endless, dark abyss. All the sounds of the ocean and war had disappeared. The boat was gone, and I was completely isolated, surrounded by nothingness, just a deep, fathomless black. Had I died with him? I looked down at my palms, which were now clean of blood.

"Kaleidos?" I shouted into the darkness. "Is anyone there?"

"My little whirlwind," came a deep voice.

I spun around and saw Kal walking off with a female with silver skin, glowing like a star. I tried to run after them, but the leaps and strides of my feet brought me no closer. I folded over, panting from exertion.

"It's not your time yet, little one," came that familiar voice.

I spun once more in search of that low, comforting voice. A voice I hadn't ever expected to hear again. My eyes blurred with tears at the sight of him, memories of losing him still too fresh.

"Papa?"

My father reached out, embracing me in his big, strong arms. I sobbed as he held me. Pride and joy emanated from him, and my whole childhood came back to me in a string of memories as seen through his eyes. Every shared laugh and comforted tear, all the way up to his lessons on spearfishing and self-defense. It was as though he was showing me every memory of my life he'd cherished and clung on to. Even the moments I wasn't proud of or the times I thought I'd been a disappointment were colored through a lens of love and empathy. When I'd terrorized my parents as a child, gotten caught sneaking out at night, my first heartbreak, he'd been there.

He hummed lullabies into the top of my head, and I cried, really cried, finally releasing all the sadness I'd been repressing since I'd lost him.

"Why did you have to leave us? I wasn't ready . . . I still need you." I inhaled deeply, taking in the scent of him, of home and safety and family. "Why did you go in Wynn's place? Why couldn't you have let him make the trade?" I looked up at him, searching.

"It was only right that it was me. You are *my* daughter after all."

"You knew the risk, and you chose it anyway. Knowing you'd leave us all behind."

"Your mother and I, we've always been a good team. She knows it was for the greater good. I know trust doesn't come easily, but I'm asking you to try."

I looked away to conceal the lingering hurt from all the secrets.

"Give her a chance, Aella. And Wynn too." He winked.

"It doesn't feel right, moving on without you."

"But you're not. Moving on does not mean leaving me behind."

And then there was more. He showed me reuniting with my friends in Concordia, learning to fly with Wynn, bonding with Ferathor, and training with my mother. He showed me visions of my strength and courage, flying into battle, and even my escape with Uncle Tal. He was showing me that he'd never left me, that he was still watching over me.

He set his hands on my shoulders. "I'm cheering you on, little whirlwind. With every wave you ride . . . or gale you soar on." His eyes crinkled at the corners. "I will always be with you, even from the stars."

I nodded, wiping away tears.

"You don't have to be strong all the time. Just remember, whatever you choose, I support you." He closed his eyes for a moment, then reopened them, his brows pinching together and rising slightly as he gave me a soft smile. "It's time to go back."

"Wait, don't leave me again."

"You need to go, Aella. You're needed for what comes next."

"I can't . . . I don't want to. I won't." I pointed in the direction of where Kal and the Argenti female had gone. "If he stays here, I must too. We are bound together."

My father shook his head. "He is Iris royalty. He will need to answer for his people's crimes."

"But, Papa, I love him."

He gave me a sad look. "Sacrifices must be made—there are some things even *we* cannot interfere with."

I furrowed my brows. "Please. Maybe we were wrong about the prophecy. Don't I get a choice in the matter? Isn't that what was foretold? How can more death be the answer?" I squeezed my eyes shut as I thought of my family and my people. I had responsibilities. I needed to end this war. I needed to help heal the world after. But what of the Iris? We couldn't just kill or imprison them all. If we did, we would be just as bad as them.

"What if I choose forgiveness?" I asked.

"You always have a choice."

"Okay." I blinked away tears. "Okay."

My father reached out, one final embrace, encompassed in his never-ending love. And just like that, he was gone, leaving me alone again in the darkness. I closed my eyes, thinking of Kal once more. *It's not his time yet either.*

Then I was falling.

CHAPTER 65

No Redemption for the Wicked

AELLA

"The stars have come to an agreement. All Iris must die to restore peace and balance on Esterra," I said to the young Iris prince standing before me.

"I understand most of us are not redeemable, but are there truly none worth saving? What of the young—those who have not yet learned wickedness? Should they too be blamed?" he asked, his green eyes pleading with mine.

"If only you knew your own history, you would understand there is no such thing as an Esterra-born Iris without a seed of evil in their hearts, watered daily by your culture of envy and hatred. You can't undo this curse on your people based on goodwill alone."

"Then tell me, how have we come to this point? How has our history condemned us?"

"The story as it has been told, the story you think you know, is false. For while there is always more than one side to a story, there is also truth." I stepped toward the prince, whose face carried the weight of the world, every regret and every sadness written plainly across it. In this realm, there was no facade—thoughts and emotions roamed freely without guard. He couldn't hide his shame if he wanted to.

"Are you sure you want to know? The knowledge comes at a cost, adding to your burden. By accepting these memories, these crimes become your own," I warned.

"There is no salvation for me if I cannot find a way to save my people."

"Why do you care to save your wretched people?"

"They may be wretched and unworthy, but I would not condemn them all without also condemning myself. While I may not stand before you to decide who lives or dies, I fiercely believe we must give them another chance. The least I can do is try." He knelt before me. "Do as you must so I can make the right choice."

Placing my hand upon his head, I infused him with stardust, every crystalized memory embedding itself into his mind so he could experience them as though they were part of his own lived story.

"*In the beginning, Esterra was a continent divided. The four races of elemental fae belonged each to their own respective corners, content in their ways and in their ignorance of each other. Water knew only water, fire knew only fire, and so forth. It was not until the Lux Verax made their descent upon the land that they learned more was outside of their small worlds . . .*" I began, recounting the true history of the Iris—the Lux Verax, as known by the stars. It played before him as if they were his own memories, his own life, implanting into him, into all of his being, all the way down to his cursed soul, if there was anything left of it.

"So, you see, born of wickedness and lies, nothing good can come from you." I removed my hand from his head, and he slowly came to stand.

The young male rubbed at his temples, wincing his eyes shut as if to squeeze away the pain of what he'd just endured. It saddened me to see him take on so much more than he already carried, that there was nothing I could do to protect him. It was he who needed to save himself. I could only pray the truth was enough, but time was running out, and a twinge of panic set in. As though he sensed my need, my other half appeared, stabilizing and strengthening me with his presence.

"You've got this," he reassured me.

"What if you gave them a warning, a message?" the prince asked, pacing now. "Granted them a chance to change? Surely, with the king fallen and the elementals triumphant, my people shall be humbled enough to amend their ways."

"Do you think we haven't tried to warn you with prophecies and signs? You've had millennia to change but have only progressively become worse. Haven't you also seen what hatred defeat ignites in your kind? The Iris have had many chances and failed all of them. Besides, only a handful of Iris managed to take over Esterra all those years ago—what makes you think it won't happen again?" I berated him.

"I thought I had a choice," the young male demanded, anger coloring his tone. When he noticed my mate beside me, his expression faltered until he realized who he was to me. His gaze shifted restlessly between the two of us.

My mate nodded to me before disappearing again. My task was complete, and it was time to lift the veil, allowing recognition between us. Like a key opening the lock to a forbidden place in my mind, everything came flooding back all at once. I blinked as I stared at the prince before me. I could see him as a child and the grown male that he now was, as a baby and as an adolescent. Flickering through his various life stages like a picture book of memories playing out before me, of what I'd known and what I'd missed out on. I choked on a sob as all the feelings of loving him rushed over me.

As though he too had been unlocked, Kaleidos fell to his knees, speechless.

"I've thought of this moment for so long," I whispered. "And now I can't think of a single word that could come close to expressing the guilt I feel over leaving you all those years ago."

He looked up through disheveled hair and glassy, red eyes. "But your blood is on my hands for my weakness. I failed to protect you from my father." His words became choked. "Forgive me, Mother, for not keeping you safe."

I dropped to his level, wrapping him in a warm embrace.

"My boy, my beautiful, precious boy. That was not your fault. You hear me?" I drew back, still holding him by the shoulders. He was a grown male now, but I'd forever see my kind, sweet boy looking back at me. "Listen to me, my son. We don't have much time left, but you can make things right. Although it comes with great sacrifice, there is still hope."

CHAPTER 66
You Look Different

AELLA

Breath filled my lungs, and a heart beat beneath mine. I opened my eyes, drawing back as warmth flowed back into my flesh. There he was, Kaleidos, my love. The wound in his chest suturing closed, the color returning to his lips. Jewel-like green eyes fluttered open to meet mine.

Where his iridescent veins of marbling had once been, only the deepest black remained, so dark, they seemed to absorb all light in their vicinity, the radiance of his skin muted and matte as though he'd lost all his luster. Even his green eyes had what looked like black ribbons in place of the metallic ones woven in through the irises.

"You're all right!" I cried.

"You can't get rid of me that easily." He gazed up at me with that cocky, stupid smile of his, and I kissed him wholeheartedly, drawing back briefly to take him in again, still shocked he was alive and well and here with me after I'd been so afraid I'd lost him.

"What's this new expression you wear?" He stroked a thumb along my cheek.

"You look . . . well . . . different." I bit my lower lip, holding back a nervous laugh. I wasn't sure how he'd take learning he'd lost all his coveted iridescence.

"Stars have mercy. What have they done to me? Is it bad?" He sat up to inspect himself, terror flashing in his eyes when he noticed his hands, then swiftly shoved them into his pockets. "That is going to take some getting used to," he said with a false laugh, attempting to downplay his momentary panic.

"I don't know, I think I like it," I said.

"You do?" he responded way too quickly.

I nodded with a smile. "It's unusual, but striking . . . Mysterious even."

"I suppose I can live with it." He sighed.

"You're ridiculous. We just died and came back to life and you're worried about your appearance."

"Never underestimate the power of good looks, Tempest. Now, you may want to remove the protective barrier you've placed over us, because that male looks like he's about to pop a blood vessel."

I turned to see Uncle Tal, who appeared to be shouting at the top of his lungs, waving his arms at us and banging on the barrier furiously. *Oops.*

"I'm so sorry. I don't even know how I did that," I apologized as the invisible barrier dissolved.

"I swear to the stars, Aella, I thought I was going to have to tell your mother I'd lost you too . . . I looked back and you were both unconscious. I didn't remember you being injured when you swam to the boat." He gestured toward Kal. "I thought maybe the prince had done something to you and started to panic." He ran his hands through his hair. "Then you were awake again with a sort of forcefield around you. Faex. Verus told me you were *different,* but I never imagined . . . Are you part *Iris* or something?" he asked the last part quietly, as though nervous he might somehow offend me or the prince.

Kal and I both laughed, then said in unison, "No."

"Thank the stormy seas, because I'm probably already in the deep bringing back one Iris. Aella, sweetheart, your father was like a brother to me, but I sure hope one of you has a plan."

"I do," we both responded, and I looked at Kal. "Stop doing that—it's weird."

"Yeah, it's super creepy, not gonna lie," Uncle Tal added.

Kal stroked the side of my face. "Aella, my darling, we need to return to the palatium. I've made a bargain with the stars to set things right, to restore balance in Esterra."

I nodded to Uncle Tal, and he turned the boat around.

On our way back to the Palatium Crystalis, though the storms and battle were simmering down, the waters were still in chaos between the floating remains of wrecked ships and the surviving Iverian and Iris fleets. I could hardly believe we'd made it out undetected, and I had no clue how we'd get back in without help. But asking for assistance wouldn't be easy, because there was no guarantee they wouldn't attack us the moment they saw Kaleidos.

He glamoured our boat to blend in as we navigated the treacherous waters, but we weren't making much headway. When I spotted Ferathor circling overhead, I took a sharp inhale, realizing how relieved I was to see him after I had dove into the palatium earlier that night.

I squeezed Kal's hand and called to my aquila with a trilling whistle. Ferathor landed on a rocky sea stack close by.

"Uncle, this is where I leave you." I gave him a heartfelt hug.

"If you get in trouble for this, I had nothing to do with it," he joked.

"Thank you, for everything."

"Anything for you, kid."

Kal showed my uncle his gratitude with a slight nod, but Uncle Tal pulled him in for a hug with a pat on the back and whispered something in his ear, which, if I were to guess, was probably aimed at making the prince soil his pants. Kal clearly had no idea how to respond, and all I could do was laugh and shake my head as he looked at me for a clue.

Before my uncle did anything else embarrassing, I grabbed Kal's hand,

and we dove out of the small boat toward the rocks jutting from the water, where Ferathor waited for us.

"Ever dreamed of flying on an aquila?"

By the time we made it to the Palatium Crystalis, we were completely surrounded.

"Hold your fire! He is under my protection!" I ordered as we dismounted Ferathor.

The rebel guards gave us wary looks, their weapons still trained on us.

"How do we know you haven't betrayed us? What are you doing with the Iris prince?"

I tore Solanos' sovereign ring from my neck, showing it to them. "You want proof? I faced Solanos, and now he's dead. Kaleidos Stellaris is on our side." My voice was full of power as it carried on the wind to all those around us. "Now escort me to our leaders."

Kal squeezed my hand. "I quite enjoy seeing this side of you. I always knew you had it in you."

I rolled my eyes, then let them linger on him again, taking in the dark veins that cut through his complexion like cracked stone filled with the fathomless black of night.

Cursed, yet somehow, he still manages to make it look good.

All eyes were on us as we strode through the Palatium Crystalis' conquered gates, star-cursed and star-blessed, hand in hand. Clearly they had no idea what to make of Kal with his new look either.

I couldn't miss his haunted expression as he took in the sight of his ruined home with splintered and cracked marble, missing chunks of wall and floor, and ceiling open to the early light of the pink and violet heavens above.

Exhausted from war efforts, it appeared few had been delegated to securing the structures that had fallen from the massive earthquakes the earth elementals had rocked through Prisma. The palatium had seen better days, but it had held up pretty well considering. All could be repaired in time.

At the entrance to one of the ballrooms, Jara was assisting in triage. One might have thought she was a seasoned healer by her quick assessments and delegations. Until her eyes landed on us and she flinched back at the sight of Kal.

"What is it? Do I have dirt on my face or something?" Kal made a show of examining himself.

"Why is he still alive? Why isn't he in custody? Or dead?" Jara asked, completely ignoring Kal's questions. Her tone was full of accusation and suspicion.

He almost answered, but I shot him a silencing look.

"Kaleidos is not our enemy," I said, stepping between them.

"Are you sure?" she asked.

"He has as much blood on his hands as the rest of them, but Kaleidos rallied against his own people. I think that should count for something."

Jara folded her arms, shifting her weight. "Is that the king's royal signet hanging from your neck?"

"Yes, I took it after I watched him die."

"Faex, girl! Tell me, was it by your spear?"

"Shadow fang." I sighed.

Jara huffed, the irony clearly not lost on her.

I turned to Kal. "Any idea how the shadow fang got in there?"

He inspected his nails. "It seemed like a fitting end to his reign. I may have orchestrated a little internal collapse . . . with the assistance of a few . . . nameless friends and Iris allies."

"They would be your only friends," Jara said, finally addressing Kal. "And to answer your earlier question, yes, you look like you've been dropped from an aquila." She eyed him up and down skeptically, then moved her gaze back over to me. "I'd get that looked at. Make sure it isn't contagious or something."

"That's a good sign," I said, squeezing Kal's hand.

"Are you saying I still have a chance with her?" he teased, and I narrowed my eyes at him.

A moment later, my mother rushed out of the ballroom, tearing off her bloody apron as she sidestepped a fallen pillar, pausing to steady herself during the aftershock that rippled through the palatium.

After it passed, she ran to me. "Aella!" She pulled me into a tight hug before holding me at arm's length, scanning me urgently and fussing over every little scratch.

"I'm okay, Mama. Save your energy for those who need it."

She looked at Kal then, and I could tell she instantly picked up on how he stood protectively near me.

"Is everyone here?" I asked. "Kal requires an audience with the leaders."

CHAPTER 67

DARK MATTER

KALEIDOS

In the dead king's councilroom, I stood at the pointed end of the triangular table once more. The three sides were crowded with leaders from the four courts of Esterra, their own council behind them. All eyes were on me and my bride as I stood trial for the Iris while whispered speculations made their way through the room. Aella stroked her thumb across the back of my hand, reminding me of her support. My once luminously marbled skin was adorned with the same markings but of darkest night, like the cracks that now riddled the walls and floors of my home. Aella's sparkling, silver skin contrasted with mine as fine tendrils of light pulsed and raced over hers.

"As I stand before you, I will not deny your accusations. I come of my own accord with a willingness to accept guilt for crimes committed against you. Convict me as you may—all I ask in return is for you to spare my people. Let me bear the burden of our collective misdeeds, for I am their leader. It falls on me to correct the wrongs. And when it is finished—"

"Why are we even entertaining this nonsense?" the Argenti leader interjected. "He was the prince, for the stars' sakes. I don't trust a word out of his mouth."

"He's not the king. Why should he take all of the blame?" one of the Aereus leaders added.

"I think it's fair—he's heir to the throne. He got all of the privileges when he was prince. Let him face the consequences now that he's fallen," said the Aurum leader.

"One male cannot serve all their sentences! Even if he were a king, it's not enough!" the Argenti leader argued.

The room erupted in a cacophony of voices and opinions, arguing what to do with the Iris, what to do with me. I cleared my throat to interrupt, annoyed at having been cut off to begin with.

"There is more . . ." I said, but none paused to listen.

Aella, sensing my frustration, used her air powers to make her voice boom and carry throughout the crowded space. "Would you so quickly judge he who killed the king yet makes no claim for his father's throne? He who kept your prophesied one safe and orchestrated her escape? Allow Kaleidos to speak."

The room hushed, and the king of the Court of Air, Aella's father, turned his attention to me. "Speak, prince. If Aella thinks you have something of value to offer, we will hear you out."

I straightened, adjusting the bloodied and frayed hems of my sleeves, unable to hold in a sigh at the unfortunate state of my attire.

"Of value to yourselves mostly, so yes, you may care to listen," I drawled, my tone laced with humorless sarcasm. "As I was saying . . . the stars themselves have cursed me with the task of restoring balance in Esterra." I held my hand up in demonstration.

I leaned in, resting my forearms casually on the table so I might see eye to eye with those sitting there, slowly taking in each and every member's face before landing back on Aella's father's. I spoke carefully then, enunciating each word, noting the impact my nearness had on them. Some couldn't help but shrivel away. "I believe it will satisfy your concerns of fairness and retribution."

I stepped back and took up my position next to Aella, *my* Aella, finding strength in the powerful female beside me. The stars had given me a choice, and I'd accepted—this fate inescapable. I was hers and she was mine, but I didn't want to share this burden. As if sensing my unspoken fear, she squeezed my hand, a sad smile crossing her face.

Returning my attention to the gathering, I concluded my declaration. "Once my task is complete, we will leave this world and return from whence we came."

"Bring forth the Iris prisoners," Aella ordered, and a small group of Iris waddled in, their strides restricted by iron chains. Aella bore a pained look in her eyes as she took in the sight of them shackled as she had once been. She waved her hand before the council. "See for yourselves."

Here goes nothing.

The first prisoner I approached was Gaelor in his heavy Faber Ludi robes. Without even touching the male, my new powers seemed to reach beyond me. Like a black hole, all of the Iris standing within a seven foot radius fell, screaming as all elemental source was ripped out of them, leaching their radiance out and into me. Pain and irrational fear sliced through every inch of me, and I was unsure what would happen next, how long this would last, or if I could even withstand it. But I had to—the stars had ordained it.

I held my breath, fighting with everything in me not to run from this wretched curse. Muscles spasmed and tensed all over my body, my heart racing to the point I considered it might just stop to free itself from the torture.

What had I been thinking, agreeing to this?

Do I truly have the strength to see this through with all surviving Iris?

Just as I couldn't take it a moment more, Aella's grip on my hand tightened, anchoring me back to where I stood. Pulling me from the terrible thoughts and feelings funneling into me from the Iris captives.

I gasped as it all came to a halt, taking a moment to collect myself. I held back the urge to sit down and retire after what felt like a tremendous amount of exertion I wasn't sure I'd recover from. But it was over. A shiver ran over me.

The Iris prisoners got up slowly, examining themselves. They looked at each other, mouths open wide, aghast.

"Gray?!" a female exclaimed as she observed that the once shimmering and iridescent rainbow of marbling in her skin had faded to shades of matte gray on a dull, non-metallic complexion. As though too stunned to say another word, she kept repeating herself like a town crier. "Gray . . . Gray?"

Gaelor lay helplessly on the floor, as though he'd lost all fight and would need to be carried out of the councilroom.

"Can they no longer wield source?" Aella's father asked with a furrowed brow.

"They are rendered mortal and without access to source or aether," I replied.

"And where does it all go? Into you? Is that even safe?" Arianwen asked.

"It is drawn in through me and released back to the stars for them to distribute as they deem fit," I said.

"If this is the will of the stars, then we should abide by it," one of Aereus leaders declared.

"Hear, hear!" voices echoed in agreement.

"Still, this does not solve the matter of the prince's punishment," the Argenti leader complained.

"Did you not see the suffering he endured while serving us just now? That was only a small number of Iris! There are still thousands more. Consider yourselves lucky he has even agreed to this!" Aella said, baring her teeth.

My fierce little tempest.

"And will you go with him when he leaves? Iris sympathizers have no place here!" the male spat.

Aella looked to her mother, whose color was leaching from her face, as though she already knew the answer, before looking back to me.

“Wherever he goes, I go.”

CHAPTER 68

THE KEY

VIERA

Walking through the destruction of the Palatium Crystalis, I was filled with a sense of melancholy. The gilded halls glimmered with the rising of the sun yet were marred by the spatter of blood and remains. I skirted the areas of the floor where cracks splintered through the marble from the earthquakes that had damaged the foundation. Sections of the palatium would need to be torn down and rebuilt.

It was over. Finally over. Why then did I feel such a sense of loss? A lack of belonging? When Kaleidos had brought me back from the edge of oblivion so many months ago, I had fallen into a hole of depression. I'd been so close to finding peace before it'd been painfully wrenched from me as my soul had been forced back into my broken body. Even after the stars had reversed the damage, nothing had felt quite the same. There was something living in my veins that differed from the source power of my element.

The prince had assigned me to a lower-ranking Iris family. I'd been lucky they were kinder than most, but servitude was a soul-sucking labor, and my lack of purpose had left me feeling adrift. Everyone had thought I'd been dead, so I'd become no one. I might as well have been made nameless. I remembered shearing the long, beautiful hair I'd once prized. It didn't matter anymore. I wasn't the same girl who'd left Iveria with intention and a plan.

The Iris king had stolen so much, and I shuddered when memories surfaced of the role I'd had to play . . . There was no returning to my former life.

I'd gotten momentary relief in Concordia, renewed motivation as we'd planned for our attack, but it was all over now. With the defeat of the Iris, what more was left for me?

I followed voices to the once magnificent throne room. From the looks of it, the leaders of the rebellion were gathered once again to discuss the next steps after the prince had explained the stars' plan for the Iris.

A weight on my shoulders lifted as I saw the familiar faces of my friends involved in the planning. Auntie Ari stood near Aella's father—it was still so odd to think of him as that.

I crinkled my nose in disgust as my own father seated himself on Solanos' throne, the lust for power gleaming in his eyes.

"The throne doesn't suit you, Father," I remarked.

"Viera, so glad to see you survived the battle," he replied, his annoyance with me evident only in the flex of his hands as he gripped the armrests.

"Get your arse off that throne, Lucris," Wynn drawled. "We may have promised you the Court of Water, but here, you have no more power than I."

"Calm yourself, Wynn," my father replied, his voice dripping with condescension. "I'm taking notes for one of my own."

Wynn rolled his eyes and muttered something under his breath. My father would be insufferable with that much power to abuse. He was selfish to the core—the last thing my people needed during a time like this.

My father leaned back, his legs spread wide in an irreverent manner, possessively running his hands along the sides of the throne. He stiffened suddenly when a hidden drawer popped open. "My, my, what do we have here?" Peering into the compartment, his brows bunched together.

A sudden realization came over me, and I cried out, "Father, don't!" then watched in horror as he pulled out the plain-looking key. I'd seen Solanos use it on my friends, and despite my father's deplorable qualities, my heart lurched the moment he disappeared in front of my eyes.

The key clattered to the floor, and my father blinked, staggering off the throne. "What's going on? Where am I? What . . ." he sputtered, looking around.

"No one touch that key," I commanded and took a step toward the confused male. "Father—"

"Am I supposed to know who you are?"

Surprised at the emotion welling up, I took another step toward him, reaching to touch his arm. "It's me, Viera. Your daughter."

He flinched away from me. "I have no daughter." His eyes scanned the space, taking in our bloodied and battered appearances. "What's going on? What is this place?" He shuffled backward.

The Palatium groaned and the earth rumbled with another small aftershock, my arms flying out for balance.

"It's okay. We'll figure this out." My voice broke as I tried and failed to stay calm, bracing myself with a wide stance on the unsteady floor. Why was he in such a state? None of the girls I'd seen turned nameless had reacted this way. Was that because they'd already been broken in spirit? Was it possible to fight the effects of the key?

Another aftershock rolled through, and the cracks in the floor suddenly split open beneath his feet.

It was as if time stood still, and I watched in slow motion as he pinwheeled his arms before dropping through the crumbling stone. Wynn and another male rushed toward him, but they were too late. Falling through the hole, my father screamed, then went silent with a sickening thud.

Time caught up with me, and I found myself numbly walking to the edge and peering down. My father's lifeless body lay in a heap, an iron bar jutting through his chest.

Someone grasped my arms and pulled me away. "Viera, don't look," Lewenne said.

I shook my head. While my relationship with my father had been icy at best, I hadn't wished him dead. "It all happened so fast . . . I can't . . ."

Lewenne squeezed me tightly, and I blinked back tears when Jara and Ona ran over, concern etched on their faces.

"Where's Aella?" I asked, my eyes scanning the room as I pulled out of Lewenne's embrace.

Jara shrugged. "I haven't seen her in a while. I think she went off with the prince to find more Iris to suck the life out of."

"Jara," Lewenne reprimanded. "No need to be so callous about it."

I shuddered, taking a deep breath. Tears could come later—not that he deserved them.

The girls pulled me back toward the throne, and I vaguely heard Wynn and the other leaders discussing what to do and how to retrieve my father's body. I thought I heard Auntie Ari expressing concern about us continuing to meet here with the risk of more aftershocks, when my eyes dropped back down to the key.

"What do you think we should do with it?" Lewenne asked, catching my gaze. "Could you bury it, Ona?"

"And risk someone digging it up? I don't want to get anywhere near it," she said. "Why not melt it?"

"Even if we melted it to something new, there's no way of knowing it wouldn't carry the same powers," Jara said.

"What about throwing it into the darkest depths of the sea?" Lewenne pondered. "Surely no one would dare to retrieve it there."

"The possibility of someone giving in to the temptation and using it for their own gain poses too great a risk." I swallowed. "Males like my father . . ." Blinking my eyes shut, I tried to staunch my emotions. "No. No one else should have to suffer losing themselves to it. From the highest mountain peak to the deepest ocean trench, if the key exists, someone could wield it again. If not in our lifetime then another."

"So what do we do?" Ona wondered.

"We need to destroy it." I rolled my shoulders back.

Jara's jaw tightened as her eyes flicked from me to the key lying on the floor. She tilted her chin toward me. "How do you propose we do that? You saw your father. He barely touched the thing and it took him."

"The king had gloves, maybe we can—"

"No!" Lewenne interrupted, her face stricken with fear. "It's far too dangerous. We can't lose you again, Viera."

"I have to do this," I gritted out. "I *can* do this, even if it kills me."

"How?" Jara asked again.

I closed my eyes, searching my body for the foreign essence that had been lying dormant inside me since the prince had brought me back.

There.

Something sparked in my veins, and instead of suppressing it, I welcomed it . . . tried coaxing it out. When I opened my eyes, I looked down at my hands, surprised my vision was as clouded as it had been when I'd come back, but there was something there, almost like an aura hovering over my palms.

I turned my gaze to Jara and said, "Aether."

"Viera!" Ona gasped. "Your eyes!"

"What in the stars," Lewenne breathed.

I reached toward the nameless key on the floor, and it shot into my grasp. The aether crackled all around me, and I screamed as the power of the key started tearing into my mind as if it were a sentient creature—seeking, searching for weakness.

"What has she done?" a male voice called out behind me.

"Stay back!" Jara yelled. "We don't know what will happen if we touch her."

I screamed again, agonizing pain lancing through my hand and all the way up my spine as the key tried to steal the last remaining parts of me, even while aether hummed and glowed. My eyes sought out my friends, and for a moment, panic set in with the realization I no longer knew their names. Memories were being stripped away one by one.

My strength waned, and my knees hit the floor. I couldn't do this. I was going to fail.

"Viera, you're not alone," a solemn voice said as a golden-haired female knelt before me, wrapping her hands around mine, lending me strength.

The key burned brighter in my hand, searing into my skin, and I wept as a warm bronze set of hands wrapped themselves around mine and the other female's. "I am with you too." A grunt of pain came out of them as the key fought back.

A third set of hands rested on top, the silver sparkling in the light shooting out from the key. "I am here."

"Viera," a familiar voice called out, and I looked up. Through the haze of my vision, I saw deep blue eyes speckled with stars. She knelt next to us and placed her hands over ours. "You can do this. Fight it!"

With the strength of my friends surrounding me, I cried out again, pouring all of my source and the foreign aether into the wretched key in our hands. Our elements combined in a surge of power that erupted in a flash, knocking all five of us apart as the key burst into a million fractals of light. A shockwave of energy flared out through the room and beyond.

I watched from above as my body was thrown across the room, flinching when my head crashed against marble, but I felt no pain. Looking down at my hands, I gasped to find they were nearly translucent as I floated higher—my spirit no longer connected to my body.

What in the stars is happening? Have I died again?

As my spirit floated out of the palatium, I gasped at the shockwave of light rippling out toward every corner of Esterra. Cries reached me from the courtyards, and with merely a thought, I was there. A group of servants clung to each other, weeping and shouting—reclaiming their names, declaring their memories had returned. Some danced in joyous celebration while others wept, broken over all the time they had lost and for what they had endured.

I closed my eyes. If this had been my last act on this earth, it had been worth it. I had only hoped to destroy the key, but seeing names restored . . . I didn't have words. We'd won back so many lives. Perhaps the stars had been merciful in this one final feat. But like a tether back into our realm, a hand reached for mine, offering me a way out of the darkness. My best friend, my lifeline.

I blinked, and I was back in my body, utterly disoriented.

"Viera!" Aella cried. "Oh, thank the stars."

I groaned as I touched the back of my head and the rather large lump that was forming. "I'm okay. I'm still me."

"You insanely foolish, brave girl," Jara said with half a grin, then surprisingly pulled me in for a hug.

"You did it! It's gone!" Ona cried tears of joy.

"We released the nameless," I said with a smile as Jara helped me to my feet.

"How do you know?" Lewenne asked.

"I'll explain later—at least, I'll try."

"Stars, Viera, does that hurt?" Ona asked, pointing at my hand.

I looked down and marveled at the key-shaped brand on my palm. "Surprisingly, no . . ."

"Faex, V. I thought I'd lost you again," Aella murmured, throwing her arms around me.

"Apparently the stars aren't done with me yet."

CHAPTER 69

THE LEDGER

AELLA

I found him standing at the bay window in his remarkably preserved bedchamber that overlooked the ruins of Prisma. After draining all the courtly Iris, he needed to rest, but he was still awake, waiting for me to get back. Kal turned to face me, pained sadness reddening his eyes. To see his city on fire, the remnants of battle and so much destruction, it wouldn't have been easy for anyone. It was evident Kal still blamed himself for the suffering of elementals and Iris alike, and there was little I could do to ease that burden.

"Seeing you endure that, Kal . . ." I buried my face into his chest, my grip so tight around him, afraid he might slip away again. As though I might keep him here with me if only I held on tightly enough.

He drew back slightly, locking eyes with mine, his brows raised and bunched together. "How is it we're allowed such a gift? To love and be loved in return. My ancestor was unable to claim it, so he stole it. You, however, have given it to me willingly. Your love and your forgiveness, they've broken a curse over my people. You're the reason we may return home to our world. You've not only saved me but all of us. You've given us a second chance, Aella. One we do not deserve. I struggle to convey the weight of what that means to me."

A small, grateful smile curved my lips, my heart swelling with his words. "Perhaps none of us are blameless." I shrugged. "But I'd like to believe that even the worst of us are redeemable. And that we all might one day laugh, smile, and dance together. That we will live. I only wish the cost weren't so great . . . The task you must now carry out, it's . . ."

"What other choice do I have?" he murmured into my hair.

I nodded, pulling back and looking up at him, brushing his lower lip with my thumb. "They're lucky it's you and not me who rules them."

"Why would you say that?" he asked, then captured my thumb between his teeth.

"You're better than I am."

Kal hummed deeply. "I'm afraid I must disagree with you on that one, but . . . you *do* make me want to be a better male."

"Oh, do I?" I traced my fingers along the black veins that marred his cheek. Rather than leaving him scarred, they seemed to enhance his stunning features. I followed one of the veins down its path to his chest. "I'm not sure I want you to be anything other than what you already are."

"And what is that?"

"Oh, I don't know . . . infuriating and arrogant for starters."

"Tell me more." He gave me a wicked smile while lifting me by the waist.

"You're a brute!" I screamed as he hoisted me over his shoulder and carried me to the bed. "You ridiculous male, put me down!" I laughed. "I can fly, you know. You don't need to carry me around."

"Oh, but it's so much more fun this way, isn't it?" He gave me a little smack on my rear before letting out a sigh and placing me gently on the bed. "And just as I've lost my future as king of Esterra, you've given me a reason to want that again."

"How so?" I asked as he climbed into the bed next to me.

"Only so I could make sure your every wish was granted, every desire fulfilled."

"Mmm, yes, I think you still have some work to do on that last one," I teased.

"Don't tempt me," he purred, pulling me on top of him.

Energy buzzed between us, our powers giving and taking from each other in equal measure. A delicious thrill ran through me from head to toe. Unwittingly, I began to float over him, our connection bringing about a surge in source. Kal wrapped his hands around my waist, pulling me back to his chest.

"Don't you go flying away from me again," he murmured against my lips.

"Stars, Kal, I thought your curse would dull the connection between us, but if anything, it's out of control now."

"I like it." He licked his lips.

"Yeah?"

"Knowing I can fill you up in more ways than one," he said with a smug grin.

I squinted at him, trying to suppress a wicked smile.

"Besides, I have ways I might tether you in case you need an anchor."

"Are you saying you can still make use of the elements?"

"Among other things."

"You're a fiend." I shoved at him playfully.

Then he softened, caressing my face so tenderly, all playfulness gone. "I do not deserve you. How is it I won your heart?"

"I was never some prize to be earned," I replied. "It was I who competed for your love, remember?"

"You never even had to try. I was yours from the very first moment you scolded me."

His words went straight to my heart. I kissed him as though I could give all of myself to him over and over and over again and it would never grow old. I couldn't help but marvel at how lucky we were to have ended up together. Despite everything we'd been through. After all we'd had to overcome. Nothing would come between us. Not even death.

Kal gave back to me in long, languorous kisses as we shared breath, aether, and source. His lips tasted of sweet nectar, as if he himself were the fruit of the stars, making me wild with hunger for him.

"I keep waiting for the moment I wake up from this dream," he whispered across my lips while holding me against himself with his broad, claiming hands. One hand sank into my hair, the other wrapped firmly around my waist. "Like what we have is too perfect to last." He kissed me harder, his breaths coming faster. With a fistful of my hair, he tugged gently, releasing the tension in my scalp. I moaned into his mouth, and he groaned in reply.

"I will fight for you, stand beside you, until my final breath." I sang the words over him. "I would follow you beyond both of our worlds, where not even the stars could find us. But if this truly is nothing more than a dream, I'm content to remain in it with you."

"I know we probably need to get up and make ourselves useful in some way, but I'd rather lie here with you all day," I said wistfully, my head resting atop Kal's chest. "Tell me, who were those friends and allies you mentioned when we spoke with Jara?"

Kal then explained how he'd continued the work we'd started. My theory had been correct—the books had given the nameless something to fight for. Even if they couldn't remember who they'd been, it had been enough to kindle a fire inside them. With help from Nephos, Kal had made his reputation more wicked than ever and rallied the nameless army against himself and the Palatium Crystalis.

"Sometimes it's the little things, isn't it? Small, seemingly insignificant acts that can change the course of destiny," he mused, his fingers tracing the star-shaped birthmark on the back of my neck, making me shiver.

"But it wasn't just the books. It all started with your mother's journal."

Then, as though an idea had popped into his mind, he rolled on top of me, pressing a heavy kiss upon my lips before climbing out of the bed.

I cocked an eyebrow while propping myself up on my elbows, and Kal pulled on a clean pair of low-slung, gray trousers.

"Stay there." He pointed at me.

"You don't have to baby me, you know."

The prince, or whatever he was now, dashed from the room. I couldn't bring myself to call him my groom. I honestly had no idea what to call him except for mine. He *was* mine. I smiled to myself at that thought.

"I'm not following your meaning," he called back from the other room, returning shortly thereafter with a sealed scroll in hand. "This is only the way a king treats his queen after a long—"

"Very long," I interrupted, sitting up quickly and moving toward him as he came to sit on the edge of the bed.

"A *very* long . . . night? Day? Has it been a week? Who can say?" he drawled.

"What is that?" I asked.

"After so much time searching for the name of my mother, after so many dead ends, I'd given up. I couldn't take any more disappointment. And then, after you left, Nephos—stars rest his soul—well, he brought me this." Kal handed me the scroll, its wax seal intact.

"Why haven't you opened it?"

"Because it didn't matter. I didn't . . . I didn't think I would survive for this to hold any meaning. But now . . ." He paused, placing a hand over the scroll in mine. "I wasn't sure if I still needed to know, but I want to. No, scratch that, I do need to know. And if this truly is what I've been searching for, then it will hold some meaning to you as well."

"I don't understand," I said.

"Who did you see in the stars?"

"My father," I said, surprising myself at the ease with which I was able to say it. Kal reached over to squeeze my hand.

"I saw him too," he replied, "but he wasn't alone, Aella. He was with his mate, he was with—"

"Your mother?" I asked, my mind drifting to the female I'd seen Kal go with in the after when we'd been with the stars. *Could it be?* My heart beat faster in my chest at the idea. It meant so much to know my father was at peace with the stars but even more to know he was with his mate. I took a deep, shuddering breath. The thought that he'd been separated from her for all of that time . . . I couldn't imagine the pain. I clutched my hand to my chest, remembering those moments when Kal had been dying.

"This is from Nephos? He found it for you?"

"It had been removed from the archive, but apparently, Nephos kept his own records over the years. He made a point to remember every contestant, even the ones my father wanted erased."

"Knowing her name, Kal . . . I'm lost for words, but this is everything. You must open it."

Kal cracked the seal, slowly unraveling the scroll that contained a ledger of names. My eyes scanned rapidly over the list, looking for something, anything that might stand out, until finally, at the bottom, circled with silver ink, was the name. Kal read it aloud, his voice cracking with emotion. I wrapped my arms around him from behind as he stared at the paper, tears of joy flowing from his eyes, that final piece of the puzzle coming into place for him.

CHAPTER 70
STARS-GIVEN PURPOSE

ARIANWEN

The aftermath of battle, death, and destruction brought about a wealth of emotions. Some elementals celebrated their liberation while others mourned the loss of their family and friends, most did both. I felt as if I'd barely had a moment to breathe in the last week, working from sunup to sundown running the makeshift medical facility in the center of Prisma.

"Ari!" a familiar voice called out behind me.

I turned and smiled at Liisa. "Are you here to relieve me?"

She nodded. "You need to take a break, dear friend."

"Easier said than done. There is so much work to do and preparation that still needs to be completed."

Liisa's eyes brightened. "So it's true? The rumors I've been hearing?"

"I've found new purpose. *This* is what I was made for. I can't go back to Iveria. Too much has changed." I sighed, wringing my hands. "Knowing Aella is leaving . . . rebuilding Concordia feels right. There are so many broken and hurting elementals who need a fresh start, and I think this is what is best for my family."

I swallowed back the swell of emotion, knowing I'd need to explain all that had transpired to my sweet children.

She squeezed my shoulder in understanding. "You definitely have your work cut out for you, but I believe in you. It's a wonderful thing, what you're doing."

"Any chance I can convince you to join me?" I asked hopefully. "I feel like I just got you back."

She reached out, and I met her halfway, hugging her tight. "You never lost me, friend. My place is in Zephyria, but please come visit me any time." Liisa pulled back, wiping a small tear from her cheek. "I'm fairly certain my king would send you an aquila whenever you asked."

"You're not wrong." I gave her a wry smile. "Some distance might be good though . . ."

Liisa sighed. "As long as you're doing it for the right reasons."

I nodded, words failing me.

"Well then, time to go check on our patients," she said, gently patting my back before walking away.

There was a heaviness in my chest—so many goodbyes, so many changes, but they were for the best. The destruction of the nameless key had brought a mass of elementals to the Palatium Crystalis looking for answers. Some desired to return to their families while others couldn't fathom the idea. My heart ached for what they'd been through as their past memories had come flooding back while they retained all the knowledge of what had been done to them in Prisma. The healing of their souls would take time.

When I'd brought up the idea of rebuilding Concordia, I'd been met with support from all of the remaining rebel leaders. Wynn had looked sad, but he'd said nothing to try to sway me. Concordia would once again be a place where any elemental could make a home and live in harmony. My dream was, while change was slow, that all of the courts would open to each other and trade partnerships could be made. Esterra would never be the same, but that was a good thing. If only the changes hadn't come with such sacrifices. I stifled a sob at all I'd lost and still had to lose.

"Ari, are you all right?"

I turned and buried my face in Wynn's chest, my body wracked with emotion. "It hurts . . . it hurts so bad."

He gently cupped the back of my head with one hand while his other wrapped around me in a gentle embrace. "I'm so sorry, Ari. You have no idea."

"I can't believe I'm losing her all over again," I cried.

Wynn held me, murmuring words of comfort while softly running his hand down my back. When the emotion was finally spent, I took a shuddering breath. I hated how much I loved the way his arms felt around me. His soul called to mine, comforting me in a way only a mate's could.

I tilted my head back to look at him, and he gently tucked a stray tendril of hair behind my ear. "I don't want her to leave either. I feel like I barely know her."

"She's fulfilling her stars-given purpose—I can't fault her for that," I said. I took another deep breath, and though it pained me, took a step away from him, hating the hurt look in his eyes that he quickly hid behind a smile.

"How's Rik doing?" he asked.

"He's grumpy like you wouldn't believe." I let out a shaky laugh. "He's the worst patient. I swear, he would sneak out of here and reinjure himself if I didn't keep constant eyes on him."

"I'm sure he'll be happy to return home." Wynn paused, rubbing the back of his neck. "Are *you* ready to head to Zephyria? Your family is waiting . . ."

I looked around the makeshift space that had essentially been my home for the last week. "Yes, I'm ready . . . but also not. The sooner we get there, the sooner we have to say goodbye to Aella."

CHAPTER 71
GOING HOME

AELLA

Icy wind bit at my nose as we hiked up the snowy mountain peak. I pulled the fluffy, white cloak tighter around myself to fend off the cold.

"Anything look similar to what she showed you?" Wynn asked Kal, looking around. Despite his rocky past with my mother, I'd developed a respect for the male. I couldn't help but like him.

As far as mountains were concerned—and I didn't have much experience—this twin peak didn't appear much different from the surrounding alps, except for the way it resembled two mountains nearly joined into one. There were no unusual markings or structures that looked anything like a door, gate, or portal to another world. I searched Kal's expression for any sense or special feeling, but it was evident he was just as lost as the rest of us. Noticing me shiver, he wrapped his arms around me from behind, allowing the warmth of his fire element to lick away at the cold.

"So the stars asked you to bring all of the Iris up here, but they didn't tell you where the door was?" Wynn frowned.

"Are you sure there isn't another possible location?" Kal asked.

Wynn sighed, shaking his head. They'd sent out scouts to search the alps for weeks while we'd been in Prisma draining the remaining Iris of their powers. When they couldn't find the door, they thought if Kal came along, perhaps it would reveal itself in his presence. He'd already searched a dozen other sites with Wynn when I'd asked to join them on their hunt.

"Maybe this means you aren't meant to leave," my mother said with a hopeful smile.

"We can try a few more sites tomorrow, but I'm really not sure what to say." Wynn scratched his head while taking a seat on an old stump. "I know these alps, and this is the most likely spot. Its proximity to the old capital, the shapes of the peaks . . . but we've checked it three times already, and no one can seem to find anything. We may need to start considering an alternative plan for the Iris."

"Tell us again what the stars told you," my mother said to Kal.

While they went back and forth over the exact meanings and histories, cross referencing them with what the Adamas and Iris kept in their archives, I wandered over to sit on a rock. If the stars really wanted us to leave, shouldn't they have made it a little easier to find the door? My legs were aching from the climb. I didn't know how I'd fare if we had many more sites to check.

"Aella, behind you!" Wynn shouted.

I turned to look, when out of nowhere, the mountains opened, revealing the outlines of a door cutting through stone in a glowing rainbow of light. It was marked with an elongated, star-like keyhole at the center, just like the one on the back of my neck. The sign confirmed what Kal had said to me. Impossible as it seemed, I was the key to the Iris' return home, like my fate had been written in the stars since the day I'd been born.

"Are you sure we're not about to become a pair of boiled shrimps?" Mila worried her lip. "There's steam coming off the top!" She gestured toward the clusters of circular, bubbling pools.

"It's perfectly harmless, sister. In fact, the baths in Prisma were a bit like these hot springs."

A spark danced in her eyes. "Really?"

I shook my head with a laugh. "And you were right, they were bigger than our entire house."

"I knew it," she muttered.

We hung our towels, then eased ourselves down into one of the empty pools.

"So? What do you think about this place?"

"About the hot bath?"

I raised my brows and tilted my head with an amused smile—she knew exactly what I was asking about.

Mila raked her fingers back and forth through the bubbling water a few times, then sighed. "I miss home . . . but in a way, staying in a palatium in a secret hidden city in the clouds . . . and then helping to rebuild a legendary lost city . . ." A small smile worked the corner of her lips. "I'm excited to have an adventure of my own."

I smiled back, my heart breaking a little that we had such a short time until Kal and I left for uncharted waters. Mila had already stepped up into my place as the oldest sibling in the year we'd spent apart, and I was so proud of her growth and resilience, but that wouldn't make leaving them hurt any less.

"I can see you getting all sad and sentimental over there. Stop it," Mila commanded, flicking her wrist, and with it, an orb of water aimed for my face.

The water diverted to the left, leaving me unsplattered, and I shook my head, laughing. "Nice try, but you've gotta stop throwing things at me."

"You're good target practice," she teased.

"Your aim is excellent. I'll give you that." At least I wouldn't have to worry as much, knowing she was as feisty and fearless as our own mother.

Mila gave me a wry look. "Seriously though, Aella, we're going to be fine."

"I know."

"I still can't believe you're actually mated to an Iris prince and running away with him."

I couldn't stop the smile that stretched my face. "He's pretty cute, isn't he?"

Mila sighed. "Yeah, I guess . . ."

"Who's the guy you've been dreaming of?"

She stared blankly at me, trying to hide her answer, and I stared right back at her.

"Okay, fine. But I'm not going to tell you who it is because I don't want you to make everything super awkward when we see him again. Let's just say he wields a couple of different elements himself, and he's so nice, Aella. So, so very nice. He's got the best smile, and the most gorgeous coppery blonde hair—"

My eyes widened, and she slapped a hand over my mouth before I could say anything.

"No guessing."

"As you command, little sister." I gave her a knowing look, and she squinted her eyes. "All right, you ready to head out?"

"Actually, I think I quite like the warm water."

"I told you you would. Just don't stay in too long or you'll turn into a raisin."

Mila shrieked, launching herself out of the pool. "A what?!"

I sputtered and laughed, and Mila widened her eyes, looking around. "Faex, Aella, they're never going to let me back in here after this."

Giggles and squeals of joy echoed down the hall as my siblings chased Rat out the door. I huffed a laugh, knowing she enjoyed the little game as much as they did. I'd been determined to sneak in as much time with them as I could before my departure, but it never felt like enough. Alone in my room now, I stood by the mirror as I rehearsed the words I'd been dreading to say.

For the first time in my life, I'd begun to feel truly connected with my mother, getting to know her and forgiving her for everything I'd held against her. I could finally see that none of her secrets had ever really mattered because they hadn't changed who she was at her core. She was beautifully imperfect, and it only made me love her more. Truly, saying goodbye to her would be hardest of all.

But I'd said goodbye before. *This time shouldn't be any more difficult, should it?*

"I must go, Mama. This is what I'm destined for. The stars confirmed it."

"Who are you trying to convince? Me or the mirror?" My mother chuckled as she let herself in.

I spun around to face my mother, who stood gazing lovingly at me from the door, my face burning from embarrassment at being caught rehearsing. Shaking it off, I crossed the distance to embrace her.

"I'm finally starting to really know you . . ."

"You could stay," she said with false hope, and then, as though reading my mind, she continued, "but your mind is made up."

"My mind, my heart, my soul . . . It's the only choice that feels right. That doesn't mean it isn't bittersweet."

"I wish I could convince you to stay." She brushed a lock of hair behind my ear.

"No chance I could convince *you* to join us?" I tried with a choked laugh and led her by the hand to the sitting area by the window with sweeping views of the surrounding alps.

"Someone needs to keep an eye on your siblings. And I think Mila has already fallen head over heels for Liisa's son."

"I knew it was him!" I laughed.

We sat side by side on a big, cozy settee facing the window, and she took my hand in hers, working her magic to calm and soothe my nerves. I could feel my muscles instantly relax, like I could take a deeper breath, like all would be well.

"Oh, to be young and in love." She sighed as she rubbed the pressure points in my palm. "Kaleidos is treating you right? His hands are huge—"

"Mother!" I snatched my hand away to cover my face.

"Faex. I just realized there's no going back. I've fully turned into my mother."

We dissolved into pearls of laughter before she pulled me into her arms in another tight embrace.

"I'll miss you terribly, Aella."

I sighed, trying to memorize her embrace, her scent, and the overall comforting feeling of being around her.

"Are you sure you'll be all right after I leave?" I asked. "I can't believe you're really going to start over in Concordia. The friendships you have here in Zephyria . . . Wynn—"

She pulled back to look me in the eye. "My whole life, I've dreamed of the day the world could come together. I get to be a part of that! I couldn't turn this down even if I wanted to, but I think you understand that feeling."

I lifted my gaze to the heavens, then back to her. "He would want you to be happy."

"I know, Aella. I really do. But my heart just isn't ready to love again." Her voice sounded choked, which made both of us start tearing up once more. "I loved your father so much."

"He loved you too," I said. "Would it give you some comfort to know that he's reunited with his mate now?" I raised my brows, unsure how she would take it. "Lyani."

Her face lit up with surprised affirmation.

"She was Kal's mother," I added.

She paused, taking in the information, then let out a watery chuckle. "The stars sure have an interesting sense of humor!" She squeezed her eyes shut before opening them and rolling her shoulders back. "I'd hoped . . . Thank you, Aella. Thank you for letting me know he's okay."

I nodded. "Well, when you *are* ready, I think you still have an admirer,"

I said, my voice caught between a laugh and a sob. "I've seen the way Wynn looks at you. The way you both look at each other."

She took a deep breath, wiping away the last of her tears. "There's no denying that we share a special bond. But I fixed my broken heart with another once, and this time, it only feels right to mend it myself before giving it away again." She held my face in both of her hands lovingly, and her eyes scanned me as though she too were memorizing my every feature. "I'll be all right, sweetheart. I promise."

I so appreciated the openness and raw honesty we shared, that she wasn't wasting a single one of our final few moments together with false pleasantries. We sat there for a long while, enjoying the view and each other's company. My head rested on her shoulder, her head atop mine. We laughed and we cried some more, and we soaked up our precious time together. And though it would take a long time to heal from all I'd been through, my mother's unconditional love and trust made it just a tiny bit easier to forgive myself for my mistakes and my flaws.

We were beautifully imperfect, and this only made us stronger.

Tears stung my eyes as I smiled at the sight of my friends together for the last time. We sat around a cozy table at Kristel's tavern near the central hearth, where the light of the fire flickered and warmed the space in an orange glow.

"Thank you for coming," I said.

"My presence ought to mean the most," Jara teased, squeezing me from the side.

"Oh, whatever, Jara. At least you can wrap yourself in a bubble of heat!" Ona laughed.

Jara tilted her glass to Ona. "You did have to travel farthest. I'll give you that."

"I'm still not sure why you don't all come help build the new settlement in Concordia with me," Lewenne said as she slammed her empty tankard down onto the table. "We could all be together, just like before the war!"

She nodded as if her enthusiasm would get us all to agree. "More glogg, please!"

I sipped the delicious spiced mulled wine and looked over at Viera, who still hadn't announced her plans to the rest of our friends. She'd been sitting quietly, simply observing, as a subtle smile lifted the corners of her lips.

"So will you be returning to Iveria to lead in your father's place?" Ona asked her.

"Actually, I'll be joining Aella in the new world."

The girls gasped.

"If only I were so brave." Lewenne shook her head.

"Lew, we all heard of how you fought in battle. You're probably the bravest of us all. But the work you'll do in Concordia will benefit all of Esterra," I said.

"Wait, you mean we could have chosen to go with you?" Jara exclaimed.

Viera laughed. "You wouldn't go even if they promised we'd be living in a fireborn mountain!"

Jara nodded in laughter, pointing a finger at Viera. "Now that . . . that's truth."

"We each have our own paths to follow," Viera added graciously.

"I'm so thankful for all of you." I raised my tankard in a toast. "To life, to friendship, and to choosing our own destinies!"

Glasses clinked, and we cheered before filling our bellies with delicious food and more drinks in the crowded tavern. It was an evening full of laughter and lightness as we sang and danced to the tunes of the old bard, who plucked away at the piano. We'd been through so much, it was a miracle, no, a gift that we had found joy and freedom after. It was a unique connection we shared, a bond over mutual suffering and pain. We were the contestants of the final Matri-Ludus. And we'd survived it together.

After long, heartfelt goodbyes to all my family and friends, Kal and I landed on a cliffside atop Ferathor, overlooking the Iris as they disappeared between the gap in the mountains, into the portal we had opened together.

"The stars might guide us, yet I still can't help but wonder what we'll find through that door," Kal remarked.

"Well," I said, "I don't hear anyone screaming, so that's a good sign."

Kal tugged me against him, nipping at my ear.

"I can remedy that if you'd like." He slipped a hand between my thighs, making me gasp.

"Kal!" I yelped. "Not where my father could see us."

"My tempest, my Aella, my darling, my queen, I'll take you anywhere. I don't care who's watching."

"And I'd follow you anywhere, but I'm *not* doing *that* here." I laughed.

Kal smothered my laughter with a kiss that had me melting into him. I turned myself completely around in the saddle to face him, hooking my legs over his, and he cupped my face in his hands, focusing all his attention on me. "Whatever it is, we'll face it together."

"Together," I agreed.

Rat squeaked.

"Yes, yes, we know—you're coming with us too," Kal crooned to the small creature, who poked her head out from a pocket in Ferathor's saddle.

And after the last Iris crossed over along with a few brave and adventurous elemental fae, it was finally our turn.

I didn't know what our future held or what was waiting for us on the other side but with him at my back, I feared nothing.

Hand in hand, star-cursed and star-blessed, we crossed through the portal into a flash of light.

CHAPTER 72

TO BE WHOLE

ARIANWEN

1 year after the Battle for Prisma

The Concordian lake shimmered as I stood admiring the sunset from my favorite dock outside the city. It was hard to believe it had been an entire year since we'd finally defeated the Iris.

The children had taken Verus' loss very hard. At times, I still found myself overcome with heartache, but I was learning to live with it. Sometimes, I didn't know if I'd ever fully recover. Through it all, we leaned on each other, working through our grief and finding purpose despite our pain. Nothing made my mama heart happier than watching my children discover joy again. Seeing them embrace this new world and learn their places in it. If they could be brave, so could I.

Losing Aella had been another grief to bear. I was so incredibly proud of all she'd done and the sacrifices she'd made, but that didn't mean I didn't miss her. I couldn't help but wonder what new adventures she was experiencing in her brand new world. She had found love, and the contentment and excitement flowing through her the last time I'd seen her gave me confidence she'd made the right choice. She was blessed by the stars, and they would continue to watch out for her. This I knew deep in my soul.

Since our move to Concordia, I had thrown all of my heart into helping my family heal and working to rebuild our world. Building something new seemed to be just what I'd needed, but I had to admit that I was lonely.

Walking away from Wynn after the Iris' exodus had been one of the hardest things I'd ever done, but I couldn't even begin to wrap my mind around what he was to me without taking time to recover.

A gentle breeze caressed the back of my neck, and a familiar scent tickled my nose. I closed my eyes for a brief moment, the sudden fluttering in my chest reminding me I could still feel.

"How did you find me?" I asked softly.

"I could find you anywhere," his voice rumbled, sending shivers down my spine as he walked up and stood beside me.

"What brings you to our little blossoming city?"

"Would it be too forward to say I missed you?"

My lips curved up as I looked at him, admiring how the waning sun reflected off his skin. "It's nice, isn't it? To be able to travel without fear of being shot down."

"The world you spoke of—it's finally happening, Ari." His eyes glimmered in awe. He cleared his throat, one hand rifling through his hair. "I hope you know that I'll never forget Verus' sacrifice."

I reached over and grasped his other hand, entwining our fingers. Surprise crossed his face, but he gently squeezed my hand.

"Neither will I . . ." I sighed. "But I don't want to live in the past anymore, Wynn. I'm ready to live and see what we can make of this beautiful new world—I know it's what he would have wanted."

Wonder shone in his eyes as he looked down at me. Almost hesitantly, he tucked one of my unruly curls behind my ear before sliding it to cup my cheek. "I'm sure you'll do amazing things. In fact, what you've done here already is incredible. This is not the same Concordia I left last year, and the reports I've gotten have been filled with so much excitement for the future."

"Thanks, Wynn." I couldn't help the blush that warmed my cheeks. "You've been keeping track, have you?"

"Of course." He grinned.

"Ah, I thought you were too busy helping set up new governments across Esterra."

His eyes lit up. "You've been keeping track, have you?"

Feeling suddenly shy, I tore my eyes from his. My heart had been yearning for his, but with him standing right in front of me, I was afraid. What if he didn't want a second chance? Had there been too much hurt between us?

"Ari." He gently gripped my chin. "Look at me, please."

I locked eyes with him, the sudden intensity sending a new wave of flutters through me.

"All teasing aside, I came here because I needed to tell you, I needed you to know . . ." He smiled, and I could sense the nerves radiating off of him.

"Go on?" I encouraged.

"What did you mean about not living in the past anymore?" His brows knit together. "Does that mean what I think it means?"

Hope welled up within me. "Yes, Wynn. I think it does."

His face broke into the biggest smile. "Ari . . . you're the light in my darkness. My guiding star. When I began to lose hope, you were there. You reminded me what I was fighting for. I was broken and lost, but I've found my way back. I offer you my heart if you'll take it. It was always yours from the start. If you don't feel the same, I will let you go, but I'm here, fighting for you, for our chance. I love you and will never stop until my final breath, and even then."

My heart thundered in my chest as I stared into his icy blue eyes and knew.

He was home.

"Kiss me, Wynn."

He pulled me into a kiss that shattered the remainder of any walls I'd built to keep him out, igniting a passion within me I'd thought might never return. His tongue swept in and carried me away, and I met him stroke for stroke, relishing in the taste and feel of him. He crushed my body to his, and I dug my fingers into his hair, pulling him even closer. Our kiss held a reminder of the past but also hope for a new and brighter future. Wind whipped around me and waves crashed below as our two worlds collided and joined as one.

Pressing soft kisses onto my cheeks and neck, he whispered against my ear, "I'd have waited a lifetime to hear those words. Stars, I thought I might never." He pulled back slightly, his eyes meeting mine. "But from the moment you came running into my life, risking everything for a stranger, you stole my heart. No one could ever take your place. My star . . . my mate."

His hand slid to the nape of my neck, and he leaned his forehead onto mine.

A tear slid down my cheek, and he gently kissed it away. My heart was so full, it felt like it would burst.

He cradled my face in his hands. "I never thought I'd kiss you again . . . Please say you'll be mine. I swear there will be no other."

I turned my face into his palm, gently kissing the spot where our oath once marked it. "Wynn, my mate . . . my love. I'm yours. Forever and always."

And we lived.

THE END

Epilogue

"Are you ready?" Aella asked.

No.

"Yes," I chirped before I could change my mind.

"Hold on tight!" She whistled a trilling call/signal.

Ferathor flapped his broad wings a few times, then leaped from the cliffside. My screams turned into laughter as we glided over shimmering, cerulean seas. So close, I could feel the spray of saltwater dust over my cheeks. I let go of Aella and threw my arms out like wings, feeling the wind swim over my skin. Aether zipped through me, connecting me to the air and the sea.

"This is incredible, Aella!"

But it was more than that, it was a connection to all things around me, living and material. To the plants and the earth, to the fire of the sun. It was everything. It was paradise. It was where I belonged.

If you enjoyed this book, please leave us a review!
Thank you for coming on this journey with us.

Acknowledgments

First and foremost, we would like to thank God for the gifts of creativity and storytelling, and our families for all of their love, patience, and encouragement.

To our children, you're not gonna read this for a good long time. ;)

Much gratitude to Holly and Lou, our wonderful alpha readers, who helped make this book the best it could be. It's always terrifying having someone read the book in its earliest stages, but your belief in our story and us kept us going!

To Rachel, our award winning developmental/copy/line/proof editor! You always go above and beyond. This series would not be what it is without you. Thank you for taking a chance on this sister duo and helping us navigate writing our first series. We seriously don't know what we'd have done without you. You're amazing and an even better friend.

Our amazing Beta Team: Karrie W., Kimberly, KL Hester, Laura F., M.A. Brown, and Sierra, thank you SO much for reading this story and cheering us on. Your reactions gave us so much life and helped us polish this baby up. We love you all!

All the thank yous to our MTP family. We're so happy The Stars Would Curse Us found a home with you. Indie publishing is no joke, and we are so grateful to not be walking this alone.

To our street team, thanks for your support and all the wonderful posts. It's amazing to have readers in our corner who love our stories!

Finally, to our readers, without you, our books would just be words on a page. Thank you for giving these characters a home and loving them as much as we do.

A note from Valerie:

This book wouldn't exist without the support of my sisters and friends who truly believed in me. Writing it has been one of the hardest things I've ever done, filled with heartbreak, doubt, and moments I didn't think I could push through. I'll never forget when my editor sent me quotes I'd written for my character, words I'd forgotten in my own struggles, to remind me that I've always had that strength inside me. To those who stuck with me and helped me see this through, thank you for being my light when the path felt impossibly dark.

A note from Stephanie:

To my other half, Justin, thank you for your endless support and belief in me. This book wouldn't be possible without you sacrificing your time to help me get this thing finished (or formatted ;)). I also love the fact that you're constantly trying to get your friends to buy my books. I love you, baby.

Publishing this series would have never been possible without the encouragement of my sister, Val, and the unending support from family and friends, old and new. Writing a book had always been a dream of mine, one I'd put to the side and thought would never happen. A whole world of possibilities opened up, and I've had to be brave. It's not been without its struggles, but I am so glad I stuck it out. I've also made some incredible new friends that I'm ever so grateful for. The indie publishing world is not for the faint of heart, and I most definitely could not do it alone. Thank you Vanessa, Hillary, Rachel, Erika, Jourdan, and Alexis for becoming part of my tribe. I'm so excited for what the future holds!

About the Authors

Meet Stephanie Combs and Valerie Rivers, a dynamic sister duo who share an enthusiasm for writing and storytelling.

Stephanie's passion for literature ignited at a young age, shaping her into an insatiable reader. Her love for writing began with crafting short fictional tales and poetry during her childhood—a spark that only intensified as she delved into writing stories for her college newspaper while pursuing a degree in Broadcast Journalism. Stephanie's sense of humor shines through her writing, infusing her work with witty banter and endearing characters. She resides in Maryland with her musical husband and four rambunctious children. When she's not sneaking in a writing session, you can find her nose stuck in a book or baking goodies for the family.

Valerie resides in sunny South Florida with her pilot husband and three children. She brings a fresh perspective to the fantasy genre, drawing from her varied experiences as a private jet flight attendant, artist, intensive care nurse, and more odd jobs than she'd care to admit. In her free time, she's writing, crafting new book covers and character art, and advancing her nursing degree online. Whether she's lost in her latest art project or in the darkest corners of her imagination, Valerie's creativity knows no bounds as she weaves fantasy worlds and narratives that transport readers to realms of magic and wonder.

You can find more on their website at:

silverflamebooks.com

Follow them on Instagram:

Stephanie - @stephdevourerofbooks

Valerie - @valerieriversauthor

More From Stephanie & Valerie

The Stars Would Curse Us Series

The Stars Would Curse Us (Book 1)
The Stars Couldn't Break Us (Book 1.5)
The Stars Could Save Us (Book 2)

More from Midnight Tide

House of Bane and Blood by Alexis L. Menard

In a city split into two opposing sides, power comes in many forms: bloodlines, money, love, and—most importantly—secrets.

An heiress in the most notorious family in Lynchaven, Camilla Marchese is doing all she can to keep her family's syndicate, the Iron Saint Railway, from slipping into bankruptcy. When the gorgeous and depraved Nicolai Attano, the leader of a rival family, offers to pay off the Inspector in exchange for her hand, she has no choice but to give up not only her throne—but her name.

Nico has his own motivations for their union beyond maintaining peace with her family. A serial kidnapper known as The Collector has been ravaging the streets of Remnant Row, stirring up mistrust between natives and descendants. If Milla can help restore safety to his streets, he'll have no need for her or her family's company. Find the Collector, prevent a war between their sides of the city, and pay off the family debt before she turns twenty-one. If Milla can fulfill her end of the bargain, she'll walk away with more freedom than she's ever had before.

But this deal plunges Milla into the city's dark underbelly where remnant magic and arcane science compete in a deadly game of depravity. When forbidden feelings rise for her new husband and dark family secrets come to light, Milla must discover the truth about her past before it gets them both killed or worse—collected.

Set in a post-industrial age setting on a magical Isle, Peaky Blinders meets the magic system of the Grishaverse in this rivals-to-lovers adult fantasy romance.

Available Now

www.ingramcontent.com/pod-product-compliance
Lightning Source LLC
Chambersburg PA
CBHW061103310726
48974CB00002B/369